Miss You
Most Of All

Miss You Most of All

Elizabeth Bass

KENSINGTON BOOKS
http://www.kensingtonbooks.com

KENSINGTON BOOKS are published by

Kensington Publishing Corp.
119 West 40th Street
New York, NY 10018

All Kensington titles, imprints and distributed lines are available at special quantity discounts for bulk purchases for sales promotion, premiums, fund-raising, educational or institutional use.

Special book excerpts or customized printings can also be created to fit specific needs. For details, write or phone the office of the Kensington Special Sales Manager: Kensington Publishing Corp., 119 West 40th Street, New York, NY, 10018. Attn. Special Sales Department. Phone: 1-800-221-2647.

Kensington and the K logo Reg. U.S. Pat. & TM Off.

ISBN-13: 978-0-7582-5880-9
ISBN-10: 0-7582-5880-1

First Trade Paperback Printing: May 2010
10 9 8 7 6 5 4 3 2 1

Printed in the United States of America

Acknowledgments

As always, I owe multitudes of thanks to Meg Ruley and Annelise Robey, my intrepid agent duo, for their patience and advice. Without them I would screw up much more than I actually do. I am also grateful to my editor at Kensington, John Scognamiglio, for his guidance and encouragement, and for being there whenever I have the urge to e-mail someone about Joan Crawford, old made-for-TV-movies, or *Pink Lady and Jeff*.

Special thanks to Linda MacCleave for knowing way in advance that a Luddite like me would need Web site help.

Thanks to my sister Julia Bass for giving the book a first reading, and thanks also to my sister Suzanne Bass for reading, critiquing, badgering, and inspiring me with her colorful East Texas vocabulary. I also owe a debt of gratitude to Suzanne and her colleague Jamon Bollock for enriching Hamilton Cho's legalese.

Finally, thanks as always to Joe Newman for technical support and cooking dinner.

Chapter 1

Chicken Fest had worn Rue down to a nub. It was only the second year for it, but the first year had been such a success that they'd had a bigger crowd than they'd expected this time around. In addition to the four paying visitors at Sassy Spinster Farm—the "inmates," as her sister Laura liked to call them—almost forty other people had shown up, one couple from as far away as Fort Worth. Two hours was a long way to drive to stare at chickens.

The day had been a soup-to-nuts crash course in raising and caring for poultry, with Rue explaining the chicken care ABCs, Webb doing a demonstration on designing and building a backyard coop, and Laura performing the gruesome honors of the sad chicken endgame. Only the true die-hard chicken freaks had joined Laura's slaughter and plucking seminar; the fainthearted majority had opted for Rue's rosemary chicken cooking demonstration. Even eleven-year-old Erica had gotten in on the act, overseeing a chicken petting zoo to show off the different varieties they raised, including the baby chicks and pullets that were for sale.

The event had gone over well from a financial standpoint, too. Webb's demo coop had been raffled off at a profit. With Erica's flare for commerce, they'd sold twenty-eight chicks. Best of all, three more people had decided to take out farm memberships, paying sixty dollars per month six months out of the year, which entitled them to a box of organic farm-fresh goods every week and a special winter box in December. The memberships, along with their farmers' market trade, were the farm's bread and butter. Those memberships were precious.

So were the boarding guests, who paid a hundred and seventy-five dollars per week to stay in an old farmhouse and learn hands-on about planting, harvesting, canning, and storing. The vast majority of the visitors were single women, but the name of the farm itself might have been a factor in the demographics. Sassy Spinster Farm wasn't exactly a moniker that reeled in the men. Most of the guests were urbanites, and frankly, very few looked like they would ever move much beyond the basil-in-the-window-box stage of agricultural endeavor, but something about the idea of living off the land lured them to this unassuming patch of East Texas. This year the farm had received an uptick in applicants because both *Texas Monthly* and, of all things, *InStyle* had given it a shout-out. As a consequence, they were booked solid all season. And this was only their second year taking in guests.

Most days around the farm were just routine—work to be done, meals to be made, and never-ending chores. Saturdays were chaos. New guests often arrived Friday night or Saturday morning. The farm had a farmers' market booth on Saturday, which was also box delivery day. Some CSA members picked up their boxes at the market, but the farm also made deliveries. Just getting through a garden-variety week was exhausting, but to stir things up and give an added payoff to the guests, every so often they had a special theme day, like Chicken Fest. Or the July Melon Thump. Rue was in charge of thinking up these and trying to get them organized. Chicken Fest this year had been bigger and more exhausting than ever, and more than it ever would be, she hoped. Three months post-chemo, her battery still felt drained.

Which was why she was only getting around to checking the weekend's e-mail and that day's phone messages on Sunday evening, after dinner. Two messages—non-messages, really—

caused her a moment's panic, followed by bemusement. She hunted down Laura, who was in the kitchen, loading the dishwasher.

"I hope you've got your wig glued down. We received two calls today from someone whose number pops up on the Black-Berry as Heidi B."

Laura unbent her lanky frame from stowing a pan in the lower rack. She was two years younger than Rue, but now the difference seemed even greater. Rue's body looked and felt like something whose warranty had expired. Yet Rue couldn't help noticing that even when frowning, her sister's face didn't wrinkle. How could that be? Laura was thirty-six. You'd think a little crow's-foot would have crept up on her by now. But no. Laura had always been in perfect health, no matter how much she abused herself. Her body bounced back from late nights and cigarettes and alcohol like one of those inflatable punching toys from when they were kids. She had the constitution of a Bobo clown. She was indestructible.

Most of the time she was immune to panic, too. But the name Heidi B. had a visible effect on her, even if she took her time drawling out her three-word response. "Oh. Sweet. Jesus."

Outside of storybooks, the only Heidi either of them had known was their one-time stepsister, Heidi Dawn Bogue. Heidi's mother, Marla, had married Laura and Rue's father five years after their own mother had died, and for three years during their teens, they had lived under her inept and capriciously tyrannical rule. Part of the awfulness of that time was Marla's constant doting on little Heidi Dawn, who was two years younger than Laura and insufferably prissy and stupid. While the sisters couldn't fight back against Marla very effectively, Heidi was always an easy target. In fact, she might as well have had a bull's-eye stamped beneath her pert blond bangs.

"Do you really think it's her?" Rue wondered aloud.

"With the way our luck's going . . ."

Doom was always perched on Laura's shoulder. If it didn't rain for a few days, she assumed they were in for a summerlong drought. When wild pigs rooted up some of her recently sprouted squash plants, as they had a week ago, she started envisioning an imminent D-day-style porcine invasion. So it was only natural that when the name Heidi B. appeared on a BlackBerry screen, it would be interpreted as an ill wind bearing down on them.

"I wonder what she wants," Laura said.

"She didn't leave a message, and I'm not inclined to call the number."

"Do you think something happened to Marla?" Laura asked. "Do you think Heidi's operating under the misapprehension that we would care?"

"I doubt it. I didn't hunt for them too hard when Daddy died." Rue shrugged. "Maybe it's just a coincidence. Heidi B.—it can't be *that* uncommon. Anyway, I've got to shove off. You'll look after the guests while I'm gone, right? And be civilized?"

Laura said something that might have been an agreement, but Rue wasn't getting her hopes up. On Laura's scale of pain, guests rated somewhere between oral surgery and Jeanette MacDonald–Nelson Eddy operetta movies. She had been dragged kicking and screaming into the scheme of taking in farm tourists at all.

Laura loved farming. Even though she had watched their father go a little further into debt and looniness each year growing corn and sweet potatoes and peaches, she'd thought she could do better when she inherited the place. She'd gone organic. She'd varied the crops. She'd added the poultry outfit. But every year had been a constant struggle to make the math add up.

After reading about community-supported agriculture, Rue, who had returned to the farm after her divorce three years ago, had suggested subscription farming. Then last year she'd hit upon the idea of agri-tourism when she'd read about a farm in Idaho that did it. If folks would go to Idaho, why not Texas? If they just spruced the house up a little . . .

The first year, despite its being more work than they had ever imagined, they had actually turned a profit. But all the money in the world couldn't keep Laura from acting as if the barbarians had crashed through the gate. She dealt with the incursion by exaggerating her normal toughness and indifference to the niceties to the level of performance art. She greeted each new batch of guests with all the warmth of Louis Gossett, Jr., meeting his recruits in *An Officer and a Gentleman*—as if they were just so many more wimpy urban nitwits to browbeat into shape.

As Rue turned to leave the kitchen, something odd caught her eye. Odd even for the Spinster Farm.

"What is a chicken doing in the kitchen?"

The chicken, a young rooster, was squatting in the corner, by a broom. The house had seen all manner of critters inside it through the years—including, one memorable Sunday, a possum under the television—but this was the first chicken who had made it inside.

"That's just Fred." Laura avoided looking at him, as if she didn't want to make him self-conscious. "He's been following me around all evening."

Rue wasn't the resident expert on chicken varieties, but she thought the white ones, the leghorns, usually were spastic and skittish. Yet, insofar as she could read bird expressions, she thought this one seemed a little dazed. "Is he sick?"

"Nah, he's just depressed. We sold Lucy and Ethel today." Catching the unspoken question in Rue's eyes, Laura lowered her voice. "Ricky Ricardo's in the freezer."

Rue felt a little depressed herself now. "Why is he following you around? Does he have a death wish?"

"Let's hope so. That'll make my job a lot easier someday."

Fred clucked listlessly and gave his wing feathers a flaccid flap. Rue felt like telling him to run for his life, to trust no one, but the sad creature didn't seem open to suggestion.

"Ice water in your veins!" she huffed at Laura as she left the kitchen.

She checked on the guests drinking sweet tea on the back porch, and then went hunting for Erica, who was due back at her father's by nine. She found her daughter sitting on the floor in her room upstairs, her long limbs folded awkwardly around her so that she bore a passing resemblance to a grasshopper.

When Erica spotted Rue, her face clouded with dread. "Can't I just stay for the movie?"

Every night they showed a movie in the living room, and Erica seemed to regret missing the movies more than anything about living at her father's house during the summer. Rue and William had agreed that she would have Erica weekends this summer, the reverse of how they usually handled the school year. Cancer had turned their custody arrangements topsy-turvy.

"You wouldn't even like the movie," Rue told her. "It's French."

"I don't mind."

"And it won't be over till eleven."

"Then why can't I just stay the night?"

Rue felt a painful tug in her chest. More than anything else, she wished she didn't have to have this discussion. She would rather debate whether Erica could have an Xbox or a television in her room, even. "I promised your dad."

Erica answered with an extravagant pout. "He doesn't care. He just knows he's supposed to care. It's all a big show."

Unfortunately, Rue suspected this was true. She wished to heaven that William would do a little better job hiding it, though.

"I don't see why I just can't stay here," Erica added. "He doesn't want me there anymore."

"Why do you say that?"

Erica bit her lip and then lifted her shoulders.

Rue tilted her head. "Is this about Ms. Dench?"

Leanne Dench was William's new girlfriend. She had been Erica's fifth-grade teacher the year before, and William probably never would have met her if Rue hadn't gotten sick. He hadn't been to a school function since Erica had enrolled in kindergarten. But Rue, who had been knocked out by her second chemo, had guilted William into attending the school's parents' night. And that night love . . . or something . . . had blossomed.

"I can't stand her," Erica said. "She's at Daddy's all the time now."

Rue didn't have a particularly bad opinion of Leanne Dench. She was a little odd—she always had an unblinking, shell-shocked look about her—but Rue assumed that was a by-product of spending nine months of the year in a classroom full of fifth graders. If anything, she was shocked that William had shown such good sense in his choice of a girlfriend. Their marriage had broken up because of his roving eye, among other things, so for years she had been bracing herself to hear that he had taken up with a barmaid or a topless dancer. Someone flashy and brainless. But no. He'd finally got serious about someone new, and it was someone who was as close to a younger version of herself as it was possible to find in the limited dating pool of Sweetgum, Texas.

Sometimes there was no accounting even for good taste.

Rue took a deep breath. "I know this is hard. You've had a difficult year. But except for when you stay with him, your father's been alone."

"Because he left us! Why shouldn't he be alone?"

"Well, we've discussed this. The divorce wasn't any one person's fault."

Erica rolled her eyes. "I'm not eight years old anymore, Mom. I know about the cashier woman at Pizza Stop."

She does? "How?"

"I have ears."

Maybe she had a satellite hooked up to those ears. Rue felt herself flailing and was glad to hear Laura's footsteps behind her.

"I thought you two had gone," Laura said.

"I don't think I should have to go at all." Erica always felt more bold about speaking up around Laura, who was Team Erica's head cheerleader. She lifted her chin loftily. "I don't think I should have to stay in a place where people are living in sin."

Rue and Laura exchanged quick glances.

"Do you mean Leanne Dench is hanging out at William's house a lot now?" asked Rue.

Erica rolled her eyes to telegraph her disdain for her mother's naïveté. "Mama, she *lives* there."

"This is new," Laura said.

"That's what I thought at first," Erica said. "But then, I started noticing that Ms. Dench's stuff was *all over* the house. This week I found her embroidery in the cereal cabinet and a pair of old panties stuck in the bottom of the laundry hamper!"

"At least it wasn't the panties that were in the cereal cabinet," Laura joked.

Erica snorted appreciatively.

Rue shuddered. She would gladly have skipped over this topic, but Laura wouldn't let it die. "How did you know those panties were hers?"

Erica made a sour face. "They were like her others I saw when she did her laundry at Daddy's—pale yellow with little blue flowers."

"Forget-me-nots," Laura guessed.

"I don't see how anyone *could* forget them," Erica said. "They're the high waist kind and sort of baggy, like the ones Great-Granny Anderson wore. I tell you, that woman is sooooo creepy and sneaky. She probably goes rushing over to Dad's the minute I come here."

Rue chewed over this tidbit. If true, the couple certainly had been discreet. Relationships were practically impossible to keep secret in Sweetgum.

"I shouldn't have to go back there now, should I?" Erica asked hopefully.

"Erica . . ." Rue hated to be the voice of doom. She would much rather have joined in the sneering at Ms. Dench's panties, but someone had to be the adult here. "There's no law that says your father can't have a girlfriend. . . ."

Erica scowled. "But she's so gross! She acts all sweet and everything, but she's really just a phony. It was the same in school. She pretended like she was the nicest teacher in the school. I should have known it was all a big act—even before she gave me a C in conduct."

Laura snorted. "As if she had any choice about *that* after you snuck into the cafeteria and put green food coloring in the mac and cheese."

"Nobody got hurt," Erica said.

No one had been hurt, but upon hearing about the green macaroni, the principal had decided that there had been at least a security breach and possibly even a terrorist incident in the cafeteria and had ordered the entire school evacuated. The meeting in the principal's office after the truth had come out was a moment in parenting Rue would have been glad to forget.

She flicked a glance at her watch. "We'd better go," she said, feeling even more dread about parting from her daughter than she had before. Not because she feared the corrupting influence of William and Leanne Dench's liaison, but because Erica was so obviously unhappy. Maybe she would speak to William. Not tonight. She wasn't up to a scene tonight. But soon. Just a word over the phone, maybe.

Erica stood with the enthusiasm of a condemned man. She could see that this was not a battle she was going to win tonight. "Can I just run and say good-bye to Milkshake?"

A part of Rue wanted to grab at any excuse to keep Erica with her. She could tell William, in the manner of a Victorian novel, that she thought he and Leanne were behaving in an unseemly manner.

But then here she was, living with Laura, the closest thing Sweetgum had to a town scarlet woman. She had been tossed out of the Carter's Springs bingo hall and had caused a scene at the all-church harvest festival by passing out in the pumpkin patch (Laura had sworn she was just tired, but Rue remained skeptical), and then there was the small matter of her having busted up two engagements. Including her very best friend's.

And of course, many people in Sweetgum just looked askance at Sassy Spinster Farm. They thought the sisters were crazy to turn their house into a revolving door of strangers from Austin to Albuquerque. They had introduced an unasked-for foreign element to the town. The first pierced nose Sweetgum had seen had belonged to one of their guests; the first openly lesbian couple had been guests, too. If it weren't for the fact that their outfit accounted for quite an uptick in commerce at Charlie McCaffree's store, who knew but that the whole town might have marched on the farm, torches in hand, like the villagers in *Frankenstein*.

"All right," she told Erica, "but be snappy."

"I'll need to feed Spunky, too," Erica replied. Spunky was an orphaned baby goat that was living in their barn. Erica had claimed bottle-feeding him as her chore. "And the kittens."

A feral cat had recently deposited four offspring in the barn. Unlike the rarely seen mother, the kittens were fat and tame from being fed and pampered by everyone. Even the dogs liked the kittens. They were in no danger of starving during Erica's absence.

Erica marched out, and Rue and Laura followed her downstairs. In the kitchen Rue grabbed her keys and let out a long sigh.

Laura, pouring out what had to be her twentieth cup of coffee for the day, looked at her with sympathy. "Want me to drive her?"

"No, I'm going to."

"You look a little tired."

"Chicken feathers in my head. I've done only a perfunctory accounting, but it looks like we made more than we expected today."

"Good. And the new subscriptions, too."

"We needed those."

Laura grunted. "Of course, if the drought doesn't end, I don't know what we'll be filling those CSA boxes with."

Rue laughed. "Mud pies, maybe."

"Dream on. We'd need rain to make mud."

"It's not really a drought," Rue assured her. "Didn't we get a sprinkle a week ago? It's just a dry spell."

"Least amount of rain we've had any spring that I can remember. Between the drought and all these people, I might just have to clap a FOR SALE sign on the place and go start a second career."

"As what?"

"A manic-depressive ex-farmer."

Laura had the same horror of selling the land that their father had had. Which was a laugh, since she and their father had had the most frictional relationship between man and daughter Rue could imagine. They had butted heads Laura's entire life, if for no other reason, Rue guessed, than that seeing another person with the same bullheaded streak was so unnerving to both of them. In his last year their father had even made noises about giving the entire farm to Rue rather than leaving anything to Laura.

"Give that gal an acre and she'll just stay a sassy spinster her whole life," he had announced at a family get-together.

But of course, he had divided everything up equally. Like Laura, he was all roar and no claw. And if he was watching them from whatever rocking chair he'd managed to plant his rear into in heaven, he would probably be more amused by the new name Laura had given the farm than by the improvements Rue had bestowed on his beloved property—giant sunflowers and other wildflowers along the fence lines, updated bathrooms and new decorations in the house, and fresh bright paint on the house and outbuildings. He would have scoffed at those things as frills, just as Laura had. It had taken some doing to convince her that these were necessities if they were going to attract paying guests.

"I honestly wouldn't mind driving Erica," Laura offered again. "In fact, I'd enjoy dropping in on the lovebirds for a moment. Just to say howdy."

"Just to drop a comment to Leanne Dench about her underwear, I'll bet."

Laura hooted. "I'll leave that to Erica. She's my girl—she'll find a way to squeeze it into the conversation before too long."

Rue shook her head. "I'm definitely going to drive her myself. You just encourage her to be like you."

Her sister feigned mystification. "What's the matter with me?"

Rue pocketed her keys. "We can go into that someday when we both have a decade to spare."

After Rue left, Laura stalked through the house, feeling at loose ends. There was always this lull at night between dinner and the movie. She was tempted to nip up to her room and hide out for a while. She didn't know why Rue was worried about the inmates. This time around they were a gaggle of porch sitters and generally stuck together. A manageable herd. They would stay out there until Rue came back and rounded them up for the movie. Then they'd all go to bed at the same time. In some groups, the people never meshed, which could be a problem. Or sometimes they'd get a few troublesome people, go-getters who were always sneaking up on you while you were trying to catch a moment alone.

She didn't have the easy way with strangers that Rue did. Laura didn't particularly want to socialize with the guests at all. But she didn't want to seem as if she were avoiding them, either.

She gravitated back to the kitchen. The dishwasher was still going, and she leaned against the counter, enjoying its companionable hum.

The after-dinner lull made her restless. It wasn't as if she looked forward to the movie all that much; she didn't love movies like Rue did. Usually about thirty minutes into a movie, Laura would start to lose focus. Something in the story would seem foolish to her—a dumb plot device, say. Or something about an actor would annoy her. (Was it just her, or was Tom Hanks slightly cross-eyed if you stared at him hard enough? Or why was it never explained why Greta Garbo, who was supposed to be French in one movie, spoke with a Swedish accent? And just who was Adam Sandler supposed to appeal to, exactly?) Rue frowned on talking during movies, so the unanswered questions would set something twitching inside Laura.

She'd start thinking about getting in her truck and driving

until she got to someplace where she could have a beer or shoot a round of pool.

For a while last winter, she hadn't been bothered by the restlessness so much. She had been busy looking after Rue and doing the farmwork besides. At night she had been too tired to move; worry had worn her out more than anything. And she hadn't wanted to leave Rue alone. Not for a minute longer than she had to. So she'd sat through every minute of *Gone with the Wind*, even though she could never understand the big deal about Ashley, anyway. And she'd made it through musicals that drove her up a tree generally, and any number of lame comedies that produced not even the slightest chuckle. Anything Netflix could throw at her, she'd endured.

But now Rue was recovered, and that old restless twitch had started up again. The guests didn't help, either. Laura seized any excuse to bolt away from them.

"Here you are."

She turned. Her old friend Webb was leaning in the doorway. She shouldn't have appreciated the way his gaze lingered on her, but she did. Sad but true. Those sleepy blue eyes of his always managed to get to her.

On the other hand, why should she be immune? Those eyes got to everybody.

"Hiding?" he asked.

"How could I be hiding? I'm right in the middle of the kitchen. I'm a sitting duck."

"Except you know everyone else is out on the porch."

"I saw *you* out there," Laura said. "Deep in conversation with . . . What's her name?"

"Jeanine."

"Jeanine! She was mooning at you."

He ambled over to get himself a glass of water. "Actually, she was asking me about composting."

"She might have had compost on her lips, but there were stars in her eyes."

He laughed. "It's like poetry."

"Face it, Webster. You're the matinee idol of Sassy Spinster Farm."

Most of their female guests seemed surprised to discover the farm had a man there at all. Some even were a little dismayed at first—the ones who had dreamed that their time there would be a sort of retreat from the world, a man-free paradise where they would shed their high heels and become can-do women of the soil. But Webb soon became a favorite with everyone. Not only was he a gorgeous specimen of human male, but he was a sympathetic listener. So that those visitors who had come to escape their problems—and so many of them did—would find themselves spilling their guts about their ugly divorce, or their latest boyfriend problems, or just the utter loneliness of their life back in Houston or Memphis or Amarillo. One or two had actually fallen a little in love with him, but the guests were here for only a week, or two weeks tops. Their boy was safe.

Laura couldn't help feeling slightly possessive of Webb. It was just the way things worked when you'd known a kid forever. The trouble was, Webb didn't think of himself as a kid. Which was only natural for a thirty-two-year-old, she supposed.

"Everyone's talking about the movie," Webb said, to change the subject. "Lots of grumbling about subtitles."

Laura didn't blame them. As if movies weren't hard enough to sit through without having to read along. "Do they have any better ideas?"

"Jeanine saw a copy of *The Wizard of Oz* on the DVD shelf. She thought maybe they could substitute that."

Laura's lips twisted into a frown. "That's Erica's. She'd be heartbroken if she found out we watched it without her."

"You could not tell her about it."

"She'd find out," Laura said. "Besides, I never liked that one much, anyway."

"You don't like anything that doesn't have Lee Marvin in it."

"I just don't like the ending," she said defensively.

His brows rose. Tell people you didn't like *The Wizard of Oz* and it was as if you had just insulted motherhood and apple pie. "The *happy* ending? Let me guess. You wish they'd all been massacred by the winged monkeys?"

She rolled her eyes. "It's the part where she's about to go home. She says good-bye to everybody, and she tells the Scarecrow she'll miss him most of all."

"So?"

So? "So how's that supposed to make the Tin Man feel? Or the Cowardly Lion? As far as I'm concerned, the Cowardly Lion's the whole show. If I were Bert Lahr, I would have turned around and said, 'Thanks for nothing, bitch!' "

"I hope you know there's a special ring of hell set aside for people who call Dorothy a bitch."

"And the worst part is," Laura continued, on a roll, "she gets back to Kansas, and suddenly she decides that there's no place like home, as if everything's hunky-dory."

Webb gaped at her. "Yeah, well, that's sort of the point of the story, isn't it?"

She stared at him, stupefied. "*No,* the point of the story was that Mrs. Gulch was going to euthanize Toto. But nobody back in Kansas ever addresses that issue, do they? Nobody ever says, 'Oh, by the way, Mrs. Gulch died in the tornado, so Toto's safe now.' As far as I'm concerned, Dorothy's just back at square one. She's going to have to run away again."

"You've way overanalyzed this."

"And that's leaving aside my opinion of Glinda, the so-called Good Witch. . . ."

"All right," Webb said. "I'll tell them to stick with the French thing."

"I don't have time to be watching movies, anyway." Laura tapped her fingers against Formica. "I should be out trying to hunt down pigs." She'd already set out twice to avenge her squash patch. But those feral pigs were elusive little bastards.

Webb put his glass down and frowned at the rooster, which was still squatting in the corner. "Is that Fred?" The chicken had its dull, red-eyed gaze trained on Laura. "He looks depressed."

"I thought that, too, at first. Now I'm wondering if that chicken's trying to mess with my head."

"Do you want me to take him back outside?"

"I will, later. I promised to stay in the house till Rue got back."

"Rue go off with Erica?"

Laura nodded. "She'll be back soon. Let her deal with everyone's movie woes." She couldn't help thinking about how exhausted Rue had seemed after the day's activities, though. It was troublesome.

"She gets a lot done," Webb said. "I can't believe it sometimes."

"The most important thing is that we don't hover over her. She got really sick of that. I wish there were some way we could spare her having to explain to every new crop of guests that comes in. Maybe we could leave a notice in their room with their towels. *Your hostess had cancer, which is why she's half bald and tired. 'Nuff said.*"

Left unmentioned were the questions about the scars on Rue's face—the old scars. Even after all these years, Laura couldn't bring herself to talk about those in any context.

"Rue doesn't mind talking about it," Webb said.

"She's just polite. Too polite."

"Or maybe she just wants to talk. Some people are like that. You know—normal."

"I just wish it were all up to her, that's all. I don't want her to feel like she has to say anything if she doesn't want to. Especially now, when she's finally gotten to the point where she can start putting it all behind her."

Webb nodded. "And what about you?"

A surprised laugh rasped out of her. "Me? I wasn't the one with cancer."

"Yeah, but they say that sometimes taking care of someone can be even harder."

"That's just horseshit." Laura had heard things like this before. Caretaker fatigue, they called it. As if helping someone was anywhere near as difficult as what Rue had been through—the strain, shock, and unfairness of being diagnosed with invasive breast cancer at thirty-seven and enduring two surgeries and chemo and radiation. The whole gauntlet.

"Probably so," Webb agreed.

But he agreed in a way that let her know that he was just giving in to avoid an argument. Or that he didn't think it was worth arguing about in the first place. He was maddening that way.

"You never put up a good fight."

"I've had enough real fighting, thanks."

He never talked much about that, either. Or about the breakup with his wife when he got back from Afghanistan. He had been discharged in January but had disappeared for a month—a month, Laura assumed, of dealing with the fact that he'd come back to a broken home and the worst job market in three decades. Then he'd just shown up to visit the farm one day in February and offered to work through the season for meals and board while he sorted himself out. What with all that had happened to Rue, and the way the farm activity had picked up this season, Laura wasn't about to look a gift horse in the mouth. But she did wonder why Webb would want to stay here, of all places. She and Webb had a long history, and not all of it was good.

"It would be gratifying if you'd occasionally hold up your end of an argument just a little bit longer," she said. "Winning all the time makes me nervous."

"You'd win anyway."

"Yeah, but I like to earn it."

He inched closer, unsettling her. "Why don't we skip the movie, Laura? Go for a walk, maybe."

"In the pitch dark?"

"Since when do you mind the dark?"

"I'm going to conk out after the movie."

He pinned her with a sleepy-lidded stare. "You won't watch the movie, and you won't sleep, either. You'll be in your truck before eleven."

She folded her arms. "Not tonight. I'm bushed."

"We could go out together," he suggested.

"Where would that get us?"

"Who knows? We could just take it as it goes."

Laura glowered at the old linoleum at her feet. It wasn't that she was a prude. In fact, the very idea of her trying to maintain some maidenly distance between herself and Webb would send guffaws rippling through Sweetgum and clear across the county. There wasn't anybody who hadn't heard about his bachelor party. The first one, at least. She hadn't been invited to the second. Understandably.

"Pick on somebody your own age," she told him.

"Is four years really so much?"

"It is when I can still remember you as a snot-nosed kid on the bus."

His mouth tensed. They'd had this discussion one too many times for him not to know that he would never win it. "I never had a snotty nose. That was Duane Biggs."

She laughed.

The front door opened and shut, and a few moments later Rue appeared. She looked all worn out. Laura imagined that there had been more words with Erica in the car, and more arguments about the necessity of Erica having to live with her dad for the summer. Which wasn't even what Rue wanted. It had to be heartbreaking.

When Rue saw them, though, she smiled. "What's so funny?"

"Duane Biggs," Laura replied.

Rue's face tensed in concentration. "That little kid on the bus who was allergic to everything?"

"Exactly."

"What made you think of him?" asked Rue.

"Webb was just comparing himself favorably to the competition."

Rue looked from one of them to the other, then shook her head. "I'm not going to step into this. It's time to start the movie, anyway. Where is everybody?"

"Back porch," Laura and Webb announced together.

"Still? I guess I'll go get them, then."

"Head 'em up. Mooove 'em out," Laura drawled.

To her delight, Webb executed a perfect whiplash sound effect.

Of course, the movie didn't have a prayer of holding Laura's attention. She dutifully took her seat next to the door and watched the beginning with all the concentration she could muster, but it was a lost cause. She thought about how good it would be to shoot a game of pool. To have a beer. To escape. Maybe there would be some guy at Chester's Lone Star to flirt with. Someone whose life she wouldn't feel so bad about messing up.

But ever since he'd appeared at her door, back from the war, Webb had taken a strange hold on her conscience. She had told Webb she wasn't going out tonight. If she proved herself a liar, she would be the target of one of his disapproving stares in the morning. He would be full of disappointment in her, only he wouldn't say so. He would just make her feel it. She would be suffused with guilt, as if she had somehow betrayed him. Which was stupid, because they were nothing to each other.

She yawned. Yawning succeeded in making her feel sleepy, which gave her an excuse to slip out.

Don't think about the truck. She deliberately left her keys on the little hook by the kitchen door, so that they wouldn't be on her dresser when she went to bed, reminding her of how easy it would be to run out the door and fire up the old Chevy. She loved the feeling of driving late at night with the windows down and warm air whipping through the truck's cab, the radio blasting.

Not tonight, though. Tonight she was just going to bed.

In her tiny attic room, which, because of the slanting roof, had about two square feet of full headroom, she tossed her clothes onto an old school desk, turned the fan to cyclone setting, and climbed into bed. Warmish air blasted her, and she closed her eyes, trying to imagine looking up through a windshield and seeing fat stars overhead and a V of roadway lighted by her headlights in front of her.

She wasn't certain how long it was before ringing woke her up.

It was hard to even think as she lurched about in the dark, feeling for her phone. As she did, she realized that there were other noises, too. Outside the dogs were barking up a storm.

"Hello?"

"Oh, thank God!" cried a voice on the other end. Though it was hard to hear for the sound of dogs barking. They seemed to be barking inside the phone, even. "I was beginning to think the place was deserted."

"Who is this?"

"It's me. Heidi!"

Laura frowned at the slightly familiar sound of the woman's voice, which was practically yelling over the dogs. She got up and went to the window.

Down below the dogs were jumping at the driver's window of a white car. And inside that car, evidently, was her ex-stepsister, one of the last people in the world she ever wanted to see again.

"It's so great to be back!" Heidi gushed.

Chapter 2

It was just Heidi's luck that Laura had answered the phone. From the sound of the less than warm reception, her old nemesis hadn't changed one itty bit, either. But this was just the sort of week she was having. It had started at Sunday brunch with her mother lecturing her about being fickle, which was akin to having Joan Rivers admonish you for having too many face-lifts. The week had then continued with what could be summarized as a very bad few days at the office, topped off by an assassination attempt.

The past two days had really been a nightmare. With nothing but a hastily stuffed duffel bag, she had loaded her battered, terrified self on the first westbound plane, had spent the night in Minnesota, and had ended up in Dallas by way of Atlanta. This morning she had missed her connection, which had put her into Dallas at eleven at night instead of three in the afternoon. Her butt hurt from being planted in various waiting rooms, cramped plane seats, and the rental car for two hours. And finally, icing on the cake, she'd gotten lost. Lost in the town of Sweetgum, pop. 117.

Sweetgum. Now here was a place that time forgot! After twenty years it still had just the one cinder-block store with a single gas pump outside, a smattering of houses along the one street, and a squat but sprawling brick schoolhouse. About the only difference in the town itself that she could detect was that it now boasted four churches instead of three. How they could add more churches without getting more people was a bit of a mystery, unless some of the same people were doubling up on their praying.

Praying extra hard to get out of Sweetgum, probably.

She'd found one positive development: the general store now had an Icee machine. She really could have used that back in '88! When she'd stopped to ask directions, she had helped herself to a root beer slush and had also grabbed a package of little powdered doughnuts off a shelf near the register. She hadn't eaten since lunch.

The man behind the counter—still Mr. McCaffree, just twenty years more ancient—had squinted at her suspiciously. "You one of them Spinster Farm gals?"

"That's where I'm going."

He shook his head. "That place just beats the heck out of me. But I guess there's no accounting for how people'll spend their dollars."

"I'd like to spend some of mine on this stuff."

He sized her up while he punched his knobby fingers into the keys of his old cash register. "You're better looking than most of the Spinster crowd." Before she could thank him, he added, "Not that that's sayin' a whole damn lot."

"Flatterer."

At the unexpected response, he eyeballed her more critically. "You look familiar."

"I should. I spent enough on candy here to fund your retirement."

"Wait a minute. . . ." For a second he looked like he was going to pop a bifocal.

"Don't you remember me, Mr. McCaffree? I'm Heidi . . . Heidi Dawn Bogue . . . I mean, Rafferty. Though it's actually Bogue again." It hadn't seemed kosher to keep her stepfather's name after her mother had run off with the exterminator.

The old man's mouth popped open. "Marla's girl?"

She nodded.

"Good God almighty! Never thought we'd see *you* around here again. Or your mother, neither."

"You won't see her."

"I bet she's just as pretty as ever."

"Mmm."

"Caused quite a stir when you two disappeared."

I'll bet.

"That was a bad time for the Raffertys all around," he said.

Heidi cringed inwardly but refused to comment. "I think I've got some change coming to me from that five I gave you?"

He dug his old leathery claw into the register for the change. "You shouldn't be wandering around so late at night. Ten minutes later and I'da been closed."

"Ten minutes longer looking for the farm and my head would have exploded."

A delighted cackle rent the air. "You mean you're *lost?*"

"I can't find the blacktop road to the farm. I must have missed it."

"First person I ever knew who got lost in this town."

"It's been twenty years." She was too tired to resist being defensive. "And I didn't drive back then. And it's dark."

But as she'd discovered after Charlie had given her directions, she'd passed the gate ten times before and missed it.

Now she sat huddled in her rental car with two snapping dogs lunging against her windows as she nervously shoved the last of her doughnuts in her mouth. For days she'd tried to keep herself from falling to pieces. It seemed like she'd hardly taken a deep breath since Thursday afternoon; the last forty-eight hours she had been entirely preoccupied with not having a nervous breakdown. She'd been hoping to put all her troubles behind her, but distance was actually having the opposite effect. It was as if her nerve endings were still attached to the East Coast and had grown more taut with each passing mile. She was just about ready to snap.

Especially when she thought about Vinnie. And Stephen. And Tom Chinske.

Poor Tom.

Oh, God.

She sucked down a last noisy slurp of her Icee.

Calm, she commanded herself as she finally saw a person—probably Laura, unfortunately—emerge from the house. From the looks of the woman as she marched rigidly across the farmhouse yard by moonlight and porch light, this wasn't a welcome wagon rolling in. Halfway to the car she bellowed at the dogs to shut the hell up.

The dogs fell silent.

Yup, that was Laura. Worse, it was Laura carrying a shotgun.

God knows she and Laura hadn't been exactly chummy, even by stepsister standards, but surely Laura didn't mean to shoot her?

She gulped back a world of anxiety, opened her car door a crack, and poked her head out into night air that was still shockingly hot and humid. It was the tag end of May, but it felt like July. She tried to feign enthusiasm. "Hey there, Laura! Long time no see!"

Laura stopped. She'd always been lanky, but twenty years had made her seem taller and more angular. Her loose white T-shirt didn't conceal her bony shoulders, and hip bones jutted out from beneath the fabric of her boxer shorts.

"Son of a bug up my butt," Laura said in her gravel voice. "It really is you. And here I was hoping this was just a nightmare."

Heidi could feel her smile flagging. "Did I get you up?"

"Yeah, you did. Not that you're probably too worried about my beauty sleep. What are you doing here?"

Heidi's sinking heart was only slightly bolstered by the sight of two more figures filtering toward them—one from the front porch, who had to be Rue (*hallelujah!*), and another, a man, who was coming around the side of the house. At least if Laura shot her, there would be witnesses.

"I thought I'd come for a visit. You know, for nostalgia's sake."

Laura coughed up a laugh. "You'd better think again."

During the long trip down here, Heidi had imagined the greeting she would receive a million times. She'd never fooled herself that anyone would actually be glad to see her, but for some reason being chased off the property at gunpoint had not occurred to her. "You mean you don't have a room for me? But isn't this, like, a hotel?"

"Yes. And right now we're, like, full."

"Oh, well, maybe—"

"We're full up till September."

A band of panic tightened around Heidi's chest. "Are you saying that I can't stay?"

"Not only that, I'm saying that it's damn strange that you'd *want* to stay. Or that you'd even come here at all. Or that you wouldn't make sure you'd talked to one of us first. And then you show up in the middle of the night and expect us to be thrilled to see you?"

Heidi didn't quite understand what came over her next. She wasn't headstrong, as a rule; she had a backbone of Jell-O, and her will was as bendy as a pipe cleaner. Yet at that moment she stood her ground. "I have to stay. I can't leave."

"Why? Something the matter with your car?"

Rue finally arrived. The sight of her almost made Heidi weep. It wasn't just that she was glad to see the nicer of the sisters, the semi-sane one, but also that she seemed so different. So old. Her bulky terry bathrobe swallowed her, and she had a knit cap on her head. A hat seemed crazy in this heat.

Then Heidi looked at the man, whose white teeth flashed at her. She couldn't tell if he was laughing at her or meant to be encouraging, but both he and Rue seemed more welcoming than Laura.

"Hi, Rue," Heidi said.

"Heidi Dawn! Long time no see!"

Laura flicked an annoyed look at her sister. "Took y'all long enough."

Rue pointed to the rifle. "What are you doing with that thing?"

The guy's smile broadened. "Locked and loaded even in her pajamas."

"It's just my pig gun," Laura said, intimating that she'd left the heavier artillery inside. "I like to be prepared."

"Well, I'm sure you don't have to wave it at Heidi," Rue said. "Or me, either, if you don't mind."

"The way the dogs were carrying on, I wasn't sure what I'd find out here," Laura told her.

"Was that the dogs?" The man feigned surprised. "We thought that was you."

Rue's more kindly presence, and the assurance that the gun wasn't about to be trained on her, gave Heidi the nerve to finally step out of the car. When she emerged from the safety of the Toyota, Rue greeted her as if they'd just bumped into each other at the mall.

"Well, my word! Look at you! It's been an age. What are you doing now? And what are you doing here? Just passing through?"

"Well . . ."

Laura didn't wait for Heidi to explain. "She says she wants to stay."

"Well, for heaven's sake!" Rue said. "I wish you would have written us. It's so good to see you, but—"

"I told her that was impossible, but she won't leave," Laura interjected.

"I can't." Heidi detected the first sign of a weepy quaver in her voice but was helpless to stop it. "I can't," she insisted, as if repetition might strengthen her position.

The other three exchanged glances.

"Look," Heidi said, "I know there's no love lost between us, but I'm not trying to take advantage. I'll work just like everybody else, and of course, I'll pay."

Rue looked almost pained. "It's not a matter of—"

"I'll pay you double!"

"I *told* you, we don't have a place for you here." Laura gestured broadly with her free hand. "You can see the house for yourself. It hasn't grown any in twenty years. And it's not like we've been keeping your bedroom like a shrine in anticipation of your return. Your *Dirty Dancing* poster is long gone, and we tossed out your Go-Go's tapes. Sorry."

God, she hadn't changed a bit. Still vicious. *I was crazy to come here*, Heidi thought.

But her gaze followed Laura's gesture to the hulking two-story frame house, painted so white it almost glowed. It looked just as it always had, only tidier. When she was a kid, she'd hated the place—she'd been so depressed when her mother had married some old man who lived out in the middle of nowhere. Now it looked like a refuge. Her last hope.

Laura and Rue had changed the farm, she knew. Back when she'd lived here, there were just fields of corn and sweet potatoes and a few fruit trees. But she'd read about the farm in a magazine, and even in the darkness she could imagine what was beyond the house from the memory of those glossy pictures: fields of vegetables, and herb gardens, and a chicken house, where fresh eggs were gathered every day. She'd been dreaming of it.

According to the article she'd read while she was at the hairdresser's—an article in a glossy magazine that had talked about agri-tourism—people came to Sassy Spinster Farm to learn how to grow things, to retreat from the bustle of urban life, and to rejuvenate spiritually by reconnecting with the soil under the guidance of the owners.

Reading it, Heidi had nearly fallen off the vinyl salon bench, laughing at the thought of Laura guiding anyone's spiritual renewal. The time Heidi had spent at this place, Laura had been her tormentor. A one-girl torture squad. Sweetgum's own Torquemada.

Yet that article had lingered in her mind. She'd wondered if the place really had changed, and she couldn't stop thinking about her old stepsisters. She had been unhappy on the farm . . .

but she had been fourteen. Maybe if she had been older or more self-confident, or if her mother hadn't been insane, they would have all had a different relationship. Maybe the Rafferty sisters would have taken her under their wing, instead of treating her like a leper. Maybe if she had learned to be a little more like Rue and Laura, she'd be a sassy spinster now instead of a gutless, quivering wreck.

The article had been accompanied by a picture of Laura and Rue, with the house in the background. The sisters had been photographed in profile, back to back. Laura was leaning on a hoe, and Rue, her face shaded by a wide-brimmed hat, held a basketful of eggs on her hip. They radiated self-sufficiency. Heidi couldn't imagine either of them bolting up in a 3:00 a.m. panic over stupid mistakes—all 236 of them, at last count—or sitting in front of a computer screen in a beige cubicle wondering what she was going to be when she grew up, if she ever grew up, which should have already happened by now but somehow hadn't. Or worrying that maybe she had grown up, and this was just the person she was always going to be, forever and ever, which was even more terrifying.

She'd stolen that magazine from the hairdresser's. And then, when the crunch had come, she'd decided that her last best hope was Sweetgum.

Big mistake (#237).

It was all too much. She sank back down into the driver's seat, letting the driver's door gape open. Where was she supposed to go now? What was she going to do? This had been her solution, her survival strategy. In her fevered thoughts during her plane flights, she'd dreamed she'd find not just refuge here, but some sort of spiritual rejuvenation through fresh eggs and dirt. And what was she getting? Bubkes.

The spigots opened, and she wept like a baby.

Rue took a tentative step forward. "Heidi?"

"I wanted to be a sassy spinster!" Heidi wailed.

Crying in front of Laura and Rue and that man was mortifying, but it felt so good, she couldn't make herself stop. She would never see any of them again, anyway. Not after she drove off into the night to God knows where. She was going to have to sleep in her car on the side of the road and would probably be killed by some psycho. Or go home and be killed by a more familiar psycho.

Neither option held much appeal.

"Uh, Laura . . . ?" Rue stepped back a few paces and beckoned her sister to join her. "Can I talk to you for a sec?"

The man, Heidi noticed, was not asked to join. He leaned against the rental car. "You don't remember me, do you?"

She snuffled and took a closer look at him. He had on jeans and boots and a loose dark T-shirt. His slight slouch against the car disguised his height, but he was probably taller than the other two, maybe over six feet. He had dark hair, a charmingly beaky nose, and one of those Cary Grant dents on his chin. A nice face. But she still couldn't place him.

"You look familiar, but I have the memory of a fruit fly."

"I'm Webb Saunders."

She gasped. "Of course!" Webb Saunders had been behind her a year in school and was one of the few boys in junior high school who had acted like a human being. "What are you doing here? Are you . . . ?"

Her gaze cut anxiously toward Rue and Laura. *Please tell me you're not romantically linked with one of the wicked step-slags.* Well, Rue wasn't so bad . . . but she shuddered to think that Laura had gotten her hooks into him.

"I'm just a hanger-on," he assured her.

"Oh, that's what I want to be! At least for a little while." She sniffed again and nodded to the powwow going on a few feet away. "Though I guess it doesn't matter. If they have their way, I'll be history soon."

"I'd say odds are even."

The two sisters flicked gazes back at Heidi, maybe to ascertain her mental state. It couldn't have looked good. A quick peek at her red eyes and streaky makeup in the rearview seconded her doubts. She dug some Kleenex out of her purse and used one to blow her nose and another to mop up the mascara damage.

"I must look like a crazy person in search of a straitjacket," she said.

"You don't look half as crazy as Laura looked when we first came out here."

In the latter stage of the conference between the two sisters, Heidi noticed more gesticulating on Laura's part. She raised her arms up, flapped her hands, then placed them emphatically on her bony hips. Heidi strained to hear what they were saying, and was pretty sure she caught the word *idiot* once or twice. She should have taken offense, but all she cared about were her chances.

She angled a pleading look at Webb. "You couldn't throw in a good word on my behalf, could you?"

"Nobody around here listens to me."

They might not listen, but Heidi would have bet money that they did a lot of looking. It was sort of hard not to look, even though tall, dark, and handsome had proven to be a deadly combination for her. Webb didn't look at all lethal, however. His expression was too open and unguarded. Maybe this was just a new good-looking guy strategy. It was hard to believe someone that gorgeous wouldn't know his own power.

The power wasn't lost on her, though. She felt its jolt and gave herself a mental slap. *No men.* At least not until she had extricated herself from the present calamity. And even then she should probably remain celibate, for her own good. It would be the equivalent of a serial debtor having her credit cards cut.

He certainly was easy on the eye, though.

Over at the powwow, Laura crossed her arms in front of her and heaved a sigh of resignation.

Heidi sat up straighter.

Rue returned to the car. "Laura and I discussed it, and since you've come such a long way and you're in such a spot . . . and since you're sort of family—"

A sound croaked out of Laura that was something between mirth and outrage.

Rue batted an annoyed glance at her sister and soldiered on. "Maybe you wouldn't mind being squeezed into a spare room?"

Heidi was on her feet in two shakes. "I'll take anything! The attic would be fine with me!"

"*I'm* in the attic now," Laura barked.

Okay, maybe it wouldn't be fine. The last thing she wanted was to share a room with the person who had put corn syrup in her shampoo bottle on school picture day.

"You might have second thoughts in the morning and decide to leave," Rue said. "But that will be your decision."

"Thank you!" Heidi turned to flash a celebratory smile at Webb, but he was already ambling off into the darkness. Before Rue and Laura could change their minds, she hurriedly leaned into the car to retrieve her duffel bag. The dogs, sensing the matter had been settled in her favor, nosed up to her, making her maneuvers a little more difficult. Still, Heidi patted one on the head and tried to sound friendly. "You're a good dog, aren't you, boy?"

"That's not a boy," Laura said. "That's Shelley Winters."

"Oh! Sorry." Bag in hand, Heidi slammed the car door shut. He, she, Shelley Winters . . . like she gave an att's rass. She had a place to stay; that was all that mattered to her for now.

Though, on second thought, it was never too soon to ingratiate herself. "Cool name!" she said as she tagged along behind the sisters.

Rue slowed down for her. "The other pup is named Monte, after Montgomery Clift. I adopted them after I watched *A Place in the Sun*. You know me and movies."

Actually, she had forgotten. Rue had always been one to stay up for the late show in those days before satellite dishes.

"I've got the movie bug, too." Heidi added quickly, "My taste has matured since *Dirty Dancing*."

"Mine hasn't much," Rue said. "If the eighties were on fire, that would probably be one of the films I'd save."

"Are you kidding? It wouldn't even make my top ten—although it might be the stupid eighties teen movie I'd be most likely to rescue." Heidi frowned. "No, that would be *Sixteen Candles.*"

"*Girls?*" Laura called impatiently from the doorway. "Are you going to stand out there all night, holding forth on Molly Ringwald movies, or are you coming in?"

They quickened the pace. Heidi had forgotten how quiet it was out here. There was no white-noise whir of cars in the distance, no air traffic, no distant sirens. When she tilted her head at all, all she heard were bugs chirping and humming. The old Sweetgum bug lullaby.

Tired as she was, a manic relief coursed through her as she was ushered up the steps to the house. Walking through the front door, she felt like a rabbit diving into a hole just before a predator could snap at it. She'd made it—she was safe. True, Laura still seemed to hate her, but she could deal with that. After what she had been through, Laura's huffing and puffing seemed downright quaint.

Rue led Heidi into the house, where they passed through the dark foyer. She could just make out the staircase. It was strange to be walking into the old house after all these years—like Nelson Mandela visiting his old jail cell. They turned down a narrow hall and stopped at the first door.

"This isn't ideal," Rue warned. "Remember the old sewing room?"

"I won't mind!"

"Unfortunately, it's the best we can manage right now," Rue explained.

She opened the door and snapped on the light to reveal exactly what she had predicted . . . only worse. When Heidi had lived here, the little room had been used as a sort of large closet. It housed the sewing machine and overflow from the house—the broken vacuum, a box of old curtains, and decades of abandoned projects. It appeared no one had cleared it out since then. One wall was lined with shelves full of old books, bric-a-brac, and odds and ends, like jars of rubber bands and old nails, but you couldn't really see all the contents of the shelves, because there were boxes piled waist-high everywhere, even on a little love seat that had a cinder block in place of a leg. The sewing machine—an old metal Singer encased in its own heavy cabinet—was there, too, next to the one window. From the position of the cabinet, it looked like it had been used as a bedside table to the bed sitting next to it. The *hospital* bed.

Alarmed, Heidi looked into Rue's face. She nearly gasped when she did.

She'd forgotten the wreck. Rue, who had always been the pretty sister, had been in a car accident with Laura when they were teenagers. Her face had been banged up, but Heidi, who had left Sweetgum right after the accident, had always imagined it would return to normal. For the past twenty years her memory had always conjured up the pre-accident Rue.

The problem started with Rue's left eyebrow, half of which was missing in action. The eye below it squinted slightly. Her cheek was mottled down to her slightly crooked jaw. Odder still, Rue's skin had achieved the feat of seeming both sallow and too red at the same time.

Only a split second passed, but Rue's eyes registered understanding. "Still a walking advertisement for seat belts."

Heidi blinked. "I didn't mean to . . ." She almost said, "Gawk," but luckily stopped herself before she compounded her faux pas. She faltered and turned her attention away, but unfortunately, her gaze again landed on the bed. The steel bed. It had the side guard up on one side, and the headrest was on an incline. "Where did that come from?" she asked.

"Dad. He was too weak to get up the stairs at the end, so we turned the library into his room. Now it's my room, so we moved this in here."

Mr. Rafferty had died in the bed she was supposed to sleep in? Laura swept into the room. "Better change those sheets."

They haven't changed the sheets since Mr. Rafferty died? Now that Heidi thought about it, that musty odor in the room had a slightly medicinal twinge to it. An old-person smell of Vicks VapoRub. Was it coming from the bed? She had to force her feet to remain planted and not back away.

Laura unfolded a top sheet with a single snap, and Heidi jumped.

"Forgive me for not asking sooner," Rue said, "but how's Marla?"

Heidi would have understood if she'd never asked at all. There had been no love lost between the sisters and their step-mother. Her mother was difficult enough to deal with as a blood relation. Heidi shrugged, wondering how little she could get away with telling them about her life in New York. *Let the acting begin.* "She's okay."

"Still have a fondness for bug men?" Laura asked.

Heidi winced on her mother's behalf. "No . . . That ended a long time ago. So did marriage number four."

Laura was shaking her head, but Rue bestowed a more kindly look on her. "We'll have lots of time to catch up tomorrow."

"Actually, that would be today," Laura said before turning back to Heidi. "How long did you say you were staying?"

"I didn't."

One sister hid it better than the other, but clearly she wasn't wanted here. This was going to be awkward.

But awkward she could handle. If she went home, she would probably be killed. The thought called up the memory of her coworker Tom Chinske, and she closed her eyes for a moment, trying to blot out the expression of pure fear that had been his parting glance to her. For all she knew, Tom Chinske wasn't even alive now.

Yeah, she could handle awkward. In her book, awkward beat dead any day of the week.

Laura followed Rue into her room after they'd put the prodigal ex-stepsister to bed. "I wish you would have let me handle that. I was doing fine before you and Webb came out."

"Oh, right. I saw how fine you were doing, Laurel Mae." Calling Laura by the name on her birth certificate was something only Rue could get away with. "You looked like you were going to strangle her."

"I was just going to shoo her away."

"At two in the morning?"

"This isn't the desert. There are hotels between here and Dallas. She'd be more comfortable in a hotel than sleeping on Daddy's hospital bed." Laura paced in a tiny circle, worrying her thumbnail against her lip. "Do you think we can get rid of her in the morning?"

"No."

"Why not?"

"Because we said she could stay. And we're not going to charge her for staying here, either."

"Are you crazy?"

"She's family."

"No, she's not."

"For God's sake, Laura, she lived here for three years. Okay, so we didn't like her mother, but she's not her mother."

Laura couldn't believe it. "We didn't like *her*, either. Have you forgotten what an annoyance she was? Have you forgotten her whining about not having ballet lessons, and practicing those horrible pieces on the piano all the time? I swear I still twitch every time I hear someone play 'The Entertainer.' "

Rue leaned forward, laughing silently.

"Have you forgotten the *twirling*?"

For an entire year it had seemed as if the kid had never been seen without a baton in her hand. Her mom had even bought her a spangled leotard, which she'd wear sometimes when she practiced in the yard. For those times when she really wanted to release her inner geek.

Rue tried to compose herself. "I remember, but also I remember that she was eleven or so when she moved here from Houston and probably thought she'd landed in the boonies, and then she had to deal with us. It wasn't Heidi's fault that our father went off to an army buddy reunion, got drunk, and eloped with her mom."

"Her mom the cocktail waitress probably had a lot to do with why Dad got drunk."

"That wasn't Heidi's fault, either."

Rue was always so damn fair. "You were older. You didn't have to deal with her as much as I did."

"Okay, but that doesn't change the fact that this was her home. The woman's not asking us to deed the land over. She just wants to visit. Why shouldn't she have a right to come back to the place she grew up if she wants to, and remember?"

"Remember what? Us stealing her homework and switching out the sugar for salt the day her mom made her birthday cake? And have you forgotten those drum majorette tryouts?"

Rue shuddered. "I had nothing to do with that."

"Don't play innocent." A frightening thought occurred to Laura. "You don't think she came here to exact revenge, do you?"

"Like a horror movie. *The Bloody Stepsisters.*"

"I'm not joking!"

"When Webb showed up in February, you thought he was here to exact revenge, too."

"I'm still not counting it out," Laura said. "Anyway, this is different. The woman just shows up out of the blue after twenty years and then starts weeping because we don't want her—as if we ever did! Didn't she seem deranged to you? A little unbalanced?"

"Yes, but that might have something to do with the fact that you had a gun and two yapping border collies were blockading her from getting out of her car."

Laura grumblingly admitted that there might be a little truth in that. "Still . . . it's fishy. This should have been the last place she'd want to visit."

"She probably saw us in a magazine and was curious about how the place had changed."

"So curious she couldn't make arrangements with us before getting on a plane?"

Rue folded her arms over her chest. "If you had picked up the phone when she called, would you have told her to come?"

"No, I wouldn't, and you know why?"

"Because you don't like her."

"Because it's a bad time. We're all full up, and it's the beginning of the busy season, and you're just recovering. . . ."

"I'm fine."

"We're stretched too thin as it is. And here comes one more mouth to feed, one more person to entertain—"

"She said she wanted to work."

That was a load of chuckles. "*Her?* Oh, she's going to be *tons* of help. Remember the time Dad sent her out to weed and she pulled up all our onions?"

"She never did it again."

"I doubt she's changed much. If life were a battle of wits, she'd be unarmed."

"She's no different than any of the other guests, except she knows this place a little better. Let's just give her a chance. She might not want to stay more than a day or two."

Rue was too damn nice. She never made snap judgments, never sniped, never kicked up a fuss about anything. No wonder she had always been their parents' favorite, not to mention every teacher's pet.

Hell, if Laura had to pick, Rue would be *her* favorite, too.

"I'll try to get her room fixed up tomorrow," Rue said.

"Don't do that. She might leave sooner like it is."

Rue sent her a big-sister, "you should be ashamed" look.

Laura didn't care. "Where are we going to put all that stuff, anyway?"

"That's a good question."

Every free inch of space in the house was guest space. "I'll think about it tonight," Laura said. Though really, even before she'd asked the question, she had already decided she'd move all the excess crap up to her room. She could shove it all in a corner. It wouldn't give her much room to move around, but she didn't have much room now, anyway. What was a few square feet less?

"*Don't* think about it," Rue said, pushing her toward the door. "Just go to sleep. Tomorrow will be a calmer day, and we can find out more then."

"Okay, but I'm still not ruling out the possibility that she's come to kill us all in our beds. You might want to lock your door, just in case."

Chapter 3

Rue loved mornings. In the old days, pre-cancer—B.C.—she had been one of those people who stumbled around in a groggy funk until the second cup of coffee worked its magic. Now each morning when her eyes popped open she understood right away what a miraculous event a new day was. Yes, there were some not-so-great moments to get through. Facing her new self in the mirror, for one. Not that her old self had been any great shakes, but there was no denying her frazzled appearance now. Her skin still had that chemical dipped look, and her little wisps of hair—curly and pale—seemed like they had sprouted from an alien's pores. She'd never been overly vain, but come on. This was a bit much to take at five thirty in the morning.

Her whole morning ritual was a trial, and she tried to get through it thinking as little as possible, except maybe to wish that she could do without mirrors entirely, like nuns in the old days. But the trouble with a mirrorless world was she couldn't risk looking like too much of a kook—not with a houseful of guests, she couldn't. So she had to put up with those early-morning glimpses of her face, which reminded her that the Rue in her head had parted ways with the Rue of reality.

But when finally she reached the kitchen, she felt like a new person. A new person with another day at her disposal. Each and every time she flipped on the lights, it felt like a lucky break.

A year ago she had been careful to be quiet in the early morning so she wouldn't wake the guests, but going through life on tippy-toe no longer interested her. Next to the toaster was a boom box, and the first order of business each day was to decide what went into it. Occasionally, it would be classical music or bluegrass, but mostly she loved singers. Laura favored country music, and Webb could listen to any station on the FM dial and not even seem to notice the difference. But Rue's CD collection, housed in what used to be their mother's spice cabinet, spanned everybody from Enrico Caruso to Amy Winehouse, though she tended to fall back on jazz singers and crooners.

This morning she put in an old reliable—Ella Fitzgerald and Louis Armstrong duets—and cranked up the volume. Then she started thinking about the menu. She had a two-week breakfast repertoire, and oatmeal was next in the rotation. She hauled out the bag of steel-cut oats she bought in bulk in Dallas and then readied the soup pot she cooked them in. She hummed along with the songs on the CD as she worked—"Stars Fell on Alabama," "Let's Call the Whole Thing Off," "Our Love Is Here to Stay."

While that was simmering, she mixed together the batter for sweet potato muffins.

Twice Laura passed through, shaking her head at the boom box and at Rue drumming along with the rhythm section with a rubber spatula. One trip was to bring in eggs, which she deposited in the second fridge in the pantry. The subject of their middle-of-the-night disturbance was not mentioned, beyond Laura's terse observation, "Well, we're both still alive."

Rue laughed. It seemed just like any other morning.

The guests ate breakfast at the round kitchen table. It was large, but now Rue wondered if she shouldn't get out the extra leaf for it. Five guests, Webb, herself, and Laura. Of course, Laura rarely sat down for breakfast. And no Erica till the weekend.

She felt a pang thinking of that and decided all she could do was *not* think of it. Denial was a skill she had perfected this past year. After the two muffin tins had been popped in the oven, she poured milk, half-and-half, and soy milk into small thermal pitchers, then arranged raisins, dried apples, brown sugar, and walnuts in bowls on the counter.

Laura came back through a little later to fill up a thermos of coffee for their two regular day workers, Dylan and Herman. Rue would also send them a bunch of muffins. "Any sign of Heidi?"

"Nobody's down yet," Rue said.

"She's probably one of those sleep-till-noon types."

"Cut her some slack. She had a long day yesterday. She probably didn't get much rest."

It was just the comment Laura had been fishing for, and now she reeled it in with zest. "I could have used a few more z's myself!"

Rue let her sister's indignation bounce off of her. Laura was one of those people who thrived on friction of one kind or another, even at six in the morning. "She'll be up. She seemed eager."

Laura stalked out with her thermos, muttering.

Ella and Louis sang "They Can't Take That Away from Me." And then the CD ended. Rue reached her hand into the CD cabinet, picked at random, and came up with Perry Como. He was crooning "Some Enchanted Evening" when the first of the guests came down; the song produced a wrinkled nose from Margaret, who looked as if she had smelled a rotten egg. Rue placed a glass of orange juice in front of her.

Margaret was one of the serious types who came to the farm; she wanted to learn absolutely *everything* in two weeks. "You don't have to wait on me," she said quickly, jumping up from lacing her work boot. "Oh! Oatmeal." She gave the pot a stir. "Look at that! You'll have to give me the recipe."

"It's oatmeal." Rue should have appreciated Margaret's enthusiasm, yet something about the woman made her want to swat her away.

Margaret looked around. "Has Laura come down yet? I could help her."

If there was one thing that drove Laura berserk, it was guests coming out to work before she was ready for them. She would be going over the plan for the day with Herman, Dylan, and Webb, and she wouldn't appreciate Margaret's *help*. One of Rue's morning duties was to keep the guests corralled in the kitchen until after breakfast.

"She's out with the guys just now," Rue said. "You'd better wait till she gets back."

"Okeydoke! Should I make another pot of coffee?"

Rue was relieved to be able to let her. Most of the guests were mellower, but the occasional live wire like Margaret reminded her of Erica when she'd been young and first started wanting to help out. Rue had had to think of flub-proof chores for times like this. Coffee making was as good as any.

The others began to filter in, thank heavens, which lured Margaret back to the breakfast table. She stood, hands planted on hips, totting up place settings. "Rue, you set one place too many."

"Maybe Laura's going to sit down, finally." Jeanine, a twenty-four-year-old hipster from Austin, slipped into the chair next to Webb's usual spot. She had been positioning herself there all week, but the strategy was getting her nowhere.

"I'm not sure Laura can digest sitting down anymore," Rue said, humming along now to "Round and Round."

Jeanine tilted her head to stare, perplexed, at the boom box. "Is this something you really like to listen to, or is this irony?"

Rue shook her head. "I don't do irony before ten a.m."

"I bet I know what the extra place is for," said Montana. She was a hospital nurse from Shreveport who had come with another nurse, named Claire. "I heard the dogs barking last night."

"I heard them, too, and there's a car out in the drive that wasn't there yesterday," Claire said.

"You can't see the front drive from your room," Montana pointed out to Claire.

"I looked out the porch window just a moment ago. It's a white Toyota Camry," Claire replied.

"A Corolla," Montana said.

"Is it?"

"My brother owns one."

"Of course," Claire said. "Well, I'm sure you're right."

"But you were right, too. It definitely wasn't out there yesterday," Montana added.

So far Rue couldn't tell if Montana and Claire were lesbians, or just very good friends, or soul mates in tedium.

Margaret hurried out to see the car for herself. When she returned, she seemed put out.

"Well, there is a white Corolla out there." She turned to Rue. "I thought y'all only took four visitors at a time."

"Normally, that's true," Rue said. "This is a special circumstance."

"The more the merrier!" Claire said.

Not a sentiment Margaret shared, apparently. "When I first called to make reservations, I was hoping to bring my friend Rachel, but you said you were all full up."

Webb strolled in at that moment, diverting attention momentarily from the unseen guest. Very momentarily. "Heidi up yet?" he asked as he took off his hat and sat down.

The name sent a wave of speculation rippling through the small group.

"Heidi?" Montana and Claire said, all ears.

"How old is she?" asked Jeanine. In her Webb quest, she seemed to consider youth her trump card.

"Why did she show up in the middle of the night?" Clearly, Margaret found this behavior highly suspect.

Laura, who had come in right behind Webb, carrying Fred, glowered first at the boom box, then at the extra empty chair. She kept walking. "I'll get her."

Margaret gaped at the others. "Was she carrying a chicken?"

"Looked like it," Montana said.

"Did the new person wake you up, Webb?" Jeanine asked. She gave her hair a flip as she turned toward him. She had platinum hair with a dark black streak through the front—a reverse Lily Munster.

He appeared unmoved by her hair maneuver. "Shelley Winters and Monte woke me."

They all stopped for a moment to listen to Laura calling through a shut door to Heidi. They couldn't hear Heidi's replies, but they exchanged amused looks at the sound of impatience in Laura's voice. Then, when it was clear Laura was on her way back, they focused their attention on their oatmeal bowls again.

Except for Jeanine. All her attention was on Webb. "Nothing ever wakes me up," she said, yawning so that her little T-shirt crept up her midriff, revealing a belly button pierced by a silver hoop. "I always sleep like a baby."

"If the sound of those barking dogs didn't wake you, you sleep like the dead," Montana told her.

Laura returned to her customary spot by the counter, set the chicken on the floor, washed her hands, and started grazing at the bowls of raisins and walnuts. "A man named Carl Bigsby lived down the road from here for years. He used to brag about being a sound sleeper, too. Then one night his house burned down, and all the firemen found of him was a charred head and a foot where his bed used to be."

Spoons clattered against bowls, and Montana brayed in disgust. "That's revolting!"

Laura's eyes widened innocently. "It's a true story."

"Did you have to tell it while I was eating my oatmeal?" Jeanine asked, even though she *hadn't* been eating her oatmeal. She always picked at her food; then Rue would clean her room in the morning and find a half dozen energy bar wrappers in the wastepaper basket. "That's really gross."

"And I really don't think chickens are supposed to be allowed in eating establishments, are they?" Margaret asked, eyeing Fred warily as he darted anxious looks back at them all.

"I'm trying to cheer him up," Laura said.

"Aren't chickens carriers of something?"

Montana and Claire looked at each other as if just remembering the punch line to a shared joke. "Bird flu!" they said in unison.

"Oh God." Margaret looked like she was on the verge of alerting the CDC. "Really?"

Perry Como sang "Hot Diggity" as charred body parts and quarantines swirled in people's brains.

Laura popped another walnut into her mouth. "You know I don't think much of your musical taste, Rue, but this is a low watermark even for you."

"Perry Como is underrated," Rue said. "I think he's due for a serious reevaluation."

No one else in the room looked convinced. And really, "Hot Diggity" wasn't his best. Rue was used to grousing, though. This was nothing compared to the morning she played Slim Whitman. A yodeling cowboy at seven in the morning had nearly caused an insurrection.

"Sleeping Beauty awakes."

Laura's amused contempt was aimed at the doorway, where Heidi stood surveying the table. Her Sandra Dee blond hair was tied back loosely, and she was wearing just enough makeup to make her look natural without looking washed out. She had very fair skin, which caused Rue to worry about the shoulders exposed by her sleeveless shirt. She expected that they would need to get out the aloe vera before the day was out.

Rue left the stove and introduced Heidi around the table, while Heidi perched uneasily in the empty chair Rue had guided her to.

"I wish I'd known that they'd accept more guests," Margaret repeated after the introductions were made. "Maybe I could have brought a friend, after all."

Heidi looked uncomfortable. "I'm sorry. I didn't mean to step on anyone's toes."

Margaret sniffed. "Don't worry about it. I'm just not pushy enough, I guess."

Rue's and Laura's eyes met, and Rue had to turn away to keep from laughing. "Heidi's not just a regular guest," Rue explained. "She used to live here. She's family."

"Sort of." Heidi sent Rue a sleepy but grateful smile.

"We're having oatmeal for breakfast this morning," Rue told Heidi. "I'll scoop up a bowl for you, and you can pick your own add-ins."

Heidi looked decidedly unenthused. "Just coffee for me, thanks."

Before Rue could explain the routine, Laura jumped in. "Coffee-pot's on the counter, and those ceramic doohickeys with handles next to it are coffee cups. Oh, and that little person in a maid's uniform you see? That's a hallucination."

A blush washed across Heidi's pale cheeks. Everyone at the table shifted uncomfortably, like kids who had witnessed some-one getting dressed down by the principal. All except Webb, who shot Heidi a sympathetic smile. "That's Laura's sweet way of saying coffee's serve yourself."

Heidi nodded and then scuttled across the kitchen to get her coffee. Unfortunately, the coffeemaker was right next to Laura. Looking at them side by side, it seemed as though Heidi were at-tempting to make herself even smaller than she was to avoid coming too close.

Meanwhile, Laura inspected Heidi's outfit. In addition to the sleeveless shirt, she was wearing jeans with the bottoms hiked up inside out to make them mid-calf length, and a pair of purple suede Mary Janes. "You intend to wear those shoes today?"

Heidi looked down in confusion. "Uh-huh. That's why they're on my feet."

"Sandals aren't practical. In case you don't remember."

"Didn't you bring boots?" Margaret asked.

"No . . ."

Margaret appeared flabbergasted by such unpreparedness. "Boots are essential."

"These really are very comfortable," Heidi insisted.

Laura slurped her coffee.

"Are *you* wearing Laura-approved footwear?" Heidi asked Webb, glancing down at his boots.

"Of course he knows what shoes to wear," Laura told her. "He works here."

"Working? Is that what I'm doing?" Webb asked, surprised. "And here I was so proud of myself. I thought I was freeloading."

"Freeloaders don't fix tractors," Laura pointed out.

"Workers don't pack away as much free food as I do, though."

"We could starve you if it would make you feel more noble," Laura joked in her favorite needling tone. "Maybe provide a bed of nails for you to sleep on, too."

"The bed I've got is plenty uncomfortable, thanks."

Heidi looked like she was about to jump into the conversation—God knows she had an uncomfortable bed to complain about—but at the last minute, something made her suck in her breath. The song had changed to the trumpet blare intro of "Papa Loves Mambo," and she twirled, trying to find the source. She spotted the boom box and then caught Rue's eye. "I *love* this! Can I crank it?"

"Be my guest." Rue tossed Laura a triumphant grin. Could she say vindication? Someone else liked Perry Como!

Or at least one song by Perry Como.

"Can anybody mambo?" Heidi yelled out over the music, searching the faces in the room, all of which were now gawking at her. Not that it seemed to matter to her. Her hips were already wiggling, and she was in her own world. With only an air partner, she did a pretty fair simulation of some kind of exotic dance.

"Looks like you're the only one," Rue said.

Heidi's eyes lit up. "Come here. I'll teach you."

Rue fell in behind her and tried to copy her steps, while Heidi called out the rhythm, Arthur Murray style. "Back-left-right-sidestep, forward-left-right-sidestep!"

Unable to resist the lure of the instructional, Margaret leapt out of her chair and joined in, so they now formed a partnerless mambo line. Montana and Claire got in the act, too, making up the tail. Webb held back, grinning, especially when Heidi let out an exuberant "Wow!" to match Perry's more reserved, cashmere-sweatered one. Jeanine remained seated because Webb did, though she was sort of sit dancing. Laura, frozen in astonishment at what had erupted right under her very nose, followed them, zagging around the kitchen with the baffled amusement she usually wore when she watched Shelley Winters and Monte rolling in cow pies.

"That's it, Rue!" Heidi yelled encouragingly, arching her neck for a peek at her students. "Release your inner Charo! Throw your hips into it!"

"And what dignity you have left," Laura added.

Rue tossed back her head and laughed. For what was left of the song, she really did throw herself into it. And why not? Her kitchen had become an impromptu dance hall. Why hadn't she thought of this before?

They mamboed en masse across the kitchen, nearly trampling Fred, who showed more energy than he had in twenty-four hours when he flapped out of the way.

When the song ended, it was with a mad, hip-swinging flourish from all the dancers. None of them were together and they were certainly not in sync with the music, but what they lacked in precision, they more than made up for with exuberance and pizzazz. When they broke their frozen ta-da positions and started laughing, Rue caught sight of another pair of eyes gaping at her.

"Erica!"

Flushed and sweaty, Erica was standing in the doorway, her face frozen in that mild horror of an adolescent watching her mother dance in public.

"What are you doing here?" Rue exclaimed.

Perry Como launched into "It's Impossible," and Laura dove for the volume knob.

"I'm coming home for the summer," Erica announced.

Rue glanced beyond her daughter's head, looking for William. He was nowhere in evidence. "How did you get here?"

"My bike."

"But that's five miles!" Rue was filled with anger. Erica had set out on her bike at six in the morning, and William hadn't even called?

Erica was thoroughly nonchalant. "I know. I'm hungry. Mmm. Oatmeal. Can I have some? With chocolate chips?"

Rue half suspected that Erica was using hunger as a way to buy time, to best figure out how to wheedle her mother into giving in to whatever demand she was about to make. As Erica well knew, Rue couldn't resist the maternal urge to push food in front of her offspring.

At that moment Erica spotted something amiss in the kitchen. She was practically pointing at Heidi, her attention so focused she looked like Shelley Winters spotting a jackrabbit. "Who is *she*?"

Rue made a mental addition to her parental to-do list. *Instill manners.* "This is Heidi. She came in last night."

Erica's forehead crinkled. "How can she stay here? We're all full." Before Rue could answer, she gasped in panic. "You didn't give her my room, did you?"

"No, no. She's in the extra room."

If anything, Erica looked even more perplexed. "*What?*"

"You know, the old sewing room," Rue reminded her. "There's a little bed in there."

"The one where Grandpa died? Gross!"

"Erica . . ."

"But it *smells*!"

Heidi, Rue saw, was grinning nervously. Confusion was written all over her face. "Erica's my daughter," Rue explained.

"Oh! I can see the resemblance."

"Heidi?" A lightbulb went on over Erica's head. "Wait. Are you *the* Heidi? The twirler?"

Laura spit up coffee, and Heidi shot an accusatory glance at her. "I put away my baton."

"Okay, enough lollygagging," Laura announced, obviously wanting to empty out the room. "How about I take the garden today, Webb?"

"Fine by me."

"How many do you need?" she asked him.

"Just one should do."

"Okay . . ." Laura inspected the people at the table one by one. Her gaze floated over Claire and Montana, then Margaret, then landed on Jeanine, who was practically wriggling in her seat at the chance to be Webb's one.

"I'll go with Webb," Erica volunteered.

"You'll stay put," Laura told her. She then looked over at Heidi. Any desire she had to crack the whip over her old nemesis evidently couldn't compete with her desire to not be in her company. "Why don't you take Heidi, Webb?"

"It'd be a pleasure." He clamped his hat on his head and beckoned Heidi with a nod.

Jeanine rocketed out of her chair. "I worked in the garden Saturday!"

"So did we all," Margaret said.

"Once you have your own farm, *you* can make the work assignments," Laura told Jeanine.

Jeanine looked at her like she was crazy. Clearly, sometime in the past week she had decided against a life of the soil. "Just so I don't have to weed again."

Laura pretended not to see Jeanine's mopey slouch. "Weeding? You must have read my mind!"

When the kitchen emptied out, Rue sat down next to Erica at the table and watched her dump brown sugar, raisins, and chocolate chips into her oatmeal. By the time she'd finished with it, the painstakingly healthy bowl of oats she'd been handed looked about as nourishing as a Pop-Tart.

Laura drifted back in and made herself look busy at the sink while she eavesdropped.

"What happened at your dad's?" Rue asked Erica. "What are you doing here?"

"I told you. I'm coming home." Erica swallowed a spoonful of goo. "I refuse to stay in the house with that woman for another minute."

There was no sense asking who "that woman" referred to.

"Your father should have talked to you about this," Rue said.

"He did," Erica replied.

But Rue didn't hear her at first. She was trying to explain it. "You see, we're so lucky here. We're all here together. When you come home, you're surrounded by us and Shelley Winters and Monte, and Milkshake, and Webb, Dylan, and Herman. But except when you're with him in the summer, William comes home to an empty house."

Erica put her spoon down in a sulk. "Not anymore. Daddy and Ms. Dench are getting married."

Chapter 4

There. Erica felt grim satisfaction at being able to render her mom and Laura speechless. It wasn't often she had a bombshell to drop, so she savored the moment. Laura even had to sink into one of the chairs at the breakfast table—something Erica hadn't seen her do since the guests had descended on them in the spring.

"When?" Rue asked.

Erica took a sip of orange juice and winced as the citrus ran smack against the sugary residue of her oatmeal. She had to swallow hard against the sour explosion. "August."

Laura and her mom exchanged looks. They did this a lot, as if after a lifetime together they didn't really need words anymore to communicate. Erica sometimes wondered if this was actually true, but not having a sibling to practice on, she doubted she would ever find out. Right now they were staring at each other as if there were some meaning to be fished out of the word *August*. Erica could have told them the meaning if they'd just gone ahead and asked. The meaning was that she now had two reasons to dread that month—school starting, and her dad ruining both his life and hers.

"August is quick," Rue said.

Laura snorted. "That depends on how far along—"

"When did you find this out?" Rue asked, stepping on whatever it was that Laura was going to say.

"Last night. This is going to ruin my birthday forever."

Rue tilted her head. "How?"

"Because they're getting married on August sixth and my birthday is the fourteenth. So every year now I'll have to endure Dad and Ms. Dench having a lovey-dovey anniversary party. By the time my birthday rolls around, I'll be too nauseated to eat cake."

Laura laughed. "It'll be a miracle if the lovey-dovey part lasts until you enter your teens."

Erica wished she could believe that. "After Mom dropped me off last night, they sat me down for a big talk in the dining room, so I knew something bad was coming. Dad hardly ever uses that room except to stack junk mail. Plus, Ms. Dench was all simpery. She'd baked cookies—like that was going to make me happy or something."

"What kind?" Laura asked.

"Peanut butter. You want one? I brought them with me."

"You swiped the cookies before you left?" Laura asked, admiration in her eyes.

"Why not? She said she'd made them for me."

Her mother hitched her throat impatiently. "What did your father say, exactly?"

"How could he say anything? Ms. Dench yapped right over him every time he opened his mouth. All about how happy she was, and how in love with Dad—as if I care about *that*. And how she knows she won't be my real mom . . ." Erica felt a choking rage building in her all over again, remembering that part. "You've got that right," she'd wanted to yell.

Ms. Dench, and probably her mom, too, would have called that starting off on the wrong foot.

"She says she wants to be Mrs. Anderson by the beginning of the new school year. She even kept saying it—Mrs. Anderson. It was so revolting! I can't believe I'm gonna have to share a name with that woman. I mean, people are going to be saying, 'Good morning, Mrs. Anderson!' and 'May I go to the bathroom, Mrs. Anderson?' And all the girls will want to see her ring! I'm sure I'll want to vomit when *that* happens. And it will, because she can't stop staring at it. It looks super expensive, too. What do you want to bet that's the reason Dad said he wouldn't buy me a television for my room?"

"There might be other reasons," Laura said. "Like the fact that Rue would kill him."

"Oh crud! I don't see why I can't have one there just because Mom won't let me have my own here. There ought to be some benefit to being from a broken home."

"Never mind the television," Rue said. "And never mind the ring, or what people will say at school. By the time school starts, you'll probably be used to it all. Besides, if the wedding happens over the summer, it will probably be pretty low-key."

"Guess again! Ms. Dench wants to have a *humongous* wedding. 'With all the trimmings,' she kept saying. She said she's been saving up for it all her life. Isn't that dumb? Imagine saving money for years and then spending it on going to church!"

There was a long silence while her aunt and her mom looked at each other again, then tried not to look at each other. It was so frustrating. If they had something to say to each other, why didn't they just say it? It was like they still considered her a child, but she was almost twelve now.

"Well!" Her mom spoke in that fake peppy tone she always used when she was trying to gloss over something really awful. "I guess it's natural that she would want a wedding . . ."

"It's not natural that she would want *me* to be a flower girl," Erica said. She still felt woozy every time she thought of *that*.

"Oh no," Laura breathed.

"Flower girl!" Erica repeated with disgust. "I told her that she could just forget that. Aren't flower girls usually, like, five or something?"

"Usually . . ." Rue said.

"I'm too old!" It was so obvious, but her mother still looked like she was trying to be neutral. "This is what I mean," Erica said, hoping to make her understand the horror of what was happening. "Ms. Dench may be a teacher, but she's so dumb, sometimes I just want to thump her on the head. And Dad just doesn't see it. It's like he's blind."

Rue nodded. "I know."

Erica knew she must have gotten through to her, because her mother had forgotten to say something positive. "He thinks everything's great. He thinks I should be *happy*."

"What an idiot!" Laura exclaimed.

"Laura, he is not," Rue asserted.

Laura looked as hot as Erica felt. "He ought to be smart enough to know that his eleven-year-old daughter—"

"Nearly twelve," Erica corrected her.

Laura backed up. "Nearly twelve-year-old daughter wouldn't want to be a flower girl at his wedding. Any being with the intelligence God gave a gerbil would know that. I feel like going over there and chewing those two out but good."

"For what?" Rue asked. "For wanting to get married?"

"They don't have to make an MGM production out of it," Laura insisted. "Just think how you would have felt if you'd been made to participate in Dad's wedding to Marla."

"No chance of that," Rue said.

Erica had heard the story of how Grandpop had gone away for a weekend and come back on Monday with a new bride and a stepdaughter, but she'd never understood the real horror of it before. Now she knew. "Is that Heidi person going to stay here? I thought y'all didn't like her."

"We don't."

Rue sighed. "Laura . . ."

"She didn't look how I thought she'd look." From Laura's description of the woman, Erica had imagined her as an overgrown Shirley Temple in a sequined leotard.

"She filed off her horns," Laura said.

"I guess it would have been worse if Daddy had sprung Ms. Dench on me all at once—and with a kid! That would be *terrible*."

The table fell silent for a few moments.

"Where *is* William?" Laura asked Rue. "Would you think he would have at least given you a phone call?"

"I'll call him," Rue said. "I'll talk to him."

Erica set down her spoon. "I'm not going back."

All during the bike ride over this morning, she had burned at the unfairness of it all. Oh, she knew she shouldn't be bothering her mother. Her mother had been through all sorts of awful things this year. But what about *her* and what she'd been through? Nobody ever seemed to think about that. She'd spent the year stuck over at her dad's, watching him become caught in some romantic spiderweb spun by her fifth-grade teacher, and all the while worrying that her mom, who was five miles away, might be dying. And now that *that* was all over, she was *still* having to go to her dad's during the week, just because of some stupid custody agreement. Never mind what *she* wanted.

While she'd been biking, though, she'd thought of arguments she could use. Really good ones that even her mom wouldn't be able to shoot down. She pulled them out now. "Why should I go back? I'm just in the way there now. And all last year I stayed with Dad when I should have been here, because you were having your treatments. I think I should be able to get some of that time back. Besides, I could be really, really useful around here. There's still the baby goat to feed, isn't there? And just last week Aunt Laura was saying that we needed another person to help on the farm . . . so why not use me?"

"Because it's summer. You've got junior lifeguard lessons," Rue replied.

"I don't care about that."

"You talked about it all spring," Rue reminded her.

Which was true, unfortunately. Erica had pestered both her mom and dad for weeks, but now she felt stupid. She'd only wanted to take the swim lessons because Jake Peavy, the only boy in her class really worth talking to, had said he was going to take junior lifeguard class. But then Jake's grandfather, a dermatologist in Tyler, had offered to send him to this really cool camp in Colorado, so Erica was going to be the only one from her school taking the six-week swimming course at a community center two towns away. Probably nobody there would like her. Jake didn't like her, either, but at least he would have felt he had to talk to her since they went to the same school.

"When I talk to William, I'll suggest that you might want to spend more time here this summer," Rue added.

"And that I shouldn't have to be a flower girl!" Erica said.

"I think you've said all there is to say about that," her mom answered. "But Erica, your father is going to be disappointed if you don't spend some of the summer at his place."

"No, he won't," Erica said. "He'll just say he is because he thinks that's how a father is supposed to act."

Her mother's eyes widened, but she didn't say anything.

"We *could* use the help," Laura broke in. "Just another eye on the chickens would be great. That damn hawk got one last night. And this way Leanne Dench will have the entire summer to herself to embroider her trousseau."

"What's a trousseau?" Erica asked.

"It's all the crap brides collect in anticipation of starting life with their new hubby," Laura explained. "Forget-me-not underpants, et cetera."

"She's already got those!"

"By August she might have a whole trunkful. Monogrammed," Laura joked.

Erica turned to her mom. "You're really going to call Dad?"

"Yes, I will. I'm going to call him right now. But I don't want you pacing around me while I'm trying to have a conversation."

Laura clamped a hand on her shoulder. "Come on. You can help me think of ways to torment Jeanine."

Erica jumped out of her chair, feeling as if she was suddenly part of it all again. It had been so awful to think of being cut off during the week—like she really didn't belong here. Now she would have the whole summer! Three whole months. Two whole months before the wedding.

Two months. Maybe if she put her mind to it, there wouldn't even be a wedding.

As she trailed after Webb toward a small metal storage shed, Heidi couldn't believe her luck. It wasn't that she was besotted with Webb or wanted to be near him because he was male and available and really, really good-looking, like that poor Jeanine person obviously felt. (Jeanine's disappointment as she had watched Heidi walk away with Webb had been palpable; her departing stare had felt like little tomahawks landing between Heidi's shoulder blades.) She just dreaded being under Laura's whip all day.

And Webb was nice. She hadn't thought about him in years—if ever—and now she wondered why. Perhaps because the last time she'd seen him, she'd been at the nadir of adolescence. Or maybe because she had spent nigh on twenty years trying not to think about the Sweetgum experience at all. Or maybe because she just hadn't shown stellar judgment when it came to picking men.

In fact, to say that she had shown lousy judgment would be giving her way too much credit. When she died—especially if she died soon—her name could go into the books as one of those women with over-the-top bad judgment in men, like any number of gangster molls, prison wives, and Liberace's fiancée.

Webb disappeared into the shed. It was new—new to her—along with a lot of other stuff around the place. She had never been much of a farm girl. She'd spent three years dreading the blazing hot days of so-called vacation, when she was cut off from socializing with anybody but Laura and Rue. As much as possible, she'd tried to barricade herself in her room with books, and she'd used piano practice as an excuse not to do more than she absolutely had to.

But the farm was different now. The old barn was still there, painted a bright red instead of the old peeling maroon on graying wood. And besides the barn and this shed, there was an even larger barn, a long greenhouse, and some smaller-looking wooden outbuilding. Behind the house, down the slight hill, there was a mammoth garden—most of it in orderly rows, accented by a few large raised beds. Beyond that was a cornfield. From a distance she recognized cornstalks, of course, and tomatoes in cages, and . . . well, that was about all she recognized. She hadn't so much as raised a potted tomato since she'd left this place.

Webb came out of the shed with his hands full of baskets—some of them obviously old Easter baskets. Wisps of plastic grass still stuck in the woven slats of a few.

"Are we going on an egg hunt?" she asked.

"No, a blackberry hunt. Follow me."

Around the corner was a little electric vehicle plugged into a jack on the side of the shed. "That looks like a golf cart," she observed.

"That's because it is a golf cart. Climb in."

She did as instructed. "Hi-ho, Silver," she said as he put the pedal to the metal and they lurched silently forward. "What's happened around here?"

He grinned at her. "Simple. First, Laura took over the farm, and then Rue took over Laura."

They came near a fence-enclosed area that contained a long hut that was half enclosed in wire, half in wood. "What is that?"

"The chicken house," Webb explained. "We'll probably have to deal with that this afternoon."

"You mean we'll gather eggs?" *Gathering blackberries and eggs. Laura Ingalls Wilder land.*

"Eggs . . . and other stuff."

"Feathers?"

"Manure," he said. "Chicken droppings make the best fertilizer."

Okay, so scooping up chicken shit didn't exactly fit into her rural idyll.

The tinny opening strains of "New York, New York" rang out, and she froze. For a split second she had the urge to throw herself off the cart and hit the ground—as if she were a commando hearing the whistle of an incoming bomb. Then she recognized the sound as the ring tone of her new phone.

Webb looked at her. "That's gotta be yours, 'cause I don't have one."

She reached into her pocket and pulled out her cell. The incoming number—her mother's—caused her to heave a sigh of relief.

She shouldn't have been worried. Nobody knew where she was. No one knew her new cell number. They couldn't know. She'd bought the phone at a store in the Atlanta airport and signed up for a new plan at a booth near the Cinnabon in the airport concourse. It had been tempting not to give even her mother her new number, but she'd decided that she wanted to have contact with *someone* from her old life. Not that she intended to tell her mother the truth about what was going on.

Webb didn't look at her, but his mouth was set in amusement.

"I'm sorry. I'll put it on vibrate."

"Doesn't matter to me," he answered in a lazy drawl. "But I've always noticed that the best way not to be bothered by one of those things is just not to have one."

"I can't believe you don't have a cell phone," she said.

"I manage."

There was a little lake not too far from the house, and they were about to cross the dam to get to the other side. She had a vague memory of picking berries along the fence lines over there when they were young.

"How long are you staying?" Webb asked.

She turned back to him. "Is that why Laura sent me with you? So you could wring information out of me?"

"We're not conspirators, if that's what you're wondering. I have no idea what's going on in Laura's head."

"Here's a clue. She's not wondering how best to make me happy."

He laughed. "I've heard stories."

"Did she tell you about the ninth-grade drum majorette try-outs?"

"I don't remember that."

Heidi crossed her arms. That incident still made her blood boil. "I spent years trying to learn to twirl. I twirled in my room, out in the yard, whenever I had any free time. What else *was* there to do in this godforsaken place back then? I twirled and I played piano. One whole summer I twirled my fingers off working up a routine to a Bangles song. You know, 'Walk Like an Egyptian.' And then, when the school had after-school twirler tryouts, Laura came by to wish me good luck."

"*Laura?*"

"Right. I knew there was something suspicious about it, but I hadn't realized how evil my stepsister was until I got out on the auditorium stage and completely screwed up. I couldn't hold the baton. It kept slipping out of my hands. Turns out, she'd put Crisco on it."

He faced forward, and she could tell by the way the corner of his lip quirked that he was having a hard time keeping a straight face.

"Oh, go ahead and laugh," she said. "It was Laura's greatest triumph. I looked like an idiot in my Cleopatra makeup, chasing that stupid stick all over the auditorium."

He shook his head. "Why on earth would you want to come back here?"

She glared out at the landscape. "Call it masochistic nostalgia."

"And where do you live now?"

"New York. Well, Brooklyn." God knows where she would end up when this was all over. She didn't want to go back to her old neighborhood and run into Stephen all the time. She had thought about moving to Stamford, where her mother lived, but she didn't want to drag her mother into all her problems. The one thing she'd worked hard at all through her adulthood was trying to keep her mother *out* of her private life.

She felt her phone vibrating in her pocket and tried to pretend she didn't. It was hard to ignore, though; her mind was now gnawing over her problems back at home. She pulled it out and looked at the little screen. Just her mom.

It was amazing how warm it could feel at seven thirty in the morning.

"You a fugitive or something?" Webb asked.

She flinched in surprise. Surprise at how good he was at reading her. *"What?"*

"You're avoiding calls like you're on the run or something."

"Don't worry. I'm not one of America's most wanted. I'm more like a fugitive from love." She chuckled, deciding she liked the sound of that half-truth. It made her problems seem harmless and trivial. "It sounds like one of those old cheesy made-for-TV movies, doesn't it? With Jaclyn Smith, maybe. And Parker Stevenson. Of course, no one I know looks like Parker Stevenson. But then, I don't look like Jaclyn Smith, either."

"Who?"

"You've never seen the original *Charlie's Angels*?"

"Oh, right."

"Of course, if I looked like any of those women, I'd be closest to Farrah, minus the big hair and the boobs." She frowned. "Which doesn't really leave much, does it?"

Webb squinted at her. "Uh . . ."

"You don't have to answer that," she said quickly. "My self-esteem has already taken a beating for the day. It's just like old times."

"Don't mind Laura. She gets snippy with everybody sooner or later."

His lips twisted into a lazy smile . . . or maybe it was a sardonic smile. Or, come to think of it, maybe it was a fond smile. She wasn't sure. All she knew was that there was something in his face that she liked. Those dreamy blue eyes, his relaxed posture. She could suddenly imagine spending the day lying on the grass, looking up at the clear blue sky, just talking all day. And then having Webb say something every hour or so.

They bumped along the narrow path across the dam. On one

side of them was water—with all manner of bugs skittering across it—and on the other was a steep drop-off into a thicket of tall, skinny trees.

"How long have you been here?" she asked him.

"Since February."

"Where were you before that?"

"Afghanistan. And before that, Iraq."

"Wow! Really? You're so . . ." She backed up and started over. "I mean, that must have been so intense, and you're so laid back. You don't seem at all . . ."

He arched a dark brow at her. "Like a crazy vet?"

"I'm sorry. I'm babbling."

"Maybe I'll bug out yet. Right now I'm just happy to be where it's green again and to be surrounded by trees. And to be sitting in a golf cart instead of an Abrams tank."

"Did you join the army after high school?"

"After a year of college. I stayed in a while, but then came back and worked at my father-in-law's garage while I attended a few more classes. Then they started calling up the reserves."

"So what's your whatchamacallit?" she asked. "Rank?"

He grinned. "Not been around the military much, have you?"

"No. I always thought it was odd that my mom never fell for a guy in uniform. I couldn't tell you the difference between a corporal and a lieutenant. I could tell you how to treat your house for termites, though, and a little bit about dentistry, too." She tilted a curious glance at him. "So what was your rank?"

"Sergeant." He smiled. "Anything else?"

"Married?" He didn't wear a ring.

"In mid-divorce. My mom still lives nearby. I guess you could say that's why I came back here."

You could say it, but something in his tone indicated that was only half the story—the half he was willing to talk about.

"I was wondering about Erica," she said. "Was Rue married?"

"Oh yeah. She moved back to the farm after her divorce a few years ago. Her ex-husband lives over on the other side of Sweetgum, but he sells insurance in Carter's Springs."

"So Rue got married. But not Laura?"

His expression turned stony. "No. She's had a few close calls, I guess."

"Oh, tell."

He cleared his throat. "Well, she eloped once with Kevin McBirney, but they wound up at a bar in the Deep Ellum district in Dallas and got into a knock-down-drag-out before they could make it to the justice of the peace. Now Kevin's married, and his wife won't be in the same room as Laura. I heard a few months ago that Alison McBirney walked out of Wanda's Chop Shop with half a haircut after Laura came in and sat down in the second chair."

"What else? You said there had been a few."

He shrugged. "I don't remember, really."

"That's funny about the hair salon. At least I'm not the only one Laura has conflicts with. You saw the reception I got last night. She looked like she wanted to kill me."

He chuckled. "I saw. I also saw the way she looked this morning, during your dance lesson."

"Like I was crazy?"

"She wasn't looking at you. She was looking at her sister. I was, too. It was like the old Rue was back again."

"The old Rue?"

"Rue had cancer. She went through chemo last fall and during the winter. It's been a tough year for her. For Laura, too."

That explained the odd hat and maybe her odd skin condition. "I didn't know."

"It's one of the things they don't talk about. One of the many."

He parked the golf cart on the other side of the lake, at the point where the land started to slope steeply down and dead-ended at a barbed-wire fence. The fence was covered in bushes whose long tendrils sagged with berries.

"We'll work this fence," he told her as he grabbed the baskets from the back. "Then we'll drive the perimeter of the farm till we have all that we can haul away. It's the first week for them, so it might take a while. Most of them are probably still red."

The moment they started walking down the hill, Heidi understood the warning about her shoes. The grass beneath her feet was as dry as straw, and blades poked at her through the open parts of her sandals. A sticker burr—she'd forgotten about those—lodged on her heel, causing her to hop a few steps until she could dislodge it. She picked her way across the uneven terrain and called ahead to Webb, who was already at the fence. "Why's the grass so yellow?" The stuff in the ground was already turning the same straw color as the baled hay.

He shook his head. "It's barely rained since Easter."

There were lots of berries. Heidi had forgotten about blackberry bushes, and after an hour or so she happily anticipated spending the rest of her life forgetting about them again. The bushes cascaded away from the fence line, their branches heavy with fruit. But they were also covered in thorns. And not long, prominent thorns, like rose thorns. These were prickly little things that practically leapt at your hands as you reached in to pick the berries.

By the time she had half a basket full, she was heartily sick of blackberries. And sunshine. She envied Webb his hat. The sun, which had seemed so sparkly and innocent when they had set out, beat down on her scalp like one of those heat lamps at a fast-food restaurant. The skin on her hands was crosshatched with scrapes. When she felt her phone vibrate in her pocket again, she didn't hesitate to check it. It was her mom.

The snap judgment she made to take the call derived as much from her need for a break as from her desire to get the inevitable conversation with her mom over with.

"Hi, Mom," she said.

"Heidi! Thank God! Where *are* you?"

"I've left New York."

"Where are you?"

Webb glanced over at her, and Heidi did a three-quarter turn for privacy. "I'm in L.A. I decided to go to Hawaii for a while. You know, to get away from it all."

"Hawaii!" her mother yelled in surprise and, it had to be said, disappointment. "Oh, Heidi-ho, have you lost your mind? Poor Stephen is just sick about what happened."

Heidi frowned. "What do you know about poor Stephen?"

A long sigh traveled over the airwaves. "Well, he called."

"He called *you?*"

"And came out to see me once."

"For pete's sake. The last time I spoke to him, he told me he never wanted to talk to me again, even if he needed a kidney transplant and I was the only donor match."

In a voice heavy with exasperation, her mother said, "He just doesn't understand what's happened to you, and frankly, neither do I. One minute everything seemed all set between you, and then you just went insane."

"Well, that's what happened—I went insane. Tell him your daughter is a lunatic and send him on his way."

"There! That's the kind of talk we just don't understand."

"*We?*"

"Stephen and me."

Great. All she needed was her mom and her ex-fiancé to be in cahoots. "Mom, I can't deal with this right now. They're about to start boarding my plane."

"Then you're not coming home?" her mother asked. "I told Stephen you had probably just needed to get away for a few days. . . ."

"To be honest, I might never come back."

"Oh, Heidi!"

"I mean it, Mom. Send him away. And don't bother calling me for a while."

"Is it okay to give Stephen your number?"

"Absolutely not."

"Oh, but . . ."

"No, Mom. I don't want him calling me. There's no point in getting away from it all if *it all* decides to keep phoning. Besides, he's said enough."

Stephen's resentment had kept welling up and then venting in puffs of anger. It would probably have helped if he had just let out his anger in one big explosion, but he was constitutionally incapable of that. When the moment of truth had come, when she'd told him that she had been seeing Vinnie, his own feelings had choked him. They'd been walking by Gramercy Park at night, and the sidewalk had been almost empty. Stephen could have raged at her at the top of his lungs; he could have called her every deserved expletive in the book. He'd *looked* as if he could have impaled her on the iron spikes of the park's privacy fence.

But the words hadn't come. He'd huffed and chuffed and finally spat out the worst name for her that he could think of. "You . . . you . . . you . . . *cheater*!"

Several days later he had followed her on her lunch break, had insisted on buying her coffee, and then, once they were seated, had announced that she was a virus in high heels and had given her the kidney transplant directive. After that he'd stood up, quaking with rage, and left.

From the moment she'd first started lusting after Vinnie, she'd been filled with guilt about Stephen. Now she felt something more painful—a feeling beyond the garden-variety I-want-him-back remorse. She didn't want Stephen back. Instead, she was pierced with the mortifying realization that there was something in her so despicable that she could dump a perfectly good guy like Stephen for a guy like Vinnie. She didn't appreciate the Stephens of the world. Maybe she couldn't. Maybe when it came to men, her judgment was as flawed as her mother's had always been.

"He feels so bad about what he said," Marla said to her in a plaintive voice. "He really does."

"Mom, it just so happens that I agree with him. Every awful thing he said is true. You can tell him that, next time you two huddle."

"But if you could have *seen* him, Heidi."

The thought of Stephen's puppy-dog eyes was too much. "Mom, I just can't—"

Eyes.

As she was reaching down to get a particularly plump berry,

Heidi found herself staring into a small beady pair of eyes—attached to a fat, brown, scaly body coiled up in the dappled shade of the bush.

She dropped the phone and stepped back in horror. Webb looked over at her.

"Something the matter?"

Her mouth felt bone dry, and she took another step back in the sandy soil. From the ground, she heard a distant, tinny version of her mother's voice calling out to her. How close had she come to sticking her hand right beneath that reptile's fangs?

Webb was at her side and saw the problem immediately. "Damn! That's a big one."

With his boot he kicked the phone toward the snake, which shot off so quickly in the other direction that Heidi let out the yelp that had been stuck in her throat all this time.

When the danger had slithered away, she felt she was finally able to breathe again. "What was that?"

"A copperhead."

"W-w-was it poisonous?"

"You bet."

Great. She'd forgotten this downside of Laura Ingalls Wilder land.

"Nothing to get shook up about," he assured her. "They're as scared of you as you are of them."

"That snake did not look scared."

Webb bent low and reached through the fence to retrieve her phone. He picked it up, straightened, and handed it over.

Heidi lifted it to her ear. Blessed silence. "The snake did manage to get rid of my mom. That's more than I could do."

"And the phone got rid of the snake." Webb nodded with grudging approval at the Nokia. "Maybe I should get one, after all." His lips tilted into a conspiratorial smile. "Be handy to have if I ever have to jet off to Hawaii."

Chapter 5

After everyone scattered to their respective chores, Rue picked up the phone extension, sat down at the kitchen table, and dialed William's cell phone. The number rang and rang, and finally his voice mail picked up. She left him a rundown of Erica's movements and whereabouts, and then hung up, feeling uneasy. She'd been annoyed with William this morning because of Leanne Dench and the wedding, but she hadn't really given too much thought to how worried he would be about Erica's disappearance. What if he was out hunting for her now?

She imagined him out in his truck, the window open, his eyes scanning the road ahead and the surrounding fields. His heart would be racing with growing panic and probably a little anger. She knew that feeling well. Once when Erica had gone out with Milkshake and not returned for hours, Rue had searched for her till almost dark, her heart in her throat and an irrational rage building in her. The anger had dissipated the minute she'd found Erica loping toward the house. "I lost track of time," Erica had said, almost blithely. "You aren't mad or anything, are you?"

"I'm furious!" At which point, Rue had burst into tears, releasing the tension and fear of the hour-long search and making herself look like a neurotic in the bargain.

That same alarm was probably building inside William right now. No matter how big an obtuse, philandering, brick-headed jackass he might have been with her, he wasn't completely without paternal instinct.

In his panic William might have accidentally run out of the house without his cell phone. That would explain why he hadn't picked up. She dialed his home number. After five rings, Leanne Dench picked up the phone.

"Oh, Rue!" she exclaimed, surprised.

Rue was caught off guard. "Hello, Leanne." She had to overcome the urge to call her Ms. Dench. "I wanted to let William know that Erica is here with me."

"Thank heavens! We were so worried."

She didn't sound worried. "I tried to call William, but he didn't pick up."

"William's at work."

Work? "I thought he might be out hunting."

"On a Monday?" Leanne asked.

"Hunting for Erica."

"Oh! Well, her bike was gone this morning, and she had mentioned she wanted to go back to the farm. *Run away* were the very words she used, but we both knew that she would only run away to a place where she'd have a warm bed and three squares per day."

"That's more than I know," Rue said, wishing technology had advanced to the point where she could wirelessly transmit her fist to Leanne Dench's sweetly uptilting nose.

"Well, we both know how headstrong our Miss Erica is," Leanne said with a sigh.

"She's had a hard year," Rue said.

"Oh, we know it. Poor thing!"

This "we" crap was really grating on Rue's nerves.

"William's bent over backwards to make allowances," Leanne added. "We both have."

Rue could already see the scenario developing. *She's always had a temper, but now she's just uncontrollable! Maybe we've just been too lax with her. . . .*

She took a deep breath. One incident did not an evil step-mother make. "If you happen to speak to William before I do, would you please tell him to call me?"

"He's at work."

"I know, but this is important."

"You sound upset." Leanne clucked as if she suddenly under-stood what could have put Rue into a snit. "Did Erica tell you about the engagement?"

"Yes. Congratulations."

"Thanks! Though I'm so sorry you had to hear it from Erica. William wanted to break the news to you himself, I'm sure."

Her tone made Rue's skin crawl. As if news of their engage-ment would be a devastating blow to her.

"William probably just didn't know where to find me," she replied a little acidly. Which she realized too late probably *did* make her sound jealous.

"Oh—"

"I've got to run, Leanne. Good-bye!"

Rue fled to her room, flung the phone headset on the chenille bedspread, then flung herself down next to it. *Good going, Rue. Every time you opened your mouth, you sounded a little bit more like a jealous, grasping ex-wife.*

She disliked William a little more for putting her in this situa-tion.

She lay there for a moment, taking stock. She felt tired and her back hurt. A month ago she'd slipped on a wet porch step. She remembered thinking as she fell, *Great. I've survived cancer only to be done in by a banana-peel-type fall.* She'd strained her back catch-ing herself, and the strain was still there, especially when she was lying down.

She pushed herself back up and reached over for her banjo. The only thing she could play on it was a few chords of "Oh! Su-sanna," although she made them sound pretty good, if she did say so herself. Back before she had been diagnosed with cancer, she'd always said that she wanted to learn to play an instrument. So one day in the hospital, Laura had shown up with a banjo. Rue had been tickled . . . or as tickled as someone could be one day after waking up with bandages where her breasts used to be.

The trouble was that during the radiation and chemotherapy, her old goals and desires had begun to pale in significance to the one goal left her. Survival. And when she did start feeling more confident about her prognosis, her thoughts about a lot of things had changed. Her wishes now were fewer but weightier. More elemental. She wanted the farm to be a success for Laura's sake. She wanted Erica to make it to adulthood with a good education under her belt and the self-confidence that she herself had lacked when she was younger. She wanted everyone around her to be happy, which she supposed was about as practical as hoping for a genie to pop out of a bottle and grant her three wishes.

She was fond of her banjo even if she couldn't play it. It was her talisman now—a sort of security blanket. She'd signed up for lessons and discovered that they made a good excuse to escape to Tyler and have a little time to herself, to think. Lately, she'd taken to cancelling the lessons and going to the movies or shopping, or just going to a park.

Summoned by the banjo strumming, Laura appeared at the door. "Sounds great."

The compliment made Rue stop. Laura didn't used to be such a liar. That was another side effect of cancer. "Sure, in twenty years or so I could almost be *Hee Haw* material."

"I'm supposed to be the sarcastic one."

"Sorry. I didn't mean to step on your toes." Rue put the banjo back in its case. "I'm so furious I can't think clearly."

Laura crossed her arms. "You're the calmest-looking furious person I've ever seen."

"I just talked to Leanne Dench."

Her sister's eyes lit with interest. "What did Our Lady of the Floral Underpants have to say for herself?"

"Only that she and William were worried sick about Erica. So worried, in fact, that William tootled off to work without even calling me. I'm not sure what Leanne was doing in her time of tribulation. Watching *Good Morning America*, maybe."

"No search party?"

"Apparently, they were pretty sure Erica was headed this way." Rue released a ragged sigh, wondering now if she wasn't overreacting. "Of course, it's not as if Erica's never out on her own. God knows what she gets into when she's riding around on Milkshake."

"He should have called."

It was true. The more she thought about it, the more it seemed odd that William hadn't at least tried to go pick Erica up and bring her back to the farm himself. It was negligent of him.

Or maybe she just wanted to grasp on to that word—*negligent*—because it would give her all the rationale she needed to take Erica for the summer. Maybe forever.

"Do you want to take the morning to drive over and see him?"

Rue looked up, startled. "What good would that do?"

"Let him know that he screwed this up. He's so oblivious, he probably doesn't even realize it. William probably has it in his head that he's Dad of the Year now that his little teacher has a bun in the oven."

"We don't know that. . . ."

"I'd lay dollars to doughnuts." They both pondered this a moment. "I wonder how long it will take for Leanne Dench to realize that her prince is actually a louse in shining pickup."

A dull ache started in Rue's head. Lately it seemed that one was never far off—allergy season had arrived with a vengeance.

"If I were you, I would at least call him up and screech at him," Laura said. When Rue didn't respond, she unfolded her arms and pushed away from the door. "Oh well. I'd better get back to the inmates. I left Jeanine pining in the chard."

Just after Laura left, the phone next to Rue's hand rang. She snapped it up. "Hello?"

"What in God's name did you say to Leanne? She's very upset!"

Rue squinted at the yellowed, peeling wallpaper. This bedroom was one of the parts of the house they'd never gotten around to fixing up. It hadn't seemed essential. "Why?"

"She said you were curt."

"I was a little annoyed. I was calling to tell you where Erica was. . . ."

"We *knew* where she was," William said.

"How?"

"Because Erica said she was going to run away to the farm before she stormed off to her room last night."

"And what if she'd changed her mind overnight and decided to run away to, oh, say, Alaska?"

"*Alaska?* Where would she have gotten that idea?"

"I don't know. I was just using it as an example."

He let out a weary sigh. "Why do you always have to complicate things? She *didn't* go to Alaska. She went home, and I'll bet she's fine, isn't she?"

"Yes."

"So . . . there's no problem. Except that now Leanne's a mess because everyone hates her."

"I don't hate Leanne," Rue said, exasperated.

"But Erica does."

He had more of an argument there.

"Or at least she acts like she does," he continued. I don't know what it is. Leanne dotes on her, and for her trouble, Erica acts like a spoiled brat. Something's got to be done about her, Rue. Leanne and me are getting married."

She wondered what Leanne thought of the lapses in grammar. Or what she would think of the lapses in fidelity that were surely around the corner. "Maybe we should keep them separated for a while," she suggested.

"What do you mean by that?"

"I mean that Erica could stay here for the summer and sort of ease into the idea of the new Mrs. You could have her weekends."

Immediately, William's dander was up. "That's not what we agreed to."

"I know that. But we can be flexible, can't we?"

"If you're trying to take Erica—"

"I'm not. This is a special circumstance. God knows you stepped up for me last winter."

"Yeah, but . . ." He sighed. "I don't want you to use this against me later, Rue—like I don't care about Erica."

"I won't."

"Because I do. She means a lot to me, even if she is a pain."

Rue flopped back on the bed. "This has been a hard year for her, William."

"*I* know that. Don't you think I know that?"

"I know you know. Which is why I'm mystified that you would drop a bombshell like your upcoming marriage on her out of the blue."

"What was I supposed to do? Wait till we were driving to the church? She had to find out sooner or later, and we couldn't wait too much later. Between you and me, it's pressing things to wait till August, but Leanne wants a big wedding. She doesn't want it to look like a rushed affair."

"Even if it is," Rue said.

"Well . . . She probably won't really show for a while yet, right?" he asked. "And you never know. It might not even happen at all. She had a false alarm once. Maybe it will all . . ."

"Just go away?" Had there actually been a time when she didn't think that this man was a complete dope? His brain had locked in place at adolescence. "William . . ."

Before she could say another word, William piped up. "Don't start in on me, Rue."

"I didn't say anything."

"It was the tone. You were being judgmental. This is none of your business, anyway."

"I've just been stressed out this morning about Erica."

"She's *fine*," he insisted. "If you want to take her this summer, okay. But don't act like I couldn't handle her myself, or like I was being negligent. Sometimes I think you think I'm a bad influence on my own kid."

"The time she got caught in school with the tobacco—"

"*She* stole that from my dresser drawer. What am I supposed to do about that? If anyone's responsible for her being a sneak thief, it's not me."

"Then who?" Rue asked defensively.

"Well, if you're going to talk about bad influences, then we might oughta start with your sister."

"Laura's never stolen."

"No, I guess not." William sniggered. "Just people's husbands, or would-be husbands. You've always had a blind spot for her, Rue, but most people think she's a lunatic. Leanne's a little scared of her. Well, hell, even most men are. At least the ones she hasn't slept with yet . . . not that that leaves many—"

"Shut up."

"She's your sister, okay. I'm just saying, if you want to talk about bad influences, don't point the finger at me. Since you're going to be watching our daughter this summer, you might take a few steps to make sure Erica doesn't turn out like Laura."

"She should be so lucky!" Rue snapped.

The conversation went downhill from there. By the time she hung up the phone, Rue was surprised William was still agreeing to let Erica stay the summer at the farm. But of course, as Laura and even Erica had predicted, that was probably what he'd wanted all along.

Now all that was left was for her to inform Erica of the good news, although chances were she wouldn't see her again till lunch. Erica would be out with the animals or hanging around Webb, Dylan, and Herman till then.

Rue felt in dire need of something to help her throat. Allergies were making her chest feel heavy. She went to the bathroom and looted the Benadryl box there. She hoped it didn't knock her out. The morning wasn't even half over and it felt like it should be bedtime.

* * *

Cleaning the barn just suited Laura's mood. Unfortunately, when she got there, the chore had already been claimed by Webb, who was standing in Spunky's stall with a shovel and a wheelbarrow. Spunky, who was mostly weaned now, was out in the chicken enclosure, acting as lawn mower.

"Back already?" she asked him. "What are you doing now?"

He didn't look up, just kept shoveling old straw. "Helping you, I thought. Call it an early Valentine."

"That would be nine months early. Sure you wouldn't rather just make it a late one?"

"I already gave you one this year."

"What?"

"Me."

She laughed. It was true. He had arrived at the farm in mid-February, after he'd been discharged from the army, and after he'd discovered that his wife was living with someone else and had put all his civilian clothes, his old CDs, his books, and his favorite recliner chair in a storage unit.

She watched him for a moment. How could she help it? The man looked great even when he was shoveling pungent straw out of a goat pen. Lean muscles rippled beneath his T-shirt, and his jeans hung loose on his hips. He was wasted out here, really. He should have been on television, or on a stadium stage, playing a guitar in front of thousands of shrieking fangirls.

"Everything okay?" he asked.

"Sure. Rue wants Erica to stay here for the summer. When I talked to her earlier, she was trying to get William on the horn."

He looked around. "Where is the nuisance?"

"Tagging after Herman and Dylan—though I think she called it helping. Poor guys. She'll drive them crazy."

"What are the chances?"

"Well, Herman's half crazy now."

Webb sent her a long-suffering look. "I mean of William allowing Erica to stay."

Laura tossed up her hands. "Who knows? That man is ornery,

contrary, and so stupid he could throw himself down on the ground and miss. I can't imagine what Leanne sees in him. Lord knows I never thought much of the woman, but I at least thought she was sane."

"What did Rue see in him?"

"Beats me."

"They stayed married for a decade," he reminded her.

"Inertia," Laura explained. "It's the secret of all so-called successful marriages, I think. If it weren't for sheer laziness, I'm convinced most couples wouldn't make it past six months."

"What about love?"

"What are they reading in the army these days? *Seventeen* magazine?" She laughed. "Anyway, it's nothing I ever have to worry about, thank God. I'm married to this place. A farm might make life hell most of the time, but at least you get a few spuds out of it."

" 'I do' isn't necessarily a prelude to disaster."

"How long did you and Denise have if you subtract your deployments? Two weeks?"

His jaw set, and she worried she had poked at an open wound a little too hard. "I just married the wrong person," he said.

"Well, why did you?"

"Because the right person walked out on me in a hotel in Guadalajara."

Laura turned away. She should have guessed Mexico would be right around the corner. "That was a huge mistake."

"Leaving?"

"*Going.* Stupidest thing I ever did—and that's saying something. I mean it. I've made a lifetime career of temper tantrums and social blunders and outright fuckups, but really, sneaking you away to Mexico the night before your wedding was . . ." She couldn't think of a word that wouldn't be a ludicrous understatement. "Well, it wasn't right."

"You make it sound like I was contraband you smuggled out of the country. I was a grown-up, remember?"

"Twenty-five is still puppyhood, and you weren't thinking straight. You were panicky about getting married."

"With good reason, apparently."

Laura couldn't help playing devil's advocate. "Standing Denise up at the altar was a rocky beginning to your marriage, you have to admit. If we hadn't behaved like idiots, things might have turned out differently."

"The stupidest thing I ever did was to go back to Denise."

"Then why did you?"

"I felt guilty as hell. I wanted to apologize. I never expected her to forgive me."

"Why did she?"

"I don't know, but if you want my honest opinion, I think it was because of the dress."

"The dress!"

"She'd spent a lot of money on it, and her mother had beaded the train by hand. I think she felt it would be a shame not to get to wear it." He sighed. "And so we had a marriage that was basically over before the dress came back from the dry cleaners. If I hadn't been overseas, it wouldn't have lasted a month. Anyone with half a brain could see that we weren't right."

"When you're talking till death do you part, no two people can be right. It's a grim idea. Forever. Till death. Who thought of that?"

"What would you prefer? Till Thursday do you part?"

She shook her head. "You're a bedrock romantic, Webster. I have a feeling you'll be snapped up again soon by someone. Probably by one of these absurd women around here, too." She couldn't help teasing him. "Maybe Jeanine."

His eyes glinted back at her. "Or Heidi?"

"Heaven help you!"

"She's okay."

"She's poison. Interpol could put her on umbrella tips."

"And you sent me out in the golf cart with her. I never knew I was in such danger."

"You just haven't noticed her toxicity yet. You're besotted by blond hair and a pretty face. If I weren't selfish and in need of a good farmhand, I would tell you to run for your life before it's too late. Get far away from here, and find yourself something worthwhile to do."

"Like what?"

"Get a real job. Be a cop."

"I might as well have stayed in the army."

"No, cop is better. You could tear up my speeding tickets for me."

"Great. I don't even have the job and already you're trying to corrupt me."

"I'm good at that."

His blue eyes seemed to travel six years and back in a single look. "I remember."

She picked at a splinter on the stall gate. "Why not go back to school? You were a bright kid. Go study architecture or medicine or art history. Anything. Didn't you have any big dreams when you were growing up?"

"Sure."

"Well, what happened?"

"I grew up." He put the shovel aside and took two long strides toward her. "We're both grown up now, Laura. We can stop this stupid routine this minute."

"Thirty-two's nothing. When you're pushing forty—"

He reached for her hand, which she quickly darted onto her hip. A frustrated sigh escaped his lips. "You're thirty-six."

"And you're rebounding." She turned away. "You'd be wasting your life here, Webb. You could be a teacher, or—"

"Or an astronaut," he joked.

"Be serious."

"I am. I'm seriously considering marrying a farmer."

She turned to stare into those blue eyes again, and a familiar, unnerving heaviness settled in her chest like an ache. If he just weren't quite so damn good-looking. If he didn't look so exactly right ambling around the place in those jeans.

But they had been friends for nearly twenty years. Sometimes she wondered when his patience with her would dry up. But patience seemed to be just another stellar quality he had in spades. Patience, kindness, forgiveness . . .

The man could be memorialized in stained glass.

It wasn't often that Laura got flustered, but the few times it had happened, Webb was usually the one who had managed to do it. Right now she suspected he was waiting for her to answer him, and she had forgotten what they were talking about. She licked her lips, trying but failing to think of something to say.

"Laura." He reached for her hand. His palm was calloused and rough—nearly as rough as her own.

"I don't see what you see in me. It sure as hell isn't what everyone else sees."

"Why would you care about everyone else?"

"Because you're my friend. And objectively, I think you could do better." Her chest felt tight, like she'd been holding her breath underwater for too long. When she made herself exhale, it came out in a kind of chortle. "There are a few billion women in the world, and if this farm is any sampling, you could have the pick of them."

"And that would be okay with you? If I picked just any of them?"

Outside, the world erupted into whoops of pure joy, and as those whoops grew increasingly louder, Webb and Laura turned toward the barn door. Knowing Erica's lungs, they were going to hear her for a while before they saw her, but Laura used the coming interruption as an excuse to pull her hand out of Webb's.

"Laura! Lauraaaaaa!" When Erica skidded to a stop in the maw of the barn door, her cheeks were bursts of red from running and excitement. "Guess what?" Not that she had any intention of waiting for anyone to guess. "Dad said I can stay here this summer!"

"Hallelujah!" Laura gave her niece a hug to let her know she meant it, and also as a silent thanks for picking such a good moment to interrupt.

Erica peeked at Webb from behind Laura's arm. "Isn't it great, Webb?"

"Great for you, maybe, but what about us?"

Despite his words, anyone could tell he was happy about the news. Erica was the only person Webb ever tried to be hard-boiled with, and she loved it.

Though he probably wished he could have heard Erica's big news ten minutes later.

Erica stepped back and sent them a wary look. "Is something wrong?"

"No," they both said.

"It's really good news for you, too," Erica told them. "Think of all the help I'll be."

Laura and Webb exchanged amused stares. "Just think of it," he said.

"I made us a lot of money during Chicken Fest." She looked around, as if intent on proving her worth that very moment. "And I can clean up, and all sorts of stuff. You know I like to take care of Spunky. Here, give me that shovel."

Laura grabbed her arm. "Whoa. You don't have to prove your mucking bona fides to us. And you're not going to waste your whole summer hanging around the barn with Herman and Dylan and me, either."

The child's jaw dropped open in astonishment. "What am I supposed to do?"

"You could read a few books," Laura suggested.

"*What?*"

Laura laughed. "It was just a thought."

"That's dumb. If I wanted to read, I would just stay over at Dad's. Leanne had a whole summer reading list she thought I should get through."

"Okay, so if you want to make yourself useful, you could help your mom."

If anything, Erica seemed even more appalled by that sugges-tion. "*Housework?*"

"Just a few moments ago you were telling us how useful you would be," Laura pointed out.

"Yeah, but . . ."

"Housework needs doing, too."

Erica's shoulders slumped.

Laura finally took pity on her. "Okay, tell you what. You can do your usual stuff—take care of Milkshake and Spunky, help with the chickens, and keep Shelley Winters and Monte from getting too stinky. But don't expect me to stick you in the work routine just to keep you occupied. We're overcrowded around here as it is."

"Overcrowded with idiots, though," Erica said.

Laura couldn't help a snort of approval. "All the same, you're not going to spend your summer a slave to the farm. It's summer. This is your break."

Erica glanced suspiciously from Laura to Webb. "Is she serious?"

"Don't look a gift horse in the mouth. Flee before she changes her mind."

"When do I ever change my mind?" Laura asked.

"Never," he said, his eyes challenging her. "But there's always a first time for everything."

Chapter 6

During the twenty years since she and her mother had fled Sweetgum, Heidi had forgotten what hot was. She was no wimp about the warm weather, but this kind of hot belonged in a class of its own. It was the kind of hot that could make a body feel both parched and as soggy as a used washrag at the same time. And this was just the tag end of May.

What was more, if you dared utter a complaint, the natives turned on you in full sneer. Once when she had moaned about the heat, even Dylan, the sweet-tempered seventeen-year-old kid working at the farm for the summer, who never said a harsh word without apologizing ten times for it, had chortled at her. "Wait till August!"

Around Laura she didn't dare utter a peep. Laura was all eyes and ears, like a souped-up bird of prey. One afternoon Heidi was working with Herman in what was modestly referred to as the vegetable patch—acres patchworked with orderly rows that created mountains of produce and endless hours of work—doing something called hilling potatoes. Evidently, on Laura's farm you couldn't just toss a potato seed or whatever in the ground and let it grow all on its own. Oh no. That would be too easy. Instead, a trough had been dug, and the potatoes planted and slightly covered, and now, as the seedlings pushed up and up, the dirt had to be piled on. And to make things just a little more laborious, the workers weren't allowed to just toss some dirt on with a shovel. They had to squat down and spade the dirt in baby scoops, as if Laura's Yukon Golds really were gold.

Getting into a comfortable position was impossible. Either her legs cramped up or her back ached. Her lower back, especially. She had never felt quite right since her near death at the hands of a car bumper, and squatting like this made her almost dizzy with soreness. Meanwhile, the sun pounding down directly overhead made it seem as if her brains were slowly stewing inside her skull.

At one point, she blew a breath out of her puffed cheeks. It didn't seem like much of a complaint under the circumstances. Even Herman, who had been doing this for years, looked sympathetic; they both had rivulets of sweat trailing down their grimy cheeks. She might have gone so far as to mutter "Phew."

This little peep of a complaint brought Laura swooping down on her and snapping at her with a sharpness that had just a touch of glee in it. "Where did you think you were going when you bought that ticket to Dallas? The South Pole?" Not waiting for a reply, she continued to stride down the row.

Heidi glared after her. "Laura Legree."

"*Qué?*" Herman asked.

Even while he talked to her, his deft hands and limber frame moved much faster down the row than she did. She had to scoot ahead to get out of his way. "Oh, never mind. It's too hot to think of explanations."

"*Agosto.*" Herman rolled his eyes. "Much worse."

Apparently, this was the programmed response to hysterical guests. She wondered what they said to the poor schmucks who had the misfortune to be here *in* August. Would the people who ran this place finally, actually, admit that yes, the weather sucked?

"I won't be here in *agosto*," Heidi said as she spaded clumps of dirt onto a potato plant. "If I am, it'll be because I died of heat

exhaustion and had to be buried here. Or maybe I'll leave instructions to have my body packed in ice and shipped to the
South Pole for burial. Remember that, will you?"

For a moment Herman looked as if he might say something,
but then he shook his head as if it wasn't worth the effort. He
took a gulp from his water bottle instead.

They worked the rest of the row in silence, although her head
seemed to be carrying on its own conversation. *Would* she be here
in August? God, she hoped not. But when exactly would it be
safe to go back home?

For an instant she saw Tom Chinske lying in the hospital. She
couldn't blame the vision on the heat, either; the specter of Tom
Chinske had been her constant companion for a week. Just last
week he had been beaten and left for dead. By the time she saw
him, he was lying bandaged and immobile in a hospital room.
Heidi had never seen her coworker at the bank in anything less
than a suit and tie, but in his hospital bed he was a vulnerable
plaster carapace with a hospital gown and a sheet thrown over
him. One cast stuck out from his right shoulder, and another jutted one leg higher than the other under the covers. There was a
large bandage crowning the top of his head, which his comb-over
usually attempted to cover. The bandaging continued around the
left side, Vincent van Gogh style over his ear, and down across his
jaw and chin. He wasn't wearing his plastic frame glasses; his
cheek was so swollen, she didn't imagine they would fit at that
moment. Without them his eyes looked rabbity and naked. Naked
except for the fear.

The fear never passed, even when it was clear he had focused
and knew who she was.

"Did you see who . . . ?" she asked him after she'd gone through
the motions of giving him flowers and sympathy.

He said nothing.

"Do you think it had anything to do with the . . . you know . . .
the case?"

Tom stared up at the ceiling. *"Uh cashe?"*

He was missing a lot of teeth, and it took her a few moments to convert the sounds coming out of his mouth into actual words. *What case?* She blinked at him in surprise. He had to know what she was talking about.

His head was turning from side to side as fast as multiple concussions would allow. He took agonizing care to make his words come out more clearly this time. "I . . . don't . . . remember."

How could he not remember? He was rumored to be the whistle-blower for an embezzling scheme at the Bank of Brooklyn, where they both worked. She knew through her boss—her panicked boss, who couldn't delete and shred his files fast enough—that Tom had already had one clandestine meeting with a DA. Apparently to blow the whistle on Vinnie.

Vinnie, who was her boyfriend as well as her boss. Which Tom Chinske knew.

"Amnesia," Tom said, swallowing with effort. Listening to him took effort, too. She leaned forward to hear him, to decipher his toothless words. "I've forgotten everything, including where I put things." His gaze cut meaningfully to hers. "Elvin Johnson."

Elvin Johnson? The name sounded familiar. Was it the man Tom was going to talk to at the DA's office?

She reached out to him but ended up just caressing the plaster shell on his arm.

"The DA's got nothing yet," he said. "Nothing. Tell Vinnie."

"I'm not here for Vinnie."

"Please?"

How could she ever see Vinnie after this? She felt sick with anger and disgust knowing that a man whom she had already shattered her life for—and Stephen's life, too—was capable of brutality on this scale. It wasn't just the casts and bruises that scared her, but the look in Tom's eyes. He was a beaten man in more ways than one.

She spent that night, Thursday night, in her apartment, weeping one moment, hyperventilating the next. She kept seeing Tom Chinske in that hospital bed and remembering that voice, which had sounded like her grandfather's when he'd taken his dentures out. *I've forgotten everything.* The phrase made her blood boil. She wanted to take up Tom's quest herself. There was probably incriminating evidence in her own files, just through letters she'd typed for Vinnie and e-mails concerning various transactions.

But then her anger would abate, and she would be left frozen in fear. She had no courage. None. Zip. She couldn't remember taking a principled stand in her entire life, and the idea of starting now, when she could either end up like Tom or maybe even floating in the Gawanus Canal, caused her to cower in a fetal ball on her futon couch. Surely the authorities would discover all the incriminating evidence they needed without her help. Eventually. Why should she put her head in a noose?

She imagined going to work on Monday and finding the place all taped off. Uniformed men would be hauling file cabinets and hard drives away in handcarts. They would probably want to talk to her. They might even suspect her as being part of the scheme. But it was okay; she was just an administrative assistant. Just a secretary. Why would she know anything? She had no background in banking herself. Embezzling was a complicated business, and she was just a music school dropout. Sure, she might have noticed once or twice that many of Vinnie's investment clients seemed on the aged side and rarely came into the bank. But they were *old*. Maybe they were shut-ins. How was she supposed to know?

She hadn't known. Not till the day before, when she'd walked into Vinnie's office and found him hovering over the shredder, muttering about someone named Hamilton Cho, and cursing Tom Chinske for trying to be a hero.

She had backed out of the office and locked the file cabinet by her desk. She didn't want any part in a crime. But who was she kidding? She'd already been a part; the authorities would know that. And her relationship to Vinnie—which they would find out, since they always found out—would throw suspicion on her.

On Thursday, the day after she'd seen Vinnie shredding, Tom had gone out to lunch and never come back. The rest of the bank thought it was a case of a middle-aged drone finally snapping and playing hooky. Heidi knew better—especially when Vinnie had come back from his long lunch slightly drunk and humming Frank Sinatra tunes to himself. He loved Frank, especially when he was happy.

As she'd listened to Vinnie humming "I've Got the World on a String" and looked at the door to Tom Chinske's empty office standing ajar, a terrible certainty had taken hold of her.

Tom was as steady as a clock, and he rarely went out to lunch. He always ate a tuna sandwich from home at his desk. He would never go AWOL.

And Vinnie wouldn't be humming about sitting on a rainbow if Tom had made it to his meeting with the DA.

She'd got up, told Vinnie she had to go to the dentist, and bolted out of the office. She didn't even wait until she'd gotten home to start calling hospitals to find Tom.

All that night after getting back from the hospital, she bunkered down in her apartment with the door bolted and chained and the shades down. In hiding. From Vinnie, of all people. Good-looking, sexy Vinnie, the man she'd latched on to to spice up her dull life. Which, she had to admit, he had certainly done.

Her phone rang twice, sending her into new paroxysms of fear, but both times it turned out to be just Stephen calling to hang up on her. Once she actually heard the anger balled up in his throat, choking him, before he slammed the phone down.

On Friday morning she put on her most comfortable work clothes, half expecting that she would end the day under hot lights in a police interrogation room. But after she got off the subway at Borough Hall and fatalistically trudged the two blocks to the building, the only policelike creature she found at the bank was Schlomo, their security guard. Around the coffeemaker, everyone was chattering about Tom Chinske.

"*Why?*" People kept asking, as if any of their number might actually have the answer.

Heidi did have the answer, but she wasn't about to enlighten them.

Lorraine, one of the tellers, had a theory that it was always the quiet ones that were involved in seedy activities. She couldn't believe that it was just a random crime.

"If he weren't involved in *something,* why would a guy pulling down his salary for thirty years have to wear the same three awful suits? And why did he always give a measly *five-dollar* Starbucks gift card for Secret Santa? What did he spend his money on?"

Plenty of other people shouted her down. Tom was pathetic, but not bad. In the city horrible things could happen to anybody. *Anybody.*

"He's lucky to be alive," said Jeff Sargent, from Loans. He caught Heidi's eye. "Don't you think?"

Heidi, who had been frozen while listening to them all, started abruptly. "Me?" She hadn't spoken a single word since leaving Tom Chinske's hospital room, and now her voice was a pathetic squeak. She could feel her face reddening to a guilty crimson, as if *she* had been the one who had beaten Tom to a pulp.

Jeff's office was right next to Tom's, which itself was next to Vinnie's. Heidi worked for all of them. She knew Jeff knew there was something between her and Vinnie. Did he also know exactly what Vinnie was up to?

And did he suspect her of being a part of it?

Her skin twitched, almost as if it was already chafing under the fifty-fifty cotton/poly blend of an orange prison jumpsuit.

"I was at the hospital last night," Jeff said. "Tom said you'd just left. From the looks of him, wouldn't you say he was lucky?"

At that moment, the scent of Armani Mania reached her nose like a malevolent shadow passing over her. Vinnie's tsunami approach to applying cologne had been one of the most disturbing things about him . . . before she'd discovered that he was an embezzling, murderous thug.

Did he already know that she had been to see Tom last night? Did he have any suspicion of all the law-abiding thoughts racketing around inside her head?

"Very lucky," she said. "Except for the amnesia."

That last word brought exclamations from everybody. They hadn't heard anything about amnesia.

Jeff looked perplexed. "He didn't mention that to me."

"He can't remember a thing," Heidi said, pronouncing every syllable carefully. "He has no memory at all of the past several weeks." She forced herself to meet Vinnie's dark eyes, which she immediately regretted. His gaze lasered right through her, and the suspicion in it shattered what meager calm she had left. "He's afraid he won't be much use to anyone anymore."

Lorraine clucked in sympathy. "Poor Tom! And I thought he was pathetic *before* all this happened. Now . . . ."

Everyone nodded. Except Vinnie. He'd already withdrawn to his office and shut the door.

Heidi turned on her heel and wobbled back to her own desk. Behind her, she could hear mutters.

"What's the matter with her?" someone whispered.

"How did she even know he was in the hospital?" another coworker asked.

She could just imagine the question their looks conveyed behind her back. *Are she and Tom . . . ?*

A week ago she would have laughed at the idea of herself and pathetic old Tom Chinske. Now she wanted to weep. She wasn't fit to file his paperwork. He was brave—or at least he had been until he'd been pummeled into hamburger—whereas she was a cheater, a passive conspirator to felonies, and a coward.

She sat at her desk for a long time, trying to think of what to do next. It seemed pointless to do actual work, since she couldn't imagine she would be a proud Bank of Brooklyn team member much longer. Even if the authorities didn't haul her away, how would she survive without a job? And how would she find another one? Getting work right now was about as likely as winning the lottery.

She had a little money saved up, but not enough to keep her going for long. Her apartment was too expensive; she'd have to move deeper into Brooklyn, or to Queens or (dear Lord) the

Bronx. Or she could go home to her mom's in Stamford and try commuting until she landed another job and saved up enough. But going home would be wretched. For one thing, her mother had been so excited about Stephen, so sure that he was finally *the one*. Marla Bogue, four times married, couldn't fathom why Heidi didn't share her enthusiasm for walking down the aisle. She had assumed Stephen was going to change all that, and had embraced him with gusto, especially since he seemed well off and reasonably normal. He was just a man who sold advertising for a major magazine publisher; unlike most guys Heidi seemed to end up with, he didn't harbor any secret dreams of being a professional bassoonist or a Buddhist monk. He wasn't recovering from anything or rebounding from anyone. He was a good guy. So, naturally, she had dumped him.

But she couldn't think about that. She couldn't think about what would happen next. For once in her life, she needed to do the right thing. Tom Chinske wouldn't have sat there cowering like a pigeon-hearted lump in a swivel chair.

At least, yesterday he wouldn't have.

She craned her neck around and looked at the door to Joe Sanfred's office, across the bank lobby. She could just go to Joe with her suspicions. He was the bank's branch manager. In fact, she wondered why Tom hadn't told him. Or maybe he had.

Or maybe Tom remembered, as she did, that Joe and Vinnie went golfing together and always palled around at the office's get-togethers. At last year's Christmas party, they had shown up in Santa suits, already eggnogged up.

She wasn't going to take any chances on Joe Sanfred.

She did a quick scouring of her computer for the names Hamilton Cho and Elvin Johnson. Hamilton Cho wasn't there. She Googled him and discovered that he was an assistant DA working in Lower Manhattan. She MapQuested his office and printed up the directions.

Elvin Johnson apparently had an active account, because Vinnie had been dealing with him. Quickly, before she could change her mind, she went down the hall to the supply room, swiped a fresh data stick, and started copying what she supposed would be the most incriminating information from her computer. Who knew if it actually was or not. She hurriedly grabbed things from her hard files—duplicates of letters, handwritten notes, anything that had passed her desk regarding Elvin Johnson's account.

She slipped the data stick a few hard copies of e-mails and the other information she'd gathered into a manila envelope, shoved it into the cloth shopping bag she kept under her desk, and picked up her phone to make an emergency dental appointment, which she knew she would never keep. Then she knocked on Vinnie's door and poked her head into his office.

He leaned away from his computer screen and looked at her. "Hey, babe."

She forced a pleasant expression. "Hey, yourself. You didn't call me last night."

"I thought you had a toothache." His gaze pinned her for a moment, like a bug on a specimen board. Then he shrugged. "Anyhow, it sounds like you were busy."

She tried to swallow but couldn't.

"Poor Tom," he said, his dark eyes lasering into her. "I wonder what happened."

She bit her lip. "The thing is, I've got to go back to see Dr. Waymire this morning. He wants to do a crown. You know how long that takes."

"Where is he?"

"Dr. Howard Waymire. East Fifty-third."

He jotted something down, then tossed his pencil aside. "See you later, then."

"You haven't taken me to dinner in ages," she told him. "Not since last weekend."

He looked up at her with his nearly black eyes. "That's right. I guess I'll have to take you out." After a slight hesitation, he added, "Soon."

Take her out, or rub her out?

After she closed the door, her legs felt like rubber underneath her. *I'll be dead by coffee break.*

If she knew what was good for her, she would sit right back down at her desk. She'd been a spineless follower all her life. Why stop now?

On the other hand, even if she wimped out, Vinnie might still want to get rid of her. He knew that she knew. If she was going to be a coward, she at least wanted to reap the benefits—the prime benefit being continuing to live. If she was going to die anyway, she might as well be brave.

She shut down her computer, grabbed her purse and the shopping bag, and left the building. Her adrenaline was pumping, but she attempted to maintain an outward calm.

It was a short subway ride to Lower Manhattan. On the way, she wondered if she could talk Hamilton Cho into giving her some sort of protection. Probably not. She doubted she rated the witness protection program. That was for serious cases—men who narced on mobsters. Vinnie wasn't really a mobster; he was more of an independent crook. She could try to get a restraining order . . . but based on what? Besides, true crime novels were littered with the sad stories of women who had gotten restraining orders against the men who eventually bumped them off anyway. Her best bet was probably just to go hide in her mother's basement.

Who was she kidding? Vinnie could hunt her down at her mother's, no problem. He would hunt her down no matter where she went.

She couldn't talk to the district attorney.

But she couldn't just do nothing, could she?

She pulled out the manila envelope and fished a pen from her purse. Across the front of the envelope, she scrawled: *Bank of Brooklyn files. Case against Vincent Cavenna.*

When she emerged from the subway, she took a deep breath and tried to get her bearings. According to MapQuest, the building she wanted was just two blocks away. She wanted to get there as quickly as possible, so she plunged in between two parked cars, preparing to cross in the middle of the street. Looking left, she glimpsed a man double-parked in an old sedan. He had dark brown hair with blond streaks in it. She never understood guys who did that—especially when the streaks came out almost orange, like this guy's. *Very unattractive.*

Just as the words *very unattractive* flitted through her mind, so did the consciousness of another sound. A motor revving. She had taken her second step into the middle of the street just as the realization struck her that she'd made a fatal error. She'd been focused on superficialities—hair—when she should have been paying attention to the car: it had her name on it.

The street she was on was a side street, but suddenly it seemed as wide as the Grand Canyon. She'd never get across it in time. Her only hope would be to hop backward.

She closed her eyes and threw herself backward as if her life depended on it, which it did. Unfortunately, she plowed right into the bumper of a parked car. Her legs buckled, and she spilled to the ground a split second before the sound of peeling tires rent the air. She squeezed her eyes shut and rolled once to get away from the oncoming wheels.

When she opened her eyes again, the car was already speeding away. She'd been expecting to die, so all things considered, she was in good shape. She felt bruised and shaken, and her butt hurt from tripping and landing on her ass.

A round blonde woman in her early forties, decked out in baby blue business casual, was running toward her. Her face was screwed up in a mask of concern.

"Are you all right?" she said loudly. "Do you need help? Should I call an ambulance?"

Heidi shook her head, both to clear it and to ward off the woman.

"Don't move!" the woman shouted. "Something might be broken."

"If it were broken, I couldn't move."

The woman grabbed her by the cheekbones and brought her face so close, they almost did an eyeball bump. She spoke as if Heidi were deaf. "What is your name?"

Heidi blurted out the first alias she could think of. "My name is Deborah Kerr."

"Are you in shock, Deborah?" The woman was obviously not a fan of *The King and I*. She grabbed her arm and started taking Heidi's pulse. "My name's Marcia Carter. I'm Red Cross trained. I saw it all happen. It was a gypsy cab. I don't know why the city can't do something about those. If they got rid of the squeegee men, they should be able to crack down on unlicensed cabs. I'm going to give the police a piece of my mind when they get here."

"Police?" Heidi asked nervously. "Forget it. I'm fine." She struggled to get up, but it was hard to get off the ground while her butt hurt and the woman was still clamped on to her wrist.

"You have to wait for the police. I got the first three letters of the license. HMT! I remember because I looked and then immediately thought, *Hello, Margaret Thatcher!* That's how I remember things—using initials."

To think she had cheated death only to be held hostage by a Good Samaritan.

"I'd better call an ambulance, too," the woman said.

"No!" Heidi needed to think. What if the streaky-haired man came back?

What if he was the same goon who had worked over Tom Chinske?

The woman finally let go of her arm and dashed out into the street to get Heidi's purse. She was almost run over herself. *I'm a jinx*, Heidi thought. *I should find a cave somewhere and hide from the world to stop myself from doing more damage than I already have.*

"You should go," Heidi told her as the woman handed over her squished purse. The shopping bag was still looped around Heidi's shoulder. "I'm perfectly okay."

"If you won't let me call you an ambulance, I'm going to hail a cab and take you to the hospital myself."

"No, please." Heidi fished through her purse. "I'll call a friend. You don't need to stay with me . . . see?" Hoping a visual aid would get rid of the woman, Heidi pulled out her cell phone, only to find it smashed to bits. Shattered metallic bits showered onto the pavement.

"You can't use *that*." Before Heidi could say anything more, the woman had stopped a cab in the street and was bundling her into it. Heidi got a last glimpse of the government building she'd been heading toward as she fell into the backseat. She should have scooched herself right out the opposite passenger door and run the rest of the way to that building. She should have bravely defied Vinnie and the goon who had tried to kill her.

But she didn't. And she couldn't say that she was sorry to have her courage fail her. This had been a close enough call for her taste. She wasn't wild to find out what Vinnie's next move would be.

"Take us to St. Vincent's Hospital," her guardian angel commanded the driver.

"I'll go by myself," Heidi insisted. Thanks so much, Margaret."

"Marcia."

"Right. You've been more than a help."

"But—"

Heidi shut the door quickly and the cab blasted off, leaving Marcia Carter thwarted in her desire to go above and beyond the call of good citizenship. "Don't bother with the hospital!" she told the driver.

"Where to, then?"

She was torn. She knew she should probably flee for her life, but she wanted to go home. To see her apartment one last time. And get some stuff. She would become her own one-woman witness protection program.

She shouted out her address in Brooklyn. "And then to the airport."

"Are you all right? Heidi?"

A large hand clamped down on Heidi's shoulder, and suddenly she was staring into Webb's deep blue eyes. She felt disoriented and headachy, either from fear or from heatstroke. The last thing she remembered, she'd been kneeling next to Herman, but now she was laid out flat between the potatoes and the broccoli.

She shook her head, inadvertently flicking a shower of sweat in Webb's direction. "I'm fine."

Sitting up made her dizzy—and embarrassed. They had an audience. Dylan, Herman, and a few of the women had formed a semicircle around her.

"We need to get her out of the sun," Claire said. "She looks like she's suffering from heatstroke."

"Heatstroke," Montana agreed.

"She's probably dehydrated."

Webb kept his hand on Heidi's shoulder. "You should go inside."

"You mean that I've done enough agricultural damage for one day?"

The problem of the sun was solved in the next moment, when the women parted and Laura towered over her, casting a long shadow. She eyed Heidi for a moment and then took in the rest of them. "Looks like y'all are busier than chiggers at a picnic."

"She fainted."

"Fell into a swoon, did she?" Laura was clearly not concerned.

Heidi stood up, aided by Webb. "Yeah, I did. Now I'm going to take Webb's advice and go inside."

"Webb's advice?" Laura lips quirked up at him. "Sassy Spinster Farm's own Marcus Welby."

God, she was loathsome. Heidi's knee-jerk instinct was to pretend she wasn't really a wimp and to keep working, but noticing the looks being exchanged between Laura and Webb, she decided there was a better way to annoy Laura. She grabbed Webb's arm and practically fell into his lap, even though she was standing. "Help me back to the house?" she asked in a breathy purr.

Webb's face looked startled for a moment, then gave way to a knowing grin. "Be glad to." He scooped her up like a groom carrying a bride over the threshold.

It was just a hundred yards to the house, but Laura looked as annoyed as if their intention was to jet off for a romantic rendezvous in Paris.

The moment they were out of her view, Heidi swung her feet happily. "It's so fun to piss her off."

"Seems to have worked on you like a tonic."

"In the old days I never won any battles. That hide of hers was impenetrable. She didn't have any weak spots."

"Still doesn't."

Heidi gaped at him.

"What?"

He honestly didn't appear to know. Did she have it all wrong?

"You can just deposit me on the porch," she told him.

He did just that but hesitated. He seemed to think she would be upset about having to go back in. "You'll be all right?"

"Of course. It's safer in the house for me, anyway. Mean sister outside, nice sister inside."

He started back to the garden. After a few steps, he turned. "She's really not that bad, you know."

Poor man.

Heidi had plenty to do in the house. She'd wanted time to have Rue's computer to herself so she could scour the Internet for news of the bank. She was still curious about the man named Elvin Johnson, too. He hadn't popped up in any of her Google searches, but maybe she just hadn't typed in the right keywords.

First, though, she needed to do laundry. In her frenzy to toss stuff in the duffel bag before the streaky-haired goon could track her down, she hadn't brought many useful clothes. What little she had brought, she'd worn already and sometimes reworn. She pulled the pillowcase off one of the pillows on her bed and stuffed her dirty clothes in it.

The laundry room was on the other side of the kitchen, off the larger pantry. Going through the kitchen, she realized that it was the first time since her arrival that she had seen it empty. Rue was nearly always there, usually with a guest or two hanging out.

The cavernous kitchen was a study in decorative confusion. The original bones were all there—the cabinets that rose to the ceilings, with their glass pulls and handles, and the three-inch molding along the edges of the ceiling, which no one would bother with nowadays. But the old counters had been done over long ago in an avocado green Formica that had looked dated when Heidi was a kid and now seemed almost as antique as the glass pulls. The appliances had been updated more recently— large stainless-steel fixtures that would be fashionable if their surroundings were at all cooperative.

The room wouldn't be attractive at all if it wasn't so homey, and that comforting warmth was primarily due to the person who inhabited it most often. The mishmash of chrome and steel and Formica and old crockery seemed just right because you could imagine Rue there, telling you to help yourself to coffee or a cookie or whatever. She had always reigned supreme in the kitchen, even when they were all kids. In fact, Heidi could picture Rue there when they were teenagers, while she couldn't imagine her mother there at all. Had her mother actually prepared meals in this room? It was hard to believe, but it must have happened occasionally. They hadn't starved, and Rue at seventeen couldn't have done *all* the work.

Now the room was empty except for half-prepped food piled everywhere. A mound of carrots sat by the drain board, half scraped. A saucepan of small red potatoes in water waited to be transferred to the stove. There were several piles of greens, some washed, some not, and another pan let out an oniony smell and steam, as if it had just been turned off.

She wondered where Rue was, then found her in the laundry room, slouched on a stool, her torso draped over the dryer. Hugging it almost, as if she were trying to absorb its heat. The knobs of Rue's vertebrae poked through her white T-shirt, but Heidi couldn't tell if the slow breathing indicated sleep or some weird kind of meditation ritual.

She cleared her throat lightly as she dropped her clothes-stuffed pillowcase to the floor.

Rue immediately straightened. "Hey!" She smiled as if it were perfectly normal to be caught hugging her appliances. "Need to do a load?"

"Is it okay?"

"Of course. Go right ahead."

"I won't bother you?" For some reason Heidi hesitated to ask the obvious. "I mean . . . Are you feeling all right?"

Rue shrugged. "Just backachy and a little tired. Now that the busy season is upon us, I catnap whenever I can."

That was understandable—but wasn't one of the advantages of working at home the ability to actually catnap on your own bed? She left the question unasked and busied herself by dumping her clothes in the washer. Rue handed her a scoop of detergent. Heidi hadn't thought to bring any, natch. Back when she had been flinging things into her bag, she hadn't been thinking, period.

"For some reason, when I packed to come here, I didn't factor in getting dirty. How stupid was that?"

"A lot of people come unprepared."

"Unprepared is my middle name, and not just in packing. Thinking ahead about anything doesn't seem to be my strong suit."

Rue folded her arms as she leaned back on her stool. "It seems to me impetuous people are the ones who end up doing the interesting things. The leap-before-they-look types."

"Actually, I'm living proof that your theory's wrong. I tend to leap into big messes."

"Are you in a mess now?"

Heidi stared at the waterfall of water pouring over her clothes in the washer before slamming the lid shut. "I'm in a little bit of a jam," she admitted. "I just need a place to stay until a muddle in my personal life blows over. That's why I'm here."

"I didn't really think you'd come here out of nostalgia."

"No." Heidi laughed. "Though I have to say, Laura's giving me a very potent reminder of what our relationship was twenty years ago."

"She's very territorial about this place, and when she's nervous, she gets up on her haunches, like a bear."

A stringy old bear with a shotgun. "Look, I know it takes crust for me to come back here. After all that we did . . ."

"*You* didn't do anything."

"My mom, then. And running out like we did, *when* we did."
Her mother had made her escape the weekend after the sisters
had been in a car accident, while Rue was still in the hospital.
Heidi had been ashamed then; now she could barely look Rue in
the face. "It was awful of us."

"We knew it wasn't you, Heidi. And Dad was more embarrassed than heartbroken, I think. Everybody knew your mom
never belonged here."

"*I* never belonged here, either. I still don't."

"Lots of people don't belong here," Rue said, pushing herself
up to a standing position. "That doesn't mean they can't enjoy it
for a little while. And, I for one, have enjoyed having you around.
It's livened things up."

"It has?"

"It's always entertaining to see Laura in full-bore paranoia
mode. She can't decide if you're trying to steal the farm or Webb,
or what. She's back to her old self almost."

"Was she ever any other way?"

"You might not believe it, but while I was going through
chemotherapy, she was a fantastic nurse."

Heidi tried to imagine it, but the thought of being sick and at
Laura's mercy was a nightmare.

"The only bad part was the food," Rue said. "Laura has a limited repertoire. One more baked potato might have finished me
off completely. But usually it was either that or her other specialty, which she called cream-of-whatever's-in-the-refrigerator
soup. And I mean *whatever* was in the refrigerator. Wilty vegetables, leftovers, tubs of yogurt on the verge of expiring . . ."

Heidi shuddered. "Maybe Laura and my mother have more in
common than they think. Remember the time when Mom was
too lazy to go to the store and she decided she could just make a
meal out of some old hamburger and a can of peeled tomatoes?"

"Hamburger soup!"

"She even tossed sliced pickles in it."

Rue laughed until she doubled over coughing. The coughing went on longer than the laughing.

"You should see a doctor about that."

"Oh God, I've seen nothing but doctors. Last time they said I was having allergies and that was what was causing the sore throat. It's always something. My immune system isn't worth beans anymore. It probably won't be for a while yet."

"That happened to my dad after he had chemo. My *real* dad, in California."

Rue's eyes lit with interest. "He had cancer?"

"Stomach cancer."

"That's terrible. How is he now?"

"Oh . . . well, he died." Heidi added quickly, "He was way gone when he was first diagnosed, though. Stage three and a half, or something awful like that."

Rue's lips twisted at the corners. "I'm familiar with stage three."

"Oh." Why couldn't she keep her damn mouth shut? Of course, *now* she didn't feel she could just say nothing. She cast about for something to cover the discomfort of just standing there. "I had my own health event a few minutes ago. Heat-stroke."

Rue's eyes narrowed. "Out in the garden?"

"It was the weirdest thing. You know how in old movies women fall into swoons? And you always think, *No way*? Well, apparently I've got more Norma Shearer in me than I thought."

"That's a good thing to find out," Rue said. "I have to say, even when I was at my sickest, I loved watching health problem melodramas. Not so much the goofy Dr. Kildare stuff, but the heavy-duty weepers, like *An Affair to Remember*."

"*One Way Passage* with Kay Francis and William Powell."

Rue snapped her fingers. "Oh . . . I know that one. They're on the ship and he doesn't know she's dying and she doesn't realize he's being taken to prison."

"Exactly!"

"And *Dark Victory*," Rue said. "Of course."

Heidi shook her head. "Okay, that one goes overboard. Bette Davis is too much. The whole end scene, where she says good-bye to the dogs and then lies down on the bed to die with the angelic choir—it always gives me the giggles."

Rue looked disapproving. "You and Laura! We almost came to blows at the end of *Now, Voyager* because she was laughing. I told her she could never watch another Bette Davis movie with me."

"That's harsh." It was also harsh being compared to Laura. "Would you do me a favor?"

Rue tilted her head. "What?"

"Let me cook dinner?"

"That would be doing *me* a favor."

"Not really," Heidi answered quickly. "I heard Laura say something earlier about wanting to take everyone out wild pig hunting this afternoon. I don't think being around Laura and firearms would be good for my health."

Rue seemed amused. "I have to think about all the others, too. *Can* you cook?"

"Sort of. I'm more of a baker, actually." Heidi added, "But I've logged a lot of hours in front of *Rachel Ray*. That's got to count for something, right?"

Rue didn't look entirely convinced, but she capitulated. "Okay. On two conditions."

"Which are?"

"Number one, I supervise."

"I was counting on it. What's number two?"

"I get to play Aretha."

"Agreed," Heidi said. "As loud as you want."

Chapter 7

All the guests wimped out on the wild pig hunt. Surprisingly, it was Margaret who cried uncle first. She didn't even make it past the yard before announcing she'd rather sit on the porch with a glass of sweet tea than chase after these elusive pigs no guest had even seen. Then a patch of bull nettle near the creek bottom took out the nurses, who started whining at the first little scrape and announced that they needed immediate first aid. Jeanine held out the longest, mostly because she was too busy jabbering at Webb to notice she was uncomfortable. But when Webb decided to escort the nurses back, Jeanine became cranky, swatting miserably at grasshoppers flying up at every step and whining about mosquitoes.

Laura could almost share her disappointment—not about the bugs, but about Webb leaving. She'd hardly had a real word with him ever since their talk in the barn. A shift had taken place. It used to be that Laura could count on catching Webb's eye when something funny happened or on his anticipating exactly when she needed a hand. Lately, though, when she tried to catch his eye, he was apt to be laughing already with Heidi. And the way he had carried her to the house like he was Heathcliff or something had been positively sickening.

"How long are we going to be out here?" Jeanine whined after a few minutes of being solo with Laura.

"Until I've gotten a good shot at a pig."

Jeanine all but stamped her little feet. "I don't think these pigs exist. They're like a mirage in your imagination or something."

"My imagination didn't root up my squash plants."

Jeanine let out a cluck of exasperation. "You've got, like, a *ton* of squash plants. I weeded the squash patch today."

Laura rounded on her. "What you weeded were the seedlings. That's all there are now—seedlings. Next week other farms will be selling squash at the market and we won't. Which means money we won't be making. Because of the damn pigs!"

"Okay!" Jeanine said. "Jeez, excuse me for breathing. The only reason I didn't go back with Webb and them was that it seemed mean to leave you out here all alone."

"I *like* to be alone."

The woman's chin shot up. "Lucky you, because it's not like people are craving your company."

Laura glared at her, then belatedly remembered Rue's many admonishments about curbing her temper around the guests. Screeching at them about squash probably wasn't what Rue had in mind. But she'd eat dirt before apologizing. "Would you like some bug spray?" she asked, trying to make amends in a less humbling fashion. "I think I have some in my backpack."

"I can't stand the smell," Jeanine said. "Besides, I've heard it causes cancer."

"Look, if you want to go home . . ."

"*Of course* I want to go home! I don't even believe in killing things, especially not with guns."

"Then why are you here? As a PETA representative?"

"I came because it was what everyone else was doing!" Jeanine said, near tears.

Because it was what Webb was doing, she meant.

"Look, you don't have to stay out here on my account. If you just want to go back, go."

Jeanine's eyes bulged. "Go back *how?*"

Laura pointed. "The farm's just over that hill where the trees are. You can't miss it."

Jeanine looked longingly in that direction. "You think I can make it?"

"*Of course* you can. It's a more direct way than the way we came out. It's a cakewalk."

Jeanine gave her one last glare, turned, and set off, still flapping her arms in front of her as if they were grasshopper wipers.

Laura let out a long sigh of relief. Alone at last.

Then guilt set in, and dread. She shouldn't have snapped at Jeanine. Rue would probably hear about it and give her one of her Miss Manners lectures.

It wasn't Jeanine she was pissed at, anyway. It was the whole setup. The guests. The drought. The pigs. And Heidi.

What was Heidi doing here? And more importantly, when was she leaving? It had been over a week.

Her departure couldn't come too soon. She was throwing the whole place out of kilter. The house was too full, Rue was overworked, and . . . well, Laura just didn't trust her. Something was not right with that woman.

Laura strode on to the next pasture, where she spied Erica sitting on Milkshake under an old blackjack oak. Her face was pinched in concentration. Laura headed over in that direction and was almost upon her before Erica noticed her.

"What are you doing out here?" Laura asked.

"Nothing."

Despite Erica's excitement at being able to spend most of her summer on the farm, in the past week she hadn't seemed quite her usual high-spirited self. She'd looked preoccupied and bored by turns, and once, when they'd been moving the chicken house and Herman and Dylan had been teasing her, she'd stepped away from her corner of the hutch and stomped back to the house.

"This is a good spot for nothing." Laura leaned her back against the trunk of the tree and examined her niece, who had a curious look in her eye. Small wonder. She was two months shy of twelve and coming off a year of stress and worry. Now her father was about to get hitched to her archenemy. And as far as Laura could tell, Erica had no one her age to talk to. That was the downside of growing up on a farm. At least when she was young, she'd always had Rue.

"Is everything okay?" Laura asked. "You've looked a little droopy lately."

Erica shrugged. "I'm all right."

"But . . . ?"

"But I was just thinking." Erica looked down at her. "What if I got my dad to fall in love with somebody else? Then he wouldn't want to marry Ms. Dench."

Laura laughed. "That explains it, then."

"Explains what?"

"The look I saw on your face just now. Like a maniacal Hayley Mills."

"I don't know who you're talking about," Erica said, clearly frustrated by Laura's lack of enthusiasm. "I think it's a good plan."

"No, it's not. If your dad wanted to fall in love with somebody else, he wouldn't have proposed to Leanne Dench."

"Maybe he just hasn't met the right woman yet to really knock him off his feet."

"Or maybe he has. Maybe that's the problem."

Erica's expression ramped up to a few degrees beyond scornful. "You've *got* to be kidding! Ms. Dench just trapped him because he was lonely."

Laura wondered if that wasn't a pretty good definition of what love was to most people—just two people snatching each other up in a moment of vulnerability.

Out of the mouths of babes . . .

She was almost afraid to probe her niece's imagination anymore, but curiosity got the best of her. "Who exactly did you have in mind for your dad?"

"How about Heidi?"

Laura bleated in alarm. "Hell's bells, have you gone mental?"

"No."

"That's the most crackbrained idea I've heard out of you yet. You'd have Heidi Dawn Bogue as a stepmother! Haven't you ever heard the saying 'Out of the frying pan and into the fire'?"

"Heidi's not *that* bad. I think Mom likes her."

"Rue's just being nice. She's always nice. That's her trouble."

Erica bit her lip. "Anyway, I don't mean that Heidi needs to fall in love with Dad. He just needs to like her so much that he sees that marrying Ms. Dench would be a . . . a . . . whatcha-macallit."

"An unsavory compromise?"

"Yes!"

"A fatal lapse of judgment?"

"That too."

"A travesty?"

Erica frowned. "I'm not sure what that is, but I guess so. Anyway, it would be a humongous mistake. Anyone can see that."

Laura was torn. Nothing would make her break into sponta-neous toe dancing faster than seeing the romance of Leanne and William go kablooey. If there was any justice in the world, that man had heartache galore headed his way. But there wasn't jus-tice; she knew that. And she didn't want Erica's heart broken by trying to undo something that was beyond her powers to undo.

"Sometimes people make mistakes and there's nothing you can do," Laura said. "I know it's like watching a train wreck, but you can't stop them."

She'd felt the same way when Rue had married William. After she'd bad-mouthed him, though, Rue hadn't spoken to her for weeks. It was one of the few times in her life when Rue had been wrong and Laura had been right, but Laura had finally had to button her lip and watch as Rue stubbornly marched down the aisle toward one of her few lapses in judgment.

"You can try to stop them, though," Erica argued. "You have to try! Otherwise, what's the use of caring about anybody or any-thing?"

"I know where you're coming from. Believe me." Laura sighed. "If you are going to try, just don't get too carried away. You know, no bridal gowns dipped in kerosene . . ."

Erica's eyes blinked wide open. "Wow!"

"I was *joking*."

"I know that." She scowled down at her. "Give me a little credit."

"I do. I credit your brain with being almost as twisted as mine."

They started back to the house. Laura didn't have too much trouble keeping up with Milkshake's lazy gait. She'd always liked this time of day—the onset of evening, when the world seemed to become quiet and still, with the heat of day giving its last gasp. It made her glad to be alive and doing what she loved. She wouldn't trade this life for anything. She loved all the spring-time prep work, with baby animals everywhere you turned and weather you could finally face without a jacket on. She loved the nonstop activity of summer, even when the horizon was wavy with heat and there didn't seem to be enough hours in the long, long day to get everything done. The mild autumns were her favorites, with the waning of the garden work coinciding with the activities of harvest festivals and Halloween and nonstop football talk. During winter she just had to keep watch over everything, do repairs, pore over seed catalogs, and strategize for next year.

When she thought about people who lived cooped up in cities, with nothing but a few scrawny parks to mark the changing of the seasons, their office work unchanged month after month, their lives untouched by the natural order of preparation, panicky activity, and then harvest, she didn't wonder that a few of them bugged out. She would want to escape, too.

She just wished they didn't have to escape *here*.

Erica's thoughts were apparently still trained on the problem of her father's marriage. "I know *kerosene* would be bad . . . but don't you think there's something I could do with poison ivy?"

"Get it out of your head."

"It wouldn't kill her."

Laura couldn't help laughing. "With those standards, you'll be attending sixth grade behind bars."

"What was it you did to Heidi when you were kids? Poison ivy in her sneakers?"

"Actually, I taped it inside her Weejuns." Next to the Criscoed baton, it had been her finest hour. But now she worried that she shouldn't have crowed about her youthful exploits quite so much to her niece. "You really shouldn't follow my example with this stuff."

"What stuff?"

"Human relations. I've never been Miss Popularity."

"So? I don't care about that!"

"Fine, but there's no sense in aiming at being *unpopular.* You'll end up like me."

"I wouldn't mind! People remember you."

"What people?"

"People in town, the old teachers at school—everybody. It's like you're famous."

"Oh sure, people will never forget Charles Manson, either. The trick is to make people remember you for good things, not the stuff you wish they'd forget."

"Who was Charles Manson?"

"Please! Seriously?" You never knew when the generation gap would rear its head. A few years ago Laura had mentioned a friend who had gone to a Queen concert, and Erica had asked if she'd had to curtsy.

"Did Charles Manson go to school in Sweetgum, too?"

"No, but come to think of it, the basketball coach sort of looked like him."

When they got home, it was almost time for dinner. Erica unsaddled Milkshake and disappeared, and Laura tried to tidy herself up a little after her long walk. She had just stuck her head under the spigot of the utility sink in the barn when Webb came in. He plucked a towel off a pile they kept on a shelf and started drying her hair with it.

"I can do that," she said.

"I know you can, but isn't this nicer?"

It certainly is, she thought, closing her eyes for a moment as he massaged her scalp. *Way nicer.* And it was tempting to lean back against him and just see what happened. She gritted her teeth, making herself stand statue still.

Sensing he was getting nowhere, Webb took her hand and plopped it over the towel, then stepped away. "Any luck after I left?"

"No."

"You're like Ahab and the white whale with those pigs."

"Uh-oh! Someone's been reading again."

"More like someone's been sleeping through the movies again. We saw the Gregory Peck movie just last week, remember?"

"I skipped out," Laura said, shaking out her head like Shelley Winters did when she came out of the lake. "I can't stand him."

Webb sputtered as he jumped out of the spray. "You don't like *Gregory Peck?*"

"I know, I know. It's like saying you don't like Abraham Lincoln. But he annoys me."

"Why?"

"Because he's so damn *bland*. He's like a big blob of boredom marching across the screen. He makes me tired."

Webb shook his head.

"Would you stop looking at me as if I were a criminal?" she asked. "Minnie Pearl on a stick! He's just an actor. You want to have me tarred and feathered just because I don't like Atticus Finch."

"That's just it! How—"

Heidi interrupted them. Almost anything was better than having to defend herself for crimes against *To Kill a Mockingbird*, but Heidi was the exception.

"Dinnertime, guys," she announced.

"We'll be along," Laura said.

Heidi looked from one of them to the other with a raised brow. "Okay. Could you let Jeanine know?"

"If I see her, I will," Laura said.

Heidi's eyes widened. "Isn't she out here?"

Laura shook her head. "No."

Webb frowned at Laura. "She came back with you, didn't she?"

A frisson of alarm shivered down her spine. "She took off right after you, Montana, and Claire left. I came back with Erica."

Webb and Heidi exchanged fretful looks.

"She's not in the house," Heidi said.

"And you just let her take off on her own?" Webb asked.

Laura hitched her shoulders back. It was like they were blaming her for losing Jeanine . . . which she supposed, technically, was what might have happened. "I showed her the way."

Heidi folded her arms. "From where?"

"It was close to that big blackjack oak in the pasture beyond the creek bottom. That's where I ran into Erica."

Webb looked astounded. "That's a mile and a half, at least."

"But you could see the house." Laura scowled. "Practically." Why should she be getting the third degree over this? Jeanine wasn't a toddler. "How was I to know that a grown woman was incapable of walking in a straight line?"

Webb let out a long sigh. "I don't guess Milkshake is still saddled up?"

"No, Erica unsaddled him soon as we got home."

He turned and started walking toward the house. Laura trotted after him. "*I'll* go with you to look for her."

He shot her one of his rare annoyed looks. "If we do manage to find her, I imagine you'll be the last person she'll feel like seeing."

"Can I go?" Heidi piped up from behind them.

"Go get the first-aid kit from Rue," he instructed Heidi. "Then meet me by the blue truck."

Heidi ran inside.

"This is silly," Laura insisted. She couldn't believe she was being shunned in favor of the useless Heidi. "Jeanine probably just stopped somewhere."

"To do what?"

Laura was at a loss.

In another second, the side screen door banged open and closed, and Rue was flying down the stairs. She looked furious.

"What the hell has gotten into you today?"

The growled question nearly sent Laura reeling backward. For one thing, she had no idea what Rue was talking about. She glanced at Webb for help, but he simply shoved his hat on his head and walked away in the direction of the truck. Abandoning her.

"I wasn't aware that anything had gotten into me." Laura attempted a casual shrug even as she mentally armored up for battle. "Up to now it's just seemed like a normal day."

"Normal? *Normal?*" Rue gaped at her in wonder. "You call it *normal* to try to kill all our guests?"

"I haven't killed *anybody*." Too late, she thought of Jeanine, whose fate was still unknown. "For certain."

And technically, she couldn't be held responsible for killing Jeanine, even if the woman was gasping her last out in a pasture somewhere. Was it her fault that a fully functioning adult couldn't manage to walk a mile without coming to grief?

Her answer nettled Rue. "First, you nearly let Heidi pass out from heatstroke—"

"I did not! I didn't even notice she was having a problem!"

"*Exactly,*" Rue said. "You were completely oblivious. Webb noticed her."

Laura snorted. "Right! She probably executed a well-timed swoon as he was passing by."

Rue didn't even deign to respond to that. "But letting one guest nearly dehydrate and pass out on the job wasn't enough for you. Oh no! You had to go drag the others out through a pasture full of bull nettle. You should see those poor nurses' legs, all covered in bumps."

"I warned them to be careful! If they hadn't been wearing shorts . . ."

"It's over ninety degrees outside! Everyone in their right mind wears shorts."

"I don't."

"I rest my case." Rue folded her arms. "And now Jeanine. God only knows what's happened to her."

"I pointed out the way to her!" Laura said for what felt like the hundredth time.

Rue rolled her eyes. "You're supposed to watch out for them, Laura! These people are as helpless as newborn bunnies. You can't just *point*."

"All right. Next time I'll know."

"Next time? We'll be lucky if there is a next time! We'll be lucky if we aren't sued for negligence and shut down."

"By whom?" Laura asked. "The agri-tourism police?"

"It might just be the regular police."

"Don't go overboard, Rue. We don't even know anything's happened to her yet."

But the mention of lawsuits and police did sober Laura somewhat. All they needed right now was to have the law come crashing down on them. Her lists of things to dread was growing: drought, guests, pigs, Heidi, lawyers.

"Not to mention," Rue added just when Laura thought the accusations against her were all finished, "as I was going to get Erica for dinner, *guess* what I found her doing?"

"Putting the finishing touches on her Leanne Dench voodoo doll?"

"No. She was on the Internet, reading about Charles Manson!"

Laura laughed.

Judging by Rue's withering look, this was not the proper reaction. "She said she'd heard about him from you."

Laura lifted her hands. "Okay, okay, I plead guilty. I just happened to mention that my old basketball coach looked like Charles Manson."

"And now her head is going to be full of serial killings, and poor Sharon Tate."

"For pete's sake," Laura said, exasperated. "You can't shield kids from famous mass murderers forever, can you? I mean, this is America. It's part of our heritage."

The look Rue leveled on her could have frozen a lava flow. "I don't know what I'm going to do. I really don't. You're hopeless."

"Rue, I'm sorry. The Charles Manson thing just slipped out in conversation. It's not like I sat her down and told her the story of *Helter Skelter* like it was the birds and the bees. And as for the rest of it, I promise I'll be more careful with the stupid inmates from now on."

"They're not stupid! And they're not inmates. They're not pests, cattle, or citified half-wits, or whatever else you call them. They're human beings, and they're paying us money to be here *on vacation*. Here's a news flash for you. People usually don't go on vacation to be dehydrated, poisoned, or killed."

"Okay, okay, I'm sorry. I'll turn over a new leaf."

The apology didn't appear to penetrate. "It's not just the guests, Laura. It's Erica, the farm, *everything*. What am I going to do if you won't be responsible? What's going to happen to everything here?"

"What's the matter?" Laura asked. "Is something wrong that you're not telling me?"

"No."

"Then . . . ?"

"Never mind." Rue looked out at the fields for a moment, thinking. "You're probably right. Five'll get you ten I'm overreacting. It's just that you get to run blithely around pissing people off and trailing them through toxic foliage, and then I have to deal with the fallout."

Put that way, Laura began to see where she was coming from. She felt a familiar twinge of remorse. "I'm sorry, Rue. I know there's no excuse. I've been screwing things up my entire life. I guess it's a hard habit to break."

"Just *try*," Rue pleaded. "That's all I'm asking. *Try*."

Laura dawdled back to the barn for a little while. When she finally talked herself into going back to the house, the place reeked of chocolate and calamine lotion. The guests were gathered glumly around the table, eating dinner; Montana and Claire had their chalky pink legs propped up on the chairs left vacant by Heidi, Jeanine, and Webb. No one said so in so many words, but it was obvious that Laura was about as welcome at that table as a rattlesnake in a prairie dog town.

It didn't help that Erica seemed to relish asking the nurses how badly their bumps itched. "That looks *really* bad," she said, inspecting Montana's calf.

"It's very uncomfortable," Montana answered. She was staring straight at Laura.

"Very," Claire echoed.

After what seemed like an eternity, footsteps were finally heard on the front porch. Everyone jumped up and ran to the hallway in time to see Webb come through the front door with Jeanine in his arms. An anxious-looking Heidi brought up the rear. The guests surged forward to find out what had happened, but a few feet away from Webb and Jeanine, a blast of foul odor sent them reeling back again. Laura considered herself pretty tough when it came to enduring stink, but even she recoiled.

Everyone refrained from stating the obvious except for Erica, who screwed up her face in her typical dramatic fashion and began waving her arms in front of her nose. "Pee-yew!"

Jeanine groaned and burrowed her nose a little deeper into Webb's shoulder.

"She fell," Heidi explained.

"She was trying to cross the creek, over where it's mostly mud, and her shoe got stuck and she lost her balance," Webb elaborated.

"And I lost my shoe, too!" Jeanine recovered some of her spirit at the thought of her ruined footwear. She swung an angry gaze on Laura. "It's all the fault of those stupid pigs of yours!"

"You mean you fell into the pig wallow?" Laura asked, amazed. "Why did you cross *there*?"

There were miles and miles of dried creek bed, or creek that had been reduced to just a trickle, which would have been a snap to cross.

"You told me to go in a straight line!"

"I didn't mean for you to take it *literally*. Crap Agnes! You could have changed course. You're not a zombie."

It wasn't until she noticed six sets of eyes glaring at her that she realized that calling Jeanine a zombie probably wasn't what Rue had meant when she'd admonished her to *try*.

Webb was one of the people glaring hardest. "She cut her foot on something in the creek," he said. "She'd hobbled half a mile when Heidi and I found her."

Everyone let out sympathetic murmurs. But apparently, they weren't sympathetic enough to brave the pig-wallow stench by stepping one inch closer.

Montana and Claire exchanged looks.

"What do you think?" Montana asked.

"Depends what was in that creek," replied Claire.

The two nurses shook their heads and said in unison, with unsavory glee, "Tetanus shot!"

Jeanine groaned again. "I hate shots."

Rue stepped forward. "We'll get you upstairs and wash it off, and then we'll see if it looks like we should take you to the doctor. There's an emergency clinic about twenty miles away, if it seems . . ."

"You'd better hurry, or infection could set in," Margaret said. "And then . . ."

"Gangrene!" Montana and Claire chimed.

"Thanks a lot," Jeanine said. "Y'all are really helping."

Rue sent a grateful look to Webb. "Could you take her upstairs?"

Webb nodded. "I'd be happy to."

The others filtered upstairs or back to the kitchen, leaving Laura alone in the hallway with Heidi. To her surprise, Heidi looked almost sorry for her.

"About earlier. Webb and Rue were just nervous, that's all. It wasn't really your fault."

From anyone else, the words might have been comforting, but

at that moment, the treacly sympathy from her nemesis rubbed Laura the wrong way.

"And I'm pretty sure that bit about gangrene was just a joke," Heidi assured her.

"Of course it was a joke!"

Heidi's eyes widened in surprise at Laura's reflexive growl, but she recovered quickly. "Sorry. I mistook you for someone who might like a little compassion. I forgot you were nice-proof. Silly me."

"Sorry to deprive you of a Hallmark moment."

"Don't worry. Where you're concerned, I gave up my hope for one of those sometime back in nineteen eighty-six. It didn't even outlast T-shirts with shoulder pads."

Heidi tromped up the stairs, presumably to offer all the niceness Laura had rebuffed to some more grateful recipient, like Jeanine. Or Webb.

Laura stalked out to the front porch and flopped down in one of the rockers there. She wished she weren't always trying to give up smoking. It just meant that she never had a cigarette when she really needed one.

The cell phone in her pocket sounded off, and she jumped to answer it. It was Buddy Slickson, one of her old partners in crime. The man used to party like a kamikaze. The last time they'd gone out, she'd ended up with a two-week hangover. But that was just before he'd moved in with a teetotaling dog groomer.

"Buddy!" she exclaimed, as if he were her long-lost friend. "Butter my butt and call me a biscuit! It's been an age."

Dollars to doughnuts Pam the poodle lady was out of town.

"Hey, sunshine. Feel like wettin' your beak?" he asked.

"Don't tempt me. If you knew the day I've been having . . ."

"Since when do you need tempting to have a friendly drink?"

"Since you almost killed me with those potions you concocted."

"Beam bombs! That was almost a year ago!"

"And my skull still feels like it's been through a wood chipper."

Buddy chuckled. "Actually, I thought we could just shoot some pool."

She was about to jump at the opportunity to escape when Webb came out the door. He saw her on the phone and pivoted slightly to give her privacy. As if he couldn't hear her if his back was turned.

Suddenly she felt less enthusiastic about Buddy's invitation. If she went off to meet Buddy and Webb knew about it, she'd have to endure his puppy-dog disappointment in the morning, when she was in the throes of remorse. (Buddy never *just* played pool.) All because she didn't want to hold hands in the moonlight and rekindle the flames of Guadalajara.

"Actually, I can't."

"Why the hell not? You gonna sit around all night watching your eggplants grow?"

"No, I'm going to go to bed at a decent hour and get up at the crack of dawn to work. You remember what work is, don't you?"

"Very funny. You're just jealous because I chose a profession that allows me to sleep normal hours."

"A junk store's not a profession. It's just a place to park your carcass for eight hours."

"Believe me, *entrepreneur* looks a lot more impressive on a tax return than *plant sitter.*"

"You're for sure going to have to play pool by yourself," Laura said. "Have a good time."

"You always were a killjoy."

Laura responded sweetly, "Speaking of which, how is Pam?"

"Visiting her sister in Denver."

"Uh-huh. And let me guess . . . She'd be brokenhearted at the idea of you sitting at home all by your lonesome."

"C'mon, Laura . . ."

She chuckled. "Sorry, Buddy. I hear the eggplants calling. Gotta run!"

After she hung up, she sank down in the chair and sighed.

"Going out?" Webb asked.

"You know I'm not. You were listening."

"Half listening."

"Then you know I'm staying in tonight, like a good little farmer." She bit her lip. "And guest killer."

"*I* never said you killed anybody."

"No, you didn't. That was Rue." She let out another long breath. "But I suppose it fell under the umbrella of constructive criticism."

"Well, it's all over now. When all's said and done, Jeanine just lost her shoe and cut her foot. No big harm done."

Laura tried to look at it in the proper light—to feel remorse, and relief that it wasn't worse, and determination to be a better person in the future. But every time she imagined Jeanine falling into that pig wallow, she wanted to laugh. Trouble was, everybody around her had lost their sense of humor.

Buddy would laugh.

A game of pool would help her unwind. Plus, she could have a few cigs. A beer or two. It wasn't as if she would have to tie one on.

Webb pushed away from the wall. "I'm going to turn in."

"Turn into what?"

He groaned in appreciation.

Webb was staying in the tiny house on the other side of the garden, which had belonged to a neighbor who had died fifteen years before. Her dad had snapped up the property because it was attached to his own, but he'd never done much with it. From time to time, when she and her father had been too much at odds to live in the same house, Laura had stayed there. Rue had made noises about selling it, but Laura couldn't bear to part with the acreage. That land was the blank page for her daydreams. She had big plans for it—blueberries, cattle, Christmas trees. The big plans changed every few months.

As Webb opened the door to the house, Heidi nearly smacked right up against him on her way out. "Oh!" she said, startled. "Just who I was looking for! You aren't watching the movie, are you?"

"I hadn't planned to," Webb replied.

"Well, then, would you have time to give me that lesson you promised? On knot tying?"

"Jesus wept!" Laura said, standing up. She squeezed past them both on her way inside and couldn't help congratulating Heidi. *Knot tying.* "That's a new one!"

She skulked back to the kitchen, feeling embarrassed at having snapped at Heidi in front of Webb. But it wasn't as if she was seeking his good opinion.

Although that was what he'd probably thought when she gave Buddy the brush-off, when really the reasons she wasn't going to go out with Buddy were, one, there was work to do tomorrow, which would be a hell of a lot easier to accomplish if it didn't feel as though there were someone playing acid jazz on a kazoo inside her skull; two, Buddy was an overgrown adolescent dipsomaniac; and three, she had promised Rue she would try. Whatever that meant.

I'm going to behave responsibly. Like a grown-up.

For once.

She would even go face down the guests, with their bumpy legs, wounds, and glares. Movie time was coming right up. She could make popcorn and show Rue that she could be hostesslike and gracious.

She went to the kitchen and banged around the cabinets, looking for their popcorn popper, which resembled a big saucepan with a flat cover and a crank handle.

Rue came in and stood watching her, hands on her hips. "What are you doing?"

"Hunting for the Whirley-Pop."

"Why?"

Was she kidding? "I was going to make popcorn. For the guests to have during the movie." *I'm being gracious, damn it.*

"No need. Heidi made Raisinets this afternoon." She took in Laura's bemused expression and said, "You know, chocolate-covered raisins."

"I know what Raisinets are," Laura said. "The question is, what kind of freak makes them at home?"

"Heidi says she likes to play with whatever ingredients she can find in a kitchen. Said it came from growing up with Marla. Which I can well imagine. So she saw we had chocolate chips and raisins, and presto!" She made a Carol Merrill gesture toward several small bowls of chocolate-covered raisins.

Laura stood for a second, scowling at them.

"Anyway," Rue continued, "you're not going to watch the movie."

Laura turned. "What?"

"You can't see this movie."

"But I *want* to see the movie tonight. I want to help. I really do."

Rue was unmoved.

"Why can't I?" Laura asked, coming as close as she ever did to whining.

"Because we're watching *The Sound of Music*."

Laura gulped. *Damn!* Why did people looooove that movie? The whole thing was like nails on a chalkboard from beginning to end. All those pink-cheeked children singing. All those saccharine songs. All that Julie Andrews.

She swallowed. *Try.* "No, really. I want to see it."

"No, you don't."

No, she didn't. *Pool with Buddy*, the little devil on her shoulder said. "Yes, I do. It's been years."

"Well, it's your house." Rue shot her a look of warning. "But I swear to you, Laurel Mae, the first smirk, snigger, or sneer, and you're out."

Laura nodded but was suddenly filled with anxiety about "The Lonely Goatherd." How was she going to sit through that with a straight face? Or that awful "Sixteen Going on Seventeen" thing, which was like chewing on aluminum? The entire movie was loaded with land mines. Watching it would be a test, and she wasn't sure she was up to it.

Still, she brazened on. "Give me some credit. I think I can behave for two hours."

But as it turned out, she barely made it past "Do-Re-Mi."

Laura hadn't braced herself properly for the pukefully precious montage sequence of kiddies in their matching curtain outfits— or for how annoyed she would feel watching Heidi and Webb come in late from their "lesson" and stretch out on the floor together like kids at a slumber party.

By "The Lonely Goatherd," she was already racking up for her third game with Buddy. He had enjoyed her recounting the series of unfortunate events at the farm. They dubbed this day Dump-on-Laura Day, and Buddy bought a round of drinks in honor of it. By the time the von Trapps made it to Switzerland, Laura had enough of a buzz on to forget all about guests, droughts, pigs, and Heidi.

Chapter 8

The next morning Rue's body felt as tired as if she hadn't slept at all. For the first time in months she would have gladly stayed in bed, if it weren't for all the guests expecting breakfast. What would happen if she didn't get it ready? She imagined all those women perched on chairs around the kitchen table, their mouths open like baby birds waiting to be fed, and she dragged herself out to the kitchen.

In the hallway she cocked her head slightly, listening to the sounds coming from behind the closed kitchen door. The kitchen door was never closed at night. Someone in there was messing around with pots and pans. And there was music . . . It sounded like the Feist CD a guest had left for her a few weeks ago.

Was she having an out-of-body experience, imagining walking into a room where she was already busy getting everything ready? Or had Laura taken it upon herself to make breakfast? Maybe she wanted to make amends for her thought crimes against Rodgers and Hammerstein.

But Laura wasn't in the kitchen. Heidi was.

"Morning!"

Rue looked around. The counters were cluttered with mixing bowls and cutting boards littered with assorted fruit peels and pits. Including, she couldn't help noticing, some peach detritus.

The sight of those peaches gave her nerves a jangle, but she decided not to dwell on it. Not just this second.

Heidi flung out her arms to do a Julie Andrews turn and belted, "The kitchen's alive, with the sound of breakfast!"

The performance was aided by the goofy bib apron with cartoon roosters on it that she wore over her jeans.

Rue approached the bowls with a curious eye. "What are you up to?"

"Waffles," Heidi said. "Cinnamon waffles with peaches, and smoothies."

Waffles weren't the best thing to attempt to serve a lot of people at once, but Rue didn't want to take the wind out of Heidi's sails. She was too happy about having help. "What did I do to deserve all this?"

"You might wonder once you've tasted it all."

"I've never met a waffle I didn't like." Rue peered into a couple of the bowls on the counter. A metal one was full of unbeaten egg whites, while a Pyrex bowl held a pile of peeled and sliced peaches. They were the earliest of the crop, and Rue knew Laura was counting on them to be the highlight of the CSA boxes that Saturday. Unconsciously, she shoved the peach bowl farther back on the counter and started clearing away the piles of pits and skins.

Rue's computer was sitting on the table, the screen showing the *New York Times*. A surprising thing about Heidi was that she seemed fanatical about checking the news. Rue had noticed that she scanned several newspapers more than once a day, every day.

"Anything in the news?"

"Not yet." Heidi looked surprised by her own answer. "I mean, nothing earth-shattering has happened since last night."

Rue sent her a sidelong glance, but Heidi had turned and was busy figuring out the immersion blender's whisk attachment.

Webb ambled in through the back door. His eyes registered amazement and, Rue couldn't help noticing, a little pleasure when he saw Heidi standing there.

"I've been usurped," Rue told him.

"Lucky you," he returned.

She wondered what was up there. As a teenager Heidi had been cute, in a geeky sort of way. Now she had a casually polished look and was good-looking by any standard, even at six thirty in the morning. Even in a stupid rooster apron.

"We're one short in the barn this morning," Webb announced. "The wild woman of Sweetgum hasn't made an appearance yet. I'm guessing she isn't oversleeping because she forgot to set the alarm."

"She might have, at that. People are apt to forget a lot of things when they stumble into bed at three a.m.," Rue said.

His jaw twitched. "That late?"

"I had plenty of time to look at the clock," Rue told him. "She sang 'Climb Ev'ry Mountain' all the way up to the attic."

"Is that what that was?" Heidi leaned against the counter. "I thought it might be rats in the walls. Laura's soprano sounds exactly like the dying shrieks of a small animal."

Webb's lips clamped into a tight smile.

"Should I go knock on her door?" Heidi suggested.

They laughed, and as he poured himself a cup of coffee, Webb said something about early morning bloodshed.

"This is one morning I could outrun her," Heidi said.

Rue looked over at Webb, who wasn't laughing now. In fact, for a fleeting moment Webb looked about as glum as she had ever seen him. "Oh well," he said. "I've got Erica hunting down eggs . . . if you need them."

"We're okay for now." When he was gone, Rue couldn't help muttering, "Laura ought to have her head thumped!"

Heidi grinned. "You're just now figuring that out?"

"She went out last night with Buddy Slickson."

"That name sounds familiar."

"The two of them have gone out carousing periodically since high school."

"Romantically?"

"I don't ask what they do," Rue said, yanking silverware out of the drawer. "They're both a couple of idiots. It wouldn't surprise me if they spent the night toilet papering houses and tipping cows."

The side door banged open, and Erica sped into the kitchen and deposited a basket of eggs on the counter. "Tortoise is gone!"

Rue frowned. "Oh no."

"Who is Tortoise?" Heidi asked.

"He's a kitten who lives in the barn," Erica explained. "His mother's wild. The other three are there, but he's gone."

"Maybe he just wandered off."

"He's *always* there in the morning," Erica said. "The kittens like to be around when I feed Spunky. They lick the spilled formula."

"I bet he'll turn up," Rue said.

"Sure," Heidi agreed. "What could have happened to him?"

Erica leveled a dumbfounded expression on her. "Anything! A coyote could have gotten him, or a hawk, or even a raccoon. He could have wandered off and gotten lost, in which case he'll probably starve or get eaten, or get run over on the road if he wanders that far. Or he could drown in the lake. Or someone could have stolen him!"

"Oh," Heidi said.

Erica shot Rue a parting glance of distress, turned on her heel, and headed back out the door.

"Sorry I asked," Heidi said.

Rue fished more silverware out of the drawer. "It's okay. There's a *Wild Kingdom*–style drama here every other day. About animals' lives, Erica has no illusions. About people, she's still a little mixed up."

"Who's mixed up?" Laura stood in the doorway. She squinted at the electric light like a vampire first seeing the sunrise, then picked her way carefully toward the coffeepot. She looked as if she were trying very hard not to take in anything going on around her, and when she finally reached the counter, she practically fell on the coffeepot in relief. She poured a cup and gulped down half in one swallow. As if her senses were coming painfully awake, she frowned into the air.

Rue held her breath, fearful that Laura had picked up the scent of peaches.

But it was the music that was bugging Laura. "Why does the kitchen suddenly sound like an iPod commercial?"

"It's Feist," Heidi said.

Laura shuddered. "That idiotic counting woman."

"I like her," Heidi said. "And I'm cooking."

For once, Rue was glad to have them sniping at each other, since it kept Laura's attention away from the bowlful of peaches sitting on the counter directly behind her.

"Webb came in earlier, asking about you," Heidi told her. "And Erica's up. She brought in eggs already."

Heidi nodded toward the little basket, and Rue found herself doing a Nureyev-style leap across the kitchen to grab it so Laura wouldn't make that fatal quarter turn and see the fruit bowl.

Laura blinked at her. "What are you, spring loaded?"

"Don't tell me I have too much energy. Finally!"

Laura sank against the counter and moaned. "I feel like death sucking a sponge."

"I don't guess you'll want a waffle," Heidi said.

Rue felt like waving her hands to stop the direction the conversation was taking.

Laura stared into the bowl of egg whites and turned a shade greener. "Is that what this is going to be?" Her nose wrinkled. "It smells like . . ." Her eyes widened.

Rue's heart sank. Game over.

Laura pivoted and gasped. There they were—a whole pile of the year's very earliest peaches sprinkled with cinnamon, glistening in their bowl. *"Who did this!"*

Heidi jumped. "Did what?"

"Butchered my June Golds!"

Heidi looked astonished. "I just told you. I'm making breakfast."

"You didn't tell me that you'd murdered our first bushel of peaches to do it!"

"I didn't use a bushel. I just used eight."

Laura's face went through every shade of red in the color spectrum. "Are you *insane?*"

Heidi looked confused. "What? They were in the pantry."

"Of course they were! I was going to put them in the CSA boxes today!" Laura raged.

Understanding dawned on Heidi's face, as well as embarrassment. "Oh."

Rue stepped forward. "Honestly, Laurel Mae. How was she to know?"

"She didn't have to know. She just had to ask! Who told her to make breakfast anyway?"

"No one," Heidi shot back. "I just wanted to help."

Laura threw up her hands. "*Help?* What the hell am I supposed to give our subscribers now? Double chard? Everybody'll *love* that."

Heidi looked so mortified, Rue almost wanted to laugh. All this Sturm und Drang over a couple of pieces of fruit. "C'mon, Laura, we can think of something."

"We shouldn't have to! This is insane."

"Yes, it is. You have no sense of proportion," Rue told her.

"*Me?*"

"Never mind, Rue." Heidi tore off her apron and tossed it on the counter. She stomped out of the kitchen and marched back to her stinky little room.

When they heard her door slam, Rue rounded on her sister. "By all means, don't let a hangover get in the way of alienating people."

"We've been alienated for twenty years. Why stop now?" Laura crossed to the table and collapsed into a chair. She scowled at the computer. "If she's so interested in what's going on back in New York, why doesn't she go back there?"

"Maybe she's just interested in the world in general. You know, news."

"The only news that would make me happy would be hearing that she's gone home. Does she intend on staying here forever?"

Rue shrugged. "I haven't asked."

"Maybe you should."

"I don't mind having her around."

Laura's brows pinched. "We still don't know what she's doing here."

Rue remained silent. A bit of a jam, Heidi had said. Laura, of all people, should be able to understand what that meant, but Rue knew the minute she mentioned it, Laura's mind would leap to the worst conclusions.

Besides, Heidi's business was Heidi's business.

Webb came back in. The only acknowledgment he gave Laura was a deadpan glance. "Where's Heidi?"

"She scampered away," Laura said. "I scared her."

"You'd scare anybody this morning," he observed. "Must have been some rough pool you played with Buddy."

Laura straightened. "It turns out that he's trying his hand at home brewing. At his store, natch. First beer I've ever drunk that was ninety proof."

"Why take it out on Heidi?" Webb asked before Rue could give him warning.

"Because she stole my peaches to put on . . ." Laura pivoted toward Rue. What was it?"

"Waffles," Rue said.

"Sounds good to me," Webb said.

"Fine! I'll just tell our customers that I'm sorry they're screwed, but we had a good breakfast."

Webb frowned. "Good God, Laura, sober up and get a life. It's just a bowlful of fruit."

Laura stood abruptly, then tottered for a moment, as if she regretted it. "I would have been just as pissed off about the peaches if I hadn't touched a drop last night."

Webb picked up his coffee cup and saluted her with it. "Right!

You're irrational in any condition. You're the town poster child for mental derangement—and in Sweetgum that's saying something."

"It's never stopped you from hanging around," Laura retorted.

"Not yet." Webb stalked out.

Laura flinched when Rue glared at her. "I know. I'm not *trying*."

"That depends," Rue said. "If you're trying to make enemies, you're succeeding magnificently."

Laura sighed. "What are you going to do today?"

"It's a banjo lesson day," Rue said.

She actually hadn't intended on taking her usual escape that afternoon, but she felt like it now. It wasn't even seven in the morning, and she was exhausted.

"It's great you're keeping at it," Laura said.

Rue squirmed a little. Now that the farm was at its busiest, she should probably give up the banjo masquerade. Trouble was, now that the farm season was at its busiest, she felt she needed her time out more than ever.

Laura sighed. "I'd better go start mending fences." She sent Rue an apologetic look. "Would you tell Heidi I'm sorry?"

"I'll tell her," Rue said. "But she won't believe me."

"Webb probably won't, either."

"Probably not, but he'll forgive you anyway. This time."

Laura blinked in surprise. "You think there will be a time when he won't?"

"Yes, I do. And I think it's coming sooner than you think."

The peaches might have been a blunder, but the waffles were mighty tasty, anyway. The guests—still limping, itching, and cranky—wolfed them down as fast as Heidi and Rue could whip them out. For once silence reigned at the breakfast table. It felt like everything was ending. It was the last day of the week, the last day of May, and all the guests would be leaving over the next twenty-four hours. Poor Jeanine looked like she couldn't get away soon enough. She sat with one tube-sock-encased foot propped up on a stool, glumly shoveling down her waffle. It was the first time Heidi could remember seeing her eat. She didn't even make her usual attempts at breakfast-table flirtation with Webb. Her resignation was sad to witness.

The peaches were a big hit. They were perfect—just the right texture and so sweet that every bite caused a little salivary explosion. It was the one thing that seemed to perk the guests up. They gobbled up most of the bowl and sang the praises of peaches loud and long. When Heidi dumped the leftovers into the blender for a last round of smoothies, she thought Laura's head would explode.

"Can't let them go to waste now, can we?" Heidi asked her, with a smile. She switched on the blender and watched Laura twitch while her final sacrificed June Golds were pulverized.

Later, when chores were doled out at the end of breakfast, Heidi discovered that she had not been chosen for anything.

"Aren't you forgetting someone?" she asked Laura.

Laura narrowed her eyes on her. "Sorry. I guess you're not needed."

Jeanine sputtered, "Am *I* needed? I mean, *I'm* the one who's wounded here."

"We're all wounded sooner or later," Laura answered her in her best Clint Eastwood growl. "I'm doing you the honor of not treating you like a wimp. But maybe you'd rather be a wimp. Would you?"

Jeanine shrank back. "No," she cheeped.

"Congratulations," Laura said. "Now, let's get to work."

The crew traipsed out, limping and grumbling, leaving Rue and Heidi alone in the kitchen with the dishes.

"You guys are really offering up a one-of-a-kind experience here," Heidi mused. "You've struck a nice balance between *Green Acres* and *Motel Hell.*"

"I get the feeling sometimes that we won't see many repeat visitors."

Heidi laughed. "Go ahead and get ready for your lesson. It seems I'm not wanted outside, so I can handle the cleanup."

"Thank you," Rue said. "And thanks for breakfast. I don't care if they were pilfered. Those peaches were awfully good."

Heidi put on Tracy Chapman and began cleaning to the song "Fast Car." She actually found putting things away and scrubbing down the counters relaxing. Maybe now that her life in banking was at an end, she could have a second career as a cleaning woman. Change her name to Madge and head for the West Coast. As far from Vinnie as she could get.

As she was finishing up, a cough heralded Rue's reappearance. She was wearing a new pair of jeans and a tank top, covered by a light green linen shirt Heidi hadn't seen yet. Lesson clothes, Heidi supposed.

"You're fast," Rue said, surveying the cleaned kitchen as she crossed to the CD cabinet and picked out a Frank Sinatra disk. *Come Fly with Me.* "You weren't planning on listening to this, were you?"

Heidi shuddered, thinking of Vinnie. "No!" Rue sent her a curious glance, and she lifted her shoulders in a casual shrug. "He's not one of my favorites."

She hadn't wanted to admit it, but her reason for making breakfast had not been entirely generosity. The fact was, she hadn't been able to sleep. And not just because of Laura's singing. She kept thinking about Tom Chinske, and that gypsy cab, and its streaky-haired driver. She was safe here; she knew she was. Nobody had followed her; nobody could have. She was fairly certain.

But even fairly certain allowed for a measure of doubt. And if there was even a tiny chance that an assassin might track her here, how fair was it to the others who lived here?

"Something wrong?" Rue asked.

"No," Heidi said. "I was just thinking . . . about Frank Sinatra. Have a good lesson."

After Rue left, Heidi went to put the syrup in the pantry. The CSA boxes were there, ready to be packed. A paper sack of onions sat at the bottom of each. Half dozen and dozen egg cartons filled the shelves of the nearby refrigerator. The half ration of peaches was ready to go. Tomorrow morning, early, Webb, Laura, Herman, Dylan, and Erica would be up with the birds, picking, cleaning, and doing the final packing.

She imagined all the people picking up their weekly box and getting double chard. Guilt gripped her. There had to be something she could do to make amends—not to Laura, but to these unseen customers. These people the future of the farm depended on.

She looked over at the chocolate chips in the pantry. Chocolate chips, apparently, were Erica's favorite condiment, because there were several sacks of them.

Ten minutes later she was elbow-deep in cookie dough.

She made a triple batch and spent a large part of the morning doing chores in ten-minute bursts while the cookies baked. She cleaned the three upstairs bathrooms this way, then came down and started working on the one she shared with Rue. Even after all the used towels had been collected, there was still room in the laundry basket, so she decided to throw some of Rue's clothes in.

She crossed Rue's bedroom, aware of something strange, but she didn't realize what exactly was bothering her until she was almost back out the door. She stopped and did a double take at Rue's banjo case. It was in its usual place, leaning against the wall near the bed.

Had Rue not realized she'd forgotten it? Heidi debated calling her cell phone number. But Rue had left a while ago, so it was probably too late for her to turn back and still make her lesson.

On the way back to the kitchen, she did a pass through the little study Rue used as the farm office. The laptop computer had been moved to the desk, and she unplugged it and stuck it on top of the laundry pile. As she rotated cookies from oven to cooling racks to sandwich Baggies, and kept an eye on the laundry, she got online and did a new search for the man named Elvin Johnson. She knew he had a bank account with Vinnie, and that as of several weeks ago it was still active. Why would Tom

Chinske have mentioned it specifically? Had Vinnie been skimming money from Johnson's account? Had Johnson contacted Tom and set the case against Vinnie in motion?

There was no sign of an Elvin Johnson in Brooklyn, or even in New York State. She couldn't find one anywhere, except a man who had gone to jail for killing a guy in the Sala Rosa bar in Cocoa Beach, Florida.

While the last few batches baked, she lettered brown sandwich bags with the words SASSY SPINSTER CHOCOLATE CHIP COOKIES. Then she practiced tying each with some rough brown string.

By the time she'd finished fifteen bags and placed them in the boxes, her neck ached from arching over her task. She had never imagined cookies could take so much out of a person.

Stepping out the side door to see what everyone else was doing, she nearly stumbled over Erica, who was sitting on the stairs with her arms wrapped around her knees and her head buried in her arms. It looked like she was in an upright fetal position.

"What's wrong?" Heidi asked.

"Tortoise is still missing! I'm sure he's dead!"

"Look," Heidi offered, "I'm at loose ends now. If we both hunt, there's a better chance of finding him."

Erica looked hopeful. "Tortoise likes to climb. Can you climb?"

"Of course. Whatever it takes."

Erica jumped to her feet. "Thank you!"

She scampered off toward the peach orchard, so Heidi headed in the opposite direction. How far could a kitten go? She had no idea. But even walking a hundred yards made her feel pessimistic about Tortoise's chances. She was approaching a clump of trees when she almost stepped on something dead with ants swarming all over it. Under any other circumstances she would have stepped right past the carnage, but now she felt like she had a duty to investigate. She bent down, trying to summon some CSI stoicism. Whatever had died, it was too small to be a kitten. A mouse, maybe. She kicked some dirt over it to give it a little burial and to keep it from panicking Erica if she ran across it.

The stand of trees in the field contained the old Kieffer pear tree she remembered raiding as a girl, and the old ash tree whose limbs long ago had held a tire swing. A scar was visible where the supporting limb had been. Heidi felt a strange pang to see it. The tire swing had been the one place on the farm where she'd occasionally felt real peace. Rue and Laura had been beyond the age of wanting to play on a swing, and so it had been a safe haven for her. Also, there was a fair prospect of the house from this small rise, and she'd enjoyed the power of being able to spy on her stepfamily.

She looked back now, almost expecting old Mr. Rafferty to come stumping out the side door in a huff, or to see her mother dashing to her car in one of the pastel tracksuits she'd favored back then for grocery runs. In those days she couldn't help wondering what her mother had been thinking, bringing them out here. Life in Houston had been touch and go—their electricity had been cut off twice in one year, and they'd had to sell their car—but surely being a divorced cocktail waitress and a single mom was better than this?

Back then she didn't know about the things people could do when fear gripped them. She didn't know that in times of stress a person was apt to run to the least likely place. Now she got it.

A mewling sound broke her reverie, and she looked up, squinting into the branches of the ash. A tiny pair of green eyes stared down at her, like those of a terrified little tiger.

Without giving it a second thought, Heidi swung herself up to the lowest branch and started, gingerly, to work her way up. The branches were dense, and the one that the kitten was perched on seemed no bigger than a twig. How had it gotten up there?

When she heard an ominous snap beneath her after she'd scrambled up a dozen branches, she questioned the wisdom of interfering with natural selection. She also feared that she was going to be naturally selected off the planet herself if she wasn't careful.

"*Heidi?*"

It was Webb's voice calling. She braced herself and looked

down. Big mistake. She hadn't lied about being able to climb, but she had omitted to clarify that anything above standing-on-a-chair height gave her vertigo.

Heidi called out to him, and he loped over.

"What are you doing?" he asked.

"I found Tortoise."

"Let me get the orchard ladder."

"Too late. I'm almost up there."

"But how are you going to get down?"

Good question. The descent would be even more difficult with a kitten in her hand.

"I know," he said. "I'll climb up right behind you, and then we can hand off the kitten as we go back down. Can you just hold still till I get up closer to you?"

"Yeah, in fact I think I'd prefer it to moving."

Webb climbed until his head was even with the branch her foot was on.

"We need to go up one more branch, I think," she said. Unfortunately, the next branch was exactly parallel to the one she was holding on to. It was going to be more than a little awkward to swing herself up there.

"Step on my shoulder," Webb said.

Heidi gaped at him. "Are you crazy?"

He raised himself, offering his shoulder as a step stool. Gingerly, she put her foot on his shoulder. Muscled as he was, he was still wobblier than a tree branch. She was about to say no way when she looked into his blue eyes and saw the confidence there, the complete lack of doubt in her skills. The completely delusional belief in her competence.

She gulped, reached for the next branch, and swung herself up.

"Way to go!" he called.

It was like having a personal cheerleader. She glanced down to see if he was for real. Incredibly, he was.

Now her challenge was that there was no branch directly above her to hang on to, so she had to shimmy out toward the middle to grab the kitten. Tortoise, meanwhile, watched her approach with growing trepidation and backed a little farther out.

Heidi inched forward until she was just within reach.

"Watch his claws," Webb warned.

Heidi watched them, all right. As she clamped her hands around the kitten's surprisingly solid little torso, she watched the front claws dig into her forearm like ten tiny razor blades. She bit out a screech.

"Mauled at thirty feet!" Webb laughed. "Go ahead and hand him down."

Heidi gulped. Trouble was, Webb was now behind her. She had to hang on to the branch with her left hand and hand down the kitten with her right.

"You can do it," he said. "Brace yourself with your knee."

She did and managed to pass off the kitten. When she had, she felt as if the weight of the world was off her shoulders. Now all she had to do was get down.

"I'll go down one branch," Webb said. "Then you do the same."

"Okay."

Webb scrambled down one branch quickly, while she inched back toward the tree trunk. This was where things got really tricky. "I think I might have to just live here."

Webb eyeballed her situation. "You need to hug the branch to swing yourself upside down, like a sloth."

"Are you crazy?"

"It will just be for a few moments, and then you'll have the other branch right under you to sit on."

She really didn't have much choice, seeing as how she didn't have any bright ideas of her own. She leaned forward, trying not to look down, and wrapped herself around the branch. Then, taking a breath that was likely to be her last, she let herself rotate to the right. Bark scraped her forearms and panic gripped her utterly. But when she was finally able to untangle her legs and sit on the branch just below the one her arms were still hanging on to for dear life, she let out a triumphant, "Yes!"

"Are you okay now?"

"Uh-huh."

"Good going," Webb said. *He* seemed to have no trouble at all scaling back down with the kitten in one hand. She managed to follow him down one more branch and then heard a thunderous snap as the branch her right foot rested on gave way. After that, there was a brief Wile E. Coyote moment of suspension as her immediate future flashed before her eyes. That future involved dropping through leafy branches and bumping against at least three large limbs until she got to the finale, which would be a ten-foot free fall to the ground.

And then she plunged.

The minute Laura heard Webb shouting, she knew something bad had happened. Very bad. Webb wasn't a hollerer by nature. And there was an uncharacteristic yet unmistakable edge of hysteria in his tone.

Her legs couldn't run fast enough. His voice came from the stand of trees where the tire swing used to be, and her first thought was of Erica. But when she arrived at the scene, Webb was hunched over Heidi's pale, unmoving form, sprawled on the loamy earth beneath the ash tree.

"We need to get her to an emergency room," he said.

"How?" Laura asked, whirling around, as if the answer might be conveniently near at hand. "Where's Rue?"

"She went to town."

"Should I call nine-one-one?"

He shook his head. "It would take them forever to get over here. Where are the nurses?"

"They're on the other side of the garden."

"Damn. Okay, just help me get her to the truck."

"But you aren't supposed to move people."

"You are when there's no help on the way."

Laura nodded. Then she cocked her head at a foreign, tinny noise in the grass nearby. It sounded like the melody to the song "New York, New York." "What's that?"

"I think it's Heidi's cell phone. It must have fallen out of her pocket."

Laura retrieved the phone. She could visualize it all now. "So what happened? She was up in the tree for some insane reason and decided to gab on the phone?"

Webb shot her an angry look. "She was rescuing Erica's kitten."

He reached down and put the kitten on his shoulder. Then he grabbed Heidi under her armpits and Laura picked up her feet, and they began to slowly make their way toward Webb's truck. Every movement of Webb's seemed focused and efficient. He'd always had a cool head in a crisis, but this was different, as if he'd practiced this maneuver a hundred times.

Maybe he had. Maybe after what he'd been through, this barely seemed like an emergency at all.

Inside Laura's pocket, Heidi's phone rang again.

Heidi mumbled something that sounded like "pain."

"She's talking," Laura said. "That has to be a good sign, right?"

Webb didn't say anything. His jaw twitched in what appeared to be a reprimand, and for a moment Laura wondered why she felt so guilty. It wasn't as if she'd sent Heidi up that tree. And Heidi had always been accident prone. There were plenty of times when they were kids . . .

Laura's brain shut down. She didn't want to think of accidents from the past or remember sitting for hours in hospital waiting rooms. The whole thing put her into a cold sweat.

"I don't imagine Rue would want me to leave Erica out here alone," she said as they approached the ancient Suburban they used for hauling things when the truck wasn't available. "Wherever Erica is."

"She went out to the lake, looking for Tortoise."

She marveled at Webb. It was as if he was fixed with an internal tracking device for each farm resident.

"You stay here." He handed her the kitten. "I'll take Heidi."

"Are you sure?"

He nodded. "I can handle it."

A few moments later Heidi was loaded and he was on his way.

When "New York, New York" rang again, Laura suddenly realized that she had forgotten to give him Heidi's phone. She looked at the number on the screen, then checked the call history. They were all the same number. She walked back to the house to call Rue, who wasn't answering her phone. Maybe she turned it off for lessons.

Laura wore a path from the coffeepot to the fridge, even though the coffee was lukewarm and no food looked appetizing. *Heidi will be fine*, she told herself. *At least it isn't your fault.*

Not this time.

When Heidi's phone rang for the fifth time, her curiosity could stand no more. She picked up and was astonished by the voice on the other end.

"Oh, thank heavens! It had been twenty long years, but Marla Bogue's Houston twang was unmistakable. "I thought you'd never pick up!"

"Hello, Marla."

There was a surprised silence on the other end of the line. Apparently, her own voice hadn't changed, either. *"Laura?"* The woman sputtered for a moment and then blurted out, "What are *you* doing in Hawaii?"

The question was so unexpected, Laura laughed. "Last time I looked, this was still Texas."

"Where?"

"Where do you think?" *Chucklehead.* "At the farm."

"In Sweetgum?"

At the moment Marla sounded like someone who had fallen from a tree.

"Yup, in Sweetgum."

"And Heidi's there . . . with *you?*"

"Well, not just at this moment. You see, Heidi's met with a little accident."

Marla gasped. "Oh my God! I knew it! They got to her!"

"Who?"

"Mobsters!"

"Cool your jets. She fell out of a tree."

Marla let out a long sigh. "Oh, thank God! From the questions the police were asking—"

Her voice cut off.

Laura squinted at the sun shining down on acres of dried grass, which made the horizon seem yellow. "The *police?*"

There was a pause. "So Heidi's okay?"

"Well, she looked sort of banged up after she fell. In fact, she looked a little . . . unconscious."

"Oh God."

All at once Laura had the horrifying vision of her stepmother descending on them, too. That would be too much. "She just had the wind knocked out of her, though," she added quickly. "Probably. The doctors are looking at her now. We'll have her call you as soon as she's all patched up."

"Oh. Well, all right." Marla seemed hesitant to let the connection go. "Be sure to have her call me. She's been acting so strange, and now . . ."

The police. And what was this business with Hawaii? Laura burned with curiosity, but she wasn't going to be reduced to picking Marla's feeble brain. It sounded like Marla didn't know what was going on, anyway. She'd always been foggy when it came to little things like facts.

"I'll have her call you just as soon as she can," Laura assured her, hanging up.

She almost looked forward to Heidi's getting back now. She couldn't wait to let Rue know the reasons behind their stepsister's nostalgic visit. *Police. Mobsters.* Someone had some 'splainin' to do.

Chapter 9

When Heidi opened her eyes, the blinding white light overhead gave her a moment of shock. People with near-death experiences always talked about seeing light, didn't they?

They never mentioned the afterlife hurting this much, though.

Come to think of it, would eighteen-inch fluorescent tubes be sold in heaven? *Doubtful. This is just the hospital.*

In which case, she was really screwed. Pain bloomed from her lower back. She was afraid to turn over, even though her body ached in the position she was in. And it wouldn't hurt to get away from that light, either. Her entire skull was throbbing.

She remembered Tom Chinske, covered in bandages, with half his teeth gone and fear in his eyes. Maybe what had happened to him had happened to her.

A figure in a pink scrub suit seemed to float past her bed.

"Excuse me," Heidi said to the scrub suit. "Am I in New York?"

She was answered by a twangy chuckle. "No, but it sounds like those meds you're taking have you flying somewhere."

The reply soothed her. She shut her eyes and fell asleep again. It was hard to say for how long. Periodically, she was aware of people jogging her awake, of the pain of being rolled over or moved. Of being wheeled down corridors.

Everything would be okay, she told herself. People looked after you in hospitals. All you had to do was sleep, slurp down Jell-O, and whine for narcotics.

On the other hand, in a hospital you were completely helpless. It would be nothing at all for someone to sneak in. Where had she last seen Streaky Hair? Standing on the street . . . just outside a hospital.

Her eyes snapped open again, but this time the shadowy form of someone stood between her and the light. Heidi shrieked.

The person leaned back, her arms crossed. Heidi started breathing again. It was Laura, which wasn't quite as bad as having Vinnie's henchman visit her.

"Nervous?" Laura loomed over her with a purse-lipped smile. "You were expecting someone else, maybe?"

Rue nudged her out of the way and peered down at Heidi in concern. "Forgive Laurel Mae's bedside manner."

Heidi tried to sound calmer than she felt. "She just seems like her normal self, actually."

"Can I get you something?" Rue asked.

Heidi nodded. "A new body. This one feels as if it's been through a meat grinder. My head . . ."

"You got a concussion when you fell," Rue explained.

Fell. Now she remembered. One minute she'd been up in a tree, grabbing a kitten; the next she'd been trampolining from branch to branch. And then hitting the ground. "Just a concussion?" It was hard to believe she could be that lucky.

"Well . . . no." Rue squeezed her hand. "They took X-rays. Your coccyx was fractured."

Heidi frowned. "What?"

Laura stepped forward again and announced with relish, "You have a broken ass."

"You need to take it easy for a few weeks," Rue said, putting a comforting hand on Heidi's shoulder.

"Hope you don't have any big equestrian events coming up."

"Will you shut up, Laura?" Rue grumbled.

"Why? I haven't enjoyed anything so much since the last Willie and Waylon reunion."

"It's not funny," Rue said.

"It is so. If it had happened to me, we would both be laughing our asses off." Laura grinned at Heidi. "Sorry. Couldn't resist."

"It's okay, Rue." Heidi was a little too worried about the repercussions of her accident to pay Laura much mind.

"See?" Laura said. "Heidi doesn't mind being the butt of a joke."

Rue groaned.

"How do they treat a fractured coccyx?" Heidi wondered aloud.

Laura crossed her arms. "The doctor's coming to fit you with a plaster ass cast in a few moments."

Heidi felt her eyes bug in panic, but then Rue sent Laura a withering look.

"Laurel Mae, if you don't *shut up*, I'm going to ask the orderlies to drag you away." Rue turned back to Heidi and spoke in a reassuring motherly tone. "There's no such thing as an ass cast. You just have to rest for a few days, and when you do get up, sit on a pillow or one of those inflatable doughnuts. You need to take it easy for a few weeks after that, but you'll be fine."

Heidi nodded. The prospect of a long plane ride sitting on a doughnut was grim, but they wouldn't want an invalid staying at the farm. Where could she go but home? And what awaited her there but certain doom?

Her gloom must have showed, because Rue reached forward and squeezed her hand again. "Erica will never forget you for saving that kitten. You're her hero."

"Aren't there guests leaving today?" Heidi asked. "Don't you need to take some of them to the airport?"

"You really have been hopped up on drugs, haven't you?" Laura asked. "It's Saturday afternoon."

"Jeanine, Margaret, and the others have gone," Rue explained. "It's a full turnover. Several new people arrived last night."

Laura circled the bed like a buzzard. "Oh!" she said, as if she were just remembering something, though Heidi could tell she'd been slavering to drop it into the conversation all along. "While you were out—so to speak—you dropped your phone, and as it happens, you received a few phone calls. I took the liberty of picking up your cell phone and answering it." She beamed a malevolent smile down at Heidi. "Hope you don't mind."

Heidi froze, but for the life of her, she couldn't think who could have called her. Her mother was the only one with the number. Unless . . .

"Don't worry. It was just Marla," Laura added.

Heidi exhaled in relief. "Did you tell her what had happened?"

"Oh sure, after I convinced her that you weren't kicking up your heels in Hawaii."

Heidi licked her lips. Her mouth was bone dry. "I . . . uh . . . didn't want her to know where I was. I was trying to get away from it all."

"By 'all,' do you mean your mom, the police, or the mob?" Laura asked with evident relish. "Because apparently all three have been wondering where you are."

Rue twisted around to glare at her sister. "Do we really need to go into this now?"

"I think we'd better ask Heidi that. *Do* we need to go into it now, Heidi? Or is hiding from the police no big deal to you?"

"I'm not hiding from the police."

"Then they're just looking for you for no particular reason?" Laura asked.

"*I'm* not in any trouble," Heidi assured Rue, preferring to direct her explanations to her. "I mean, the police might be looking for me, but they're not looking *for me.*"

"Who, then?" Laura asked.

"If you must know, they're probably looking for my boss. Who was sort of my boyfriend." Heidi added, "And also sort of a crook."

"*Sort of?*" Laura asked.

"Okay, I believe he was embezzling some money from the bank where we worked. I don't know where you got that stuff about mobsters."

Laura eyed her implacably. "From Marla."

"Mom doesn't know anything. That's why I left town so suddenly. I didn't want to involve her or anyone I knew in New York in what was going on."

"But I guess involving the people you knew here was just fine and dandy."

"What *was* going on?" Rue asked.

"Well . . ." Heidi took a deep breath. "I'm pretty sure someone tried to kill me. A whistle-blower at the bank—or the guy who had intended to blow the whistle—was beaten up badly. I visited him in the hospital and decided I should copy my bank files and take them to the district attorney. But when I was taking them over, a gypsy cab tried to run me over. It wasn't Vinnie. It was . . . an associate, I guess."

"But *Vinnie's* not part of the mob or anything," Laura drawled.

"He's not! He's . . . well, he might be a crook, who happens to be Italian, yes, but he's an independent crook. As far as I know."

Laura crowed. "That's showing excellent judgment there, Heidi Dawn. And I thought your mother took the cake when it came to men!"

"I've heard some stories about the company you keep," Heidi shot back.

Laura glared at her. "What does that mean?"

Heidi returned the hostile stare. "Pot, kettle, black."

"As far as I know, none of my friends have tried to kill me!"

Rue stepped between them. "Girls, this isn't the place for fighting." She grabbed Laura's arm and tugged her toward the door. "I'm going to go ask the RN outside when she thinks you're going to be released. And I think you're due a pain pill."

Heidi's thoughts were in a stew. All her secrets had been discovered. *Now what?*

She supposed she should be happy that she had just been discovered by the people on this end, and not by the people in New York.

Except now her mother knew, which was definitely not good. Marla had never been renowned for her discretion. She needed to swear her mother to secrecy. Immediately.

An industrial beige phone was perhaps two feet from her shoulder, on the table next to her bed, but from her perspective it might have been two continents away. In slow motion, she lifted herself to her elbows. Just sitting this far up made her nauseous.

She gripped the metal side bar of her bed, draped herself over it, and reached one arm for the phone.

Her mother picked up on the first ring. "Heidi! What have those Rafferty girls done to you? Why did you lie to me? And what on earth made you go *there?*"

"Which question should I answer first?"

"Are you all right? Laura said they were taking you to the hospital."

"Don't worry. It's just a concussion and a broken ass."

"A what?"

"I'm all right."

"Stephen and I have been so upset!"

Stephen and I? Was that still going on? "I hope you haven't told him about all this. . . ."

"Of course! What else could I do when the police came knocking at my door? And then you weren't answering your phone. . . ."

"What did the police want?"

"They wanted to know where you were, of course."

"Why?"

"Because you're a *missing person.* According to your bank, you just walked away from your desk one day. Did you think no one would notice? Your coworkers called the police, and the police called me because I'm listed as the insurance beneficiary in case you died doing banking business during office hours." She paused. "Thank you for that, by the way."

"Why were you talking to Laura about mobsters?"

"That was Stephen's idea. He said Vinnie looks like someone out of *Goodfellas,* and I knew it had to be on account of Vinnie that you ran away. Am I right?"

Heidi decided to dodge that question with a question. "What about Vinnie, Mom? Is he in jail?"

"Not as far as I know. Should he be?"

Heidi grunted a nonanswer. She couldn't help feeling disappointed. She had hoped that the police contacting her mother meant that the case against Vinnie was proceeding.

"Having the police at my door was bad enough," her mother went on, "but then calling you and finding myself talking to that awful girl!"

"The girl is thirty-six now," Heidi reminded her mother. "But she's still awful."

"I'm worried sick about you, and so is Stephen."

Heidi groaned. "Mother, this is none of Stephen's concern."

"You wouldn't say that if you had seen his face. After I told him the police had come by, he went straight down to the bank to make his own inquiries."

Heidi lurched up and regretted it immediately. She was definitely becoming more coccyx cognizant. "Mom, you need to tell him to stop. *Now.* And don't tell the police anything, either. You didn't give them my cell number, did you?"

"I just told them you were in Hawaii." Her mother gasped. "Does that mean I'm guilty of perjury?"

"Uh, I don't think so." Heidi lay back, cradling the phone in the valley between the pillow and her ear. Holding it required too much effort. "Mom, listen. You—you and Stephen—need to forget you ever found me. As far as you know, I'm still on a beach in Maui."

"Still?" Marla asked, confused. "Were you ever?"

"No . . . but you don't know that. I'm frolicking in Hawaii. Do you understand? Visualize grass skirts and ukuleles. And stop calling Stephen! You're just putting him at risk, too."

"Risk?"

"Just tell him not to get involved."

"Darlin', you're scaring the bejabbers out of me."

"Good. Now do as I say. You know nothing. I'll handle the police when I get back."

"When will that be?"

Heidi squirmed. *When Laura packs me onto a plane. When I grow a spine.* Something told her that the former was more likely than the latter. "I'm not sure. I had a little accident. I climbed a tree and it spat me out."

"I was afraid Laura had pushed you. You remember how she was."

"She hasn't changed."

"Why did you go *there*?"

"Because I was hoping you would think it would be the last place I would be."

"It is!" A frustrated sigh rattled across the line. "I don't understand you at all. Why do you have to hide?"

Heidi felt exhausted. "Mom, I think I need to go back into a coma now."

"Coma?"

"Go back to sleep, I mean."

Tired as she was when she hung up, she couldn't sleep. She played with the controls on her bed, lifting herself up to almost sitting. It soon became apparent, however, that her sitting days were over for a while, and she was flat on her back again when Rue came in and announced that she was going to be discharged.

"Remanded to my custody," Rue said.

"And Laura's?"

Rue laughed, but Heidi imagined that the sisters wanted nothing more than to send her back to Brooklyn, pronto. Rue might have too much kindness in her to make her sit in coach for four hours, but Heidi could imagine Laura crating her up and shipping her off in freight if necessary, like they did dogs and corpses.

The word *corpse* gave her pause. It was apt. If she went back to Brooklyn, she was a dead woman. "Where can I go?"

"Back home." At Heidi's questioning glance, Rue clarified, "To the farm."

"Are you sure?"

"Of course. Why not?"

"Well, because I'm in hiding. And I didn't tell you."

"Yes, you did. You told me you were in a mess."

"Was this the mess you imagined?"

"I'm embarrassed to say I never thought about it all that much. I've been preoccupied with other things. Besides, a person has a right to keep things to herself."

Heidi swallowed with effort. She didn't deserve this much understanding. "If Vinnie finds me . . . if he manages to track me down to Sweetgum . . ."

Rue brushed off this possibility—the source of all Heidi's terror—with a chuckle. "If that old boyfriend of yours comes down here, it'll just give Laura something to shoot at besides pigs."

"Y'all must *love* it here. Love, love, *love* it!"

Rue and Laura stifled yawns as they looked up at the sky to examine what exactly was sending their newest guest, Becca Stanbury, into rhapsodies.

"Look at those stars! Some of them are as big as my fist!" Metal flashed in the moonlight as Becca punched numbers on her cell phone. "I've *got* to tell Jackson about this."

Laura, sprawled on an Adirondack chair, seemed unmoved by the magic of the night sky. She obviously had something on her mind; otherwise she wouldn't be there at all. It was past midnight, and she'd been twiddling her thumbs for the past quarter hour, alternately glaring at the poor woman and dropping pointed hints.

The evening movie, *The Women*, had ended an hour and a half earlier. Most everyone had enjoyed it, except Jenna, a high school English teacher from San Marcos, who had left in the middle, weeping. It was an odd reaction to a thirties comedy, but then again the woman had just endured a five-hour drive in a seventeen-year-old Geo Metro. Rue was prepared to cut her some slack.

Jenna hadn't been seen again that night, and Luanne and Susan, the two women who were visiting from Tulsa, had seemed more interested in their Audubon guides than in dinner or the movie; they had emphasized several times that they were early risers and had yawned through the last half hour of the film. Then there was Becca. Becca was an attorney. And evidently a night owl.

"Jackson!" she yelled into the phone. "You should see it out here—in-fucking-credible. House like *The Waltons* and stars as big as my fist." She listened for a moment. "Oh, were you asleep?"

"Imagine that," Laura drawled.

"Oh! Sorry!" Becca chimed. "Guess I got carried away here. You go back to sleep. I'll give you a buzz tomorrow, and we can catch up. Night, tiger!" Setting the phone on the chair's ample armrest, she leaned back again.

"Is tiger the boyfriend?" Rue asked.

Becca cackled. "Better than that. He's my assistant at Gainey, McGibbon, and Emhardt."

"I'll bet he was glad to hear from you," Laura observed.

Becca released a sigh. "Well . . . I suppose guys just don't appreciate nature like we gals do."

"Anyone would think you'd never seen a star," Rue said.

"Not as big as these!" Becca folded her arms, looking like she was really ready to settle in. She closed her eyes. "We never experience peace and quiet like this."

Laura swatted at something on her arm. "Nothing but the sound of the mosquitoes gulping down our blood."

"I could spend the night out here," Becca said.

"That's not advisable." Laura looked over at Rue. "Especially not alone . . ."

The woman's eyes blinked open. "Why?"

"It's nothing," Laura said quickly. "I don't want to scare you."

"Are there wolves or something?" asked Becca.

"Oh yeah, but they're nothing much to worry about," Laura told her. "*They* hardly ever attack people."

Becca leaned forward. "You mean there is something out here that eats people?"

"Well . . ."

"Y'all don't have bears up here, do you?"

"A neighbor said he spotted a bear once, but I think he'd just been hitting the Jack Daniel's too hard." Laura chuckled. "Anyway, bear attacks aren't so bad, as long as you keep your wits about you and play dead. Which isn't always easy to do, since they tend to bite your skull first."

Becca fell silent.

"I've never seen a bear," Rue assured her.

"Me neither," Laura agreed. "*They're* not really what you should worry about, either."

"Well, what then?" Becca asked. "You might as well go ahead and spit it out, because you've already scared the crap out of me."

Laura leveled a dead serious gaze on her. "Cougars."

"Cougars!" the woman echoed. "Here? I thought they were only in the mountains."

"Used to be," Laura told her. "Used to be we hardly had any big predators at all, until the wild pig infestation. The pigs have lured the cougars, and if a cougar can't eat a pig, he's apparently just as happy to have a person. There have been attacks in the area. Large cats seem especially partial to women and children. They stalk them, then attack from behind."

The woman didn't move a muscle, as if there might be a cougar poised to pounce in the hydrangea hedge right at that moment.

"That's why Rue and I thought we should stay out here with you, even though it's been such a long day and we're both dog-ass tired. Wouldn't do to have our paying guests turned into cougar cat chow."

The woman sprang to her feet. "Well, sugar buns, I guess I'll turn in. I'm awfully tired, after the drive and everything. . . ."

Rue felt a lot more friendly toward her now that she was finally turning in. "Good night, Becca. Breakfast is usually between seven and eight."

The woman was inside the door so fast, not even the spriest, hungriest cougar could have caught her.

"You're shameless," Rue said to Laura when they were alone. "The woman's going to be seeing cougars behind every bush."

"Got rid of her, didn't it?" Laura sank down in her chair. "When I learned that tiger was a coworker, I was worried she might start calling everyone on the payroll at Gainey, McWhosit, and Whoever. And I didn't hear you piping in with any caveats or corrections."

Rue sighed. "I'm too tired. I wouldn't have contradicted you even if you'd said there were man-eating crocodiles in Kickapoo Creek."

"Maybe you should just start spiking the sweet tea with Sominex."

Rue yawned again. "Speaking of which, I'm about to pass out myself."

She started to get up, but Laura stopped her. "Actually, if you don't mind, I wanted to get rid of Sugar Buns so we could talk."

"About what?"

"You know . . ."

Actually, Rue didn't know.

"Heidi?" Laura said, as if she were dropping a hint.

"What about her?"

"Come on, Rue. Hospitality is one thing, but that woman's dug in like a tick." She backed up and started over. "I mean, okay, the woman fell out of a tree on our property. It's only fair that we should put up with her for another day or two. But you know and I know that she has to go."

"Why?"

Laura looked incredulous. "Because she *lied*. She made out like she was just here for a friendly visit."

"You never believed her," Rue pointed out.

"But I didn't think she was a fugitive from justice!"

"She's not."

"So she says. How do we know the police aren't really looking for *her*? She might be an embezzler, too. It wouldn't surprise me if she was in on the scheme. She admitted that guy was her boyfriend."

"Then why would he have tried to kill her?"

"Maybe because she was going to turn him in so she could cop a plea," Laura said. "Or what about this? Maybe he never did try to kill her."

"I doubt she would make something like that up. Why else would she have come here? And you remember how nervous she was."

Laura backed up and relaunched her argument from a different angle. "What would happen if it got out among the guests that there's a fugitive among us?"

"She's not a fugitive," Rue repeated.

"Okay then, a woman being hunted by a psycho embezzler mobster." She laughed. "An *independent* mobster."

"Heidi says there's no way he can trace her here."

"What if she's wrong? Forget the guests. What about *us*? What about Erica? What's William going to think about your putting his daughter in danger?"

"There's no danger. No one's after *us*."

"I hope you're right, but it still just doesn't seem worth it to have her here. Why not just send her on her way?"

"Because I don't want to." Rue looked her sister in the eye. "*I* want her to stay."

"But why?"

"Because I like having her here. She's helped me."

"Look, if you need some help, we can hire someone."

"You don't understand. She's my friend, and I don't have a whole lot of those right now. I *need* to have her here."

In the yellow porch light, Rue could see the muscle in Laura's jaw twitching. "What do you mean you don't have friends? Jesus, Rue, you've lived here all your life. You know everybody."

"But I don't *see* everybody," Rue pointed out. "During the day I'm too busy to run around socializing, and at night I don't have the energy to go out, even if I could. Some Sundays I don't even drag myself out of bed for church. But none of that matters, because I lost half the people I used to hang out with after the divorce, because they decided they were William's friends, not mine. Then several of the ones who stuck with me through the divorce bailed on me during cancer. It's like I was contagious—or maybe they just didn't like the way I looked in caps."

"Then they're bastards, and you're better off without them."

"I know."

Laura stared at her feet. "It's not like you're all alone out here."

"I know. Sometimes it feels like I can't move without bumping into a guest."

"I'm not talking about guests. You've got Erica. You've got me."

"Maybe that's it. We're so isolated, we both know exactly what the other person is going to say before she says it. Even with all the guests, it sometimes feels like I'm going to go nuts without somebody to talk to."

"I see."

"Of course you do. Isn't that why you go roaring off in your truck several times a month?"

"I just need to blow off steam sometimes. It's a nice break from sitting around worrying about when this place is finally going to go broke. I don't analyze it beyond that."

"Maybe you should. Maybe you should take a good look at what really matters to you, and who."

"I don't need to! I certainly don't feel the need to start shipping people in to be my friend."

"What about Webb?"

"He's just camping out till he figures out what to do with himself. The other day I was trying to convince him to become an air traffic controller. He's got the nerves for it."

"He's here because of you."

"He's just mixed up. He's just out of the army, and he's going through a divorce. You know how that is. Any port in a storm. That's why *you* came back to the farm."

"I came back because you were here. And that's why Webb's here, too. You didn't see the look on his face when he found out you'd run off with Buddy the other night."

Laura let out a whoop of disbelief. "I'm sure he was heartbroken—the Valentino of Sassy Spinster Farm! He's got every woman on the place after him, including your new best friend. Maybe we should warn him that she's a gangster's moll."

Rue studied her for a long moment. "I can't shake the feeling that you're the one who needs warning."

"Why?"

"You never seem to see the curves coming."

The moment the words slipped out, Rue's face went hot. She sucked in her breath, as if by doing so, she could call the words back. But she couldn't. There was no getting them back, and immediately the atmosphere crackled with tension.

Laura leapt out of her chair, nearly overturning it.

"Laura . . ." Rue struggled to get up herself.

"Forget it!"

"You know I didn't mean that how it sounded."

"Forget everything."

"I'm sorry."

"I said forget it." Laura shook her head, then did what she always did when confronted by a charged emotional situation. She changed the subject. "And for all I care, Heidi can stay till she gets hauled off to the hoosegow!"

She turned sharply and went inside, letting the door slap loudly behind her.

It wasn't often that Rue felt ashamed of herself, but now she writhed with shame. Ached with it. How could she have let what was supposed to be a heart-to-heart talk devolve into a spat? How in just one offhand instant could she have cracked open a Pandora's box that had been tightly sealed for twenty long years?

Chapter 10

When Laura crept out of bed at dawn, her midnight conversation with Rue was still whirring through her brain. It felt as if their talk had been on a loop in her head since she had gone to bed, keeping her fidgeting all night. Now she was so jittery with exhaustion, it took an effort just to rake a toothbrush across her teeth.

You never seem to see the curves coming. . . .

Finally. There it was. Almost two decades in the making. She had been waiting for it ever since the accident—the little chink in Rue's armor of perfect niceness. All these years she had thought it would be such a relief if Rue just lashed out at her. But Rue had never uttered a blessed little word of reproach about the accident. No hint of bitterness or accusation or resentfulness had ever crossed her lips.

Until last night. Laura hadn't known how to respond. Contrary to expectations, the oblique gibe had brought her no relief at all.

She went downstairs early enough to miss Rue and let herself out the side door. She practically tripped over Becca, who was perched on the top step, lacing up a complicated white and blue sneaker that looked like it had been designed by NASA.

"Morning, sweet cakes!"

Laura wasn't sure which was more unsettling—seeing a guest up this early or being called sweet cakes.

"Weren't we just talking about five minutes ago?" One good thing about rising at the crack o' dawn was that it gave her an hour or so to be guest-free.

"I'm an early bird." Becca sprang to her feet, hopped a few times, then began a hamstring stretch. Her skimpy black and purple Lycra jogging outfit seemed ridiculously out of place here, but the muscles straining on her otherwise twiggy limbs made it clear that she never missed her morning jog. The woman was a compact powerhouse, like a flea.

She shot a resentful look at Laura. "I looked up cougars online last night. That was a load of bull, wasn't it?"

"Somewhat," Laura admitted. "In any case, you have nothing to worry about. You're probably not enough of a snack to warrant chasing down."

Becca looked annoyed and still a little distrustful. "I guess it wouldn't hurt to stick to the open, anyway," she said before she bounded off toward the lane.

"Crazy way to live," Laura grumbled to herself as she opened the gate to the chicken yard. In the coop she checked all the nests for eggs and found nine. Fred followed her out, as usual, shaking out his feathers as he dogged Laura's heels ahead of Shelley Winters and Monte, who were impatient to be fed. From the barn she could already hear the robotic voice of Dylan's NOAA weather radio, which announced that the day's forecast called for sun and temperatures in the lower nineties with no chance of rain, and that the long-range forecast called for sun and temperatures in the lower nineties with no chance of rain.

That radio was maddening, but the guys loved it. Listening to it drone on, she couldn't help thinking that the whole world was getting the moisture sucked out of it. It was just June, and they'd already started pumping water from the lake to irrigate. By July the fish would need flea collars.

If yields weren't good, by the end of the summer the farm

bank account would evaporate, too. Then their problems would really begin. Just as her father had predicted all along, she would be an utter failure.

Webb was up, and his eyes shone with amusement when he got a load of her and her entourage. "You look like a cranky pied piper."

"I feel like hell," she said.

"Do your hangovers have a forty-eight-hour delay?"

"I'm not hungover. I'm fed up. This is a stupid way to make a living." Mr. NOAA was sawing away about the long-range forecast again. "Do we really need that thing on all the time?"

He reached over and turned down the volume. "Don't worry. Yesterday Herman told me that we were going to have rain soon."

"How in Hades does he know that?"

"He says his bones are telling him."

"Well, from his ulna to God's ears," she said. "Anyway, it's not just the weather that's making me mental. It's all these damn people. I just tripped over one as I was coming out of the house. A jogger. I'd really like not to have to tippy toe around my own house in the morning. And I'd like to have a bowl of cereal in the a.m. without having to listen to the inane chatter of strange women."

"If only the strange women didn't give you money . . ."

"They don't *give* it. We earn it by offering up our lives to them. We're farm whores."

Finally succumbing to Monte's and Shelley Winters's silent but heartfelt pleas, she opened a tub and scooped some kibble into their bowls. The dogs wolfed down the nuggets like they were filet mignon.

"This place is turning us all into crazy people," Laura said.

Webb shook his head. "You didn't actually start out at ground zero on the mental health scale."

Laura let out a halfhearted laugh. "Now Rue's going strange, too. She's decided she and Heidi are best buds. She wants her to stay indefinitely."

She watched Webb's face closely for his reaction. It wasn't very heartening. He smiled. "Really? And what do you say to that?"

"Far be it from me to deprive my sister of her friend." She bit her lip. "Or you, either, apparently."

"I admit it. I like her."

"Well, don't like her too much. She's bad news."

"Yeah, she looks real threatening."

"It's no joke. She's got all sorts of little secrets."

"Oh, I know about those," Webb assured her.

"What do you know?"

"That's she's hiding from somebody."

Laura was flabbergasted. "You knew? Since when?"

"Since the first day she got here. I heard her on the phone telling her mother that she was in Hawaii."

"Why didn't you tell me?"

"It was none of my business. I only heard because I was eavesdropping."

"You and your ethics." Laura could have spit. "She's *living* here!"

"And that makes you entitled to . . . what, exactly?"

"To know what's going on!"

He laughed. "What are you? The KGB?"

She scowled at him. "I thought you'd at least be on my side."

"I didn't know there was a side to be on."

This was just what was so irritating about Webb. He was always striking an evenhanded, nonjudgmental pose. Which was fine when he was holding back judgment of *her.* But sometimes she just wanted someone to sling a little mud with. And she certainly wanted to know if there was dirt to be had on her archenemy. Was that too much to ask of a friend?

She remembered Rue's vague hints of Webb's imminent defection and took perverse pleasure in bursting any bubble that might be developing there. "She's already got a boyfriend, you know."

"I know. Stephen."

She felt a flash of triumph. "No, his name is Vinnie." She frowned. "Who's Stephen?"

"Stephen was the name she mentioned to her mother on the phone."

"Well, the boyfriend's name is Vinnie. I'm sure of it. Maybe this Stephen is another sucker she's stringing along."

"Sounds like she's been living a *Peyton Place* existence."

"More like *The Godfather.*"

Webb chewed this over for a moment. "I doubt she's got it in her to be a lawbreaker."

Laura let out an exasperated sigh. "You're as bad as Rue. When I told her I didn't want Heidi here, she threw the accident in my face. Practically the first time she's mentioned it in twenty years!"

"So that's it."

"That's what?"

"Why you've got such a bee in your bonnet about Heidi."

"I do not have a bee in my bonnet!" It would have sounded more believable if she hadn't been shrieking. She attempted to ramp it down a notch. "I just don't know why everyone wants to jump to Heidi's defense. What's she done to endear herself to anyone?" She narrowed her eyes on him. "What's she done to endear herself to you?"

"Jealous?"

Unfortunately, she couldn't think of a way to answer that question without either incriminating herself or sounding more like a hothead than she probably already seemed. She settled for, "Don't be ridiculous," and marched out of the barn.

In the kitchen Rue was up and listening to Willie Nelson. It was Laura's CD; Rue had never liked him all that much.

"What is this? Penance?" Laura had planned to be conciliatory, but the words came out grumpy.

Rue looked up at her with tired eyes. "I am sorry about last night, Laura. You know I didn't mean it how it sounded."

"Sure."

Rue's stare mirrored the question running through Laura's own mind. *So why are you so angry?*

Laura filled a thermos with coffee and a cup for herself and went back outside, where she ran into Herman and Dylan, newly arrived and yukking it up over something or other. When they saw her, their happy faces vanished. *Do they think I'm an ogre?* She exchanged crisp good mornings, handed Herman the coffee thermos, then got into the golf cart and headed for the lake.

Sometimes a tactical retreat was essential. The farm wasn't safe this morning. She kept ricocheting from person to person, getting irritated. She needed to get a grip on herself, and she couldn't do that with all those damn people around her.

She careened the golf cart full speed ahead over ruts and old, dried-up wheel tracks, sending bugs flying. At the dam she stopped and looked out over the lake. There wasn't a wave or any movement on the water at all except for the occasional ripple when a dragonfly buzzed too close to the blue-green surface.

She climbed out and walked to the old diving board, which had broken in two in the nineties and now looked like a sawed-off shotgun jutting out over the water. When they were kids, she and Rue had always hurled a rock into the water "to scare away the snakes." Later they'd just tossed in Heidi. Whether the snakes were all that scared of rocks or Heidi had never been proven, but since she didn't have Heidi handy, she tossed a stone in, anyway. Then she peeled off all her clothes and dived in.

The water was surprisingly refreshing. She hadn't swum since August, and that late in the summer the lake stank of algae and tended to be the temperature of spit. Now, as she stroked through the water, she could almost imagine that she was gliding through a gleaming spring-fed pool like Esther What's-Her-Name, whose movies bored the snot out of her.

She Australian crawled until she was dead center of the lake, then rolled onto her back and floated. There was work to be done, and she scolded herself for not doing it. But what did it matter? All the work in the world wasn't going to keep the farm going if it didn't rain soon.

She felt torn between guilt and resentment. In the kitchen Rue was busy making breakfast. Rue wouldn't have run away and jumped in the lake when there was work to be done. Rue never ditched her responsibilities. She was better for this land than Laura had ever been. Laura had been burning to take over the farm since she was a girl and had begged her dad to let her ride with him on the tractor. But the only reason the place was at all solvent now was because of Rue. In fact, if Rue hadn't gotten divorced and decided to come back, Laura would have probably ended up declaring bankruptcy years ago. There would be no farm. Nothing. The paying guests, the CSA memberships . . . all Rue.

That was the nagging constant in her life—the feeling of being the inferior one. In kids' books, if there were two sisters, one was usually pretty, while the other one was smart. But in their family Rue had received the brains *and* the beauty. And all the goodness. Rue had always done her homework and made straight As. She'd helped their mom around the house, while Laura had sneaked off to the woods to play. She had been the one with the tidy room and impeccably ironed clothes, whereas Laura had worn clothes until they were stiff with grunge and managed to evade the bathtub for days on end. Small wonder, then, that when they were older, even after Laura had discovered the joys of good hygiene, the boys flocked to Rue, while they looked on Laura as just another kid in FFA.

The strange thing was, Laura had never been jealous. Not seriously. They'd been so isolated, Rue had always been her best friend. Envying her would have been laughable, like envying the person you were adrift with on a lifeboat.

And how could you be jealous of someone who always covered for you when you forgot to do some annoying chore, like vacuuming? How many people had a sister who, even though she was only two years older, would bake lemon squares for you to take to the school bake sale because your mother was too sick to get out of bed? And then, after their mother had died, Rue was the one who had made sure Laura got new clothes for school, who had explained—however sketchily—the birds and the bees, and who had stood up for her to their dad when he decided, frequently, to take his anger at the world out on Laura.

Rue had been Laura's brick when their house had been invaded by Marla Bogue and Heidi Dawn.

And she had taught Laura how to drive.

Laura flipped over into a dead man's float, as if by holding her breath, she could also hold back the memories. But they flooded in anyway; they always did. Sometimes when she was completely absorbed in some task, unaware that awful thoughts were stirring in her mind, the sound of metal crunching and glass shattering would explode in her ears, as sickeningly real as the moment it had happened. Suddenly she would be sixteen again, and Rue eighteen, and their lives would be shaken up all over again in that noisy, terrifying instant.

During the last days of Marla's reign, home had become a hell. Their father and Marla argued constantly. Several times a week Laura and Rue begged to borrow Marla's car and run some errand for her so that they could escape for a little while. They would do the errand and then just drive down the back roads, listening to the radio and laughing. They laughed like maniacs at anything. Laura would sneak cigarettes, hanging out the front window like an Irish setter so that there wouldn't be a telltale smell when they returned the car. Sometimes she would ask Rue to let her drive, even though she didn't have her learner's permit yet.

Rue was a good teacher, but the two of them differed in their view of cars. Rue saw them as transportation. Laura saw driving as a thrill ride. Going fast and scaring the bejesus out of Rue, and even sometimes out of herself, made her feel alive. Powerful. After sixteen years of being cooped up and doing what she was told—or not doing what she was told—she could suddenly seize her own destiny. Rocketing down back lanes that she'd known all her life was pure liberation, however short-lived.

One afternoon, when the atmosphere at home was particularly charged, they had skipped out of the house and taken the car without permission. At the end of the farm's lane, they switched places, and Laura hurtled them down winding country roads at speeds that made their stomachs lurch as they crested hills. Usually, Rue would halfheartedly advise her to slow down, but Laura always suspected her sister was a closet speed freak. This was one of those days when she was game for a little bit of derring-do. Laura could remember her whoops of laughter.

She was laughing, too. She remembered the Clash cranked on the radio, and the split second of stunned fear as she rounded a tight turn and saw a cow standing in the middle of the road.

Her frantic hand-over-hand turn kept them from hitting the animal but sent the car careening off the road on two wheels. Tires shrieked. They cartwheeled off the road, slid, and finally landed sideways and nose down against a concrete drainage pipe in a ditch.

When the world was still again, Laura felt as if someone had bludgeoned her in the chest with a baseball bat. It took her a moment to understand it all, to realize that she'd crashed Marla's car. The pain she felt was where her lap belt had let her pitch forward into the steering wheel.

Then she heard a moan. She wrenched her neck and saw Rue piled up against the shattered glass of the passenger window. Rue, the careful and conscientious one, had not been wearing a seat belt. Her face was a horror; blood dripped down her skin like melted wax down a candle.

"Rue?"

She moaned again.

She's alive, Laura thought. *I haven't killed her.* "Rue? Are you all right? Can you move?"

Obviously she wasn't, and couldn't. Laura wasn't sure that she could move, either. When she finally tried, she was surprised how easily she was able to reach across and touch Rue's shoulder.

Her sister recoiled from the gentle touch as if Laura had slugged her. She whimpered and sank even farther against the passenger door.

"Rue, can you hear me?" Hysteria rose in Laura's throat. "Rue, say something . . . please say something . . . *please* . . ."

Rue's eyelids fluttered; she didn't turn her head to look at Laura but stared blandly ahead and spoke in a hoarse whisper. "Get help."

Even in disaster, through a veil of pain, Rue was the one thinking clearly.

Laura was still in a panic. How could she get help? They were in the middle of nowhere. What if Rue died while she was gone? What if the car exploded? Cars exploded after crashes in movies all the time. All the time.

"I can't leave you," she said.

"Go."

Laura looked at the blood on her sister's face. Rue was right; on this isolated road they could wait an hour for another car to come by. She would have to fetch somebody.

She turned to see if she could push her door open and ended up sliding against Rue, who let out a shout.

"I'm sorry!"

She clambered over the backseat to get out of Rue's way, rolled open the left side window, and heaved herself out of the car as if she were pulling herself out of a manhole.

When she tried to stand, it felt as if her right knee was going to give out on her, but she managed to limp a few paces before adrenaline kicked in for real and she started jogging down the road. It seemed like hours but was probably only minutes before a truck came toward her. She waved it down and recognized the driver from seeing him at McCaffree's store. After she blurted out her story, the man helped her into the truck and then sped toward the car. He hopped out to look at Rue, then said he would go to the next house and call an ambulance.

From that point on, time crawled. It took forever for help to come and then to get Rue to a hospital. The hours in the waiting room while Rue was being looked at by a doctor seemed endless, too. In addition to the damage to her face and jaw, Rue had broken her right arm and fractured her collarbone.

Their father, when he finally arrived at the hospital, was blazing mad. It didn't help that Laura had made it through the accident with a few scratches, a sprained knee, and a broken rib. None of these injuries were serious enough to make up for her grievous faults. She had been driving without a license in a car they had taken without permission. She had almost killed her sister.

And it *really* didn't help that their father had just discovered that his wife was sleeping with the bug exterminator. Laura didn't piece that together till later. All she knew was that her father railed in front of anyone within earshot that Laura was no good and never had been, and now she'd as good as tried to murder her sister. He couldn't resist adding that it would have been better for everyone if their positions had been switched. Laura was the one who deserved to be deformed for life.

That word, *deformed*, terrified her. Surely he was just raving. Rue was so pretty—nothing could take that away.

But when Laura finally saw Rue with her jaw wired and her skin pocked with cuts and gashes, she knew her father was right. Nobody would be calling Rue the pretty one anymore. From then on, people would stare and then pretend not to. Strangers in stores would feel compelled to ask what had happened. The worst of the damage was worked on in two surgeries, one to build up a crushed cheekbone and the other to fix her jaw, but their father only had catastrophic health insurance and certainly didn't have the money to keep paying for plastic surgery out of pocket.

Through it all, Rue never uttered a word in anger to Laura. Ever. Even when Laura stammered out apologies, Rue shrugged them off. "You didn't know there was going to be a cow in the road," she'd say.

In the midst of all this trouble, Marla and Heidi disappeared. The event Laura had wished for had finally come to pass, but there was no moment to savor it. Mr. Rafferty's moods swung more violently than ever, and his drinking increased correspondingly.

After the accident, Laura vowed to be a better person. She would work hard to be more like Rue. But once Marla and Heidi were gone, all their father's bitterness came down on her, and it became harder and harder to be like Rue when she felt so damn angry. Sometimes she even wanted to get mad at Rue for being so nice about it all, so forgiving. Life would have been easier if she could have hated Rue for being a walking billboard for all her mistakes, her recklessness. No one in Sweetgum would ever forget that Laura Rafferty had wrecked her sister's life. No one except Rue.

But how could Laura hate the person who had to wake up every day and face in the mirror the repercussions of her biggest mistake? How could she hate someone who had to start every single day of her life forgiving her?

Laura lifted her head out of the water and gasped in a deep breath. She had no idea how long she had been floating there, although her fingers were starting to prune.

She began to swim back. Halfway to shore, she stopped. Webb, hatless, was perched on the sawed-off diving board, his face squinting up at the morning sun and one dangling leg swinging a lazy figure eight beneath him. The dogs sat on the dam behind him, like sentinels.

Laura breast-stroked until she was in talking distance and looked up at him warily. "It's a little early to work on your tan, isn't it?"

A smile spread across his face as he squinted down at her. "I'm not the one with all my clothes off."

"So that's why you're here."

"As a matter of fact . . ." He turned to grab something and held up a folded towel with the tips of his fingers, like a waiter holding a tray of aperitifs. "I thought you might appreciate this."

"How did you know where I was?"

"From Luanne and Susan. The bird-watcher women? They came in to breakfast and announced that there was a naked lady swimming in the lake. Apparently, they got up early to go bird-watching and had quite a morning. They spotted a hairy woodpecker in a cottonwood and a loon in the lake."

Laura's head spun to see if they were still out there.

"Don't worry," he said. "They're gone. It's making for interesting conversation around the breakfast table, though."

Breast-stroking again, Laura complained, "A person can't even take a morning dip in her own lake." She stopped when she'd gone as far as she could without having to rise out of the water, unclothed, like a weather-beaten Venus. "Would you mind turning your head so I can get out of here?"

"Isn't it a little too late for modesty?"

"Just trying to save you an early morning fright." As she touched ground, he dutifully turned his head and handed her the towel. "Thanks."

While she struggled into her clothes again, he leaned back on the board and looked up at the sky. "What happened?" he asked. "One minute we were having a typical morning bull session, and the next you disappeared."

"I wanted to be alone, to think."

"Care to elaborate?"

She didn't want to rehash her trouble with Rue, so she fell back on her usual complaints. "I was thinking about this place, and how I'm going to survive another year like this. And about all these people poking around all the time. If I could just think of a way to make the farm pay better."

"If it doesn't rain again soon, you might not have to worry about people. The whole place might just dry up and blow away."

"Very comforting!"

"You could always become a camel rancher."

"Erica would love that. A new kind of critter to ride."

"Start an aloe vera farm."

She zipped up her jeans. "Thank you for your very kind suggestions. Now I have several new ideas for going broke."

Webb stood up. "It's the least I could do." He stopped inches away from her, and she held on to him for balance while she dug her foot into her boot. His arm was solid muscle. "You're always trying to come up with plans for my future," he said.

"But *my* ideas are all good."

"No, they're not. They're lousy."

She laughed. There was an uncomfortable charge between them; she could feel it in the tension in his arm. "When you come up with something better, I'll be the first to tell you so."

"Really?" He looked down at her, and the eye contact stirred her in a way she wasn't ready for. He was smoldering. Smoldering looks like that weren't supposed to happen at eight in the morning. At least not between two people who had spent the night in separate houses. "Let me know what you think about this."

She still had one foot in just a sock when he took hold of her free hand and pulled her to him. In all the months since he'd come back, this was just what she had been trying to avoid. Now here she was, caught off guard and off balance, so that she leaned right into him when he kissed her. All of it was a surprise—the rough feel of his skin, the warm orange-juicy taste of his mouth, the lingering smell of the alcohol he used as aftershave. She looped one hand around his nape. When he'd first come back, he'd grown out his hair after years of having it military short. Now it was lopped off again for summer, and she fluttered her fingers over the soft bristles.

The fuzz gave him a vulnerability that surprised her. It was like baby chick down.

She slid her hands, palm out, down his chest and gave him a gentle push. "We shouldn't have done that."

He let out a tired breath. "You're as predictable as the sunrise. I had a countdown going in my head. Three . . . two . . . one . . . denial."

Sharp hunger gnawed inside her. She stared into his eyes and moved her mouth a moment before working herself up to words. "It's not denial. It's the opposite. It's accepting reality."

"Your reality doesn't seem to be matching up with mine. My reality says we're two adults. We've been orbiting around each other for years, occasionally meeting up but never quite managing anything permanent. This could be our chance."

She swallowed. "I can't have this conversation right now. I've still got one shoe off."

He looked down at her foot encased in its now-damp sock, and then his eyes slowly moved up the rest of her. She flushed under the gaze, which, she couldn't help noticing, wasn't entirely lustful. There was a hint of criticism in the way he was looking at her, which she wasn't used to receiving from a man who'd just kissed her.

"Your shirt's buttoned crooked," he said.

With nervous fingers, she set about righting herself as he watched her with a hint of amusement. When she was done, he crooked a brow and asked, "*Now* can you have a conversation?"

"I'm hungry," she said. "Swimming always does that."

"I'll drive you home." He'd dropped his hat into the driver's seat of the golf cart, and once there he picked it up and smashed it on his head while she settled herself into the seat next to him. She assumed they were back to normal, until he grabbed her hand.

"Laura, what's wrong with us? All these years. You have to have known how I feel. I—"

"Don't say it."

He stopped. "What?"

"Whatever you were about to say. Don't."

"Why not?"

"Because when people say those words, it's usually a blunder. Rue loved William, you loved Denise, and Heidi probably loved the guy who tried to mow her down with a car. Those words don't mean what people want them to mean. They don't mean as much as what we have now. They don't mean as much as friendship."

His face cycled through a series of expressions, from puzzlement to anger. "I don't feel friendship toward you," he said. "In fact, right this moment I feel the opposite. I feel pissed off."

"Good." She stared forward, wishing like hell he'd get the damn cart moving.

He gaped at her. "And that's all you have to say to me? Just a kiss and then shut your piehole?"

"What else? We made a mistake once before, remember? I practically ruined your life. That's what I excel at. Ask anyone."

He spent an uncomfortably long time staring at the farmhouse in the distance before replying. "I was wrong to come back here. I thought maybe you would see things differently."

"You thought I'd go all warm and fuzzy in my old age?"

He didn't answer.

She fixed a stare on his profile, wanting to see into those eyes again. He didn't oblige her. "What are you thinking?"

"I'm thinking I'll stay the summer, like I promised. I like the work. After that I'm leaving."

"What will you do?"

"I'm not sure," he said, turning the key in the ignition. "Maybe I'll take your advice and become an air traffic controller, after all. It'd be a hell of a lot easier on my nerves."

Chapter 11

The third night Jenna was at the farm, the movie was *Mrs. Doubt-fire*, and the poor woman had bolted from the room in tears.

This batch of guests was an odd mix. There was Becca, the steamroller, relentlessly businesslike even as she called everyone tiger and sweet pea. The two vegetarian bird-watchers, Luanne and Susan, seemed more interested in exploring the woods than farming. And then there was Jenna, who had barely shown her face except at mealtimes. Rue had convinced her to give the movie a try, but that was obviously a big mistake.

"She cried all last night," Susan whispered. She had the room right next to Jenna's.

Luanne shook her head. "D-i-v-o-r-c-e."

Susan went on in a regular voice. "She told me her husband had just left her for an older woman."

"*Older?*" Becca asked.

They all stared at each other.

"That's gotta hurt," Luanne said.

Becca clucked impatiently. "Sugar bun needs to stop boo-hooing and start filing."

Erica's brows knit in confusion. "Filing?"

"Divorce papers," Becca said. "*Now*. That's the trouble with women. We get all emotional just when we need to be looking out for ourselves."

"Well, it's hard not to get emotional when your marriage is swirling down the toilet," Luanne observed.

Becca wasn't moved. "Men don't cry. They litigate."

That night Rue couldn't sleep. She had a backache, and she felt like she was having an asthma attack. *It's a panic attack*, she told herself as she sat up and sucked in breaths. But the words didn't comfort her, or fool her.

Ever since she'd been diagnosed, any bodily twinge made her stomach lurch in fright. A headache was a brain tumor; indigestion meant imminent death. If she woke up at night with a sore back, imagining kidney disease sent her into a feverish sweat. Once she had run to her oncologist between visits—and she visited every two months—sure that her sore throat was the beginning of the end. "Allergies," he'd said.

Of course it was. She'd always had allergies. Allergies brought on asthma, which she'd suffered from as a kid. It was just that now any symptom seemed sinister.

It's nothing, she told herself again and again. *Nothing.*

She got up and padded out to the kitchen in her slippers. She poured herself a glass of cranberry juice and looked out the back window; she could have sworn she saw something out there. Pressing her nose against the pane, she took in quite a spectacle: Heidi was lying in a pair of shorty pajamas on her stomach, backward, on a lounge chair. Rue poured another glass and went outside.

Heidi cricked her neck up to see who it was.

"That position looks painful," Rue observed. "I thought you deserved a drink for accomplishing it." She set the cranberry juice on the ground, near Heidi's right hand.

"Thanks. Actually, it wouldn't be all that bad if my breasts weren't getting smashed. Do you think anyone makes Adirondack chairs out of memory foam?"

"Would you like a cushion for your legs?" They were bent at the knee, her calves pressed against the backrest.

"No thanks. I've got a pretty good thing going here. I don't want to mess it up." Heidi sighed. "If I ever recover, so help me God, I'll never take a pain-free butt for granted again."

Rue settled herself into a chair—the right-side-up way. "I should have offered to switch beds with you. That old thing of Dad's is probably torture to you right now."

"It's okay. Especially if I lie on it backward. I have a whole new perspective on furniture now."

"Maybe I could get you to switch with Erica for a few days."

"I doubt she'd go for that. She says my room still stinks." Heidi craned another look up at Rue. "What are you doing up?"

"I couldn't sleep."

"Problem?"

"No." Rue gave her head an adamant shake. "No, it's just . . ." She swallowed.

"Just what?"

"I think . . ." To Rue's horror, her voice cracked as she blurted out, "I think I'm dying!"

At first the outburst shocked her almost as much as it did Heidi. But as she sat there fighting back tears, she realized the words had been scrambled in her head for a couple of weeks now; she'd just been avoiding sorting them out. She'd certainly avoided giving voice to them.

Heidi unbent herself into a normal sitting position. "Why do you think that?"

"I'm sorry. That sounded so melodramatic. I don't know why I said it."

"Because it was on your mind, obviously."

"It's just a feeling I've had."

"Have you seen a doctor?"

"A while ago. My GP. He gave me an inhaler for this nighttime asthma I've been having," Rue said. "I had asthma when I was younger, too, but it's been years . . ."

"And?"

"And it seemed to work at first, but I think that was just wishful thinking. Now I'm terrified—not just of being sick again, but of how it will change everything. I don't know how we could function around here. I know now how . . ." She swallowed; she didn't want to go any further down that path.

"What's the next step?" Heidi asked.

"I don't know."

For a moment there was no sound but the crickets.

"You have to go back," Heidi said.

"I know."

"Soon."

"I know."

"It might be nothing. You might be worrying for nothing. But you're not going to stop worrying until you find out for sure."

"I know that, too." Rue leaned back in her chair, gripping the arms tightly. "On the other hand, it might be bad news. And what comes after that would be a nightmare. Not just for me, but for everybody." She tried to swallow and couldn't. When she thought of Erica, her throat clamped shut.

"But it wouldn't help matters to wait, would it?"

"No." Rue knew Heidi was saying all the things that she would have said had their positions been reversed. "You're right."

"Call."

Rue assented to the plan in silence.

"Do you want me to go with you?"

"No. Thanks, but I don't want the others to worry. Laura's got enough on her mind as it is, and Erica . . ."

They sat quietly for a moment, listening to cicadas and a lonely frog somewhere nearby.

"Thank God I've got good health insurance," Rue said. "William might not have been much of a husband, but as an insurance agent, he's pure gold."

"So it's your breathing that's bothering you?" Heidi probed. "Nothing else?"

"There's not much left. After they discovered I had stage three-B cancer, they hollowed me out as best they could, in stages. Double mastectomy, hysterectomy. I asked them if they could take out my appendix and maybe do a little liposuction while they were at it, but my oncologist didn't seem amused."

"Hysterectomy! But why?"

"A, because estrogen is associated with breast cancer. B, because recovering from multiple surgeries is so much more fun when you get to deal with hot flashes, too. Plus, it gave me two fewer organs to worry about cancer metastasizing to."

"I didn't know," Heidi said. "About the estrogen thing, I mean."

"No, it's one of those subjects that doesn't come up until you're sitting on a metal slab in a surgeon's office in a complete panic. My mom had breast cancer—died of it—but I didn't pay attention to the details." She took a swig from her glass. "Ignorance was bliss. This has been one education I could have done without."

Heidi grunted in assent, and Rue started to regret bringing this up. Why had she?

"It's probably nothing," Heidi assured her.

"That's what everybody says. It's what they said when they found the lump. My friends, Laura, people at church. Even the doctor. 'Probably nothing,' they all said. They even had me believing it. And then, when it turned out to be something—something big—I felt like I'd been sucker punched."

"All right, I promise not to say anything positive or peppy."

"Thank you."

"Except"—Heidi cleared her throat—"I never thanked you."

"For what?"

"For letting me stay on, even after you learned about Vinnie. I know Laura would like to see the back of me."

"Laura would like the whole place cleared out. Sometimes I think she wants me gone, too, so it can just be her, a few chickens, and Herman and Dylan to boss around."

"I'm not like the other guests. And now I'm really useless."

"Not to me, you're not."

Heidi looked surprised. "What have I done for you?"

"Well, for one thing, you turned up Perry Como. You risked

your life to save a kitten. And you've made me laugh more than I have for a while." Rue frowned. "And there's something else, too. I guess I've always felt guilty. We weren't very nice to you back when we were kids, were we?"

"*You* weren't so bad."

"I have a confession," Rue said. "The salty birthday cake? That was my idea."

Heidi laughed. "Well, I was probably an obnoxious little snot. With an annoying mother."

"You're a forgiving soul."

"I'm just somebody who's screwed up a lot. This latest episode is the most dramatic, I guess, but the way I've bumbled through life up to now, something like this was bound to happen. The only time I knew what I wanted was when I was studying piano. I *knew* I wanted to go to music school and be a concert pianist."

"What happened?"

"I realized I lacked something—talent."

Rue shook her head. "You were the best musician at our school."

"There are thousands of schools across the country, and they all have someone who's the best." She took another drink. "Don't get me wrong. I thought I was great. But my idea of great and Juilliard's are a little different."

"So what did you do?"

"I kept switching colleges, and majors. Then I finally ran out of money and started doing the same thing with jobs. Switching, I mean. I never finished my degree, so that sort of hampered me, advancement-wise. That's how I ended up working as an admin assist at a bank. Now I need to figure out something else. Preferably something *not* in an office, where I feel my life drip-drip-dripping away and my brain shriveling like an old apple core."

"There are a million jobs that don't involve offices. You could work for yourself."

"Doing what?"

This, Rue couldn't say.

"That's the problem," Heidi said. "I always draw a blank, too. When I was younger, I assumed that I would just stumble across my destiny. Now I have a sneaking suspicion that you have to be a little more proactive than I've been up to now."

Rue understood. She'd always had an idea of how the world worked, too. You studied, worked hard, married, had kids, and lived to collect Social Security and have card parties with your cronies. Now she was beginning to suspect that this was just how the world worked for the lucky ones.

Despite being awake half the night, first worrying about herself and then worrying about Rue, Heidi was up with the birds the next morning. She forced herself out of bed at the ungodly hour of six, but she still didn't manage to catch Becca before her jog. Unfortunately, she did catch Laura. They had a near collision as Heidi rounded the corner at the side of the house.

Laura couldn't have looked any more surprised if she had run into the Sasquatch. "What are *you* doing up?"

Heidi wasn't about to discuss her problems with Laura. "I wanted to get up early and exercise."

"Since when do you exercise?" Laura asked.

"I heard Becca does, and she's in great shape."

"So you're going to go jogging?" She glanced down at Heidi's feet. "In your sandals?"

"You've got to walk before you can run," Heidi said. "Anyway, walking is all I can manage right now."

The two of them continued to stare each other down. "Well, go ahead, then," Laura finally said. "Far be it from me to stifle anyone's inner Jack Lalanne."

Heidi scooted around her and hurried toward the lane. She was fairly certain Becca wouldn't be jogging through open pasture. There was a stand of trees halfway between the house and the main road, and she planted herself on the other side, out of sight of the house, to wait.

She hadn't been up this early in a long time. The air almost reminded her of what normal temperatures felt like. A little dew glistened in the grass, shimmering in its short life before it burned off. And out of the corner of her eye, Heidi saw a flash of reddish brown and turned just in time to see a fox disappear into some bushes.

She kept her eye out for more wildlife sightings, but all that presented itself was a squirrel and a few crows.

Where was Becca? It felt as if she'd been standing there for an age. How long could a person run before they ended up with respiratory failure or shin splints?

About the time she was going to give up, Becca crested the small hill and began her final descent toward the finish line. Just as she was passing, Heidi stepped out.

She had assumed that Becca had seen her and was just ignoring her, but apparently this was not the case. At the sound of her voice, Becca hopped about two feet up in the air and let out the blood-chilling screech of captured prey.

Heidi froze.

When Becca snapped out of her terror, her face flushed with anger. "I thought you were a . . ." She swallowed. "What are you doing out here?"

"I'm sorry." Heidi put out her hands to calm Becca down and approached with the caution of an orderly approaching a psychotic. "I just wanted to talk to you."

Becca sputtered, "Can't it wait? I'm jogging!"

"You're almost finished, aren't you?"

"Almost," Becca said impatiently.

"If we could just talk on the way back to the house, I'd be really grateful. It's a private matter. . . ."

"Oh, I get it." Becca rolled her eyes. "Do I get to bill you?"

Heidi had no idea what they charged at Gainey, McGibbon, and Emhardt, but she doubted it was within the reach of an unemployed bank secretary. "I was hoping we could speak more informally."

Becca crossed her arms. "All right, sugar bun. Let's hear the sob story."

"Well, I've got this friend."

Becca snorted. "Okay."

"My friend knows someone who was involved in a crime. A

white-collar crime. And she knows this someone isn't above beating the crap out of her or even attempting to kill her if he finds out that she is going to the district attorney with any information."

"Does your friend have any information to give the DA?"

"She might, but she's not sure how useful it would be. It might not even be worth putting herself at risk."

"Sounds like your friend is a real pillar of courage."

"He tried to kill her."

"Then she should go to the police."

"But what if the police can't protect her?" asked Heidi.

"Well, maybe they can and maybe they can't, but it's a cinch they can't if she doesn't report him. And about this other thing— the white-collar crime."

"It's not even for sure it's beyond the investigation stage. Maybe they'll never press charges. . . ."

"Does the DA know she has the evidence?"

"She doesn't think so."

"Because if they know, they can subpoena you—excuse me, *her*—and she'll have to come forward, anyway."

"Oh."

As they approached the house, Becca regarded her with a sidewise glance. "Sounds like someone's got herself in a pickle."

Heidi nodded. She hadn't considered that she might be hauled back to New York against her will. "But at least if the thing did go to trial and she were dragged into court to testify, the guy would know she was a hostile witness."

"Would he care? If he's the kind of guy who would have murdered her just on the chance that she might come forward, he seems like an endgame man."

The little shred of hope that Heidi had been clinging to disappeared.

"Did that help you at all?"

"Yes, it did," Heidi said. "It helped me see that my friend is just as stuck as I thought she was."

"Maybe even more stuck, honey bunch. If I were your friend,

I'd try to find out if there's a case at all and how it stands. Then your friend can gauge whether it's safe to come out of the woodwork."

On the second day of junior lifesaving class, Erica was supposed to rescue Maggie Robichaux, the only other girl in the class, but if it was up to her, she was pretty sure she'd go ahead and let her drown. Maggie was one of those popular girls who seemed to have dropped in from a different planet from the one Erica lived on. Both days she'd shown up at the pool in a bikini. Her mother ran the Mairzy-Doats Dress Shop in Carter's Springs, so she probably had a million of them. It wasn't like there was a whole lot for those little halter tops she wore to show off, either, but from the way the boys reacted to those two measly bumps, you would have thought they were frolicking in a pool with Jessica Alba.

There weren't many among these boys that Erica would have wanted to rescue in an emergency situation, either.

In fact, she was coming to the conclusion that she wasn't cut out for lifeguarding.

She might have wanted to save Jake Peavy if he hadn't abandoned her and gone to Colorado. Though, to be fair to Jake, he didn't have a clue that she liked him, so he was probably unaware of the fact that he had abandoned her. Most likely he didn't even remember she was taking the class, although she'd made a point of telling him that she was signing up, too. Several times.

But even if he did remember, why would he care? Jake was really popular.

Come to think of it, if Jake were here, he would probably be in the pool, ogling Maggie Robichaux's breast bumps, too.

It was so demoralizing. In Sweetgum she at least knew where she stood. She knew everybody and everybody knew her. In Carter's Springs she was really the odd man out. All the other kids knew each other, because they were about to start sixth grade at Carter's Springs Junior High, whose student body nearly topped a hundred. She felt alone and backward. Sweetgum was a dinky town compared to Carter's Springs. It was a dinky town compared to almost anywhere.

She tapped her hands against a red flotation tube while their instructor, Randy, directed Maggie and a boy named Kiefer to swim to the deep end. At the sound of the whistle, Maggie and Kiefer started flailing in the water—Maggie was hamming it up way more than was called for—and from the other side of the pool, Erica and Luke Trotter had to jump into the shallow water, swim across the pool as fast as they could, and then tow their drowning victims back to safety.

Erica could swim like a fish, so it was no problem getting over there, but Maggie was being a drama queen and wouldn't take the flotation device. She splashed and flapped her arms helplessly, and when Erica came close to her, she grabbed her and pulled her under the water, practically by her hair.

"Ow!" Erica yelled.

"That's good, Maggie!" Randy called out. "Now, Erica, what do you do?"

Erica bonked Maggie on the head with the floatie.

"Hey!" Maggie called out.

"Take it," Erica growled.

Maggie took it, sputtering pool water in indignation as Erica grabbed her by an armpit and started hauling her back. Even with Maggie being such a pain in the neck, they still managed to make it back before Luke and Kiefer. But Maggie was furious.

"You didn't have to hit me!"

The boys waiting their turns in the shallow end were laughing. "Barkie fetched Maggie!" one shouted.

The boys called Erica Barkie. *Ha-ha.*

"Good job, Barkie!" another boy yelled.

"Y'all are so funny." Erica lifted her chin and turned away. *"Not."*

"You're lucky she didn't give you rabies, Maggie!"

Sometimes Erica thought she wouldn't mind if she never saw another boy again. Even Jake Peavy. *Especially* Jake Peavy, since he was the one who had got her into this mess. To her mind, his being completely unaware that she had joined the class because of him did not clear him of guilt.

While the last lifesaving efforts took place, the kids who had already finished huddled together in the shallow water and talked about what they were going to do for the rest of the day. Two boys discussed some Xbox game involving killing armored space monsters—that was all they *ever* talked about—and the others talked about walking to the Dairy Queen for an ice cream, if they could get away from their moms and various chores.

Erica stood apart from them, where her toes could just barely touch bottom. She folded her arms on the rough concrete lip of the pool and rested her chin on her wrists. She wished she were invisible so she wouldn't have to feel so awkward about not being one of them. And strangely, she found herself wishing she was one of them. Carter's Springs wasn't exactly a metropolis, but on the farm she just couldn't stroll over to the Dairy Queen and meet other kids. She couldn't run over to a friend's house at the drop of a hat. In fact, out in the country, where she lived, she hardly ever saw her schoolmates from May till the end of August, except in passing at McCaffree's store or when her mom or dad made her go to church. She lived on a farm with lots of oddball women coming and going. It wasn't normal. And her parents hardly ever drove her anywhere. Just figuring out who would take her to and pick her up from these junior lifeguard lessons required four phone calls, usually.

Of course, she liked living at the farm and hanging out with Webb, Dylan, and Herman. Herman was teaching her Spanish. And she had Milkshake and all the animals. But she couldn't talk to Milkshake . . . or if she did, it was really just one step away from talking to herself, which was probably just one step away from being crazy.

The kids in the huddle were whispering about her; she pretended not to hear. When she couldn't stand pretending anymore, she pushed off from the side and submerged herself until she was squatting at the bottom of the pool. She could hold her breath for a really long time, but eventually her chest started to feel like a balloon that had all the air sucked out of it.

When she surfaced again, Maggie was waiting for her with her arms crossed and a smirk on her lips. "Have you ever had a boyfriend?"

Erica's first instinct was to tell her that it was none of her beeswax, but after hearing the sniggers from the boys behind Maggie, she heard herself bragging, "Of course. I have a boyfriend now."

Maggie tilted her head. "Who?"

"You wouldn't know him." Erica had intended to leave it at that, but in the next second she heard herself blurt out, "His name's Jake Peavy."

"Jake Peavy!"

One of the boys, Luke Trotter, scowled. "I know him. He used to go to our school!"

"When?" Erica asked.

"He left in third grade."

"I remember Jake," Maggie said. "He was cool."

Could a third grader be cool? Erica was doubtful, but as Maggie looked her up and down with a little more interest, she began to change her mind. It was as if Jake's leftover third-grade coolness was rubbing off on her. Even the boys seemed to back off a little—although Kiefer looked as if he was trying to square *cool* with having Erica for a girlfriend. Maybe they wouldn't call her Barkie anymore, now that they knew the Jake connection.

The false *Jake connection*, Erica reminded herself.

She raised her chin, trying to dismiss the twinge of discomfort her lie had caused. "Jake was going to be in this class, but he got to go to camp instead. In Colorado. It's one of those places in the mountains that costs about a zillion dollars, but Jake's family's rich."

Luke's eyes were narrowed on her. "I see Jake sometimes, but he's never mentioned you."

Erica stared right back at him, never flinching. "He never mentioned you, either."

"How long have you been going together?" Maggie asked her.

"A while." Erica was surprised how easy it was to create fiction once you got wound up. "Jake and I were voted most popular in our class last year. We got our picture in the yearbook." This was another lie, but it only felt like half of one. They didn't actually pick most popular at her school, but if they did, Jake would be it.

"How many girls were in your class?" one of the other kids taunted. "One?"

Erica rolled her eyes, as if to convey that she wouldn't bother answering him, but she couldn't help muttering, "Nine." Her school wasn't *that* small.

Maggie turned her back on the boys. "What's Jake like now?"

Erica shrugged. "He's really good at math and science and stuff. Last year he stuffed a Mr. Potato Head with firecrackers and some ingredients from his chemistry set and exploded it in the boys' bathroom on standardized-test day. The whole school got sent home."

"That's cool."

To Erica, it had been beyond cool. It had been amazing—especially since no adult ever figured out it was him. To her, he was like the James Bond of Sweetgum Elementary.

"Did he ever kiss you?"

Erica shifted from one foot to the other. "I said he was my boyfriend, didn't I?"

Thankfully, Randy interrupted them before Maggie could probe any more about her imaginary romance with Jake Peavy. For the rest of the lesson, though, she could feel Maggie's eyes on her, sizing her up, even while they did kickboard relays across the length of the pool.

When it came time for the class to end, Erica looked over toward the parking lot and saw her dad leaning against Ms. Dench's car. She hoped Ms. Dench wasn't with him!

Her dad, who already looked impatient as he waved her over,

had arrived early. Which probably meant he would be cranky from waiting for her.

As she was getting out of the pool, Maggie tapped her on the arm so hard, Erica felt like she was getting vaccinated. "Is that your dad?"

"Yes." Erica shivered, even though it was already almost ninety degrees outside.

"I've seen him before," Maggie said. "My mom pointed him out to me. I remember because he looks like Johnny Depp."

Erica wrinkled her nose. "No, he doesn't!"

"Well, almost."

Not even.

"Does your mother know my dad?" It seemed unlikely that her father hung around the Mairzy-Doats Dress Shop very much.

"They dated once. She showed me a prom picture," said Maggie.

It was hard to imagine her father going to a dance. "Weird."

"My parents are divorced."

"Mine, too," Erica said.

Maggie turned back to her and stared some more, just like she'd been doing in the pool. "You should wear lip gloss. It'd make you look a lot better."

Erica was at a loss for words.

"Don't get all offended," Maggie said. "It was just a suggestion."

"I'm not offended."

"Good." Maggie smiled. "See you next time!"

Of course I'll see you next time, Erica wanted to say. *I don't have any choice.* But it didn't matter what she'd thought about saying; Maggie had already scampered away to the locker room.

Erica shoved her feet into her flip-flops, grabbed her towel and tote bag with her clothes in it, and headed straight to the parking lot.

"I've got a meeting with a client in a little bit," her father said, prodding her along with his impatient voice. "We need to hurry."

Erica eyed the car with suspicion, as if Leanne might pop out of it at any moment like a demented jack-in-the-box. "Where's your truck?"

He let out a huff. "I'm having a brake job done today, which I forgot until your mom so kindly called to remind me that it was my turn to pick you up! So I borrowed Leanne's car. Try not to leak on the seat covers. You know how she is."

Did she ever.

Erica opened the door and draped her towel over the passenger seat before sitting down. Her father was peeling out of the parking lot almost before she had the door closed again.

He wrinkled his nose at her. "You smell like chlorine!"

"I was swimming."

He lowered the windows. "Don't they have showers?"

"You looked like you were in a hurry."

"I am. You're not soaking through that towel, are you?"

"I don't think so."

"Next time I'm bringing a Hefty bag to put under you."

They rode in silence for a few minutes. "A girl in junior lifeguard class said you looked like Johnny Depp."

A grin spread across her father's face. "No kidding! Who? That girl I saw you talking to?"

"Her name is Maggie Robichaux. You took her mother to the prom."

Her father's head swung around. "What's her mom's name?"

Erica frowned at him. "How many girls did you take to the prom?"

"There was more than one prom."

Erica gripped the armrest as her father shot around a sharp curve bobsled style. "It said twenty-five around that curve."

"They always underestimate," he said. "Does she live around here?"

"Who?"

"The mom of your little friend."

"She's not really my friend."

He bit out a sigh. "Okay—the girl I saw you talking with."

"Her mom runs the Mairzy-Doats Dress Shop. Mrs. Robichaux."

"Jessica Stubbs?" he asked, surprised.

"I don't know what her name used to be," Erica said. "You must see her, though. She lives in the town you work in."

"Yeah, but I don't spend office hours socializing." He shook his head, still smiling. "Jessica Stubbs. Really. She thinks I look like Johnny Depp?"

"No, Maggie thought that."

"Huh!" He laughed. "I think I like your friend."

"She's not my friend," Erica repeated. "I don't have any friends in that class. How could I? It's not like I could hang out with any of them. I don't even live in the same town. I might as well live on the moon as far as they're concerned."

"I thought you were happy on the farm. You sure made a fuss about staying out there for the summer."

"I am," she said quickly. "I like it out at the farm. I'd be just as bored at your house all summer."

"You shouldn't be saying you're bored. You know what Leanne says. 'Boredom comes from within.' "

She clamped her mouth shut. He was already starting to talk like her! It was bad enough when Leanne said stupid things like that. But having her dad parrot Leanne's words was doubly frightening. He was becoming a Dench zombie. And maybe, if she had to live with them half the time after the dreaded wedding, she'd become one, too.

She just had to figure out a way to stop the August catastrophe.

Chapter 12

Part of Laura's stress came from the fact that while she was being eaten alive with worry and generally walking through the valley of the shadow of doom, Rue was in a parallel world. A pink lollipop world of obliviousness. She and Heidi were best buds. The two of them were always together in the kitchen, making soup or fudge and listening to music.

Forget worrying about the farm. It wasn't even seven yet, and when she brought the eggs into the kitchen, the two of them were listening to Maria Callas, fixing French toast, and seemed to be in the middle of one of their annoying movie challenges.

"*Gandhi,*" Heidi was saying. "It's gotta be *Gandhi.*"

"*Around the World in Eighty Days.*" Rue flicked a glance at the egg bowl and then said as an afterthought to Laura, "Hey."

"Hi. You know I—"

"*Gandhi,*" Heidi repeated insistently.

Rue shook her head. "You're crazy. That was a good movie."

"Tell me this. Would you ever want to see it again?"

It was like walking into the middle of a pitched battle between Roger Ebert and Rex Reed. And just as irritating. Especially since Laura actually had an idea she wanted to run by Rue.

"What's the topic?" she asked, refilling her coffee cup.

"Worst movie that ever won a Best Picture Oscar," Heidi said.

"That's no contest at all," Laura said.

Both Rue and Heidi groaned.

"What?" Laura asked. "I haven't even named a movie yet."

"But you're going to, and it's bound to be something really fantastic, like *It Happened One Night*."

Erica sped into the kitchen and made a beeline for the fridge, and the orange juice. "What's *It Happened One Night*?"

Heidi and Rue groaned again.

"I've never seen it, either," Laura told Erica.

"But she has youth as an excuse," Heidi pointed out.

"Well, it doesn't matter, anyway," Laura said, "because the worst Best Picture was *Titanic*. Hands down."

"No way," Heidi said.

"That was a good movie," Rue said, then looked at Heidi and added, "Like *Gandhi*."

"Then why was I rooting for the iceberg?" Laura asked. "And that ending! We're led to believe this is some grand love story, and then in the end she just pokes Leo down into the ocean as if he were an ice cube."

"I don't remember her poking him," Heidi said. "He sank because he was drowning, and it was sad."

"I'm telling you, he was pushed, and about an hour too late for my money." Laura grabbed a piece of bread away from the pile that was waiting to be frenchified and chewed it as she said impatiently, "But I was going to tell you, Rue, I've got an idea for making money."

"What?" asked Rue.

"Pigs."

For a moment, the kitchen was filled with *Carmen* and skepticism.

"Pigs." Rue repeated the word, obviously trying not to look or sound too doubtful. But of course, both were as plain as day to Laura.

Heidi was just sitting down with a plate when Webb walked in from outside. "I thought you were at war with pigs, Laura," she said.

"With *wild* pigs. I'm talking regular domesticated pigs. Maybe they could teach their cousins some manners."

"I love pigs!" Erica exclaimed. "Especially little piglets. They're so cute."

"And smart," Laura said.

Webb smiled. "And tasty."

Susan and Luanne came in together and plunked themselves down. "What's tasty?" Susan asked, having caught just the last snippet.

"Pigs." Erica seemed a lot less enthusiastic now that she'd been reminded that the cute little piglets she had imagined as pets were destined to become breakfast.

"Did our big cheese finally catch a pig?" Becca asked in her usual crisp way. She took her chair, then sighed in exasperation when she remembered she had to get her own coffee.

"No," Heidi said, getting them up to speed, "she's decided to raise domesticated pigs. And slaughter them."

Irritation flashed across Laura's face. "Just pretend I didn't see you scarfing down a ham sandwich yesterday."

"I have a hard time with this," Becca announced, dumping two packets of sweetener from home into a mug. "*Charlotte's Web* was my favorite book when I was a girl."

"Wilbur." Erica expelled a heavy breath.

The room took on the character of a wake.

"Laura's probably the only person who read *Charlotte's Web* and sympathized with the farmer," Webb said.

Laura cleared her throat. "Earth to breakfast table. *Charlotte's Web* or no *Charlotte's Web*, you have to be realistic. If we had pigs, we wouldn't be sweating bullets because of the drought. And they'd eat all the kitchen scraps, too—they're like living composters."

"Living," repeated Susan.

Heidi shook her head. "But doomed."

All the guests, who for the past twenty-four hours had been looking at Laura as if she were the resident stripper, now viewed her as the resident murderer.

"From a financial standpoint, would it help all that much in the short term?" Rue asked. "We'd have to build a pen for them and lay out the money to get ourselves started. And then, with the drought—if you want to call it that—feed's going to be more expensive."

Feeling perturbed, Laura turned around and poured herself some more coffee. She practically upended the sugar bowl into her cup. "It was just an idea. If anyone's got a better one, I'm open to suggestions."

The room was all aria again until Webb piped up. "Maybe this is a little off topic, but I was buying gas at the Sweetgum store yesterday and had two people come up to me to talk about the cookies. Sally Colley asked me for the recipe."

"Cookies?" Laura asked.

"The chocolate chip cookies that were in the CSA boxes last week," he explained.

Laura's brow furrowed.

"Heidi made some cookies and put them in," Rue told her. "Didn't you know?"

"No. I didn't."

"It was because of the peaches," Heidi explained. "I wanted to make amends."

"So you put *cookies* in our produce boxes?" Laura asked. "The key word in that question, in case you missed it, was *produce*. As in fruits and vegetables. Organic fruits and vegetables. Not some lame Toll House cookies."

"Toll House cookies!" Becca exclaimed. "I love those!"

Erica looked at the others. "*Yum!*"

Even their depressed divorcée perked up a little.

"We've received three customer e-mails about the cookies," Rue told Laura.

"I don't care if we got fifty," Laura said. "This is a farm, not a bakery."

Webb gaped at her. "You were just asking if anyone had any bright ideas for making money."

"Oh, and *that's* a bright idea? Chocolate chip cookies in the veggie boxes? Of course! Why didn't I think of it?" Laura drummed her fingers for a moment before exclaiming, "Oh, that's right—because cookies in the farm boxes makes about as much sense as tits on a lawn mower! I'm a farmer, not Mrs. Fields."

"It wouldn't have to be cookies all the time," Heidi said cautiously. "It could be something more related to the farm. Like Rue's sweet potato muffins. Or zucchini bread. Or sun-dried tomatoes."

Suddenly the table was buzzing.

"What *I* was thinking," Heidi said, warming to the encouragement, "was that we could also include a newsletter in the boxes."

"*We?*" Laura asked.

"Well, I guess Rue or someone else could write it. You know, just a friendly note saying what's going on at the farm, and what's going to be harvested the next week, and maybe a few hints or recipes for what to do with all that chard, say."

Laura's lips flattened into a straight line. "Like one of those noxious Christmas letters people send out."

Jenna looked stricken. "I used to send those out every year, before . . ." Her lips started to tremble.

"*Everybody* sends them out, puddin' cake," Becca assured her.

"I can't believe I didn't think of that," Rue said. "A newsletter—it's so basic."

Heidi shrugged modestly, but Laura could tell she was pleased that her idea had met with approval. "It's just an idea. And not a particularly original one."

Laura was mad enough to eat bees. "And who would be making all this zucchini bread and writing all these chatty newsletters?" She lasered a glare at Heidi. "You? Are you moving in permanently, or are you just thinking of more work for the rest of us to do while we wait on you hand and foot?"

"I'm more than happy to do my fair share," Heidi said.

"Lately, all I've seen you do is your fair share of loafing," replied Laura.

Webb's chair shrieked as he abruptly scraped it back and

stood. He aimed a hard stare down at Laura. "I believe what she's been doing is resting, which is what a person generally does after she gets out of the hospital."

"Who are you now?" Laura asked. "Florence Nightingale?"

"No, I'm just a guy who's had a lot of buddies come out of the hospital with long recoveries ahead of them." He mashed his hat on his head and walked out the door.

Laura watched him stomp out, feeling the sting of his last withering glance.

The rest of the table, except for Heidi, Erica, and Rue, stood and followed Webb out the door like ducklings following their mother. Or children escaping their dysfunctional home.

When they were gone, Rue rounded on Laura. "You should apologize."

"Why? What is this—*Mister Rogers' Neighborhood?*"

"No one needs to apologize to me," Heidi said. "I can do more in the kitchen now. It feels better to stand up than sit down, anyway."

"Shame they don't have a standing section on airplanes," Laura said. "Maybe then you'd want to go back to New York and visit Stephen."

Heidi froze. "Who told you about Stephen? Did you talk to Mom again?"

"No, another little bird told me," Laura said.

Erica frowned. "Who's Stephen?"

"Someone else Heidi's not telling us about," Laura said.

Heidi rolled her eyes. "He's no one. Just my ex-boyfriend."

"Then why would you want to go back to see him?" Erica asked.

"I don't."

Erica scowled, confused, then stood up. "Will you show me how you paint your nails?" she asked Heidi.

Laura felt almost light-headed with surprise. Since when did Erica ever care about her nails? She exchanged bemused glances with Rue.

"Sure." Heidi stood and followed Erica upstairs.

When everyone else was gone, Laura stretched her long legs out in front of her and sighed. "Peace at last."

"Peace!" Rue almost spat the word. "What would you know about *that*? You stomp around like you're on the warpath. Even when someone does something good for us, you jump down her throat."

"I just didn't like the idea!"

"You wouldn't like *anyone's* ideas," Rue said. "I know you. You've worked yourself into one of your moods. I don't know what's triggered it this time, but I wish—"

"You know."

Rue stopped. "No, I don't. I honestly don't."

"Almost twenty years, and you never said a word. Then, out of the blue, you make a nasty remark about the accident."

Rue was astonished. "It was just a slip! I told you that."

"Subconsciously, you meant it."

"No, I did not."

Laura's eyes flashed. "Well, why not?"

The question confused Rue. "Why not what?"

"Why don't you ever get mad at me?"

"Oh, I do. I'm mad right now."

"But not for the right reason! Who gives a damn about Heidi or the stupid cookies? Why don't you for once just look me in the eye and tell me I ruined your life?"

Rue looked like she could be knocked over with a sneeze. "Is that what this has been about?"

"What?"

"All these years of your recklessness and moodiness. And you think you've ruined *my* life?" Rue laughed.

Laura's eyes bugged out in astonishment, then narrowed. "It's funny?"

"No," Rue said, sobering. "It's not funny. It's hilarious! You've been moping around for two decades, all the while thinking that *I* was to be pitied. All because I got my face smashed up?"

"It was my fault."

"It was the cow's damn fault!"

"The cow wasn't speeding."

"Then it was my fault for not wearing a seat belt! I wasn't a kid." Rue shook her head. "For God's sake, Laura. Just think for a moment about the life I've had. I went to college and got my degree—and I had fun in college, too. Did I ever tell you that? I fell in love several times and then got married—to the wrong person, granted, but I'm not the only one who picked a loser. And, anyway, I have Erica. And a great home here. And I *like* what I do. I like all the people who come through here. I enjoy feeding them and listening to them talk about their lives. I'm *happy*." Rue shook her head. "If there's anyone to be pitied in this house, it's you. You're the most pathetic thing on two legs around here—stuck at surly and sixteen for twenty years. You don't even know what happiness looks like. You've got every reason to be happy—the ingredients are all around you and you're too stupid to know it."

Laura's chin rose; she could tell Rue was trying to let her off the hook, however gruffly. She wasn't used to Rue lashing out. "You sound angry."

"I am! Stop pitying me. I never asked you to. I never blamed you."

"Dad did."

"Dad was a bitter old drunk. For God's sake, Laura, you're as tough as an army boot, but you still fall apart over the thoughtless needling that man gave you. Let it go. For everyone's sake."

"Let it go." Laura sneered. "That's Oprah-speak. I don't operate that way."

"The way you're operating now doesn't seem to be working out too well."

Laura pushed away from the counter. "I have to go."

Rue nodded. "Of course you do."

"What does that mean?"

"That's how you react when things get the least bit uncomfortable. You snap your mind shut and dart away."

"I have work to do," Laura insisted. She left without a back-

ward glance, and certainly without a glad-we-had-this-little-talk
moment.

Pity me? That was a joke.

And she hadn't wasted her life, either. She had never wanted
to do anything but what she was doing. Farming this patch was
the only work she was fit for. She'd go nuts anywhere else. Rue
was just doing some kind of jujitsu to try to make her think otherwise.

What the hell was the matter with her?

Maggie noticed Erica's red nails with the yellow polka dots
right away and pronounced them cool. But in the next instant
Erica's hair was found lacking. "Have you ever thought of French
braiding your hair?"

Erica touched her hair self-consciously, hoping she didn't look
as clueless as she felt. She didn't have the first idea what a
French braid was, or how it was any different from a normal
braid.

"I know, it's hard to do by yourself," Maggie commiserated.
"You don't have any sisters, do you?"

"No."

"Neither do I. It's really difficult sometimes when you're all
alone."

"Yeah." Erica didn't tell her that even though she might be an
only child, being alone wasn't exactly what she had to worry
about. If anything, at the farm it could be difficult to get a moment to herself. People were always there. And if you decided to
change one little bitty thing about yourself—just to wear a little
nail polish, say—someone was always bound to notice. And make
fun of you for it, like Dylan had. And Laura.

She didn't tell her, because she had a feeling that their being
all alone at home was her bond with Maggie.

"Pigtails don't really look right on you," Maggie said, studying
her. "They're too babyish."

The other kids were studying them curiously.

"You don't wear jewelry, either, do you?" Maggie asked, although it was obvious that Erica didn't. "That's probably just as well. Most kids just wear fake stuff, which just looks dorky, anyway. I'd rather not wear anything than have a cheap ring or a cheesy locket on a chain."

Maggie was full of opinions on the way people should look. But it was nice to have someone in class who didn't treat her like an outcast. Especially since it was someone who everyone liked and who got to live in town.

"I always wanted a sister," Maggie said later as they kick-boarded through the water. "It's so boring being alone all the time."

"Yeah."

"Is your dad picking you up today?"

"No, my mom." Erica blew out a breath. "I hope."

At the end of the pool, they finished and handed their kickboards to the two kids who were waiting for their lane.

"Does your dad have a girlfriend?" Maggie asked.

Erica could feel her teeth grinding. "Yes."

"Oh."

"Worse, she's not just his girlfriend. She's his fiancée. And she's awful."

Maggie's eyes lit up. "Oh, tell!"

It was hard to know where to begin. Once she got started, however, Erica had a hard time knowing how to stop. It would take hours to catalog all of Ms. Dench's faults. But for the first time she felt like she had a truly sympathetic audience.

"Wow! It sounds like you don't want them to get married *at all*," Maggie said once Erica had finished.

"I don't. I'd do anything to stop it."

"Why don't you?"

Erica shivered a little and shrugged. "How?"

"Oh, I bet there's a way," Maggie said. "Just give me a little while to think about it."

A whistle blew, which meant that Maggie and Erica's group was supposed to dive and swim underwater at least half the length of the pool. Some kids had trouble with this, but Erica surfaced past the halfway point and sliced through the water toward the other end.

Maggie finished just behind her. She flopped her elbows over the lip of the pool, breathing hard. "You want to come over to my house today?"

Erica hesitated. She had said she would give Shelley Winters and Monte tick baths when she got home. If she canceled, she would look irresponsible. Also, for some reason, she didn't want to say the words *tick bath* in front of Maggie.

"We can figure out a way to pry Ms. Dench away from your dad," Maggie said, making Erica's indecision more agonizing. "Won't your mom let you?"

"Of course. It's just that I'd have to ask permission first."

"So? Call her."

"How?"

Maggie hopped out of the pool. "C'mon."

Erica stared at her as she walked coolly up to their instructor and whispered something to him. Then she pivoted, gestured impatiently to Erica, and mouthed the words, *"Come on!"*

Erica pulled herself out of the pool and hurried after her. She didn't catch up until they were almost to the locker room. "Where are you going?"

"My phone's in my locker. You can call your mom."

Erica was in awe. No fifth grader in Sweetgum had his or her own cell phone. And Maggie acted as if just getting up in the middle of a class was no biggie.

"What did you say to Randy?"

"I told him that you were having a girl-mergency and needed my help."

Erica's jaw dropped. She could feel her face turning scarlet. "But I haven't even started yet!"

"So? He doesn't know that." She opened her locker, dug around in a pink gym bag, and handed Erica her pink and white phone.

Erica hesitated. "Shouldn't you ask your mom first?"

"My mom won't care. She's working, anyway. We can walk over to her store, let Mom know I didn't drown in class, and then go to the Dairy Queen and talk over your stepmother threat. Really cute high school boys sometimes hang out there. That sound okay?"

It sounded unbelievable. Like how kids lived on television shows. "Okay!"

Over the phone, her mom sounded equally amazed. "You're not up to anything, are you?"

"No!"

The one sleepover she'd gone to, she'd gotten in big trouble for putting peanut butter in a girl's hair. The trick hadn't even been her idea, but she was the one who'd taken all the blame. The worst part was, the victim had been the girl having the slumber party. It made for an awkward moment when her mom had arrived to pick her up.

After class they walked the four blocks from the high school to the Mairzy-Doats Dress Shop, which was just off the courthouse square. A few of the stores on the square were boarded up, but there was still a café and two antique stores there, and next to Maggie's mom's shop was a place that sold beauty supplies and wigs.

"I know about every bald person in town," Maggie told her in a low voice as they walked past the window full of Styrofoam heads topped with fake hair.

Erica eyed the faceless heads warily. "It's sort of spooky, isn't it?"

Maggie nodded. "You should see all the cancer people. You catch all kinds of poor women going in there—some of them look half dead. That's *really* spooky."

Erica flushed. For a split second she felt almost ashamed—and then she felt shame for feeling ashamed. "No, it's not." She lifted her chin. "My mother had cancer."

Maggie caught her breath. "Oh my God, why didn't you tell me?"

Because I don't know you, Erica thought. But she was sort of flattered by the insinuation that she should feel free to divulge all sorts of personal stuff to Maggie. It was a sign of real friendship. "I don't like to talk about it."

"Your poor mom!"

"She's better now."

Maggie thought about this. "Did she wear a wig?"

Erica shook her head.

"Maybe she didn't have the real serious kind."

"It was really serious, but she wore caps."

Maggie blinked. "That must have been really hard."

It was difficult to know whether she was referring to the cancer or the caps.

They went inside Maggie's mom's store, and Erica's focus shifted to meeting Mrs. Robichaux. Erica had seen her before but hadn't thought all that much about her. The Mairzy-Doats Dress Shop was where kids were dragged when they needed "an outfit." Going there always seemed like a punishment to Erica, whose definition of a bad day was any day she couldn't wear jeans or jean shorts. The only jeans sold here were really expensive ones that no one in her right mind would buy.

Mrs. Robichaux was so petite, it was almost hard to believe she was anyone's mother. She had black hair and dark button eyes and was probably the best dressed woman in Carter's Springs, maybe in the whole county, even though her dress shop didn't sell adult clothes beyond the junior sizes, except prom dresses. Mrs. Robichaux definitely went to Dallas for her own clothes.

"Me and Erica want to go to the Dairy Queen," Maggie announced, causing Erica to wince. She knew what was coming.

"Erica and I," said Mrs. Robichaux.

"Erica and I," Maggie parroted impatiently. "Is that okay?"

"I guess. I spoke to Erica's mother, and she said she would pick her up here at two, so don't lose track of time."

"We won't," Maggie said. "And now I have a requestion. Can I have some money?"

"What happened to your allowance?"

"I promised to buy Erica an ice cream sundae."

Erica was startled. "Oh, I—"

Maggie gave her friend a sharp kick. "I can't go back on a promise, can I?" Maggie stared beseechingly at her mom.

Mrs. Robichaux shook her head and reached around the back of the counter for her purse. "You shouldn't promise other people's money."

Erica was about to protest against anyone having to buy her anything, but her words choked her when Mrs. Robichaux held out a twenty. Usually when she begged and wheedled, she was lucky to get a five! But Maggie plucked the twenty from her mom's red fingertips and practically skipped to the door, as if it were no big deal.

"Thanks, Mom! We'll be back in a little bit!"

She took Erica's hand, and they burst out of the store, laughing for no reason and running as if someone were chasing them until they reached the shell of the old Piggly Wiggly two blocks away. It was a community center now, where two nights a week they had bingo. Erica knew because Laura and her friend Buddy had gotten kicked out once for bringing in vodka-spiked Mountain Dew.

Erica wondered if Maggie knew about Laura, or anything about the farm, which a lot of people thought was weird. A lot of people in Sweetgum, at least. Her mom and Aunt Laura certainly weren't anything like Mrs. Robichaux. They might be from different planets.

"I wish your father was picking you up," Maggie said as they approached the Dairy Queen.

"He has to be at his office."

"I know. It makes things difficult."

Erica was going to ask what things, but then they were inside the cool air-conditioning, and decisions had to be made. Erica just ordered a vanilla cone, because Maggie really did insist on paying. They chose a table by the window, but Maggie wanted to face the counter because she thought the guy behind the register was really cute. Erica just thought he looked really bored.

"Now," Maggie said. "You need to tell me more about this Ms. Dench. Are she and your dad really engaged?"

Erica nodded. "There's a ring and everything."

Maggie sipped at her Diet Coke. "You shouldn't give up so easily. Engagements fall apart all the time. We need to tackle this in an organized way."

That *we* gave Erica a little surge of hope. "How?"

"That depends. How long till the wedding?"

"About six weeks."

"That's plenty of time."

"Plenty of time to what?"

"To bust them up." Maggie grabbed a purple pen out of her purse and wrote down a large 1 on a napkin. "Now. First off, I need to check out this woman."

"How?"

"I need to observe her and your father up close. Which means I need to get into your house."

"When?"

"There's no time like the present. Call your mom and tell her that you're going to your dad's. Then call your dad and tell him to pick you up at my mom's store after work. And then tell him that you have a charming new friend who's dying to visit Sweetgum."

She seemed so sure of herself, so sure that everything would work out just the way she wanted. For the first time in a long time, Erica experienced a real surge of hope. Finally, someone was on her side. Finally, she had a real friend.

When Heidi had insisted on coming along to the doctor's appointment, Rue had thought it was a silly idea. There was no reason why she couldn't face up to a simple appointment at her GP's by herself. Especially after what she'd been through. A year ago she'd walked into a hospital with a near certainty that she was going to come out minus two breasts. An X-ray was a skip through the park by comparison.

But as she sat on the edge of a chair in the waiting room, she was glad Heidi was there, calmly flipping through a *People* and occasionally breaking into Rue's thoughts to point out something silly. If only momentarily, celebrity gossip displaced the worries on the march in Rue's head. Who else but Heidi would know that Lindsay Lohan rehab stories would calm her nerves?

Unfortunately, nothing could blunt her discomfort when the outside door opened and Leanne Dench sailed in. She headed straight for the little appointment desk and checked in, but the moment she turned around, she spotted Rue and released a surprised yip in greeting.

"How great to see you!" Leanne grinned at Rue and then looked curiously at Heidi, obviously unsure whether they were together.

"Nice to see you, too." Rue tried to keep her voice neutral when she introduced the newcomer to Heidi. "This is Leanne Dench."

"Hi!" Heidi's lips turned up and then froze as recognition dawned. "Oh! I hear congratulations are in order."

Leanne rolled her eyes, chuckling. "Word gets around."

"In my case it didn't have far to go. I'm staying at the farm," Heidi remarked.

"Oh, you're one of the—"

"Actually, Leanne, this is Heidi Bogue. She's my stepsister."

Leanne's face wrinkled in confusion.

"Ex-stepsister," Heidi said, clarifying.

"She's visiting for a while," Rue added.

"How nice! Not that you were hurting for company . . ." Leanne chortled. "I swear, that house of yours is like one of those mesh tote bags that looks so little but you can just keep stuffing things in. I thought you'd be overcrowded when Erica insisted on spending the summer there."

"We're full, for sure. But it's nice," said Rue.

Leanne nodded. "Of course! And don't think for a second that my feelings were hurt by Erica's decision. I understood completely that it had nothing to do with me."

"Well . . . good."

For a few uncomfortable moments, they stared at each other, brains feverishly lurching for some topic of conversation. Leanne looked especially panicked, but then again it was hard to tell for sure. She was one of those people who never seemed to blink, so her expression always appeared slightly surprised. As a result, talking to her always made Rue feel edgy.

Leanne leaned toward them and said in a low voice, "I'll bet you can guess why I'm here."

"No," Heidi said. "Why?"

Leanne dropped her eyes and patted her tummy. "Mind you, it's supposed to be a secret, though heaven knows that won't last around here!"

"No." *Especially not if you're going to blab about it in public.*

"And what are you doing here?" Leanne asked Rue, a concerned frown pinching the bridge of her nose. "Nothing wrong, I hope?"

"Just a checkup."

"Well, good. You *look* fantastic!"

Rue was used to this. People who never would have noticed her looks before were always reassuring her now that she looked good, even when she knew she looked like yesterday's dog dinner. "Thank you, Leanne."

"And you're so slender!" Leanne shook her head. "Although in your case it's like cancer brought coals to Newcastle, weight-wise. This might sound kind of crazy, but sometimes I just envy people who shed pounds for medical reasons. I mean, at least you didn't have to count calories and all that jazz."

"I'd still recommend Weight Watchers over cancer," Rue said flatly.

Leanne trumpeted out a laugh. "I'll bet!"

Providentially, the nurse called Rue's name. She leapt at the chance to escape; then she remembered she was leaving poor Heidi behind. "This shouldn't take long."

Heidi nodded. There was an unspoken good luck message in her gaze. "Don't worry," she said. "For entertainment, I have a whole tableful of stupid magazines."

"And me!" Leanne said, settling into the chair that Rue had just vacated.

Heidi's face elongated in alarm, and Rue had to dart past the waiting nurse so she could laugh out of sight of Leanne.

It was the last time she laughed that day.

Forty-five minutes later, sitting out in the hot car, with the large manila envelope containing the X-ray in her lap, and with Heidi perched in uncomfortable silence next to her, she felt as far from laughing as she ever had in her life.

Don't cry, she told herself. It wouldn't help anything.

But the more she reminded herself of how useless crying would be, the more she wanted to blubber like a baby.

"One spot on an X-ray isn't conclusive," Heidi said. "That's why he told you to see someone else."

Rue blew out a breath. "He didn't just tell me to see someone else. He sprinted to his phone and dialed the specialist's number as if there wasn't a second to lose."

"You're seeing him on Monday?"

"Yes. I have a whole weekend to angst. And to try to keep it from Laura."

"Keep it from her!"

Rue took a breath. She had just been lecturing Laura for being evasive, which took a lot of nerve, considering the secrets she herself was keeping. But she just couldn't face Laura with this. Not yet.

"What's the use of having the whole house on pins and needles?"

"What's the use of going through it alone?" Heidi returned.

"You know. You can be my designated worrier."

"I'm happy to be, but I still think keeping Laura in the dark's a little . . ." She either couldn't find the right word or couldn't bring herself to say it. "And you know there's no love lost between Laura and me."

"Have you looked at Laura lately? She's a wreck. It seems that every time I see her, she's a little closer to the end of her rope. She's worried that if it doesn't rain soon the farm will go under." She's got enough on her mind."

Heidi faced forward, sweat beading on her forehead. The car was like a convection oven. "What do we do now?"

Rue turned the key in the ignition. "We've got thirty minutes to kill before we have to pick up Erica."

It looked like Heidi was about to suggest something when Rue's cell phone rang. The sound sent a crazy hope leaping inside her. Maybe it was the doctor, calling to tell her that it was all a big mix-up with the X-rays. Hers showed nothing, nothing at all. . . .

She didn't recognize the incoming number. "Hello?"

"Hi, Mom!" Erica's voice surprised her.

"Do you want me to pick you up early?" Rue asked.

"Uh . . . no, actually, I was hoping I could spend the night at Dad's house."

Rue had to repeat the sentence to herself to make sure she'd heard right. "Your dad's?"

"He said it was okay."

"Are you feeling all right?" Rue asked, worried. "I mean, is there anything wrong?"

"Everything's fine," Erica said.

Rue frowned at the steering wheel. "Well . . . if it's okay with your father, it's all right with me."

"Good! Maggie's coming with me. We're going to have a sleepover."

Rue flashed back to an encounter with an angry mother who'd spent part of a night shampooing Skippy out of her daughter's hair, but she decided not to mention it. "That should be fun."

"Yeah! Mom, I need to go. Maggie and I are going shopping."

Shopping? Erica hated shopping. "Give me a call tomorrow to let me know when you want me to pick you up."

"Okay. Bye, Mom!"

Rue hung up, utterly flummoxed. "That was Erica. She and another girl are spending the night at William's."

Heidi looked puzzled, too. "I thought . . ."

"I know, but that's Erica for you. I'm just glad she's made a friend. And it'll give me time to calm down. I was worried about the drive home."

But during that drive home she more than once regretted not having the diversion of Erica's chatty stream of consciousness coming from the backseat. The few stabs at conversation Heidi made weren't enough to pry her mind away from that spot on the X-ray. At least not for long. And so they spent twenty minutes in gloom punctuated by a few futile stabs at perkiness. It was a relief to finally turn into the farm's lane.

As they neared the house, Rue spotted an unfamiliar car in the drive.

"Oh God," she moaned. "Did I screw up and overbook the guest rooms?"

"Have you ever done that?"

"No, but I've been so distracted lately. . . ."

The newcomer was hard to miss—a sandy-haired man of medium height, dressed in tan slacks and a sports jacket. He was surrounded by women on the steps of the front porch. He also had Laura's rifle practically poking him in the ribs.

Heidi sucked in her breath and braced herself before Rue hit the brakes.

"Vinnie?" Rue asked her.

"No." The dread in her voice made it clear that she considered this visitor just as bad, if not worse.

But how could it be worse?

"It's Stephen."

Chapter 13

Stephen at the farm was such an oddity that in the first moment Heidi couldn't quite wrap her mind around it. It seemed more likely that she was hallucinating than that he was actually standing there on the front porch with Laura's pig gun trained on him. Adding to the plucked-from-her-nightmares feel of the situation was the fact that his hands were lifted like a cornered burglar's, and that he was surrounded by dogs and the women guests, and that Fred the chicken stood just at Laura's heels like Laura's second in command.

But in the next moment the surprise dulled and alarm took over. Did Laura intend to kill him?

She hopped out of the car before Rue had brought it to a full stop and charged toward the front porch. "What are you doing!"

Laura pivoted, though the gun remained pointed at Stephen's side. "This guy showed up looking for you. From New York. I wasn't going to take any chances."

The guests were all huddled a safe distance away from both the questionable visitor and Laura's gun. Heidi looked at them cowering and rolled her eyes. "This is *Stephen*," she told Laura. "Stephen, not Vinnie."

Stephen's arms, still raised, gestured in exasperation. "I told her that."

"How was I to know you were telling the truth?"

"I showed you ID!" said Stephen, irked.

Laura scoffed. "Do you think I just fell off the turnip truck? IDs can be faked."

"A whole walletful?"

"Where are Webb and Herman and Dylan?" Rue asked.

"They took a load of trash to the dump," Laura replied.

What a mess. "Put the gun away, Laura," Heidi said. "This is not a predator."

"That's what I was trying to tell Annie Oakley there," Becca piped up. All the guests seemed a little braver now. "This little tiger doesn't have the look of a mobster."

"*Mobster?*" Heidi glowered at Laura. "What have you been telling people?"

"You should be thankful I'm not letting people waltz up to the house and shoot you," Laura said.

Poor Stephen. His pale lips quivered in indignation, but even his anger wasn't the least bit threatening. In New York Heidi had always considered him a pleasantly solid guy, but here in the noon sun, standing right next to lean, rope-muscled Laura, he seemed almost Pillsbury Doughboyish.

She smiled at him apologetically. Some gesture was probably in order, but she couldn't quite figure out what that would be. A hug seemed way too intimate, but shaking hands would feel weird. Having six curious women witness their reunion wasn't making things any less awkward.

Rue saw the problem and jumped into the breach. "Well! I'll bet everybody's ready for a tea break."

Watching Rue herd the guests inside, Heidi felt renewed admiration. That X-ray had to be lodged in the forefront of her mind. In her shoes, Heidi wouldn't have given a damn about the arrival of some strange guy from New York. She sent her friend a silent thank-you.

And then there was Laura, who would not be budged. She loomed above Stephen, sizing him up with her cool stare. "So this is your non-mob paramour?"

Heidi knew Laura was just trying to get a rise out of her. Unfortunately, it worked. "Would you drop the mobster crap already? I told you Vinnie wasn't—"

Before she could finish, a machine-gun fire of outrage burst from Stephen. "I can't believe you! I've barely said hello and already you're defending that scumbag!"

"There! Thank you!" Heidi turned, more concerned with battling Laura than soothing Stephen. "*Scumbag*. That's the appropriate word. *Mobster* is just inaccurate."

Laura snorted. "Pardon me."

"She's just being annoying, Stephen, which you'll have to get used to if you stay here for more than half an hour." Heidi squinted at him. "How long *are* you staying?"

"He can stay as long as he wants as long as he takes you with him when he goes," Laura said.

Heidi sighed impatiently. "Yes, you've made your point. You hate my guts. Now would you please leave us alone?"

Stephen stared from Heidi to Laura and back again. "Who *is* she?"

"Oh, sorry." Heidi finally remembered Stephen had no idea who these people were. "Stephen, this is Laura Rafferty. My stepsister."

"Ex-stepsister," Laura said.

"The one with the Crisco?" Stephen swung around to gape at her with heightened interest.

Laura was delighted. "My reputation precedes me."

"Hovers around you like a spore, more like," Heidi said.

Rue came out the front door and made a beeline for Laura.

"And this is Rue Anderson," Heidi told Stephen. "Laura's sister."

He shook Rue's politely proffered hand. "I can see the resemblance."

"Don't worry," Heidi told him. "It's only skin deep."

Laura's hostility meter ramped up a few notches, signaling she was about to go on the attack again, but Rue, bless her, cut her off at the pass. "Could I bug you for a minute, Laura? If you can believe it, we're out of onions."

"Okay, I'll go grab some." Laura leaned down and picked up Fred. "Come on."

Shelley Winters and Monte loped after Laura, and Rue turned her attention to Stephen. "I hope you're staying for dinner." Both Heidi and Stephen started to contradict her, but she wasn't taking no for an answer. "You can't leave without letting us show you a little hospitality. It's not all shotguns and insults around here. And male visitors are scarcer than hen's teeth. You'll be the center of attention at the supper table."

He looked doubtful that this was actually a good thing, but finally relented. "Thanks."

Rue glanced at Heidi, arched a brow in curiosity, then turned and went inside.

Stephen was still darting glances at the corner around which Laura had disappeared. "Was that woman talking to a chicken?"

"It was just Fred. He's an orphan." Heidi pointed to the rockers on the porch. "Want to sit down? And take your jacket off, for heaven's sake. Haven't you noticed it's hot out here?"

"Like a sauna." He shrugged off his blazer and then settled himself on the edge of a rocker, so that it looked like it was going to tip him out. He glanced up at the blue painted ceiling of the porch, where dirt daubers had defied the screening and were making a nest.

Heidi rocked for a few moments, wishing she had some tea. It would give her something to do besides watch Stephen silently work himself into a state.

She cleared her throat. "You came all this way. You must have something to say."

A muscle in his jaw twitched. He sat for a moment, looking like he was practicing deep breathing exercises, until he finally exploded. "Your mother was right! You're insane!"

"Couldn't you have just written that in a note?"

He reacted to her lame response with pure exasperation. "Oh sure, make jokes! Very funny! I should never have come here!"

"No, you shouldn't have. And Mother should never have told

you where I was." Stephen looked hurt, and she tried to smooth over her curt words. "I told her not to."

"Why?"

"Because it serves no purpose. I can't leave, and it's just putting people at risk."

"Because of that . . . that man at the bank?"

"Yes."

He scooted his rocker toward her. "Then you *can* leave. That's what I came here to tell you. They've arrested Vinnie."

It seemed too good to be true. "When?"

"It was in the papers this morning."

"But you're here right now. How . . . ?"

He shrugged. "Okay, I've called the prosecutor's office a few times. Mr. Cho."

Heidi groaned.

"I didn't tell him where you were," he assured her. "Even though he's *very* interested in talking to you. They think you took some things with you when you left. They searched your computer after you disappeared. It looks sort of bad, Heidi—but I assured him you had nothing to do with any of it."

"And I'm sure he just took your word for it."

"I think he did." He seized one of her hands in his two. "I know you didn't want me involved in all this, but it seemed to me— and your mother—that you were making very bad decisions."

Heidi had to bite back a laugh. "My mother wouldn't know a bad decision if it was waving at her from a convertible in a ticker-tape parade."

He frowned. "She's genuinely worried about you. In fact, she was the one who suggested I call Hamilton Cho. He thinks you should come back, too. On account of the missing files."

She looked out at the pasture, but she could feel his eyes on her.

"Then you do have them?" When she didn't answer, he asked, "Did you ever think about giving them to the DA? The more evidence he has, the more chance there is for a conviction."

"I was taking them to him when I almost got killed."

"*Killed?*" He gaped at her. "Your mother didn't tell me that!"

"Because I didn't tell her."

He looked down at his feet. "I went to see Vinnie, too, you know."

She buried her head in her hands. "Oh no. Please tell me you didn't."

"I couldn't help it. I went to the bank. I told him that he should leave you alone."

"Stephen . . ."

"Don't worry. He didn't seem all that interested in killing me. He just asked me where you were."

Her heart stopped. "You didn't tell him?"

"I didn't know. Not at that point."

"Good." It was hard to imagine the courage it must have taken for him to walk into that bank and face down Vinnie. "You didn't happen to talk to anyone else while you were there, did you?"

"I talked to some sort of receptionist near the door."

"There's a man there—"

His jaw dropped. "*Another* man?"

"Just a coworker. His name's Tom Chinske."

"The only fellow I saw around that day was some poor guy in a wheelchair."

Her breath choked. "Wheelchair?"

"Yeah. I saw him peering at me through his door, which was just cracked open. When he saw me, he slammed it shut."

"That's Tom Chinske. He must have finally worked up the nerve to blow the whistle on Vinnie, or they wouldn't have arrested him."

Poor Tom! He must have been in a living hell these past few weeks. Now that Vinnie had been arrested, he had to be relieved.

She supposed she should be relieved, too. If Vinnie was in jail, surely it was all over. Except he still had to worry about someone testifying against him. A horrible possibility occurred to her. "Did you notice anyone following you after you left New York City?"

His eyes widened. "Why would anyone follow me?"

"To get to me."

"Heidi! This is crazy! You're not the kind of person who gets involved with oily thugs or has to hide out!" He slapped a mosquito on his arm. "Doesn't this screen work at all?"

"It's got a few holes. And maybe the mosquitoes just like you. Some people are like that—their sweat glands attract bugs."

He turned toward her and grasped her hand. "Heidi, come with me to New York. It's so obvious you know you made a mistake coming here."

She bit back a wry smile, focused her eyes in the distance, toward a haystack on the hill. When they were younger, Laura had pushed her off one of those and she'd sprained her ankle. She remembered back then praying for a miracle that would deliver her from Sweetgum. The miracle had come in the form of an exterminator. Now deliverance was being offered in the form of Stephen, who was not only forgiving her, but boldly stepping up to the plate to be her protector.

But how could he protect her? She remembered Tom Chinske in the hospital, and that split second of terror when she'd realized there was a car barreling down on her. How could anyone protect her?

She shook her head. "No. I can't."

His jaw stiffened. "I see."

"If I went back with you, it would be like repaying your kindness by signing your death warrant."

"Is that all?"

All? Wasn't that enough?

But she could see from the high color in his cheeks that he wasn't thinking about the danger. He hadn't seemed to grasp that angle yet. He was stung because he was being rejected. Again.

"I need to stay here a while longer," she told him. "Even if there wasn't the danger, I can't leave just now."

"Why not?"

"There are people here—well, one person in particular—who I care about."

"What?" he sputtered. "A person *here* you care about?"

"Stephen . . ."

He shot to his feet abruptly, sending his chair rocking so hard that the back nearly whapped him on the rear. She made a move to stand up, too, but he stopped her. "Don't." He put a palm out toward her; he looked like an indignant crossing guard. "I shouldn't have come here. You'll never change. You've got this sweet, winsome exterior hiding a gnarled little pebble of a heart."

"It's not what you think."

"No ethics! That's your problem."

"You obviously think there's some guy, but there isn't."

"Then what's keeping you here?"

"It's . . . well, it's Rue, if you must know. She had cancer."

"So? You barely know her."

She blinked. He said it so matter-of-factly, as if she were just making up excuses. As if friendship didn't mean anything. He assumed that now that Vinnie was out of the way, the path before her was clear. The path that led back to him. This indicated a healthier ego than she'd ever given him credit for.

Rue wasn't the one she barely knew, she realized suddenly. She and Stephen had been together for a year, but they had never been through any kind of trouble together. They'd talked about their day-to-day lives, but never anything deeper.

"Your mother warned me you were stubborn, but I didn't listen," he said after a few moments of silence.

"I find not listening is the wisest policy when Marla Bogue starts dishing out advice."

"Or when anyone does, apparently." He let out a long sigh. "Well! So much for trying to help you. I might as well go back to Dallas now. My flight is tomorrow. And if you do ever come back to New York, don't even think about looking me up. I never want to see you again."

"Wait, Stephen. Before you go, I should at least give you the ten-cent tour. Let me grab a hat. One of the guys might have an extra out in the barn for you."

She sprinted to her room, but by the time she had retrieved

the floppy straw hat that Rue had lent her as a sunbonnet and hunted down Stephen, he was surrounded again. He'd found his way to the kitchen and had a glass of sweet tea in one hand and a forkful of peach pie in the other.

"You can't mean that you're going to drag tiger here out in the sun after he's been traveling all morning," Becca told Heidi, almost accusingly. "Give the man a rest!"

Stephen shrugged, as if he were completely helpless in the matter of what to do with his afternoon, and allowed himself to be coerced into a chair. Jenna darted into the seat next to him, offering him her most vulnerable, melancholy smile.

"I can wait," Heidi said, taking off her hat.

After Rue's tea the guests piled on the golf cart with Stephen and went joyriding. Dylan, Herman, and Webb ended up doing most of the picking for the farmers' market, so Heidi felt obligated to go out alongside them and gather cabbages, the first of the peppers, and cucumbers. In the morning, just before the market, the guys would be up first thing picking the leafier plants—lettuce and chard.

The extra work didn't make Heidi feel any more kindly toward Stephen. Especially since she was worried about Rue.

As the afternoon wore on, Laura seemed to be getting more and more annoyed, too, even though what seemed like the first clouds Sweetgum had seen in a month had materialized overhead. The guests, back from the lake now and hanging out on the back porch, drinking buckets of tea, started calling them Stephen's clouds.

Dylan delivered a new weather bulletin every time he passed by the NOAA weather radio in the barn, and Herman announced that his bones had named the next day as the moment for the big downpour.

Laura set her jaw and clung to her skepticism. "It's not going to rain."

"Thirty percent chance!" Dylan chirped.

"I'll believe it when my hair's wet," Laura retorted.

At dinner, as Rue had promised, Stephen was the center of attention. He wasn't an outgoing person, but he seemed to enjoy this gaggle of women surrounding him. Considering they were treating him like visiting royalty, what was not to enjoy? Occasionally Heidi would catch his gaze, and she could read his thoughts. *See, some people appreciate me.*

Battle-scarred Jenna seemed to have attached herself to him like a baby duck attaches itself to the first moving thing that crosses its path. Or like Fred had attached himself to Laura.

Or maybe that wasn't fair. Maybe she really saw something in Stephen she liked. After all, not too long ago, Heidi had seen that same something. Why couldn't she see it now?

What was wrong with her?

After dinner, the group did its usual migration to the back porch, even though the cloud cover made it even more stifling hot than ever. Stephen was telling them about the last Broadway show he'd seen, a musical. He looked so manic, Heidi suspected he was on the brink of breaking into song himself.

She felt like he was putting on this performance for her. One of the few things they had argued about when they were going out was that he hated the theater.

She left the porch, hoping her absence would give him the leeway to relax a little. In the barn she bumped into Webb, who was giving Milkshake a going-over in a stall. He was cleaning his hooves with a curved hoof pick, something Heidi could never imagine having the nerve to do. She liked horses in theory, but she retained what she considered a healthy fear of them. Webb's hard work had paid off, though. Milkshake's coat was already gleaming, his mane beauty-parlor perfect.

From the counter, the weather radio man droned on about a 30 percent chance of showers.

"Aren't you generous!" Heidi said. "The horse-care fairy. I'm not sure Erica deserves it."

"Where'd she go?"

"She's having a sleepover at William's house, if you can believe it."

He shook his head. "That knucklehead. Just when she's needed around here most."

"What do you mean?"

He sent her a pained look. "I'm not blind."

She lowered her voice and stepped closer. "You know, then? About Rue?"

"I don't know anything. I'm just guessing. And I'm guessing it's not good. You guys disappeared today without saying why, and then a few minutes ago, when I was in the kitchen, I caught Rue standing in the pantry, looking dazed."

Heidi leaned against the stall as Webb unhooked the tethers from the horse's halter. "A chest X-ray she got this morning showed a spot on her lungs. She has another appointment on Monday, in Dallas. She doesn't want anyone to know."

He nodded. "I won't say anything."

"But do you think all this secrecy's such a good idea?" Heidi asked. "I don't. It seems wrong to me."

"It's her decision."

"I shouldn't have told you, I know. I don't know why I did, except . . ."

Unaccountably, Heidi felt tears in her eyes. Maybe it was the thought of something awful happening to Rue, and the burden of bearing her secrets. Or maybe it was the stress of Stephen's sudden arrival and having to listen to his blistering assessment of her character.

Or maybe it was just the sticky heat. She wiped moisture off her face. Sweat, or tears. Or both.

"Hey." Webb saw her distress and walked up to her, looking down at her with those blue eyes. She felt like collapsing against his broad, solid chest and weeping like a child. Either that or throwing her arms around his neck and kissing him. She settled for leaning into him and allowing him to wrap a sturdy arm loosely around her.

"C'mon, now. What's the matter?" he asked.

His low voice was a soothing purr—probably the same tone he

used with Milkshake—but she couldn't deny its effectiveness. She gulped in a breath. "I shouldn't have blabbed. I'm just worried how Laura will react."

He rubbed his thumb on her chin, like a transference of calm. "Don't. Laura's not your problem. Besides, she's tough."

"But when she finds out . . ."

A scraping sound startled them both and practically sent Heidi vaulting over the stall door.

Laura was standing at the barn's open door, her cool squint in their direction belied by the high color in her cheeks. "When Laura finds out what?"

She spoke in such a deadly cold growl, Heidi shrank back instinctively. The look in Laura's eyes was one that typically preceded events like pins getting shoved under toenails. But Rue had specifically asked Heidi to keep her secret from Laura, and Heidi didn't want to disobey that request.

Webb wasn't saying anything, either.

Laura's lips curled into an angry smirk. "Never mind. Laura just found out."

She turned on her boot heels and steamed back toward the house.

Heidi felt like her knees were about to give way. Clearly, Laura had misunderstood everything. "What a mess."

To her astonishment, Webb let out a hoot of laughter. "Hell hath no fury like a woman scorned. Even when it's all in her own head."

"It's not funny. What am I going to do?"

"Nothing. If she's going to jump to conclusions and run off half-cocked, she doesn't deserve explanations. Let her stew in her own juice."

"Easy for you to say. You don't have to live in the same house where she's stewing."

Webb led Milkshake back out to the field next to the chickens, where he and the lone goat were serving as grass cutters. They took turns feeding him carrots.

Heidi sighed. "I guess I'd better go back and check on Stephen."

"Last I saw, he looked like he was doing okay."

She grinned at him. "Don't worry. You don't have a rival for heartthrob status. He's leaving tonight."

"Alone?"

Heidi searched those blue eyes to see if it would matter to him. She didn't kid herself that Webb was in love with her, but she couldn't deny wanting him just to feel a little regretful over the prospect of her leaving. Or even a lot regretful.

"He'll be alone, unless Jenna managed to snag him sometime in the past thirty minutes."

"I thought Jenna had sworn off men."

"She probably feels a special bond with Stephen. The league of the ill-used."

When they were out of carrots, she and Webb headed for the back porch. The voices coming from there fell silent when they rounded the hydrangea hedge.

Stephen stood up and looked from Heidi to Webb and then back at her again. His posture stiffened into an injured hunch. "Excuse me." He turned sharply and hurried inside.

"Let me show you your room," Rue said, following him.

"His room?" Heidi looked around at the others.

Becca answered unsmilingly, "Rue offered him Erica's room for the night."

The vibes coming from the guests were making Heidi uneasy. "That was nice of her."

"Yes, wasn't it?" Luanne's voice dripped with hostility. "Very considerate."

"Unlike some people," Jenna said.

Heidi and Webb exchanged glances. Everyone was looking at them as if they had been caught in flagrante delicto.

"Why is everyone acting as if we ought to be standing in the naughty corner?" Heidi wondered aloud.

Luanne eyeballed her coldly. "Laura just came through here

and informed me and Susan that if we wanted to identify some lovebirds, we could find two in the barn."

"Oh, for God's sake," Heidi said. "We were just *talking.*"

Four pair of eyes blinked at them.

Heidi looked again at Webb, who seemed almost amused by the farce they'd set in motion. "I'm going to find Rue. Maybe movie time will calm everyone down."

Everyone was coaxed into the house to watch *The Painted Veil.* Everyone except Laura, who five minutes into the movie marched through the living room with her rifle in one hand and a brown paper bag in the other and announced she was taking the golf cart out. A moment later the back door slammed.

The rest of them settled into watching the movie, which seemed really good until it sank in that the plot was about an adulteress and the man who couldn't forgive her for being un-faithful. Halfway through the movie, Heidi realized that while everyone else was watching the screen, Stephen had a steady glare fixed on her. The last part of the movie was punctuated by distant gunshots, which continued periodically into the night, long after they'd all gone to bed.

Heidi got dressed for bed, but then started worrying that Stephen would drive off in the morning, before she had a chance to speak to him again. She pulled on a robe, crept upstairs, and rapped lightly on Erica's door.

Not hearing a reply, she peeked inside. "Stephen?"

A light snapped on. Stephen was sitting up in a twin bed, sur-rounded by posters of horses. "What?"

She slipped into the room and shut the door behind her. "I didn't want you to go back to New York without telling you I was sorry."

"For what? For finding someone else?" He let out an annoyed sigh. "*Another* someone else, that is."

"Webb isn't someone else," she said. "I don't even think he likes me very much."

"Unlike the guy who ran you over?"

"He didn't actually do it himself."

"For God's sake, Heidi!"

She tried to calm him down. "I'm not condoning his behavior. I was just trying to be accurate."

"Good. Because I have to say, something at that bank didn't seem right . . ."

She tilted her head. "Like what?"

"That old guy—Tom Chinske, you said his name was? *He* sure seemed scared of something."

She frowned. "I wish I was better at research. I think the linchpin of the whole scheme of Vinnie's is someone named Elvin Johnson. But I have no idea who he is or where he lives. I can't find him on the Internet."

Stephen frowned and switched positions several times, as if he were wrestling against some inclination. "I could look," he finally said.

"Oh no." She shook her head. "Don't get involved."

"If you don't find out what happened to the guy, how are you going to know whether it's safe to go back?"

She bit her lip. *Or whether the information in my files will be at all meaningful in putting Vinnie behind bars.*

"I can help you," Stephen said.

"No. That's crazy."

"I know a few journalists. They would be good at this kind of thing."

"The last thing I want to do is alert the press! I'm trying to *hide* here."

He frowned. "Then maybe I could poke around a little on my own."

"I would think you would be glad to know that I am half a continent away from you."

He shrugged and said, "Just because I hate you doesn't mean that I want you to be unhappy."

She half laughed. "That's generous. Especially since the last guy who said he loved me apparently wants me dead."

Stephen flinched, and she realized what an impolitic thing that was to say.

She got up and backed toward the door. "Well . . . I should let you get to sleep now."

"Good night," he said.

She turned toward the door.

"Oh, and Heidi?"

She looked back at him.

"When this is all sorted out," he said, "I *really* never want to see you again."

Chapter 14

Laura heard a scream and bolted up in bed, completely disoriented. Light spilled through her window, and for a moment
the fact that she was fully clothed confused her. The large green
numbers on her clock read 10:00.

Now *she* felt like screaming.

Actually, what had awakened her wasn't exactly a scream so
much as a continuous shout of indignation, which lasted as long
as it took Erica to run downstairs from her room, circle the house,
and then dash back up two flights to Laura's room.

This gave Laura plenty of time to brace herself for her niece to
appear. But she still wasn't prepared for the new and improved
Erica. Her ponytail had migrated to the crown of her head, and
now hair spilled down into her face, making her resemble Cousin
Itt from *The Addams Family*. Which was probably just as well.
Erica pushed her hair back, revealing bright red lips and smudges
of blue on her eyelids.

Maybe this was all a nightmare, Laura thought, falling back
against her pillow.

Erica jumped on her bed. "What's going on?"

The effect of the shouted words on Laura's eardrums was
fierce. "I was wondering the same thing myself."

"Dad just dropped me off. I can't find Mom or Heidi or anybody! And someone's been staying in my room!"

"Oh." The reminder of Stephen brought the previous night back to her in its entirety.

Erica's face swooped closer to hers. "What's the matter with you? Are you sick?"

"I'm tired."

"But it's ten! You never sleep this late!"

"I didn't get to sleep until almost six."

"What were you doing?"

"Shooting pigs."

"Did you get one?"

"No."

"You never do!" Erica said. "Who was in my room?"

"Stephen Whatsiwhosit."

"*Who?*"

"Some guy who came to visit Heidi. Rue told him he could stay in your room."

"I knew it would get rented out sooner or later!" Erica exclaimed. "I'm going to be banished, aren't I?"

"It was just for the one night. He's leaving today." For all she knew, he was already gone.

"Good."

"What happened to you? You look like you OD'd on Color Me Beautiful."

"That's what Dad said—or something like it—but Ms. Dench said she thought I looked good."

Laura crowed raspily. "Seeking Leanne's good opinion now, are we?"

"No, but . . ."

Laura attempted sitting up again and went so far this time as to swing her legs over the side of the bed. There. She was committed.

Come to think of it, sleeping fully dressed saved a few steps in the morning. Now if she could just make it to her toothbrush . . .

"Where is everybody?" Erica asked.

"I have no idea. I don't even know what day it is."

Erica looked at her as if she were as crazy as a bag of frogs. "It's Saturday."

"Oh." Laura stood up and then felt such horror and mortification that her knees nearly collapsed under her. "Saturday!"

Erica's eyes widened in understanding. "Omigod! The market!"

Laura dashed into the bathroom and ran out ten seconds later with her toothbrush in her mouth, shouting instructions at Erica, which Erica miraculously was able to understand.

In three minutes they were in Laura's truck, and in twenty they were at the farmers' market outside Carter's Springs.

The farmers' market was set up under a giant green canopy tent, which wasn't even needed today, because Stephen's clouds were still hanging in there. Still stubbornly unproductive. Laura parked as close as she could and quickly wove through the crowd to the Sassy Spinster table. The market was in full swing and busy. Laura skidded up to Rue, her boots sending the sawdust on the ground flying up into the stifling air.

"I'm so sorry," Laura said. "I slept late. That's all there is to it."

Three of the guests turned in her direction. It was Becca who spoke, but she seemed to be voicing a common complaint. "It's nice to know *someone* slept!"

Laura frowned. "Why? Did something happen last night?"

"Yes," Rue answered wryly, "some lunatic was out shooting pigs."

Yet everyone seemed to be in better shape than Laura herself, and the guests apparently had done a bang-up job selling. They were down to their last two bushels of peaches, which Dylan and Herman were unloading from the farm truck. And the rest of the produce along the table was beginning to have that end-of-the-morning, picked-over look.

"Looks like you guys have been as busy as a whorehouse on dollar day," Laura observed. "I really am sorry. You should have gotten me up."

"Don't worry about it," Rue said, handing someone change for a basket of tomatoes.

Laura was burning to know exactly how big an ass she had made of herself the night before, but she was too embarrassed to ask Rue. Besides, asking would be an invitation to be lectured on the dangers of mixing Jack Daniel's and pig hunting. And if she promised to give those up, what pleasure would life hold?

She sidled up to Dylan. "Hey there!"

He looked at her warily.

She took off her hat and fanned herself with it. "You wouldn't happen to know what became of Stephen, would you?"

"The New York guy?" Dylan asked. "He went back to New York."

She nodded. A faint hope stirred in her breast. "Heidi's not around, I see."

"She and Webb volunteered to do the box deliveries."

"Oh." It was hard not to read something into that statement, though Laura knew it would be jumping to conclusions. How many times had she and Webb driven around the county, making deliveries? It wasn't exactly an activity ripe for romance.

Dylan squinted at her. "Are you feeling okay? You don't look so good."

"Not surprising. I feel like death eating a cracker."

"Rue's got a thermos of coffee, if you need some."

She circled back around to the front of the table, hoping to find some fault with how the guests were running things. Some reason for thinking that her presence was absolutely essential to the success of the enterprise. Apparently, it wasn't.

"Heidi-ho's zucchini cakes all sold," Becca informed her.

As if she should be doing handsprings. "I thought those were going into the boxes."

"We decided that the beet brownies were even better," Susan said, "so we included those instead."

"Terrif," Laura said, falling about twenty degrees short of enthusiasm. She addressed Rue. "I should probably just go back to the farm. I haven't done squat doodle this morning."

"Don't worry about the chickens. Webb let them out, and Heidi fed them."

The Webb-Heidi team strikes again.

She didn't know why she was so bent out of shape. She poured herself a cup of coffee from the thermos and leaned on the table next to where Erica was sitting, swinging her legs. Erica's eyes were riveted on the old silver and turquoise ring on Rue's right hand.

"Why do you always wear that ring, Mom?" She leaned in and frowned as she inspected it more closely. "It's not very pretty. Is it an heirloom?"

Laura sniggered.

"What?" Erica asked.

"It's a ring Laura brought me back from a trip she took with our grandparents once," Rue explained. "They stopped at the Alabama-Coushatta Indian Reservation, and Laura bought this for me as a souvenir."

"Is it real? I didn't know silver got so skanky looking," said Erica.

"It's supposed to be a turquoise stone set in silver, but I think it might just be greenish rock in pewter," Laura said. "It set me back thirty-eight dollars, though."

"So it's not really worth anything," Erica noted.

Laura gave her a swat. "Hey! When was the last time you gave something to somebody worth thirty-eight dollars? It's nothing to sneeze at, especially when there were Supertramp records to buy and a Space Invaders machine at the Stop-Four-Gas in Carter's Springs ready to take all my spare dollars."

"Anyway, I like it," Rue said. "It's my good luck charm."

Laura grunted. "Just goes to show what thirty-eight bucks of luck'll get you."

"Maggie Robichaux said you should wait to wear jewelry until you have something real," Erica said.

This Robichaux kid sounded like a real gem herself, thought Laura.

"Another school of thought is that things are worth how much you value them yourself," Rue said. "I like my skanky little ring. It reminds me of my skanky little sister."

Laura laughed. She studied Rue more closely as she served a new customer. There were dark circles under her eyes. She waited for the customer to leave before speaking again. "You look like hell. I guess I kept you up, too."

"I had a fitful night," Rue admitted.

"Have you been using the inhaler the doc gave you?"

Rue shook her head.

They were alike in disliking the idea of being medicated. That was partly the reason Laura was so impressed by how Rue had managed the past year. She'd had a Monsanto warehouse of toxic chemicals dumped down her.

"I can see you don't need me here." Laura pushed away from the table. "So I'll be off like a prom dress."

She still felt out of sorts on the drive home, but she tried to shake herself out of it. Probably when she saw Webb, he was going to rib her mercilessly for last night's shenanigans. He always did.

The strange thing was, though, when she finally did see Webb, he didn't say a word. He just waved at her from across the field and kept going. Laura dropped her hoe and hurried to catch up with him before he got to his truck.

"Y'all get the deliveries all done?"

"Sure. No problem." He tossed a couple of shovels into the back of the truck.

"Where are you going now?"

"I was going to repair that patch of fence on the other side of the lake. Otherwise, we're going to be invaded by the Williamsons' cows."

"Oh. Good."

She was about to volunteer to help when Heidi came skipping around the corner of the outbuilding on the path from the house. She was wearing Rue's floppy straw hat and a rapturous expression.

"Ready!"

Webb tossed her a pair of gloves. "Try these."

They were too big for Heidi's hands, and she got a kick out of showing them off. Her smile faded a little when she caught Laura's stare.

"Oh, hi, Laura. I made some fresh coffee. It's in the kitchen."

"Novel place to find coffee." The two of them sent her unappreciative looks, and Laura made a point of mending her tone. Sort of. "I mean, thanks. I could use some."

"Yeah, you look it." Heidi was halfway in the truck when she poked her head out again. "Hey, if Rue gets back before I do, tell her to take a nap." She ducked in and then bobbed back out again. "No, don't tell her. *Make* her. Tell her I'll be back in time to help with dinner."

The truck roared to life, and Laura watched the two of them bump across the pasture. When they were out of sight, she went inside, downed two cups of black coffee, and then restlessly walked back outside again. The farm rarely felt so deserted. There was only herself and the dogs, and they were already hard at work snoozing under the shade tree. Laura freed Fred from the chicken hold and let him follow her out to the garden.

"It would be nice if you'd learn to talk," she said to him as he strutted after her. "Or at least crow every once in a while. Otherwise, you won't earn your keep, and you know what that means."

Fred pecked at the ground, heedless.

"You're a chicken on thin ice," she said. "You may think you're indispensable, but you're not."

After noon people started filtering back from the market. First, a carload of the guests, some of whom dashed inside to get packed up to leave. (Laura sent up a short prayer that Becca would be one of them.) Then Rue came back with Erica, and Dylan and Herman followed in the truck after having donated the leftovers to the Methodist church food bank.

Dylan brought over a box of what they termed the leftover leftovers—the damaged, the bruised, the bumper crop proceeds that even the Methodists didn't want any more of. There were onions—couldn't have too many, in Laura's estimation—bruised tomatoes ready for saucing, some very dirty spinach, which would wash up nicely, and swiss chard.

Laura frowned. "We need to cut back on the chard next year."

"Rue likes it," said Dylan.

"Too bad Rue's not a customer."

Laura hauled the leftover leftovers box inside, to the pantry. Walking from the sauna heat into the air-cooled house made her head ache. Rue appeared at the pantry door, with a wooden spoon in her hand.

"Heidi told me to tell you to take a nap," Laura informed her. "She's giving orders now."

"I might after Susan and Luanne leave."

Laura let out a moan of disappointment. "*They're* the ones? Not sugar bun?"

"Becca leaves tomorrow."

"What about Jenna?"

"I can't remember."

Great. Stuck with the dreary divorcée. "She is going to leave eventually, isn't she?"

"I imagine so."

Another hour dragged by, as sluggish as the humid air. Laura thought she might go insane if there wasn't a breeze soon. If it got any more humid, she was going to need a bellows to keep her lungs going. The air seemed to cling to her and smother her pores as she mulched hay around the cabbages and cukes.

She finally gave up and headed toward the house. Most everyone with a lick of sense had already migrated inside for the AC, so she was surprised to hear laughter on the back porch. She was even more surprised to discover that it was coming from Heidi and Webb. She hadn't seen them come back. They were draped in the chairs, dripping wet and obviously sharing some hilarious joke.

"What happened to you two?" she called.

When they saw her, their laughter faded.

"The truck got stuck," Webb said.

"In the lake?"

"No, in a sand dune," Heidi said, breaking up again.

"It was a gopher hole, *not* a sand dune." Still smiling, Webb turned to Laura. "We tried to push it out and just ended up getting overheated, and then Heidi here jumped in the lake."

"You pushed me!" Heidi said with mock indignation.

He turned on her. "Who pushed whom?"

Laura bit her lip. "Rue's by herself in the kitchen," she told Heidi. "Let's hope she's not depending on you any more than I was depending on you to get the fence fixed."

The giggling stopped, and the two of them were as still as the tepid air around them. In the next instant Heidi sprang up and came so close to Laura that for a moment she wondered if Heidi intended to trample right over her.

"The fence *is* fixed," Heidi said.

"Good," Laura replied.

"Now apologize," Heidi demanded.

"For what?"

"For being an asshole."

"Whoa," Webb said, pushing himself out of his chair.

"No!" Heidi said. "No whoa." She spoke to Webb, but her eyes never left Laura's face. The stood toe-to-toe like mongoose and cobra. "I've had it up to here with her rudeness and insults. I'm tired of people letting her off the hook. I want an apology, and I'm not going to leave this spot till I get it."

Laura smirked. "Would you like your meals sent out to you?"

"Apologize!"

Laura put her hands on her hips. "Won't your intention to stay out here till hell freezes over—"

"Just until you apologize."

Laura paused to let Heidi know she understood her conditions. "Like I was saying, until hell freezes over. Won't that cripple your social life?"

"I don't care. Apologize," Heidi repeated.

"Why should I? I see what you've been doing."

Webb attempted to step in between them, but it was a danger-ous place to be. "Okay, you two . . ."

"No!" Heidi barked at him. "I want to hear this. What exactly have I been doing, Laura?"

Laura looked once at Webb's beseeching expression and hard-ened herself against it. He hated conflict, but this wasn't his fight. This was something that reached back twenty years, and neither she nor Heidi was going to let it go now. "You've been wrapping Rue and Webb around your little finger, to get at me. Or around me."

Heidi first looked befuddled and then blasted out a laugh that had not an ounce of humor in it. "You've got excellent powers of observation! You see everything. Everything except what's right under you damned nose."

"Tell me, then. What am I missing?"

Heidi hesitated just a moment, then asked her, "Have you ever once heard Rue play a note on the banjo?"

The question came at her so far from left field, it took Laura a moment to digest it. "What's the banjo got to do with anything?"

"Banjos. Rue."

"So?"

Heidi was so incensed, she practically bounced on the balls of her feet. "So she's been taking lessons, hasn't she?"

"I guess." Laura frowned. "I'm not the FBI. I've got a farm to run here." She lifted her chin. "*I* don't have the kind of life where I can just run away from everything and hide out from my problems."

Heidi sneered. "Why would you need to, when you can hide from them just by sticking your head in the sand right here at home? When you can just assume that your sister, who's obvi-ously *not* getting better, is just feeling a little low? That way you can stamp around, pouting about your lack of privacy and the drought and all the stupid people around you, and *never once* no-tice that Rue is sick again!"

Laura started at her, flabbergasted. Her first instinct was to say that Heidi didn't know what the hell she was talking about. But there was something in Heidi's angry stare now that gave her pause. She detected a nugget of pity that hadn't been there before. It was worse than anger. And more convincing.

Laura pulled her gaze away from Heidi and sought out Webb's eyes. "Is it true?"

"I went to the doctor with her yesterday," Heidi said. "She had an X-ray. There's a spot on her lung. There's a possibility that the cancer might have metastasized. If that's true—"

"You don't have to tell me." Despite the heat, Laura suddenly felt clammy all over.

Back when Rue was diagnosed with cancer, Laura had stayed up nights surfing the Internet until her eyes burned, looking for all the information she could find about invasive ductal carcinoma. She'd sneak off to the library and read medical tomes, plowing through dense passages of scientific jargon to gather not just knowledge, but also hope. There had been little to be had. Rue's cancer had been discovered late. She'd had two Grade III tumors, which were aggressive and fast growing.

In all her reading, Laura had tried to skirt the passages on recurrence, but it had been impossible to avoid them completely. Even after mastectomy, cancer at the stage Rue had been found at could metastasize practically anywhere. If this happened, the prognosis became light years more grim. What she'd learned of recurrence, she had tried to forget, not because she was a Pollyanna, but because she was the opposite. It was Rue's misfortune that her main caregiver was a person who could see the cloud in front of every silver lining. For those months while Rue was undergoing hellish treatments, Laura had tried to back-burner her own anxieties.

The fears had been on the back burner so long that she'd almost forgotten them entirely. Now they came flooding back full force.

And Rue—what was she going through? She was sure Rue had done her own research. Rue had seen the same statistics she had.

When Laura spoke, she hardly recognized the rasp that was her voice. "How long?"

"What?" asked Heidi.

"Rue feeling bad. How long have you known?"

"Not long. Not even a week."

Prickly heat stung Laura's eyes. Just this morning she had asked Rue about her asthma. *Asthma!* And Rue hadn't said anything, hadn't felt the need to confide in her at all. No need to, apparently.

Anger, devastation, worry, and jealousy raged inside her. The sticky air made it hard to draw breath.

"They're still not one hundred percent certain there's anything really wrong." Heidi's voice was softer now, but that very softness grated on Laura's nerves more than their confrontation had. In that moment Laura loathed her more than ever. "With something like this, she has to get more tests and another opinion."

"I know that!" Laura snapped. "I went through this with her before. I—"

I was with her through it all, until I decided she was out of the woods and started worrying about other things. Until I stopped paying attention. Their lives had been on parallel tracks in the same house. She hadn't really been there for Rue.

And she'd thrown that hissy fit about the accident. The bitter things she'd said, and the words Rue had flung back at her, filled her with shame. Going into a tizzy about ancient history, when Rue had probably been worried sick about what was happening right that second.

Why hadn't she said anything?

Laura turned, hands in fists at her sides. When she started walking toward the house, Webb called after her, but she answered with a shake of her head. She marched through the back door, not caring if it banged shut behind her. Not caring about anything but getting to Rue as soon as possible.

She went directly to her sister's room, wheeled through the door without knocking, and shut it behind her.

Rue sat up in bed, startled.

Seeing her there, so obviously pale and painfully thin—everything about her appearance screamed *sick*—Laura could barely contain her anger at herself. Rage was a bitter molten brew boiling inside her, and she struggled not to erupt.

Several questioning expressions flashed across Rue's eyes before she silently hit upon the right one. "You've been talking to Heidi, haven't you?"

"Yes!" Just the name made Laura shake. "I had to hear it from her."

"She wasn't supposed to tell. At least not till after Monday. Dr. Morris found a spot on my lung, so I'm having a procedure done in Dallas."

"So I heard."

"It's called a bronchoscopy. They put you into a twilight sleep and stick a tube down your throat and take little scrapings from your lungs. They say it's not too bad, but I read on the Internet that I might cough up blood for a few days."

Laura couldn't believe this was happening. Most of all, she couldn't believe Rue was just perched there with folded hands, telling her about lung scrapings and hacking up blood, as if she were a parent trying to calm a small child about getting a flu shot.

"And you were just going to have this done without telling anyone?"

"Heidi's coming with me."

"*Heidi?*" Laura tried not to explode. "Why? You barely know her! I'm your sister!"

"I was trying not to worry you."

"What am I? Just some passing acquaintance you happen to share a house with? A complete stranger it just so happens you've known for thirty-six years?"

"I didn't tell Heidi, exactly. She figured it out."

"Of course! You're such pals."

"Are you angry because I've made a friend or because it's Heidi?"

"Neither!" Laura flung herself into an old armchair. "I don't give a shit about Heidi right now. I'm mad because you're sick, because it's not fair! I'm mad at the world!"

"So am I."

"You don't sound like it."

"I've had more time to deal with it than you have." Her eyes registered that this was not a reminder tailored to pacify Laura. "It didn't even come to me all at once. I thought I was just run down. For all my panicking, I fooled myself into ignoring the warning signs."

"How could you? Time means *everything*."

"I know."

"You have to fight."

Rue thought about this for a moment. "I needed to be ready to fight, though."

"That's horseshit! I wish I had known what you were going through. Or better yet, I wish it was me. If it were me, I would be doing anything and everything ASAP. No matter how radical. I'd be moving mountains—"

"But it's not you," Rue fired back. "It's never you."

"What does that mean?"

"It means nothing bad ever happens to you—just good things you don't even appreciate."

Laura felt as if she'd been slapped.

"Do you honestly think I need a lecture at this point?" Rue asked. "A pep talk? Do you think I want to give up? Do you think I wake up every morning wondering whether I want to live or not? Do you think I look at Erica . . ." She stopped and gulped to calm herself. "That I could look at Erica and not want to steal every spare second available?"

Laura focused her eyes on her boots, blurs on the ends of her legs. She couldn't speak. Every time she opened her mouth, she just seemed to blurt out wrongheaded, hateful spew that was the exact opposite of what she really wanted to express. Why was she like this? She didn't want to be. She wanted to be one of those people who knew what to say to comfort someone. Someone who knew how to express feelings, like a mom on a stupid sitcom. More like Rue, and less like an old troll.

"I'm sorry if you're offended because you weren't the first to know," Rue told her. "I wasn't going to be—"

A bone-rattling crack shook the house. Rue and Laura froze and blinked at each other in surprise. It took them a second to understand what they'd just heard. And more important, to realize what it meant.

Thunder.

Rue's eyes widened just like they used to do on Christmas morning when they were kids. She jumped up and ran through the hallway in her bare feet, with Laura close behind. The front door almost blew open on its own when Rue turned the knob.

A blast of cooler air knocked them back a bit before they stepped out on the porch. The rain was just starting, heavy intermittent drops blowing through the air with the leaves that gusts of wind had dislodged from the trees surrounding the house.

A carnival had spontaneously erupted in the front yard. Luanne and Susan had been packing their car to leave, but now everyone was out. The guests, Herman, Dylan, Heidi and Webb, and Erica had all migrated to the front yard. No one ran for cover even when the tempest let loose and the rain poured down in sheets. The drenching rain was greeted with outstretched arms. Lightning just brought shouts of joy.

Luanne, Susan, and Becca performed some sort of impromptu bacchanalian dance, while Shelley Winters and Monte dashed around in mad figure eights. Erica cartwheeled across the grass. Behind her Herman, Heidi, and Dylan took turns locking arms and swinging each other around in square dance circles. And then there was the strangest sight of all—Webb, with Jenna sitting on his shoulders, their faces pointed directly up to greet whatever the sky saw fit to toss down at them.

Rue, who'd run inside again for a moment, reappeared with her boom box, blasting the CD she'd played that morning. It was her favorite singer of all, Ella Fitzgerald. When she cranked up the volume in the middle of a noisy swing version of "Ding-Dong! The Witch Is Dead," the sopping wet revelers went nuts. Jenna, of all people, started singing and nearly toppled off Webb's shoulders, and the rest of them joined her. Even Herman seemed to know the words. Rue ran out in the middle of it all, still in her bare feet. She stopped Shelley Winters from knocking her over by grabbing the dog's muddy front paws, and she and the dog started doing something that looked like the twist.

Laura stepped out but stopped in the middle of the porch stairs. For a moment she just stood there being pelted with rain and watching them all act like lunatics. She started to laugh until she caught sight of Rue again, her arms flung out and neck cricked back so she could catch the rain on her face. Her expression was pure joy.

Rain was flooding from the crown of Laura's head, mixing now with the tears flowing freely. She hadn't cried in years and didn't want to now. It felt as if a steel band was squeezing her chest, and that if she could just exhale or scream or hit something, she could bust free of it, superhero style. But there was nowhere to scream here. Not with all these people.

She leapt off the porch and ran for her truck.

She sped out of the driveway, tires spitting gravel and mud behind her. Only a few of the front-yard revelers stopped what they were doing or understood why she was peeling away in such a frenzy. Rue knew, and Webb and Heidi had a good idea.

To everyone else, it was just another of Laura's moods. The woman had no joy in her, no heart.

Chapter 15

To Erica, the worst part of Six Flags had always been all the time spent standing in line, watching other people having a lot more fun than she was. Usually, she'd come with just her mom and Laura. She remembered patiently sucking down Cokes and wilting in the sun while she watched kids who had come with their huge families or, even better, in mobs sponsored by various groups. Sometimes they wore matching T-shirts. The big groups were always obnoxious, talking too loudly, laughing too much at stupid antics, and generally shuffling along collectively like a hormone-laden amoeba and getting in other people's way. She'd envied them.

But going to Six Flags with an actual friend was entirely different. Maggie never ran out of stuff to talk about, and she was full of opinions, even about which rides were cool and which were lame.

El Sombrero, which Erica had always ridden first off every time she'd come here, was pronounced *definitely lame.* "I haven't been on that Mexican hat thing in years," Maggie announced as Erica was making a beeline for it. "C.W.O.T."

In Maggie's world, this translated into *complete waste of time.*

Erica stopped in her tracks, feeling a surprising disappointment, considering they were just talking about a merry-go-round shaped like a giant sombrero.

"I always skip the Mexico section when I come here," Maggie went on. "It's *very* lame. It's best to go straight to Texas, or Modern. That's where there are the coolest rides, and the cutest boys."

It was hard to argue with such emphatic opinions without feeling like a geeky idiot. Erica had always thought Six Flags was about rides and gulping down food her mother would declare off-limits otherwise, but Maggie's focus centered on one thing: cute high school boys.

Cute high school boys were everywhere at Six Flags—they worked at the concession stands and were the guys who stuffed people on rides. Boy visitors walked around in pairs and packs, and occasionally one would just be alone, minding his own business, unaware that two almost twelve-year-olds were eyeing his every move. No cute high school boy escaped Maggie's notice, not even the ones that, frankly, really weren't all that cute. She even took special glee in pointing out the boys who were definitely *not cute*. Basically anything that seemed male and over thirteen had to be checked out, speculated about, and ranked for hotness.

Rides were chosen specifically for their popularity with cute high school boys, so that they spent the afternoon standing in line for flume rides and the most sinister-looking roller coasters. The roller coasters scared Maggie to death, but apparently conquering fear was the price she paid to put herself in the vicinity of her prey.

Not that these cute high school boys took the least notice of them. Why would they? Maggie was cute herself, but she was still just a sixth grader. And Erica felt all the more gangly and awkward every time Maggie poked her in the ribs and started whispering about the popcorn-ball vendor or the guy yanking nauseated riders off the Tornado.

By one in the afternoon, she felt hot and a little cranky. She convinced Maggie to stop for a Coke.

"Thirty more minutes before we have to meet up with Mom and your dad," Maggie said when they had finally claimed a seat under a giant candy-striped canopy. "I wonder what they've been doing."

She grinned, as if Mrs. Robichaux and Erica's dad could be kindling a wild romance in the middle of a packed amusement park.

Erica still couldn't believe that her father had agreed to come at all. Her mother had promised her this trip a while ago, but of course, she couldn't make it, so she'd guilted William into taking her. He'd agreed reluctantly because he felt sorry for Rue, but mainly because Leanne was going to be gone for a weeklong curriculum conference in Austin. And then Maggie had finagled her mom into going, too.

Maggie grinned, looking very pleased with herself. "Isn't it great how everything's worked out?"

Erica mumbled something like an agreement. It was hard for her to say that her mother's not being able to come because she had cancer again was evidence of anything "working out." But, of course, she hadn't told Maggie all the details about her mom. She'd had surgery that removed part of her lung, and now she said her back was a problem, too. There weren't guests at the farm now, which seemed weird, and they'd canceled the July Fourth watermelon thump. People from Sweetgum came out to the farm now, some of them bearing food. They usually left with a small sack of produce; her mom didn't like to send anyone away empty-handed. She felt sort of guilty for being here, even if her mother had insisted she go and have fun.

Getting her father out of Leanne Dench's iron grip *was* great, but she wasn't so certain Mrs. Robichaux was too much better. Erica always felt self-conscious around her because Mrs. Robichaux commented on how "Wal-Marty" certain people looked. This was the term she applied to people who dressed in T-shirts and jean shorts—Erica's year-round wardrobe. Erica feared that when she left the Robichaux house, Maggie's mom criticized her daughter for bringing home such a Wal-Marty friend.

Yet Mrs. Robichaux had certainly jumped at the chance to come here when she heard Erica's mom couldn't chaperone them. Mrs. Robichaux was really cool, but there was something odd about her. She gave Maggie whatever she wanted, which was great for Maggie; but Erica got the feeling that every dollar, every gesture of affection, had a little desperation in it. Maggie and the store were all that Mrs. Robichaux had. So she could see why Maggie was so psyched to do a little matchmaking.

Erica sucked on her straw and listened as Maggie went through their time line.

"By the time Ms. Dench comes back from Austin," she was saying, "your dad needs to realize he's made a mistake."

"If he doesn't realize it now, I don't see how he ever will. It's been clear to me all along."

"He just didn't know what his options were. He hadn't met my mom."

Erica frowned, remembering what she'd heard about the woman at Pizza Stop. Had she been the Mrs. Robichaux of her parents' marriage? She didn't even know what had happened to that woman. She apparently hadn't lasted long.

"Do you think your mom really likes my dad?"

"I know it." Maggie leaned closer. "Your dad kissed my mom the other night."

Erica gasped—mostly because Maggie had managed not to mention this before now. It was certainly more interesting than the pimply guy at the orange-drink stand, who had taken up a quarter hour of their time. "When?"

"Two nights ago. He came by our house on account of I'd left my flip-flops in his car when he picked us up from the pool the other day. *He said.* Actually, they were *your* flip-flops."

"He kissed your mom?"

"Uh-huh."

"How did you find out?"

"I was spying on them through my door."

"What did your mother do?"

Maggie shrugged. "She just stood there. But I think she enjoyed it. I mean, I couldn't see all that much. It wasn't like a close-up in the movies where you can actually see tongues. . . ."

Erica shuddered. She didn't want to think about tongues, especially her dad's. "I can't believe it."

"I told you it would work."

"But how did you know?"

"My mom had talked about your dad a couple of times before I met you. She said he flirted with her once at a chamber of commerce meeting."

Erica wished he had pursued Mrs. Robichaux in the first place, instead of Ms. Dench. Adults didn't seem to have any idea what they were doing. Her parents hadn't been able to stay together, and Webb's marriage had busted up, and while it used to seem like Webb liked Laura, lately Erica wondered sometimes if he wasn't more attracted to Heidi. They'd become pals. And then Erica had heard weird things about Heidi and all sorts of men back in New York, including the guy who had stayed in Erica's room and then fled the next day.

Maybe the whole world would be better off with Maggie Robichaux making their romantic decisions for them.

"I wish we were spending the night in Dallas! Then we'd have to stay at a hotel, which would really move things along." Maggie drummed her fingers on the table. "Maybe if one of us got food poisoning . . . or pretended to. Do you think you could start throwing up, maybe if you ate a lot of hot dogs?"

Erica blinked. "Yuck!"

"I know it's gross, but I can't throw up on cue. And this is for a good cause." Her brows rose. "Unless you've changed your mind and decided it's not."

"I haven't changed my mind." Doubts weren't the same thing as changing your mind, were they?

Maggie pouted at her. "You haven't been a lot of fun today. It was like you were barely interested in what I was saying half the time."

"It's just . . ."

"I know, you probably wish you were here with Jake instead."

"Jake who?"

"Jake Peavy!" Maggie said. "Don't tell me you've forgotten all about your boyfriend."

"Oh." Erica tried not to look as foolish as she felt. But the truth was, she hadn't thought about Jake in weeks. "I haven't even heard from him since he went to camp."

"Boys are so awful! Serve him right if you found somebody else."

"Yeah."

"Do you like any of the boys in lifeguard class?"

"No."

"Me neither. They're all so immature. All they're interested in is stuff like games and sports and goofing around."

"Yeah . . ."

Then again, games, sports, and goofing around pretty much summed up her favorite activities in life, aside from horses. Erica sucked down the last of her drink in a noisy finish, and for the first time in a day of doing nothing but chasing boys, she thought that being around one might actually be nice.

"It's like we're at war with squash." Laura sent a despairing look at the tangle of plants that seemed to sprout by the second. Every year she always seemed to make an overestimation with one thing or another. This year it was squash. She blamed the pigs. Their early incursion on her squash patch had panicked her and made her overcompensate.

Dylan, leaning on a hoe, nodded. "And the squash is winning."

"I'm experimenting with putting more of it in the chicken mash."

Dylan's nose wrinkled. "Those poor birds. I can't stand that stuff."

"You didn't like the squash soup I made for lunch the other day?"

The expression that crossed Dylan's face before he caught

himself told Laura all she needed to know about her recent kitchen improvisation. *Damn.* She'd thought the soup was pretty good, especially after she'd thrown in the ham chunks and jalapeños.

"Actually," Dylan said, "I didn't mind those squash fritters Heidi made the other night. I told her she should include the recipe in the next CSA boxes."

Laura tapped the toe of her boot in the dirt. "Of course they tasted good. They were dredged in butter and bread crumbs. Any jackass can do that. But if we fried everything in butter all the time, we'd all be dead of heart attacks in a few months."

"Yeah, I guess." His tone indicated it would be worth the sacrifice.

"But we'd all be dead of starvation if we had to eat squash soup every night," Webb's voice piped up behind her.

Laura spun on her heel. "What are you doing? Sneaking around?"

Webb laughed. "Yeah. I sneaked across an open field."

"While I had my back turned." She looked down at a brown paper bag in his right hand, which looked like it had a flask inside it. "Have we finally driven you to drink?"

Webb shook his head. "Not yet."

Dylan frowned at them. "What now?"

Laura squinted as she looked a few rows over. "We'd better pick some more of those tomatoes. They're getting away from us, too."

"How's Rue?" Webb asked once Dylan had walked away.

"She feels like hell. She was taking another bath last time I checked." She was always taking baths these days. It helped with the bone pain the chemo caused, and she said it relieved the backache caused by the tumor the oncologist in Dallas had found on her spine.

He held out the bag. "I was in Carter's Springs and bought her some bath salts. Could you give them to her?"

Laura nodded, took the bag, and lifted it to smell. Verbena.

She cleared her throat. "Nice of you. She'll like it. Rue doesn't bitch and moan like I would, but I can tell she's having a harder time since the operation than she had last fall and winter."

"How are you holding up?"

She stiffened. "Me? I'm fine. I'm just trying to keep my head down until Rue's better."

He looked toward the lake. "Heidi said you're working round the clock now. That you never go out."

The idea of them gabbing about her rubbed her fur the wrong way. "There's too much work. Typical summer."

"I guess that's why I haven't seen much of you."

"You see me every day. And every night you're running off with Heidi."

"Not every night—just a few. She needs a break every now and then. And she doesn't have a car of her own since she took the rental back."

"She should have taken herself back along with the car."

He pushed his hat back on his head so that she got a better look at his blue eyes. "I think you might be getting your wish finally. Just last night she was telling me that she felt like she was in the way here."

"She's just now figuring that out?"

"I worry what could happen if she went back."

He looked truly anxious. He didn't want Heidi to leave. Laura felt her throat tighten.

"There's more to her than you think," he said.

"There could hardly be less."

He joined Dylan in the tomato row, and Laura went inside the house. She found Rue wrapped in towels and her bathrobe, lying flat on her back diagonally across her unmade bed. Her skin looked gray and her eyes were closed.

Laura stood over her head, peering down until Rue's eyes popped open. She jumped back. "Tarnation! You scared me."

"Scared *you*? You looked like you were about to hold a mirror under my nose."

Her eyes were red and watery, but Laura couldn't tell if she was just tired or if she'd been crying. Something peculiar was going on.

"Why are you lying around in wet towels?" Laura asked.

"Don't ask."

"I just did."

"There was an incident." Rue swallowed. "A vomiting incident."

"Oh."

"I was sitting in the tub." Rue closed her eyes again, and Laura saw a tear squeeze out of one eye. "I didn't make it out in time. That's never happened to me before."

"You need something?"

"I need a new stomach. In fact, a whole new body would be good. Think you could manage that?"

"Dr. Frankenstein I'm not. Would a ginger ale do?"

Rue flung her forearm over her eyes. Her mouth was a slash of pain.

Laura leaned toward her. "Rue?"

"Where's Heidi?"

"I think I heard her in the kitchen."

Rue swallowed and sniffed, then pushed herself up to her elbows. "I haven't cleaned up the bathroom yet."

"Forget about it."

"I can't just leave it there."

"Yes, you can. You look like one whiff of Ajax would send you back to the hospital. I'm going to bring you some ginger ale, and you're going to swallow a Zofran and take a nap."

"Oh boy. I haven't had a nap in two hours."

"When you wake up, everything will be shipshape. I'm doing laundry, too, by the way, so give me your grungies."

Rue's lips ticked up at the corners, but Laura didn't get the reaction she'd expected. "Give me your grungies" was an expression their mother had used when she made the rounds of their rooms, picking up laundry baskets. It usually cracked them up.

"Shouldn't you be outside, seeing to things?"

Laura grabbed the laundry basket from the closet. "I'm learning to delegate."

Rue closed her eyes. Laura wasn't sure whether she'd fallen asleep, passed out, or decided to shut down and ignore the world, but she didn't seem to notice when Laura tiptoed out.

She stopped at the bathroom to scope out the damage. One step inside sent her reeling out again.

Heidi was in the kitchen, listening to Patsy Cline. She was up to her eyeballs in tomatoes. The yearly tomato crisis was upon them, and she was having to handle it mostly on her own, with the occasional directive from Rue. There were two pots on the stove, several cutting boards of chopped tomatoes waiting their turn, mason jars stacked all over, and red-stained utensils of every kind.

"Anything wrong?" she asked Laura. "Do you need help?"

Laura began rifling under the kitchen sink for cleansers and rubber gloves. "No, I've got it."

"Got what?"

"Never mind."

"Is Rue okay?"

Laura straightened. Anger at the unfairness of it all surged through her. "No, she is not okay. She's been pumped full of poison."

"I know."

"Then why ask such a stupid-ass question?"

She stomped out of the kitchen with her supplies, stopped at the bathroom door, and took a deep breath. She remembered the first time she'd gotten roaring drunk. She'd come home in the middle of the night and puked all over the staircase before passing out. Rue had cleaned up after her before their father woke up.

Payback time.

Five minutes later Heidi stopped at the door. "What are you doing in . . ." Her senses kicked in and her hand lifted to her mouth. "What happened?"

"Don't ask."

"Can I help?"

Laura rolled her eyes. "It's not exactly a two-person job."

Heidi frowned at her and backed off. Minutes later Laura heard "I Fall to Pieces" coming from the kitchen.

Laura liked country music, but Patsy Cline always seemed so pathetic to her. The woman was forever falling to pieces or going crazy or walking after midnight, searching for lost loves. It was music to slit your wrists by.

Unfortunately, it seemed to fit her mood now. She wasn't falling to pieces, but it did seem as if the whole rest of the world was cracking up. Since the rain, the farm had been puttering along, but now they didn't have the guests. Or the guests' money. Canceling their guest bookings had been a wrenching decision, especially for Rue, but what else could they do? Rue was the key to the whole hospitality operation, and she just wasn't up to it.

Laura's throat constricted. Maybe the cleanser chemicals were making her brain go haywire, but suddenly the thought of there being no more guests in the house made her depressed.

Heidi thanked heaven for tomatoes. They gave her something to do with herself, some excuse for being here.

The problem was, she didn't know where else to go. Despite the fact that Vinnie had been arrested, she still didn't believe the coast was clear. And didn't want her hunch confirmed by having the police pull her cement-shod body out of the East River.

Her cowardice in not returning to Brooklyn preyed on her mind, as did the thought of that manila envelope stuffed with documents and the data stick with her files on it. Evidence. But how could she know what evidence might or might not be useful at Vinnie's trial? If the case ever went to trial. Sometimes these things were settled or plea-bargained, or the charges were dropped. She didn't want to stick her neck out for nothing.

After Stephen had left the farm, she had called him several times to see if he'd found out anything about Elvin Johnson. He hadn't, and even though he was the one who had volunteered to investigate, he always sounded a little grumpy when she checked up on him. Their latest chat had been no exception.

"I talked to that guy on the phone," Stephen had said. "Tom Chinske. He was tight-lipped. Said he couldn't talk about it. He sounded interested in you, though."

"He was the one who mentioned Elvin Johnson to me."

"Well, he wouldn't talk to me." Stephen had sighed. "Look, Heidi, I think you're overreacting. They've got Vinnie. What can he do to you now?"

She got the sense that Stephen was ready to wash his hands of her. And who could blame him?

She finally decided to call the bank herself. The person who answered the phone was Lorraine, the biggest busybody there.

In a moment of panic, Heidi attempted a vaguely Eastern European accent to disguise her voice. "I'd like to speak to Mr. Chinske, please."

"*Heidi,* is that you? Where have you been? And what's with this 'Mr. Chinske' stuff?"

Obviously, her accent would fool no one. Or maybe she normally sounded more like Bela Lugosi than she'd ever suspected. "I need to speak to Tom, Lorraine."

"You can't. He's disappeared."

Oh God. "*What?* Where is he?"

"We don't know. He just didn't show up one day. And then the cops have been picking through every file drawer in this place...."

"Do you think Vinnie got to him?"

Lorraine lowered her voice. "Actually, most people around here think he's like you."

"Like me, how?"

"You know . . . in witness protection."

Heidi almost choked. *If only!*

"You aren't trying to find Vinnie, too, are you?" Lorraine asked.

"Why? Do you know the number for the Kings County Jail?"

"Vinnie's not in jail."

"*What!*"

"He got out on bail. He put up twenty percent of eighty thousand, they said. God only knows where *that* money came from. His trial's in September. Everyone around here is buzzing about it. Do you think they'll call us as witnesses?"

Vinnie was out. Out. Free.

So much for peace of mind.

When she hung up, she sat on the floor for several minutes, breathing hard. What had happened to Tom?

A few days ago she had come in from outside and discovered a message on her cell phone. The message was from someone named Max Warren, a paralegal working in the office of Hamilton Cho.

"Ms. Bogue, Mr. Cho would very much appreciate it if you called him at his office here in New York, in regards to a case involving your employer—or former employer—the Bank of Brooklyn."

How had they found her number?

Heidi had listened to the message five times and written down Cho's office number. But she hadn't called back. Nor did she intend to until she got what course she should take clear in her head.

Had the DA really put Tom in some kind of protection program? That seemed unbelievable. But if it *was* true, maybe the situation was even more perilous than she knew. Maybe she'd actually be safer going back and throwing herself on the mercy of the DA and asking for protection herself. Or maybe that was a snare and a delusion, and she would just be putting herself closer to danger, back in the land of killer gypsy cabs.

Eventually, she would have to go back. She couldn't sit around canning tomatoes forever. She needed to kick-start her life, find a new job. After the plane fare, she hadn't spent much here, but her savings wouldn't last forever. Not while she was still paying rent for a place in Brooklyn and bringing in exactly zip.

She couldn't stay, especially now that Rue was sick. The guests were all gone, but she remained. The last holdout.

No one had said anything to her yet—at least not directly. But she had the distinct feeling that she was overstaying her welcome.

With great reluctance, she called her mother. If she couldn't go back to Brooklyn, she could at least count on her mother giving her a bed.

"I was wondering when you would get around to calling," Marla said, sounding put out even before Heidi had gotten a word in.

It wasn't an auspicious beginning to a conversation in which she was going to ask a favor. "I'm sorry, Mom. There's been stuff going on here. . . ."

"Here too!"

"Really? Well, I guess I've been a little involved with Rue. Things turned out worse than the last time I talked to you. They think her cancer has spread to her lungs and her bones."

"Oh no."

"Well . . . but she's being as aggressive as she can in treating it. She had surgery to have one of the tumors removed."

"One *of them?*"

Heidi sighed. It sounded bleaker when she was talking about it on the phone with her mother than when she was dealing with it in person with Rue. She veered onto a different subject. "The thing is, I feel like I need to get back, but I can't go back to my place yet, and I was wondering if I could stay with you."

"I don't think so."

Heidi blinked. At first she thought she must have heard her wrong. "You mean . . . no?"

"There's no room," her mother said simply.

"What about your spare bedroom?"

"Tom's sleeping there."

Heidi frowned. "Tom who?"

"Tom Chinske."

Heidi felt slack-jawed with astonishment. "What is Tom doing at your house?"

"Well, you should know. It was all your doing. Didn't you tell Stephen to investigate some man called Elwyn Johnson?"

"Elvin."

"Yes . . . Well, he couldn't find anything on his own, so he consulted Tom, who *did* know. He'd found out that this Johnson man had turned up dead in an empty parking lot in New Jersey a few years ago."

"Oh God."

"It didn't seem so worrisome until Vinnie got out on bail." Marla added in a stern voice, "You should never have gotten involved with that person."

"I figured that out."

"Well, when the news about Vinnie came out, Tom was frantic. He couldn't think of what to do, and then he remembered Stephen had given him his card and told him to call if he found out anything new. So he called him in the middle of the night and asked him to put him up for a few weeks. But apparently, he and Stephen didn't get along, and Stephen was a little resentful, anyway, because why should he put up with the tuna-fish-munching coworker of a woman who doesn't even want to go out with him anymore? So he thought of bringing him here. So far it's worked out fine."

"Why didn't Stephen tell me this?"

"Well . . . I guess he just assumed I would tell you."

"Why didn't you?" Heidi asked hotly.

"Because you never called," her mother argued. "Couldn't be bothered to pick up the phone. It's always up to me. Communication is a two-way street, you know."

"Mom, that's ridiculous. I'm in hiding down here."

"I know that."

An idea struck her. "Did you give my new phone number to the district attorney's office?"

"Of course not!" her mother said. "Stephen might have, though."

Stephen. She hadn't thought of him ratting her out.

"Anway, Heidi, there's no extra room now, and I don't think you should come back, anyway."

"But what am I going to do here? Just nothing?"

"You don't have to do nothing. Tom is taking advantage of the time here. I'm taking him to Ned's."

"Your ex-husband? Why?"

"Not to his house, to his office." Ned, number four, was a dentist, which was how her mother had ended up in Stamford. "He might have an eensy problem with the booze, but cold sober, no other dentist on earth does a better bridge than Ned Neely."

Heidi hung up, feeling very shaky. So now she was stuck . . . unless *she* wanted to be found in an empty parking lot in New Jersey.

Later in the afternoon, Rue came out to the kitchen in her bathrobe. She had a greenish hue and looked painfully thin as she padded toward the CD player and put in Nina Simone. "Love Me or Leave Me" seemed to perk her up.

"I was thinking of making something tomatoey for dinner," Heidi told her. "Pasta, maybe? Tomato soup?"

"I'm not sure. . . ." Rue lowered herself into a chair. "Tomato soup, maybe. I feel like comfort food. That's all I feel like now—comfort food, comfort movies."

"What's a comfort movie?"

"Fred Astaire. Last year Laura gave me a Fred and Ginger box set. I thought I'd break it out tonight."

"Sounds great. Although I'm more of a Gene Kelly fan myself."

Rue sat up straighter. "How can that be possible? I thought I knew you. . . ."

"It's the wolfish smile. I'm a sucker for it."

"But that's so wrong. He just doesn't compare."

"Singin' in the Rain?" Heidi reminded her.

"But what else?"

Rue had a point. None of his other movies equaled that one. Heidi did what she always tried to do when she was losing an argument—she changed the subject. "Oh! I have a present for you."

She went to the computer and unplugged her iPod from the USB port. "I've been downloading. It's got all your faves."

Rue fingered the little rectangle as if it were solid gold.

"Thank you! This is incredible. Are you sure you want to part with it?"

"I haven't used it all summer."

Heidi inserted the earphones into the jack and then hooked one bud up to Rue's ear and took one for herself. When the first song came up, Rue grinned. "Billie Holiday!"

Laura came in and stopped in front of them, doing a double take at the sight of them sharing an iPod like a couple of teenagers. "What's that?"

"An MP-three player," Heidi said.

Laura rolled her eyes. "I know that. When did you get that?"

"Just now," Rue said. "Heidi gave it to me."

Laura looked so flabbergasted, it was hard not to laugh. It was as though she had never considered the idea that Heidi might *give* someone anything. "Those aren't cheap."

"Room and board isn't cheap, either," Heidi told her. "You guys never cashed the check I wrote you."

"This is better than money," Rue said, rubbing her metallic blue rectangle like she would a good luck charm. "I don't have to sit in that damn chemo room, listening to other people's dismal conversations. I can just veg out in my own world."

Heidi had gone with Rue for her first chemo treatment after her surgery. She had been expecting grim, but the reality had been even worse—two rows of people hooked up to IVs, sitting in recliner chairs. "What?" Heidi asked Rue. "You don't want to listen to Denture Man telling the nurse about his hemorrhoids?"

Rue fell forward, giggling.

Laura gaped at them. "Why's he called Denture Man?"

The question just made Heidi and Rue laugh more. Rue tried to answer once, but couldn't get beyond "His teeth" before collapsing again. She put her head down on the kitchen table, and Heidi draped an arm across her bony shoulders.

"His teeth click when he talks," Heidi said, sucking in a breath.

Rue convulsed. "Like c-c-castanets!"

Laura smiled limply and stalked out.

They didn't see her again until the movie, which was *Top Hat*. Laura hated musicals, although she couldn't complain about this one too much, since she had given it to Rue. Besides, it had a narcotic effect on Rue, who dozed on and off throughout, leaving Laura and Heidi watching together, each aware of the fact that they would rather not be sitting in a room together, but not wanting to abandon Rue.

Heidi left as soon as the end credits started to roll. She found Webb lounging on the back porch steps and sat down next to him. "What are you doing?"

"Just thinking."

"About what?"

"About you, actually."

Heidi felt a dangerous kind of adrenaline at the idea that she had occupied even a tiny corner of his thoughts.

"I keep thinking about that other guy . . . What's his name? The one who was here."

"Stephen."

"Right. I keep wondering what happened there."

So much for being the object of Webb's dreams. Turned out he was just curious about how she had managed to screw things up so badly. "*I* happened. I've been bumbling all my life, and occasionally I bumble into someone else's world. And unfortunately they usually regret it."

"I doubt that."

"Do you want names? I could give them to you. Better yet, my mom could provide you with a list. And probably their phone numbers, too. She takes my failed personal life harder than I do, even."

"Your mom? I thought—"

"That she was my prototype? She doesn't see it that way. *She* settled down, you understand. The fact that she settled down four different times in three separate states doesn't seem to faze her. All she can see is that I haven't ever gotten that ring around my finger. It's how she measures success."

He laughed.

"I liked Stephen, but there wasn't . . . a spark. Does that sound stupid?"

"Of course not." He sort of waggled his brows at her. "You gotta have spark."

He was just joking with her, but her stomach fluttered nevertheless. "I don't know," Heidi said. "I'm beginning to wonder if spark is overrated. I had sparks galore with Vinnie. Then he tried to run me over with a car."

"Too much spark," he said.

"Sometimes I think that I just shouldn't go back at all, ever. That I should try to find a new niche for myself."

"Doing what?"

"That's the jackpot question." She looked at him. "You're in the same spot, aren't you? What are you going to do?"

"Don't you start, too."

"People pester you about your future?"

"Laura does. She's always trying to figure out what I could become."

"Oh."

"It's her gentle way of telling me to shove off, I guess. It's taken me a while to figure that out."

"Weird."

"Why?"

"I can't imagine anyone trying to get rid of you." Their eyes met as the sound of her words rang in her ears. She blushed. "I mean . . . you're so helpful around here."

"Hmm."

She swallowed. "And I always thought you and Laura were . . ."

"Sweet on each other?"

"Laura, sweet?" Heidi was amused, then frowned. "But, yeah, I guess that's sort of what I meant."

"She's let me know in no uncertain terms, countless times, that we're just friends."

Heidi couldn't believe it. Or maybe she could. Here was proof that Laura was certifiable. "So . . ."

"Yeah. So, I guess that's it. I'm a free man."

He hardly looked like a carefree bachelor. In fact, if the expression in his eyes was any indicator, the man was a wreck inside.

She knew that feeling. She put her hand over his. "It doesn't last."

"What?"

"What you're going through. That feeling that someone's taken a jackhammer to your heart. It goes away."

"I know. God, I really do know. My wife told me our marriage was over while I was in Afghanistan. I got an e-mail."

"Nice."

"But you know what was really awful? Just a few days later I was glad. Relieved. I never should have married Denise in the first place. Suddenly I couldn't wait for my tour to be over. I was homesick. For here."

She squeezed his hand.

"Laura and I see each other completely differently," he said. "To her, we're just old pals, but complete romantic misfits. But to me, it feels like we were meant to be. Does that make sense?"

Heidi nodded slowly. "That's what I thought about Vinnie. For about five days."

He let out a ragged sigh. "I should let it go. Otherwise, I'm just going to go crazy. Sometimes I wonder if it's not some new variation of post-traumatic stress."

"Laura Derangement Syndrome. LDS. Laura has that effect on a lot of people, believe me."

He laughed.

A shadow passed over them. They both looked out of the corner of their eyes to the figure looming just feet away.

Heidi was so startled, she jumped back. The only other time she'd seen an expression like Laura's was when a hawk had swooped down and picked off a baby chick near the henhouse. She guiltily pulled her hand away from Webb's.

Which was stupid. What did she have to be guilty about?

"I need to talk to you," Laura said.

Heidi shivered. The announcement had been aimed at her. *"Now?"*

"Now," replied Laura.

"I'll go," Webb said.

"You don't have to leave," Laura told him.

Heidi nodded fiercely. "Yes, stay."

"Heidi and I are leaving." Laura kept her gaze trained on Heidi, whose heart sank. "Let's you and me take a drive."

Chapter 16

Heidi gulped. The phrase had an ominous ring to it. "Couldn't we just talk here? Or better yet, in the kitchen?" *Where there may be witnesses . . .*

Laura didn't seem open to suggestions. "C'mon."

Heidi rose slowly to her feet, whispering to Webb, "If I'm not back by morning, call the police." She turned to Laura. "Just wait a sec while I get my purse."

"You won't need it. I'm buying," Laura told her.

Heidi knit her brows. "Buying what?"

"Drinks."

"That's a first," Webb joked.

Heidi regarded her warily. "You're taking me out for drinks?"

"You have a problem with that?"

"I'd still like to have my purse on me. In the event someone needs to identify my remains."

Laura grabbed her arm. "They can send off for your dental records."

Heidi dug in her heels. What could Laura possibly want to talk to her about? It probably had something to do with her never-changing desire to see Heidi gone. But what did she intend to do to achieve her ends?

Curiosity finally got the best of her. Very reluctantly, Heidi traipsed after Laura and climbed into her truck, which smelled of decades of oil and cigarette butts. "Isn't this your dad's old pickup?"

"Yup. Still runs great."

Heidi had to yank the squeaky door shut. "Ten miles to the gallon?"

"Eight. It's only money."

"And the world," Heidi said under her breath as they peeled out of the drive.

"What?"

"Nothing!" Heidi fastened her seat belt. "So where are we going?"

"A bar."

"There's not a bar until you get to the next county."

"I felt like a road trip."

Wonderful.

Turning onto the paved main road, Laura cranked up Willie Nelson singing "Bloody Mary Morning." Any attempt at conversation after that was pretty much impossible, both because of the stereo's volume and because Heidi was too terrified to take her eyes off the road. It wasn't that Laura drove too fast so much as her tendency to forget to slow down for things until it was almost too late. Then she would nearly jerk to a stop and hit the gas again the next moment. Heidi kept a white-knuckle grip on the armrest.

After what seemed like an eternity, they pulled up to something called Chester's Lone Star Sports Bar. Heidi spilled out of the passenger door and could have kissed the cigarette-butt-strewn ground.

Everybody at Chester's knew Laura, including the guy behind the bar, who wasted no time putting a beer in her hand. Heidi eyed the room self-consciously. Aside from the bright white lights over two pool tables, the only real illumination came from a big-screen television playing baseball highlights, which no one was watching. Probably because everyone was staring at her. She felt eyes on her from the tables along the wall; through the dark and smoky haze, they felt like rodent eyes piercing through the night. The few guys in gimme caps slumped on stools at the bar turned and ogled her openly. She wished she'd taken the time to change into jeans. In her tank top and shorts she felt oddly exposed.

This stood in stark contrast to the chummy greeting Laura received.

"We haven't seen you around lately. Glad to see you survived that night with Buddy." Heidi assumed the beefy guy was Chester, since he was bartending. He seemed to be the only employee here.

"Just barely," Laura said.

He swung toward Heidi, expectantly.

It took her a moment to pick up the cue. She was busy trying to banish the Jodie Foster movie *The Accused* from her thoughts. "Oh! I'll have a gin and tonic, please. Thank you."

Too late, she realized she probably should have just ordered a beer. A few of the guys at the bar chuckled, as if she had just ordered a Shirley Temple.

The requested drink passed from Chester's hands to Laura's to Heidi's; then Laura tugged her toward an empty table. The wood booth had a thick, waxy varnish, which made a squeaking sound against Heidi's legs as she scooted in.

"So this is where you disappear to nights," Heidi said.

"Sometimes."

"Friendly folks. Full of curiosity."

"Not exactly a girly hangout."

"Is that guy a friend of yours?" Heidi asked, nodding discreetly at the bartender. "Chester?"

Laura shook her head. "That's not Chester. That's Wade. Chester's been in jail since his meth lab blew up."

She seemed to relish the redneckiness of it all almost as much as she enjoyed Heidi's discomfort.

"So." Laura took a swig of beer. "Business."

Heidi sighed. "I know what you're going to say."

"No, you don't."

"I can guess. Hands off Webb, right? But honestly, that holding hands on the porch thing . . . You just caught us at a weird moment. He doesn't—"

Laura cut her off. "What happens with you and Webb is none of my business. He's a big boy, and if he wants to throw his life away on you, so be it. The fact is, I brought you here to tell you, beg you even, not to leave Sweetgum." She set her beer bottle down for emphasis.

The speech caught Heidi completely off guard. Instinct told her that it was all a trap. "Let me get this straight. You want me to *stay?*"

"That's what I said."

"A month ago you said I couldn't leave fast enough to suit you."

"What I want doesn't really matter." Laura folded her arms and glowered at her beer bottle. "Rue wants you to stay. She needs you. She would never ask you, because that's just how she is. I know it might sound strange since you've only been here a little over a month, but if you left Rue, I think it might . . . well, I think she'd miss you. I haven't seen her so happy as when you've been around. At least not in the past year. You two seem to have developed some kind of kinship." As if to wash away the rancid aftertaste of that last word, Laura took another swig of beer. "So that's it. I'm asking you to stay. Please."

Heidi turned her glass in her hands. She'd been looking for an excuse not to go back to New York, and here it was. A gilded invitation to put off her problems until some faraway date in the future. *For Rue.*

And she wanted to stay. She did. It would have been hard to leave Rue while she was so ill.

Laura bit her lip. "The thing is, I'm afraid if you leave, she won't get better."

Heidi couldn't help but wonder at that statement. Did Laura actually think that Rue was going to get better? No one had said anything, but in the reading Heidi had done on the Internet, and just from observing Rue, this illness wasn't going to have a positive outcome. The surgeon had even been hesitant to operate on Rue's lung, because he believed at that point the cancer had spread too far to stop it, and that was before they had found a tumor on her spine, which was inoperable. All he could do was remove the largest lung tumor and hope the chemo and radiation would shrink the tumor on Rue's spine, or at least slow its growth. But every time Rue went into a hospital or clinic now, she seemed to come out another degree diminished. And her pain got worse every day.

"I don't think my staying or leaving will . . ." Heidi stopped herself. She didn't know how to put it diplomatically. "It's cancer."

Anger snapped in Laura's eyes. "I know it's cancer! But it's also a matter of will, isn't it? Of not wanting to give up? It requires a good mental attitude."

She couldn't believe she was sitting here listening to Laura praise the powers of positive thinking.

"People have survived years beyond what doctors say," Laura added.

"Of course."

"And she *enjoys* life when you're around. For some reason, I just don't have what it takes. The joy gene skipped me."

Heidi deliberated. She could stay. Her mother could oversee moving her stuff out of her apartment, and she could stop paying rent. Then she would be cut loose from everything. Sure, she would have to stay in Sweetgum until . . . until . . .

Her chest felt tight.

Laura raised an eyebrow. "I guess the answer's no."

"No!" Heidi said quickly. "I mean, no, the answer's yes. Definitely. Only I worry a little about Rue. Isn't she going to wonder about why you're suddenly being nice to me?"

"Who said anything about my being nice to you?"

"Oh." Heidi tried not to dwell on that statement. "But she knows that I've been thinking about going back. She thinks I should go back. What reason could I give her for staying, aside from your lacking the joy gene?"

"I thought about this. You can say you want to do a cookbook."

"A cookbook?"

"A Spinster Farm cookbook. You and Rue could work on it. It would give her something to think about besides her health."

"That's actually not a bad idea," Heidi said, sipping her drink. "A cookbook."

"Are you kidding?" Laura guffawed. "It's a ridiculous waste of time."

"People *like* cookbooks." Heidi's enthusiasm for the plan grew. "We could have pictures of the farm and the chickens and Dylan and Herman. . . ."

Laura snorted. "Right. Now you're talking best-seller material."

"I'm *serious.*"

"It's your baby. If you want Dylan and Herman to pose as centerfolds, it's all the same to me. As far as I'm concerned, this is more of a make-work project." Laura thrust her hand across the table. "So it's a deal?"

Heidi eyed the hand warily. There had to be a catch. In spite of their conversation, she was still expecting the joy buzzer in the handshake.

But she didn't have it in her to snub a friendly gesture, even if the old proverb about shaking hands with the devil echoed in her head. "Deal."

Laura's hand squeezed hers like a tourniquet. "Just remember this—you're there for Rue. If you let her down, if you skip out again without a word, like you and Mommy Dearest did in the way back when, I'll be down on you like stink on a skunk. Got it?"

Heidi swallowed, forced a smile, and shook. "Got it."

"A Sassy Spinster Farm cookbook?" Rue looked at Heidi in amazement. "You never talked about that before."

"I never . . ." Heidi bent over and wedged a cup into the already full dishwasher. "That is, it's actually been in the back of my mind for a while. I just wasn't sure I had the confidence to do it. And also, it's not my farm."

"Of course it is."

Heidi laughed. "I don't think Laura would be well for making me a partner."

"She'll go along with the idea, though. If it actually got published, it would be great publicity."

"If it got published and if it was any good."

Rue let out a wry chuckle. "Well, yes. It would help if the recipes didn't poison anyone." She leaned back in one of the kitchen chairs, thinking. "And the handy thing is, we could work through e-mail if we have to."

"E-mail?"

"When you go back to New York."

Heidi turned away again and transferred the sugar bowl from the table to a counter on the other side of the room. "Actually, I was thinking I could stay here until we finished working on it."

Rue couldn't help feeling torn. Much as she wanted Heidi to stay, she began to wonder if this new project didn't have some other motive behind it. "You're not telling me the truth, are you?"

Heidi's eyes bugged out. "What do you mean?"

"This isn't just about writing a cookbook, is it?"

"Of course it is!"

"It's about your not wanting to go back and get involved in the case against Vinnie."

Heidi let out a breath and flopped into the chair opposite Rue. "Okay, maybe a little. But I've asked myself, what good would I do there, really? They won't need me."

"They might."

"Well, they're not going to get me. I don't want to go back and be picked off like a duck in a shooting gallery. And for what? What purpose would I have served?"

"You might help put a criminal in jail."

"*Might* is the key word. I'm not all that sure I have much to contribute. I was just an admin assist, and believe me, my heart was not in my job. It's not like I was actually paying that close attention. It was just a paycheck."

Rue listened, nodding even though she couldn't agree.

"Anyway, what I was thinking was, we should start taking pictures of the farm, and the booth at the farmers' market, and the CSA boxes. We need to spruce them up. What we really need is a logo."

Rue nodded. Why hadn't she thought of this before? For the past two years, they had just been using a plain label with Old West–style lettering and clip-art vegetables in the four corners, which suited Laura's unfrivolous nature. A better logo would be fun, and a good attention getter.

"But, of course, the real work will be assembling everything," Heidi added.

Erica came bounding in. "Assembling what? Can I help?"

"We're thinking about writing a cookbook," Rue said.

All of her daughter's enthusiasm ground to a comically abrupt halt. "Why?"

"Because people like cookbooks," Heidi told her.

"Really? Who?" asked Erica.

Rue smiled. "People who like to cook. They can make good gifts."

Erica scrunched up her nose. "Ew. Getting a cookbook for a gift would be seriously weak. For my birthday—which is only a month away, you know—I'd rather have a television for my room."

"You're more likely to get a cookbook," Rue said.

Erica hung back, less enthusiastic now about helping. "Would it be okay if I took Milkshake out for a while instead of helping y'all?"

"Sure. You haven't been riding him as much as you used to." Rue tilted her head. Erica was chewing gum and had the same preoccupied expression on her face that had been there for the past few weeks. She hardly seemed like the same girl who had been so happy to be staying at the farm in May. For one thing, every day seemed to reveal the results of the latest makeup experiment. Today it was eyeliner. Half moons of midnight blue stood out on each eyelid.

Erica shrugged. "I've been busy."

"It's summer," Rue said.

"I know, but there's so much going on. I've got junior life-guard, and Spunky and the kittens to take care of . . ." She suddenly remembered something. "Oh! I was supposed to ask you, is it okay if I go to Maggie's tomorrow after the pool?"

"You've been over there a lot lately."

"Maggie's mother doesn't mind."

"Should I call her?"

"I don't see why. She's busy at the store all day. She hardly notices we're there."

"That's why," Rue said.

"It's not like we can get into any trouble in Carter's Springs," Erica said. "We just go from the pool to Maggie's mom's shop, then to the Dairy Queen and back to Maggie's mom's shop, and then to their house to watch a video or something. Maggie has a cell phone, and her mother calls her all the time."

"I might call her just in case."

Erica lifted her shoulders as if to say, "If you want to waste your life, fine by me."

Rue couldn't help smiling. It was wrenching to see Erica enjoying someone else's home more than her own, but it was good that she had a new friend, even if Maggie seemed a little sly and Eddie Haskellish. She was grateful Maggie's mom had stepped in for her when she couldn't take the kids to Six Flags.

"You could invite Maggie here, too, you know."

Erica looked alarmed. "Here? Why?"

"Because you live here. You've invited her to stay with William and Leanne, right?"

"Only a couple of times. And only because she wanted to look at Leanne."

"Well . . ." Rue sighed. "Your friends are always welcome here, is all I'm saying."

After Erica was gone, Rue was afraid to look at Heidi for a few minutes. Erica had all sorts of reasons for not wanting to have Maggie visit the farm—vague ones, mostly, but Erica was getting to that age when she didn't want to say too much, at least not to grown-ups. Yet Rue couldn't help wondering if the real reason wasn't that Erica didn't want to be around while she was sick. Her heart constricted at the thought; yet it made perfect sense. Last fall Erica had stayed mostly with William. She was getting a more complete picture of illness this time around. Rue tried to stay on an even keel, but when she felt half dead, it was hard not to get irritable.

In a way she was glad Erica had a place to escape to. She remembered that feeling of wanting to escape from home sometimes when she was a girl, when her mother was sick.

But that didn't make their separating any easier to accept emotionally.

Heidi shook her head, chuckling lightly. "When I was Erica's age, I wanted to spend every hour at my friend Amy's house. She lived in a real house, not an apartment, and her parents had cable television. To me, it was as if she was living in the lap of luxury. The grass is always greener at that age."

"It's especially greener when your friend's mother doesn't have cancer." The words escaped before Rue could stop them, and hearing them, she winced. "And when your mom's not a self-pitying whiner."

"You're allowed. I complained more after I fell on my ass than you have about getting a chunk of lung removed and chemo. I wish you'd whine more, to tell the truth. Too much stiff-upper-lipping is disgusting."

"If I start, I might never stop." Rue looked out the window and saw Erica in the side pasture, holding a carrot in her palm to tempt Milkshake closer so she could bridle him. "You're right. It's just normal. She's growing up and pulling away from her mom. She would want to cut the apron strings even if I didn't have cancer."

"Exactly," Heidi said.

And probably I would have this same wrenching feeling inside to see my daughter finding happiness away from me, Rue thought.

But if it weren't for the cancer, she might have more resistance and be more stoic. She would know there would be time.

Chapter 17

Walking back from the pool, Maggie gave Erica a full update. "He came by the store once, saying he was going to buy a present for you. I was there. Don't forget to thank me when you *don't* receive ladybug hair clips for your birthday."

"What did he get?"

"I'm so not going to tell you that."

"Why not? I'd tell you."

"I can't. It would, like, violate the ethics code of store owners or something. Think about it. I could run around spoiling the birthday surprises of half the girls in town."

Erica supposed she had to accept a little secrecy. "Anyway . . . you said they met again, right?"

"Uh-huh. Mom mentioned that they just happened to bump into each other at the gas station."

Erica frowned. "Maybe they *did* just bump into each other."

"It's too much of a coincidence."

"But . . . a gas station? That doesn't sound very romantic."

"Of course not. That's why it's the perfect place. Because it's not at all suspicious."

"It doesn't take long to fill up a tank with gas. What could they do?"

Maggie expelled her breath in a huff. "They could make a

date to meet each other in secret somewhere else. That's the way these things work."

Erica felt embarrassed. She didn't know about this stuff. What was more, she didn't know how Maggie knew. "Did they make a date?"

Here Maggie hesitated. "I'm not one hundred percent absolutely positive, but I think so. Mom's been humming. She only hums when she's happy."

Erica nodded.

"Have you noticed your dad acting differently?"

"Not really. Anyway, it sounds like you've seen him more than I have."

"Men don't show their emotions as much," Maggie said, knowledgeably. "They're enigmums."

They stopped by a Coke machine in front of the pharmacy. Maggie dug through her little purse and sighed in frustration. "Please tell me you have a dollar."

Erica dug in her shorts pockets and came up with four quarters, which she forked over into Maggie's outstretched palm.

"Thanks!" Maggie put the money in the machine and punched the Diet Coke button, which disappointed Erica. She couldn't stand that stuff. Maggie took her first slurpy sip and sighed. "Much better! It's going to be so great when you live here. We'll have so much fun all the time. Last year I always felt so bored after school."

Erica could feel her brows beetling. "Live in Carter's Springs?"

"Of course. They'll have to buy a bigger house, probably farther out from town than where we live now."

"But my dad lives just outside Sweetgum."

"Right. But since both your dad and my mom work here, it would be really stupid for us all to live in the boondocks. And if you had to choose between the two, why would you live in the smaller, more boring place?"

Erica didn't have a good argument for why. "Mostly, I live on the farm, with my mom and my aunt."

"Right. But now you won't have to."

"But—"

"There will be boys here, too, you know. Your little heart won't be broken forever."

Erica blinked in confusion. "My heart?" *Boys?*

"Because of Jake Peavy."

Erica sucked in her breath. "Oh yeah."

"You see? It's been just two months since school let out, and you've practically forgotten him already. So it's not like there's anything to keep you in that dinky little school."

Before Erica could analyze why exactly this disturbed her—it was not like anybody else had even mentioned moving yet—they arrived at Mairzy-Doats. Mrs. Robichaux was in the middle of trying to find something for a little redheaded girl to wear to her great-grandmother's hundredth birthday party, so she suggested that Maggie and Erica go to the house and watch a DVD or something.

They hung around Maggie's house for two hours, watching television, and then Maggie announced she was bored. "There's no point in our staying around here and then just having your mom come pick you up tomorrow," she said. "You should call your dad and tell him that we want to go to his house."

Erica frowned. "Why? You've been there. We'd have to deal with Ms. Dench."

"I know, but I've got a plan."

Erica was not at all enthusiastic about this idea—and she was sure her dad wouldn't be, either—but she didn't know how to say no to Maggie.

And as it turned out, her dad was very chipper. Anyone would almost think that he actually wanted Erica and her friend to stay at his house. "When should I pick you up? Five?"

Erica held the phone against her shirt and turned to Maggie. "Should he pick us up at five?"

Maggie shook her head. "My mom doesn't close the store till five thirty."

"Five forty-five," Erica said into the phone.

"Okeydoke!"

When Erica's dad showed up that evening, Maggie wasted no time tugging Erica out the door. "Hi, Mr. Anderson. Erica and I will wait out in the car."

Her father drew back in surprise—and also so he wouldn't be whopped by Maggie's duffel bag. "Wait for what?"

Maggie turned. "For you to talk to my mom. To figure out how to get me back here tomorrow?"

He nodded. "Oh. Right."

They didn't have long to wait. Only a few minutes passed before Erica's dad was making his way across the lawn to the driveway. Maggie sputtered in exasperation, "What's the matter with them? They're not making the most of opportunities!"

"How do we know? It's not as if we could see through walls to tell what was going on in there."

Maggie scowled. "Nothing interesting can happen in two minutes. Is your dad retarded or something?"

Erica was taken aback. And a little offended. "What?"

Just then, her father ducked into the driver's seat. "All fired up, girls?"

They stared at him.

"Great!" he said, as if they'd actually responded to him.

"Well, what a surprise," Ms. Dench said twenty minutes later, when they all tromped into the living room. She darted a stony look at Erica's dad. "William, you didn't tell me we were having company."

"It's just me and Maggie," Erica said.

Leanne acted as if having two junior high girls in the house was a big inconvenience or something.

"Just the girls," her father echoed, beating a hasty retreat to the back of the house.

"We've eaten," Maggie said, "so you don't even have to feed us."

Leanne pasted a smile on. "You sure you don't want something?"

"No thank you." Maggie walked around to the oval dining-

room table. Over the course of the summer, it had become cluttered with projects Leanne was working on, usually involving
pastel fabrics.

"What's this?" Maggie asked, fingering a pile of pale green.
"You're not going to get married in a green dress, are you?"

Leanne released a blast of laughter. "Heavens to bleepin'
Betsy, no! I bought my wedding dress already, in Dallas. But
since the dress really broke the bank, I thought I'd save money
by making the bridesmaid dresses myself. Erica's, too."

"Cool. Is Erica's dress going to be green, too?"

"No, I picked out a special color just for her." Leanne held up
several yards of shiny pale purple cloth. "See? It's lilac."

Erica shuddered. *No way. No way, no way, no way.*

"Pretty!" Maggie exclaimed.

She was such a liar. But Leanne didn't even seem to notice.
"And since I'm so pressed for time, I thought it would be a fun
learning experience if Erica-bug and I worked on her dress together."

Erica gaped at her. "I don't know how to sew."

"It's the simplest thing," Leanne replied.

Was she crazy? Really, truly crazy?

Or did she just want her stepchild to look like a freak? An
oversize, badly dressed purple flower girl.

"Wow," Maggie said. "Sewing. That sounds *fun.* Can I learn,
too?"

"Of course!" Leanne said. "Who knows? Maybe you'll become so good at sewing, you could start making things to sell in
your mother's store."

"That would be H!" Maggie exclaimed.

Leanne's face went slack. "What?"

"Hard core," Erica translated, shaking her head. *Not.*

"Really? I've never heard that. In my day *H* just stood for . . ."
Leanne's brow puckered for a moment before she was able to get
that glassy smile back in place. "Well! See, you'll be able to teach
me some things, too!"

In Erica's bedroom, Maggie dove onto the bed as soon as the door was shut and screamed with laughter into a pillow. Her face was flushed. Erica collapsed on the floor.

"Oh my God!" Maggie exclaimed. "That woman is *such* a tool."

Erica rested her back against the bed. She couldn't get the purple satin out of her mind. "I'm not going to be in that wedding. I absolutely refuse."

Maggie clucked her tongue. "Of course you're not. There's not going to be a wedding. Not for Ms. Dench, at any rate."

If only! "Seeing her working on those dresses makes it seem like it really is going to happen."

"Don't panic. We haven't put part two of this evening's plan into action yet."

"I didn't know there was a part two."

"Did you think I came all the way out here just to hang with Ms. Dench?" Maggie pushed herself to the edge of the bed and explained it all very carefully.

Five minutes later, Erica ran into the kitchen, where her dad and Leanne were eating one of Leanne's spaghetti casseroles, a really gruesome dish Leanne always referred to as her specialty. To Erica, it always just looked like worms in red sauce.

"Something bad's happened," she announced.

Leanne gasped. "Is Maggie all right?"

"Well, she's okay, but she's crying," Erica told them.

"Why?" William asked.

"Because she's embarrassed," Erica explained. "See, she forgot to bring her asthma medicine, and even though she's not having an asthma attack, she's worried she will have one, but she's too embarrassed to say anything about it. She's worried her mom'll be mad at her."

"Jessica?" William asked. "Why would she be mad?"

"Who's Jessica?" Leanne asked.

"Mrs. Robichaux," Erica said. "I guess I could call her and ask her to bring it, couldn't I?"

Her dad bolted up out of his chair. "Don't do that."

Leanne gaped at him. "Why not? We don't want the girl to have an asthma attack without her inhaler."

"I'll just pop back to town and pick it up myself. It won't take long, and y'all are so busy with the dresses and stuff. And I had meant to swing by the car wash, anyhow."

"The car wash?" asked Leanne.

"That white paint on your car shows every little speck of dirt," he explained.

Knowing that it was her car that was going to be washed caused Leanne to reconsider. "That's nice. But maybe you should call Mrs. Robichaux first."

"I don't even know her number," William said quickly.

Leanne reached for more casserole. "I meant Erica could. Or Maggie."

"Oh." William nodded. "Well, yeah. Of course. That would make more sense."

Back in her room, Erica and Maggie exchanged high fives, although Erica didn't feel quite as triumphant as Maggie. There was something about the whole thing that made her uneasy. When they had been plotting out everything, it had sounded great. But her dad was acting so dodgy. Could he really be falling in love with Mrs. Robichaux while he was engaged to Ms. Dench? She hated Ms. Dench, and she certainly didn't want to traipse down the aisle at the Methodist church, tossing rose petals in a shiny purple dress . . . but she'd sort of expected things to work out differently. She'd expected her dad to call off the wedding and then pursue Mrs. Robichaux, or maybe even someone else. She hadn't expected him to start two-timing.

Why wasn't Maggie a little freaked out, too?

When they heard William leave, Maggie grinned at her. But the grin faded when Leanne stuck her head through the door. Without knocking, which drove Erica crazy.

"Y'all doing okay?"

"Uh-huh," they said in unison, hoping to chase her away with indifference.

No such luck. She folded her arms and leaned against the door frame. "Have I mentioned how hard I've been looking to find a caterer? They're so expensive—even for the relatively modest spread I'm envisioning. And I've already nearly broken the bank on the wedding cake."

"That's too bad," Erica said.

Leanne went on. "I just don't know. I'm half tempted to try to do it all myself. Does that sound crazy? I guess it does. I'm already so busy that I feel like if I take one more thing on, I'll just snap."

Maggie and Erica exchanged glances, then looked back up at Leanne.

"You know who I was thinking of asking just the other day?" Leanne asked. "Your mother."

Erica could feel her face screwing up in confusion. *"Mom?"*

"People just rave about those goodies she's been selling at the farmers' market and putting in those boxes."

"Heidi does most of that. Mom's sick."

Leanne nodded. "All the more reason to throw a little business her way, I was thinking. Everybody knows the farm had to turn paying guests away. They've got to be hurting for money over there."

Are they? Erica hadn't been paying all that much attention.

"And their stuff is mostly organic, right? I like the idea of having a green wedding." Leanne shot a sharp look at Erica. "As long as organic doesn't mean more expensive."

Erica blinked at her in astonishment. Here she was trying to prevent the wedding from happening, and Leanne was thinking of getting Sassy Spinster Farm involved in it. How had that happened?

Leanne continued. "Of course, since they're not a real catering company, I wouldn't be able to pay them what the big places in Athens and Tyler are asking. But I would certainly like to do your mother a favor if I could."

Erica wasn't so sure her mom would consider it a favor. She was sure her aunt Laura wouldn't. She hardly knew what to say. "Does Dad think this would be a good idea?"

Leanne dismissed that concern with a wave of her hand. "He's not contributing a dime toward this shindig. Typical man. Couldn't care less! I swear, it's amazing that weddings ever come off at all."

"It sure is," Maggie said, grinning.

Erica gave her a punch in the side.

Maggie could make jokes, but Erica had an unsettled feeling churning away inside her.

Chapter 18

"Your red blood count is very low. It's a concern."

Rue clutched her tote bag to her side and frowned. She had been waiting for the blood test results so she could keep her chemo appointment at noon. Not that she was looking forward to the chemo, but she had mentally geared herself up for it. Now she felt thwarted.

Last year her red blood cell count had never been too low. And she'd had only one chemo treatment so far.

"What am I supposed to do?" she asked the doctor.

Dr. Ajay, who seemed always to be on guard against giving any facial clues whatsoever, kept her eyes focused on Rue's chart, even though she had to know what was there, since she'd written it herself. "I'm going to give you a Procrit injection and send you home. We'll test you again next week."

"What if it doesn't get better?"

"It will." The doctor's forehead scrunched a little, which Rue interpreted as a frown. "I'm actually more concerned about your white blood cell count, which is low, too."

This seemed baffling. "If I'm low on red and white, what's circulating around in my veins and arteries? Mineral water?"

Dr. Ajay paused, as if to process this information, and then gave a curt nod. "Still have your sense of humor. That's good."

Rue smiled, but in the back of her mind, she wondered. Was Dr. Ajay's comment just the product of someone who was socially awkward, or was a loss of humor one of those unspoken cancer milestones? She imagined doctors noting the humor stages of illness. Peppy, sharp Groucho for stage one; moving to mordantly humorous Jerry Seinfeld; winding down to stage three Richard Lewis; and then, finally, Carrot Top and death.

Hopefully she was still a long way from Carrot Top.

She got her shot, made her next appointment, and hurried out of the building with an uneasy feeling. Half of her felt as if she'd been given a reprieve; the other half felt like a shirker. So many accommodations had been made for her at the farm. They'd turned away all the paying guests. During the busiest time of the year, she felt too wiped out to do all the canning and preserving, which she usually managed. Heidi was doing most of that now, and the cooking too. Even in taking care of Erica, she felt like she'd been slacking off. Erica seemed to spend half her time either at her friend Maggie's or at William's house. All Rue had to do was go through treatment, rest, and get better . . . but instead of getting better, she felt like the drugs were sapping her. She couldn't even recuperate right.

Heidi tagged after her as they left the building. "What's wrong?" She hadn't asked any questions when she saw her in the waiting room, obviously realizing that something was wrong but not wanting to ask what in public.

"My red blood cell count is too low. I have to postpone this round of chemo."

"You're upset about that?"

"I want to get this over with."

"But if it would just wipe you out . . ."

Rue opened the passenger door to her car. "What's Laura going to say?"

Heidi looked perplexed. "What?"

"She'll be disappointed."

"Oh, for heaven's sake. *She's* not the one going through chemo!"

"But she's the one bearing the brunt of my treatment." To Heidi's raised-eyebrow look of disbelief, she added, "Workwise."

Heidi got inside, clicked her shoulder belt in place, and started the car. "Don't worry about Laura. She finally has the farm just how she wants it—all to herself, with a few lackeys around her." She backed out of the lot and pulled into traffic. "If she could just get rid of me, her life would probably be perfect."

They drove in silence for a while. On the drive up, Rue had been dreading chemo and the days of feeling like hammered meat to follow. But now, when she wasn't even going to have it, her emotions were starting to unravel. Why was this happening to her?

Not that she wished cancer on anyone else, but why her?

Heidi cleared her throat and looked over at her expectantly. "I've got a movie challenge. Are you ready for it?"

Given the direction Rue's thoughts had been headed, the distraction was welcome. "Okay."

"Movie character dream date. Who would it be?"

It was too easy. "Cary Grant, *The Philadelphia Story*, C. K. Dexter Haven."

Heidi nodded. "Good one. He was a little preachy about the booze, though."

"It doesn't matter. He's Cary Grant." Rue crossed her arms. "You?"

"Mine's easy, too. William Powell, *The Thin Man*, Nick Charles."

Rue made a buzzer sound. "He's married."

"So? He's fiction! I mean, this is all hypothetical."

"And you want to be a hypothetical home wrecker? Busting up Myrna Loy's marriage? I don't think so. Try again."

Under pressure now, Heidi choked.

"This was your question," Rue reminded her.

"I didn't know you were going to disqualify my dream date!" Her face tensed in concentration. "Oh, okay, I've got it. Paul Newman. *Hud*."

"*For a date?*" Rue asked. "He's a rapist!"

Heidi frowned. "Oh. Yeah, he is, but . . ."

She murmured something under her breath about him being extremely good-looking, which left Rue shaking her head. "He made other movies. Didn't you like him in anything else?"

"Okay! Got it! Butch Cassidy."

"He was a *bank robber.*"

Heidi sagged against the steering wheel again. "Fast Eddie?"

"I think we could be zeroing in on your problem," Rue told her.

Dinner was on the table when they finally arrived home. Unfortunately, Laura had been busy in the kitchen. She'd concocted her new specialty: whatever's-in-the-refrigerator pilaf. The dish's one benefit was that it was easier to shove around a plate than whatever's-in-the-refrigerator soup. The pilaf was wild rice mixed with chunks of canned salmon, cooked cabbage, pecans, and something that on closer inspection turned out to be dried apricots. Rue spied Erica maneuvering a pile of it under a slice of the wheat bread Laura had set out "to fill in the cracks." Then she took two more pieces of bread and quickly gulped them down.

Heidi followed her example.

At least Rue could claim nausea as an excuse, but even so, Laura looked a little hurt. "I put the salmon chunks in for you. It's good for you."

Rue nodded. "I know. I'll probably get up in the middle of the night and gulp down whatever's left over in the fridge, but right now I'm just wiped out. The day did me in."

"The chemo hitting you already?" asked Laura.

Rue shook her head. "They wouldn't give it to me. My blood tests all came out subpar. I'm anemic *and* I have a white blood cell deficiency."

"Oh." Laura frowned at the tablecloth, thinking this through. "Y'all didn't get home till late."

"We went to a movie," Heidi explained.

"What movie?" Erica asked.

"You would have hated it," Rue said. "It was in German."

Erica wrinkled up her nose. "Why?"

"Probably because it had German people in it," Webb said dryly.

Erica did not appreciate the joke. "I meant, why would you go see a movie in German? There's all sorts of good stuff out now. I wish I could go see PG-thirteen movies. The boys at the pool all do already."

"We were trying to find the one movie in the multiplex that no one would want to go see," Rue explained. "And we found it. We had the whole theater to ourselves."

"It was like having a private screening room," Heidi said. "No one talking or crinkling candy wrappers."

"Or checking messages on their cell phones," Rue said.

Webb grinned. "It's nice to know you're just as finicky about movie-watching behavior in public theaters as you are in your own home, Rue."

The determined way in which Laura was shoveling down pilaf indicated that a disturbance was brewing. "Was that smart?" she finally asked.

"What?" said Rue.

"Going to the movies when your white blood cell count was low. It means you're immuno depressed. What if you catch a cold and it turns to pneumonia?"

Rue put her piece of bread down. "Maybe I shouldn't have gone, but it was a spur-of-the-moment thing."

Laura sniffed. "With Heidi egging you on."

"I didn't egg!" Heidi protested.

Webb got up and cleared a few plates.

Erica's eyes were as big as saucers as she stared from Laura to Rue. Rue wanted to take her sister by the neck and shake her. Maybe she had been a little irresponsible, but where did Laura get off lecturing her and worrying Erica this way?

Heidi stepped up to their defense again. "We'd driven all that way, and Rue looked tired."

"Tired!" Laura huffed out an indignant laugh. "You should

have just brought her home. Didn't you see her? She was too exhausted to eat."

Heidi could barely hold back. "Hmm, there seemed to be a lot of exhausted people at the table tonight."

Laura squinted. "What do you mean?"

"I mean *nobody* wanted to eat your stinkin' pilaf. Talk about a health hazard!"

Laura was so angry, she looked like she just might levitate. "If I'm going to go to the trouble to cook, I don't want to be insulted."

"Then don't cook," Heidi retorted.

"I won't!" Laura stood up, and for a moment Rue worried that she might do something drastic and theatrical, like yank the tablecloth off the table with all the dishes still on it. Instead, she lifted her chin, stomped out of the dining room, and kept going out the side door. It banged behind her.

"I always rise to the bait," Heidi said, slumping in her chair. "I'm sorry, Rue."

"Don't be. I had a good day, and I'd expected to have an awful one."

"Yeah," Erica chimed in. "Don't be sorry. Thanks to you, we'll never have to eat whatever's-in-the-refrigerator anything ever again!"

Rue, Heidi, and Webb looked at one another and laughed.

Scones were a bone of contention between Rue and Heidi. No other bread caused so much discord. About biscuits, they were in complete agreement. Corn bread, they both allowed, should have a slightly rough texture and no sugar. Muffins were a nobrainer; muffins practically begged for improvisation. But on the question of scones, the daggers were drawn.

Heidi was an enemy of the scone. "They're nasty."

"Not if they're good," Rue insisted.

"But they never are good," Heidi said. "Almost never. They're the stale things you find bandaged in Saran Wrap at the deli next to the cash register. Desiccated triangular biscuits with currants or"—here she shivered—"or even chocolate chips embedded in them."

"Chocolate chips sound good," Erica interjected. She was perched in one of the kitchen chairs, painting her toenails. The scent of the polish was sharp and slightly nauseating to Rue.

"Why do we even need scones?" Heidi asked.

"Because people *like* them," said Rue.

"Masochists."

"They expect them."

"Then we'll surprise them by *not* having them."

"Y'all should flip a coin," Erica said, carefully dabbing pink lacquer onto her little toe. " 'Cause it really doesn't sound like you'll ever agree."

The tart chemical scent of nail polish floated Rue's way. She put her head in her hands and breathed deeply through her mouth for a moment.

"Rue?" Heidi jumped out of her chair. "Rue, are you all right?"

Rue nodded. God, she hated this.

"Do you need a drink of water?" Heidi asked.

Rue lifted her head again and leaned back, still trying to breathe through her mouth. It was just a sensory thing. She could get over it. *Mind over matter.*

Erica's eyes bugged out in panic, and the fear Rue saw there was like a knife in her heart. People watching her, hovering, walking on eggshells. Irritation bubbled up in her.

"Do you have to do that in the kitchen?" she asked.

Erica glanced over at the nail polish and dumped over the little bottle in her hurry to put the cap on. "Sorry." She leapt for a roll of paper towels and started mopping up the mess.

"I don't see why you're painting your toenails, anyway. You never did before," Rue pointed out.

"Because Maggie and I wanted to go to the pool tomorrow and hang out."

"You can't swim with normal toenails?" asked Rue.

"Maggie always paints hers." Erica frowned. "I don't see why it should be a big deal."

"It wouldn't be if you'd put it on where I can't smell it."

"Sorry," Erica said. "Is it okay if I do it in the living room?"

Rue nodded, and Erica gathered her things and stomped away.

Guilt pierced Rue. Lately, she'd been lashing out over the stupidest things.

Heidi studied her for a long moment, and Rue could feel red rising in her cheeks. She'd been irritable and irrational. It had nothing to do with anything anyone was doing—it was just that she didn't feel well. Having other people buzzing around, doing business as usual, was hard to bear sometimes. But that was no excuse.

"I'm sorry," Rue said, even though she was saying it to Heidi when she should have been apologizing to Erica.

"That wasn't a pity ploy to get me to agree to the scones, was it?"

Rue laughed. "No."

"Because I'm standing firm on this point."

"Me too."

"We're at a standoff, then." Heidi frowned. "Maybe we really should flip a coin."

"I'm willing." Rue started digging in her shorts for a quarter but couldn't find one. Laura came in from the side of the house, holding Fred under one arm and her cell phone in the opposite hand. Something was obviously on her mind, but Rue stopped her before she could get a word out. "Do you have any change?"

"Not on me." Laura stopped, wrinkling her nose. "Jesus Pete, are you guys putting nail polish in the soup or something? The smell in here could gag a moose."

"I might have a quarter," Heidi said. She began digging in her pockets. The shorts she had on had about a dozen.

Laura looked at her with just a passing disdain. "Is there a reason for all those pockets?"

"Is there a reason you have a chicken attached to your hip?" Heidi retorted.

"I like to keep him close in case I need a quick dinner idea."

"You are despicable!"

Laura sucked in a breath. "Oh, but I forgot! I'm not cooking anymore." Not waiting for Heidi's reaction, she turned to Rue. "Troubling news. We just got a call from Leanne Dench. She wanted to know when she could come over."

"Over here?" Rue asked. "Why?"

"Something about food and her wedding. I told her she was nuts, but she insisted you would know what she was talking about."

Rue gaped at her. "But I don't."

"Maybe you should call her," Heidi said.

"Or maybe we could just ignore her and hope that she goes away," Laura suggested. "I'll do a better job screening my calls."

"But she must have had some reason to call," Rue said, although it was a strain to figure out what that could be. Suddenly she caught sight of Erica hovering in the doorway, darting sheepish glances from one of them to the other. "Erica?" she asked, cuing her.

In a rush, Erica confessed. "Okay, the thing is, Ms. Dench wants you to cater her wedding, and I forgot to mention it. I'm really sorry."

Laura repeated the words slowly. "Cater. Her. Wedding."

"*Us?*" Heidi asked.

"She said she thought it would be good for you all—since the guests are all gone." Erica swallowed. "As long as it doesn't cost too much. She doesn't want to spend much money."

"Just what anyone is looking for in a client," Laura said. "A patronizing cheapskate."

"When did she tell you this?" Rue asked. *And how can we cut her off at the pass?*

Erica shifted her feet and concentrated on the floor. "Um . . . a few days ago?"

"And you just forgot to mention it?" Laura's voice looped up a notch. Anyone would have thought that *she* was on the hook here. "For a few days?"

Erica lifted her chin. "I've been busy."

"Right. Hanging out with that Robichaux kid," said Laura.

"What's wrong with Maggie?" Erica asked.

"She seems like one of those mean girls to me," Laura said.

Heidi hooted with laughter. "What is this? An irony refresher course?"

"Maggie's my friend!"`

"Okay, okay," Rue said, trying to calm them all down. "This isn't about Maggie. It's about what we're going to say to Leanne."

Heidi gaped at her. "We're going to say no, surely."

"Why?" Laura asked.

Both Rue and Heidi swung around to gape at her, astonished.

"Because, as you would say, this is a farm, not a catering company," Heidi explained, as if she couldn't quite believe she was having to point this out to Laura, of all people.

"Still afraid of rolling up your sleeves?" Laura taunted her. "Can't take a little pressure?"

"It would be a lot of work," Rue said.

Heidi slanted a perplexed look up at Laura, who was casting an especially pointed glare back at her. A glare that said that the consequences for crossing her would be dire. "I guess it would give us an opportunity to give some of our recipes a trial run. . . ."

"Exactly," Laura said.

Rue shook her head. "A good opportunity to have a nervous breakdown."

Laura grunted. "Well, do what you want. I've said my piece."

When Laura was gone, Erica came forward and sank down into the chair next to Rue. "I'm sorry, Mom. I totally forgot about Ms. Dench."

Rue leaned forward and gave her a squeeze, which was all Erica would put up with these days when there were other people around. "It's okay."

"I didn't think you'd be interested, anyway," Erica added.

"Why not? The more I think about it, the more it seems like a good idea," Heidi said.

Rue turned to her in surprise. "You do?"

"Who knows, we could even transform this into a real gig. A paying concern. It might just be what I've been looking for."

"The Sassy Spinster Catering Company," Rue said, mulling it over. "I don't feel prepared. Or qualified."

"Welcome to my world," Heidi said.

"But you don't want to get involved with Ms. Dench, do you?" Erica asked, looking at one and then the other. "I mean . . . yuck."

"Just making some food for her wedding wouldn't make us all best friends," Rue pointed out.

"I know, but . . ." Erica's leg jogged nervously. "But what if something goes wrong?"

"Like what?" Heidi asked.

Erica bit her lip. "Well . . . for instance, what if the wedding doesn't actually happen?"

Rue had been a little nervous ever since Leanne had declared her intention to have Erica involved in the wedding. Once or twice she'd bolted up in the middle of the night, awakened by nightmares of wedding sabotage. Honey on the vestry floor. Frogs in punch bowls. Now she worried that Erica had more ambitious dreams. "Why would you say that? It's less than a month away."

Erica sighed. "People call off weddings, don't they? I mean, you see it all the time on television. I heard Webb's wedding to Denise was canceled at the last minute the first time he was supposed to marry her."

"Who told you that?" Rue asked.

Erica shrugged. "I just heard. And Ms. Dench is so hard to deal with. I'm sure you don't want to be around her. I know I don't."

"I thought maybe you'd gotten over that," Rue said. "You've been spending more time over there."

"That's just because of Maggie," Erica said.

"Maggie likes Leanne?" asked Rue.

"Gosh no. She just . . ." Erica swallowed. "She thinks Ms. Dench is funny."

Rue began to wonder if Laura wasn't right about Maggie. "You know, if you don't like people, you really aren't supposed to hang around them just to laugh at them."

"I know," Erica said. "So . . . if you decide to cater the wedding and if for some reason the wedding *doesn't* come off, then would you still get paid?"

"I'm not sure. I suppose so . . . if the food had been delivered," said Rue.

Erica frowned. "And how far in advance would you prepare everything?"

Rue exchanged a puzzled glance with Heidi. "That would depend. But most of it would probably get done the day of and the day before."

"So it would really only be a complete waste of your time if the wedding were called off on the day it was supposed to happen, or maybe the day before. Right?"

Rue began to worry that Erica was building herself up for a letdown. "Erica, I know you don't like Leanne, but you can't live in a dream world. Weddings get called off at the last minute in movies, and occasionally in real life, too, but chances are that in August your father and Leanne are going to tie the knot. Sitting around hoping for everything to fall apart at the last minute isn't generous. It's not healthy, either."

Erica shrugged and stood up to leave. "I was just worried about you guys."

Rue watched her daughter stalk out of the room. "Please tell me I'm wrong to wonder if there's arsenic in Leanne Dench's future."

"You're wrong." Heidi drummed her fingers on the table. "I think we could do this. I really do."

"I'm not so sure. Leanne might just be putting out feelers, anyway. Why on earth would she want to hire us?"

"Why not us?"

Rue tilted her head and studied Heidi for a moment. Her face was tensed in concentration, as if she were already preoccupied with the details of the Dench-Anderson wedding.

"Because I'm the ex-wife of her husband-to-be?" Rue reminded her.

The words didn't seem to penetrate. "We should have a menu

plan drawn up when she comes over. Do you think she'd want us to do the cake?"

Rue laughed. "I don't think she'll want us to do anything, really."

"O ye of little faith."

The statement struck Rue as particularly on target. It wasn't that she didn't have faith in their abilities; she didn't have faith that in a month she would still feel up to giving her life over to hors d'oeuvres and finger sandwiches. She wasn't entirely sure she was up to it now. But a month from now . . . where would she be?

Heidi felt herself being drawn deeper and deeper into life on the farm. She'd already been keeping the kitchen going for Rue, and doing the inserts and baked goods for the CSA boxes, and noodling around with the cookbook idea in her spare time. Now there was the wedding, which had pushed the Sassy Spinster Farm cookbook to the back burner.

At the same time, New York just wouldn't let her go. She had ignored several messages from the office of Hamilton Cho. In fact, she had taken to setting her phone to vibrate and stuffing it into a drawer in a table by her bed in order to avoid being plagued further by that man and his office minions.

Then she received an envelope in the mail with the seal of New York on it. She was glad she herself had picked up the mail that day. This was definitely a letter to open in private. She deposited everyone else's mail on the dining-room table and scurried upstairs to the room she'd moved into after all the guests had left.

The letter was dated July 14.

Dear Ms. Bogue:

Regarding and in respect to this office's repeated calls to you, none of which you have returned or acknowledged, I am again respectfully yet urgently requesting your cooperation in a matter of utmost importance, viz: potential evidence in People of the State of New York v. Vincent Cavenna. *Ab initio, certain individuals*

*interviewed in this matter have indicated that you have informa-
tion and perhaps documentation arrogated in the course of your
serving in an administrative capacity to Mr. Cavenna. At this
point in time, I believe I need not elucidate or elaborate as to why
your assistance in providing the putative information and documentation would be beneficial to the State.*

*Furthermore, I feel bound to caution you that in the event that
your contumacious behavior continues, additional action on the
part of the State (e.g., subpoena duces tecum and/or subpoena ad
testificandum) must and will be taken to compel you to disgorge
pertinent material documentation and information you may pos-
sess or have knowledge of.*

*In other words, Ms. Bogue, if you have any evidence shedding
light on alleged criminal activities of the above-mentioned
Mr. Cavenna, it is incumbent upon you to produce said evidence
forthwith, pursuant to New York General Business Law § 352(2).
Respectfully,
Hamilton I. Cho
Assistant District Attorney
P.S.: While you may not have been aware of the necessity of provid-
ing the information described supra in this letter, I'm sure you
agree that* ignorantia facti excusat, ignorantia juris non ex-
cusat.
—*HIC*

Rereading the letter, Heidi began to tremble. The Latin in
particular struck fear in her heart. She had no idea what any of it
meant—except that she was marked for persecution. She envi-
sioned herself being hunted all her life like that poor slob in *Les
Miserables* . . . except her tormenter would hound her in legalese
and words she hadn't seen since taking the SAT. Hamilton I. Cho
woud not rest until she had disgorged.

What should she do? She could mail him her evidence, but she
worried that that would just be like tossing chum to the sharks,
and that lawyers would start circling her in earnest. They would

want her to come back to New York to testify. And if the prose-
cution used the evidence, wouldn't the defense have to see it,
too? Wouldn't they have the right to question her before trial?

How had Hamilton Cho found her address in the first place?

She didn't have to ponder that question overly long. She dug
her phone out of its drawer and dialed her mother's number.

"Did I, or did I not, ask you not to tell anyone where I am?"
Heidi asked as soon as her mother picked up.

"I haven't told anyone."

"So you've never told my whereabouts to a person named
Hamilton Cho?"

"Oh!" Her mother chuckled. "Well, yeah. Of course."

"What do you mean, *of course?*"

"I mean he's on our side, isn't he?"

"I'm not even sure I want to take sides. I don't want to be involved at all."

"You would if you saw him. He's really quite a good-looking
man, Heidi. He's got a little salt and pepper going on. I always
think that looks distinguished. And do you know how much
lawyers make?"

As if Hamilton Cho, a man who used words like *contumacious*
and *forthwith*, was interested in romance. "What worries me is,
who else have you told?"

"Nobody. Just those two."

"*Two?*"

"Mr. Cho and the other man from his office."

Heidi started breathing again. She probably meant that Max
Warren guy, who had left her messages.

"Don't tell anyone else, Mom. Not another soul."

"Of course I won't. Who else is there to tell?"

Heidi sighed.

"When are you coming home?" Marla asked.

"I don't know. I have a job here now. I'm catering a wedding."

"Back to waitressing?"

"Rue and I are the caterers, Mom. We're cooking."

"Someone *hired* you?"

Heidi laughed. "No, we're just going to show up at some random wedding with a vanload of food."

A moment of dead air crackled over the line. "You need to get out of there. You're getting as unpleasant as Laura."

When Heidi hung up, she wondered if she would ever get out. Or where she would go when she did. She didn't miss New York like she would have expected. Of course, the fact that she had spent her last days there in terror might have something to do with that fact. But while she didn't feel quite rooted in Sweetgum, it was beginning to feel more like home than any other place had seemed in a long time.

She took Hamilton Cho's letter and tore it into tiny little pieces. And then she tried to forget all about it. Forthwith.

Chapter 19

During the movie that night, *Sabrina*, a horrifying realization struck Laura: She really missed the guests. Really. When the troops of strange women had been in the house, they had seemed like a plague. But she had become accustomed to being entertained by their irritating presence. They had been the other, the enemy, the outsiders. Now, as she sat in an armchair in the corner of the living room while Rue and Erica lay on the couch, with Erica snoozing away, and Heidi and Webb stretched out on the carpet, having a silently flirtatious mock battle over a bowl of popcorn, who was it who didn't belong?

The movie wasn't helping. Why did Rue never put Westerns or action pictures on her Netflix list? This one had the imprimatur of a charming old classic, meaning she was supposed to love it, which only made her more critical of its flaws. Which were legion. For one thing, who believed William Holden as a blond? And Humphrey Bogart! God knows she loved him—she would have given her left eyeball to be watching *The Maltese Falcon*—but next to Audrey Hepburn, the man was clearly AARP material. It gave her the same creepy feeling she'd had when she'd watched *Funny Face*, which featured Audrey Hepburn and an ancient Fred Astaire. Or watching Hepburn sip Geritol cocktails with Gary Cooper in *Love in the Afternoon*. Even Cary Grant in *Charade* had been reaching the expiration date of his professional shelf life.

"Is there an Audrey Hepburn movie where she isn't blinking those doe eyes of hers at some poor guy who looks like he's ready for the actors' retirement home?" she blurted out. "It's like she tries to seem more gamine-like by positioning herself next to old men."

Curt responses ping-ponged between Heidi and Rue.

"Roman Holiday."

"Two for the Road."

"The Nun's Story."

Laura grunted at the last effort to shoot down her theory. "Any nun is up against the world's oldest leading man."

Webb chuckled, but Heidi and Rue only flicked annoyed glances at her before turning their attention back to the screen.

Laura tried; she really did. Her favorite scenes were the glimpses of the kitchen, which featured both Grandma Walton and Miss Jane Hathaway from *The Beverly Hillbillies*, one of the best shows ever, in her opinion. She won no goodwill for pointing out this rare intersection of TV talent to the others, though.

"Shh!"

Laura sighed and thought about the guests again. She missed the presence of other people who could absorb her irritations. The guests had been her hostility sponge. Who would have guessed that being surrounded only by people you liked would be so irksome? Heidi was still here, of course, but she was being treated like visiting royalty. Say a cross word to Heidi and it was as if you had spat on Mother Theresa. She'd even won over Erica.

She tried to focus on Audrey Hepburn, who was spinning in an office chair and looking adorable. All at once it was just too much.

"My God, she's nauseating," she blurted out.

Three heads snapped toward her. The comment even seemed to rouse Erica.

"What?" Heidi asked.

Laura gestured toward the screen. "C'mon, the woman's revoltingly cutesy. She's all pixie haircut and fake smile and big, blinky eyes, and that voice of hers is really grating."

"*What?*" Heidi repeated.

"She enunciates every line like she's practiced it for maximum adorableness. It's so phony."

While Heidi gawked and gasped like a beached fish, Rue grabbed the remote and froze the screen. Unfortunately, it froze on a close-up of Audrey's precious doe-eyed face.

"See?" Laura asked, gesticulating.

"You are a monster," Heidi said.

"Why? For pointing out the obvious?"

Rue rounded on her. "You need to leave now."

Laura laughed. "Are you giving me a time-out?"

"No, I'm banishing you. Forever. You are no longer welcome in this room during movie time."

Laura gaped at her. "You can't be serious! Is this Castro's Cuba? I was just expressing an opinion."

"You were *talking* during the movie, which is bad enough. But worse yet, you were just trying to get a rise out of us."

"No, I wasn't," Laura argued. "I just *really* don't like Audrey Hepburn. I'm sorry. I just don't."

"Monster," Heidi muttered.

"Go," Rue said.

"Fine." Laura jumped to her feet. "I was just watching the damn thing to be sociable."

Webb chuckled.

Laura glowered at him. *Traitor.* Even Erica, who should have been sticking up for her, seemed more interested in burrowing into the couch and finishing her nap. What was happening to the world?

Rue shot her an impatient look. "Do you mind? We'd like to finish the movie."

Apparently no one—and here Laura couldn't help darting a pointed look at Webb—was going to play the Audrey hater's advocate. It was difficult to exit a room with dignity after you'd been verbally tossed out of it, but Laura did her best to hold her head high.

"Monster," Heidi repeated when Laura stalked past.

"Suck-up," Laura hissed under her breath.

Once she was out of the room, she kept going out the front door. She was ready to plop onto a rocking chair when the sounds of dog paws against screening beckoned her. She'd always liked it better out in the open, anyway. The screening had been Rue's idea, to have an outside sanctuary that was somewhat free from bugs. But Laura wasn't sure she didn't prefer to stretch out on the steps leading down from the porch and stare up at the constellations while Monte and Shelley Winters used her legs as a snout prop.

Her heart was still jackhammering away, even as her anger began to lose focus and double back on her. What had riled her up? She didn't give a damn about Audrey Hepburn. And now she'd acted like an idiot and been expelled from movie time, which was one of the few times she and Rue relaxed together. Of course, with the movie going and everyone else around, it wasn't very intimate, but she hardly ever got to see Rue without Heidi anymore.

Rue obviously preferred Heidi's company to hers.

And given the fact that she couldn't keep her trap shut for the running time of a movie, who could blame Rue for that?

What was wrong with her? It was as if she was missing the gene for sustaining any kind of intimacy with people. She always had to blow her stack at the wrong moment, or needle someone, or shoot her mouth off. Psychiatrists probably had a name for her defect, and therapy for it no doubt involved a gruesome combination of padded cells, getting in touch with one's inner child, and looms.

She closed her eyes, trying to imagine herself some other way. Maybe if she could see herself as one of those sunshine-and-lollipops kind of people, she could become one. Even though the thought nauseated her. Did creative visualization have a prayer when the thing you were visualizing made you want to spew chunks?

Probably not.

She sighed and kept her eyes closed, anyway, just because it felt good. She hadn't realized how tired she was. The day had been a broiler, and she had been out in it since morning. They were starting to turn over some of the finished patches of the garden, getting it ready to either be fallow or to rotate in the winter crops. The only thing that kept her awake at all was the intermittent sound of Monte smacking his chops in anticipation of nodding off.

After a while she heard people coming out onto the porch. Heidi and Webb. Of course.

"She looked tired," Webb said.

"She's always tired, I think. She just hides it well. I think she doesn't want to miss out on things."

"I can see that."

"So can I," Heidi said. "But I don't think I'd have the fiber to keep going like Rue does."

No kidding, thought Laura.

"I worried about Erica," Webb said, "but she seems to be handling everything okay."

"I think she's entered the teen zone. She spends so much time with her friend Maggie, but Rue doesn't mind. She's just happy that Erica has a social life going—one that doesn't involve the farm."

"What, Herman, Dylan, and I don't rate as companions?"

"Herman and Dylan are okay."

Webb laughed and a moment of silence followed. Laura tensed, wondering what was going on just above her head. And if she should make herself known. Of course, they might wonder why she hadn't spoken up before.

"You might not believe it, but the one around here I'm really worried about is Laura."

Heidi's words made Laura's eyes pop open.

"You're right. I don't believe it."

Me neither.

"Seriously, she's racing right past cranky and is fast approaching the gargoylehood. I mean—Audrey Hepburn? Honestly!"

"Not everybody likes old movies," Webb said.

Thank you! Finally! He hadn't been in any big damned hurry to defend her when she was under attack, though.

"But . . ." Heidi sighed. "Okay, it's not just the fact that she's a gargoyle that's bugging me. I've always known that. I guess I never realized how pathetic she was. That's it. She's pathetic. A pathetic gargoyle." There was a slight hesitation before Heidi began again. "This morning we found out Leanne Dench is thinking about asking us to cater her wedding."

"Good Lord."

"That's what I said. But Laura, of all people, seemed to think it was a great idea! I could tell she thought it would be another way for Rue to try to keep her mind off the cancer."

"What did you say?"

"Well, what could I say? Laura shot me one of those contradict-me-and-die looks, so I did a one-eighty and agreed with her. I'm not a complete fool."

"Maybe Laura's right about catering the wedding," Webb said. "Could bring in a little money."

"She wasn't thinking about money. All I saw in her eyes was denial. She thinks that if Rue keeps baking muffins and coming up with squash recipes, she'll live forever."

"I doubt that. Laura knows Rue better than anyone, and she's not blind. She can see how things are."

"This might be one of those cases where the things we're closest to are the hardest to see changing. Anyway, I get the feeling Laura thinks she can pull Rue through this on sheer willpower. *Her* willpower."

"If anyone could, it would be Laura."

For a moment there was no sound from the porch but rockers rolling against the floorboards.

"It's a funny thing," Heidi said. "I started out the summer disliking Laura."

"And now?"

"Now I still dislike her."

Same here. Laura felt like hopping up and announcing herself. She would have loved to see the looks on their faces. But her limbs had gone noodly on her, and her thoughts weren't clear. Where did they get off talking about her and Rue this way? What the hell did they know?

"But I feel sorry for her, too," Heidi continued. "I think when it finally dawns on her, the truth is going to devastate her."

"She's tough."

"Not when it comes to Rue. I remember right before Mom and I cut out, just after the car accident. We went to the hospital once. Mr. Rafferty was okay—he just had an extra belt of Johnnie Walker on his way over—but Laura was coming apart at the seams. I'll never forget her face. Chalk white skin and eyes that made her look like something hunted.

"I thought at first that she was scared of the trouble she would be in for taking Mom's car and wrecking it. But as I was sitting next to her, she whispered something in an awful voice. It sounded like her heart was being torn out of her. She didn't want to confide in me. She just couldn't keep the words in. She said she wished *she* had died in the accident—and I believed her. It wasn't getting in trouble with her dad that scared her, and I don't think it was even guilt. It was a life without her sister that terrified her. It was staring into a future without Rue."

Another moment passed when the only sounds were those of the night, the gentle rolling crunch of rocking chairs, and the erratic thump of Laura's heart. Her eyes stung, and she gulped in breaths. Of course she'd been terrified. She'd thought she'd killed her sister.

"She's no more ready to face that future now than she was then," Heidi said.

What the hell are they talking about? They were writing Rue off as if it was all over, as if there was no hope at all. As if they thought Rue should pack it in.

"She's an old hand at denial," Webb said. "Maybe she won't figure out how things are till . . . well, for as long as possible."

"You act as if that would be a good thing."

"I don't want to see that look in her eyes that you described. I don't know if I could take it."

Heidi sighed. "It's no wonder I get nowhere with you. You're a lost soul."

"I'm snapping out of it. I'm even beginning to be glad it's hopeless. I must have been insane to come here."

"So you started out the summer madly in love with Laura, and now . . ."

"Now I guess I'm like you. I feel sorry for her."

Heidi yawned. "Well . . . she'll always have Fred the chicken."

"Till she kills him."

They laughed.

Thanks, old friend.

"I'd better go home," Webb said. "I want to get stuff done early tomorrow. It's supposed to be a scorcher."

"And what was today?" Heidi asked. "Ninety-eight degrees doesn't qualify?"

Laura was too busy scrambling away to hear the reply. She dove behind the rose of Sharon tree next to the porch. When she squatted down, her hand touched something slimy on the ground.

"What was that?" Heidi asked.

"The dogs, probably. Shelley Winters likes to hide the newly dead things she catches behind the rose of Sharon."

Laura closed her eyes and tried to keep her gag reflex in check.

"Think I'll go out through the house," Webb said.

The door opened and shut, and Laura crawled out from behind the tree, wiping her hand on her jeans.

Instead of going inside, though, she lay back down on the porch steps. The boards poking against her back felt just right at the moment. Her own bed of nails.

She looked up and the stars started to blur. *Screw them,* she thought. *Screw their pity.* They had no idea what was going on. They knew nothing about her or Rue. They hadn't seen Rue last fall and how sick she was then. They didn't know what a strong person like Rue could survive. But she knew.

She also knew that after Heidi and her mother had skedaddled, she had pulled herself out of her funk and been there for Rue during her long recovery. She would be there this time, too, after Heidi and Webb were gone.

"I'd like to have a sit-down dinner for my reception—that's what my cousin who lives in Houston had—but I think that would be just a little too formal for the reception hall at the Methodist church. I don't want to look like I'm putting on airs.

"But, of course, I don't want to look like I'm being stingy, either. So I'm thinking buffet, but a *really nice* buffet. That would have the added benefit of saving on tons and tons of serving staff, too. I don't mind telling you right up front, I'm not one of those money-is-no-object girls. And I'm not one of those bridezillas you hear about, either. I want this to be a low-stress, enjoyable event for all my friends and family. Well—it's really for the whole Sweetgum community, isn't it? I know everybody, and practically everyone's invited."

Laura, who had been lurking by the pantry door, took a long swig from her iced-tea bottle and then wiped her mouth with her T-shirt sleeve. "Our invitation must have gotten lost in the mail."

Leanne's startled eyes panned from Rue to Heidi and then back again. Nervous laughter wheezed out of her. "I didn't mean I invited *every single person* in the phone book."

Rue wrinkled her nose at Laura before returning her respectful gaze to their potential client. "Of course your wedding is going to be an event. You're a very popular teacher. That's a big deal around here."

"Just imagine if you were marrying the football coach," Laura said dryly. "That'd really get the dogs out from under the porch!"

Smiles of varying degrees of civility/hostility darted Laura's way before the three women turned back to the matter at hand, although Rue couldn't help shooting her another warning glance. What was Laura thinking? She had wanted them to talk to Leanne Dench, and now here Leanne Dench sat in their kitchen, and Laura couldn't stop oozing sarcasm.

Laura lifted her shoulders in an "I just can't help myself" gesture before pushing off through the back door. When she was gone, Rue breathed a sigh of relief, if only momentarily.

Leanne Dench had decided ideas about catering, and she wasn't going to be selfish and keep them to herself. "My biggest belief about something like this is that it should appear gracious. But I want to emphasize quality, not quantity. There should be an appearance of abundance, but not excess."

Rue held a pen poised over a yellow legal pad, but so far all that was written was "Methodist church." "If we could get some specifics . . ."

"The reason I thought of coming here was that I want the thing to seem homey, not fussy. You know, a down-home, farmy feel. Not that I don't want style, too. I do expect a little pizzazz." Leanne stared unblinking from one to the other. "Y'all can do that, can't you?"

Heidi tilted her head. "Do what?"

"Pizzazz," said Leanne.

"We can certainly . . ." Rue frowned. "What do you mean by pizzazz, exactly?"

"Well . . . like the things in magazines," Leanne explained. "For instance, I saw this adorable Maine wedding, where they had lobster, of course, and also these miniature metal pails full of blueberries at every place setting. The little buckets I thought were a great touch. I thought that would be awesome, only with something more Texasy."

Rue couldn't think of a response, so she nodded and wrote, "Little bucket substitutes?"

Heidi looked perplexed. "Buckets aren't Texasy? There seem to be a lot of them around here."

The look Leanne sent Heidi made Rue remember what it had

been like watching classmates being sent to the principal's office. "It doesn't matter if a bucket is Texasy or not. The bucket idea isn't exactly original now, is it? Not once it's been in a magazine. What I want is something similar to little buckets, but completely different." She allowed that desire to hang in the air before continuing. "As another example, I saw this other caterer who made these itsy cracker sandwiches with tiny square crackers like Wheat Thins . . . although I suppose you could use any kind of cracker, really. Even a rice cracker. The chef had sliced smoked salmon very thin and put it and a piece of cheese between two crackers, and then wrapped chives around the crackers like a ribbon. They looked like little bitty presents. Isn't that cute?"

"Crackers . . . chives . . . pizzazz . . . ," wrote Rue.

While Rue scribbled, Heidi asked, "Is that another similar but different idea?"

"No, that's the sort of thing you could just flat-out copy."

"We would be relying heavily on food that's in season, from the farm," Rue told her. "Unless you have a specific food request."

"I'm very flexible," Leanne assured them.

"So there probably wouldn't be stuff like smoked salmon. . . ."

"Wait a second." Leanne frowned. "Really?"

"Unless there was something you specifically wanted," Heidi added. "We're flexible, too."

"What about the wedding cake?" Rue asked.

"Oh! I've ordered the big bride's cake," Leanne said. "Practically busted my budget on the thing, to tell you the truth, but I will need you to make the groom's cake. Chocolate, of course, and no more than three layers."

"Don't want the groom to overshadow the bride," Heidi joked.

"No worries there." Leanne raised a brow at her. "It's the cost I'm worried about."

Rue looked up. "Speaking of cost . . ."

Leanne cut her off. "You can give me an estimate. Though I

should warn you, I'm not paying a penny over two hundred and fifty dollars."

Heidi darted a quick glance Rue's way. "And how many people?"

"About eighty to a hundred," Leanne said.

Rue put down her pen. "Leanne, that comes out to two dollars and fifty cents a head! That's bologna sandwich and Kool-Aid territory."

"Well, as I said, I'm flexible. I'm sure you'll do your best." Leanne stood up. "Though I'm not going to pay one penny above three hundred dollars. It's just a buffet, for heaven's sake. What do people expect to eat at Sweetgum United Methodist? Filet mignon?"

When she was gone, Rue and Heidi wandered back into the kitchen and sank back into their chairs. Heidi propped her elbows on the table and dropped her head into her hands. "I have a bad feeling about this."

Even though Heidi wasn't looking, Rue shrugged. "I guess there's no harm in giving her an estimate."

"There would be if she accepted it." Heidi looked up at her. "The woman wants pizzazz and little cracker sandwiches with herb bows, and she wants us to do it practically pro bono."

"Everyone in town's going to be at that wedding. If you seriously wanted to pursue this, then this would be a good launch-pad."

"Or a good place to flame out if we screw up."

"We wouldn't screw up. What could go wrong?"

"That's a dangerous question to ask when I'm around," Heidi said.

Laura spotted Leanne Dench walking to her car and decided that, for the sake of Rue and Heidi's business, she should try to schmooze a little, God help her.

She ambled across the yard. "Hey, Leanne. Leaving so soon?"

Leanne dropped her big purse on the Ford's hood and started digging through it. Her movements were jerky, agitated. It wasn't until Laura looked at those big eyes of hers that she noticed that Leanne was crying.

"Heidi's recipes upset you that much?" Laura asked her.

Leanne pulled out a Kleenex from a purse pack and flapped it open. Her words were hard to make out at first, since she was blowing her nose and talking at the same time. Coherence was also an issue. "I was just so surprised . . . it had only been a month or so . . . and . . ." She gulped in a breath. "I wasn't expecting . . . Bless her heart!"

Laura began to understand. "It's the chemo. The last round made her so sick, she didn't want to eat."

Leanne kept blowing and folding her Kleenex until there was just a little postage-stamp-size area of virgin tissue for her to aim at. "I knew she was sick, of course. I just had no idea how bad it was."

"She's feeling better," Laura said, with growing irritation. "She went through this last year, too. That's what happens with cancer. If they catch it in time, it's not even the cancer that makes a person sick. It's the radiation or the chemo."

Leanne nodded. "I know, but . . ."

"I certainly hope you waited until you were out of the house to start blubbering," Laura said. "Did you all get around to talking about the wedding plans at all?"

"Of course!" Leanne sniffed. "I'm not tactless. I was very businesslike. It's not like I'm asking all that much. It's just a buffet. And a cake. But then there was Rue, just as thin as a straight pin, and every time she wrote something down, the veins in her wrists and the tops of her hands looked like they were going to pop through her skin. And so I tried not to look at her hands at all, but then, when I looked in that beautiful old scarred face of hers, I started noticing that she has to paint her eyebrows on now. And she'd painted right through the scar where her real eyebrow was broken up." She started tearing up again.

The urge to grab Leanne by the shoulders and give her a shake was hard to resist. "Losing hair is normal. Eyebrow hair, too."

"I know, I know." She sucked in a breath. "I know."

"Did you end up hiring Rue and Heidi? What happened?"

Leanne's eyes snapped open farther. "Of course not. They have to come up with some specifics and a bid first."

It wasn't easy to wheedle and beg, but Laura was almost willing to do it now. "Rue would do a great job. And I think it would be a great help to her to have a big project like that. She's been sort of at loose ends since the guests left."

"Well! Be that as it may, my wedding is not a charity event or a make-work project. I have guests to consider."

Laura stepped a little closer. "They'll do a good job. Understand?"

Leanne's uptilted chin slowly lowered as Laura stared her down. "Well of course, I'm going to hire them. Of course. But you don't want me to just agree right off the bat. They might suspect it was a pity hire or something."

Laura had to admit, she had a point.

"Poor Rue! And here I thought she was being such a slack-off mom all summer, letting Erica practically live at that unpleasant little Robichaux girl's house. Now I can see why." A tear slipped down her cheek. "When I think about how hard it must be for her. And it's not hard for me to put myself in her shoes right now, believe me. I am *very* keyed into maternal feelings, probably more than anybody around here. And not just because I'm going to be Erica's stepmom soon, either."

"Really?" Laura said.

There was no one else visible outside, but Leanne lowered her voice to a whisper. "I'm going to have a baby. Surprised?"

"You could blow me over with a bug fart."

Leanne absorbed Laura's reaction to her big news with equal parts disappointment, disgust, and distrust, but then decided to let it pass. "I would really like to help Rue out in any way I can, especially with Erica. In fact, busy as I am, I am really going to knock myself out to do more."

Laura tilted her head. "More in what area?"

"With Erica," Leanne explained.

Uh-oh.

Leanne went on. "Now, I know you look a little skeptical, but Miss Erica and I are becoming good pals. I'm teaching her to sew. Did she tell you that?"

"No."

"She's quite a little seamstress . . . if you keep a close eye on her."

"She has gone girly this summer, hasn't she?"

Leanne flashed a frown at her. "Don't make fun of her. Teasing is the worst possible thing you can do to girls that age. It wounds them."

"A lot of things wound a twelve-year-old. It's been a hard year for her."

It was the wrong thing to say. Leanne turned on the waterworks again and had to start digging through her purse for another Kleenex. "So sad . . . She's so young . . ."

Laura stood scowling as Leanne demolished another tissue. "She's dealing with everything fine. She knows as well as I do how strong Rue is."

Leanne shook her head to and fro for a moment. "Of course. But there's no reason why any of y'all need to cope on your own. We're all family now. I am going to be putting my shoulder to the wheel trying to think of ways I can help out." When Laura opened her mouth to say something, she steamrollered right over her. "Now, I won't let you thank me, and I certainly won't let you stop me. I am stepping up to the plate. And when I step up to the plate, I aim for the stands."

Leanne executed a crisp turn and got into her car. As Laura watched her go, she felt as if she had missed an opportunity to stick her thumb in the dike and hold off the flood.

Chapter 20

The more Erica thought about it, the clearer it became that wedding or no wedding, things were going to be a mess. Ms. Dench had called her mom to tell her that she wanted the farm to do the catering job. So now if the wedding was canceled, her mom and Heidi would have done a lot of work for nothing. And if the wedding did come off, she would be unhappy, and so would Maggie and Mrs. Robichaux.

Then, just a couple of days later, Rue announced that Leanne had asked—no, practically begged—to be allowed to take Erica back-to-school shopping.

"But *why?*" she asked her mom after hearing about Leanne's offer.

"She thought it would be a good bonding experience for you two, I imagine."

Erica crossed her arms. "Haven't we bonded enough over the wedding and that stupid dress?"

"I'm very curious about this dress," Rue said. "Did you really make it?"

Erica rolled her eyes. "I sewed a couple of straight seams on the machine, but somehow I ended up doing the hem backward, and she had to rip it out and take the skirt up some more to hide my mistake, so now it's nearly up to my kneecaps. It looks dorky."

"Well, it's still good to know your way around a sewing machine. It comes in handy sometimes."

"You didn't tell Ms. Dench that I would go shopping with her, did you?"

"Of course I did. I thought it was nice of her. She's very busy, and she's taking time out to do this with you."

"But I didn't ask her to. I don't want her to!"

"You usually like going to shop for school supplies."

"With *you*, not Ms. Dench."

"I actually don't think . . ." Her mom stopped and looked down at her hand for a moment. "I'm so busy with Heidi and getting ready for the wedding."

"What's to get ready for?" Erica asked. "You can't cook the stuff now, can you?"

"Some of it we can. And we're experimenting, trying to see what will work."

Erica bit her lip. *That stupid wedding.* "Couldn't Laura take me?"

Rue inhaled a deep breath and held it for a moment. "Tell you what I'm going to do. I totted it up this morning. Last year we spent two hundred and twenty dollars on your back-to-school stuff. That was for everything—one new pair of shoes, jeans, shirts, underwear, school supplies, and a new jacket. This year I'm going to give you two hundred and fifty dollars in cash, and you get to choose whatever you want."

Erica gasped. *"Two hundred and fifty dollars!"*

"You have to buy school supplies, remember. And you have to buy new shoes."

"Two hundred and fifty dollars to spend on whatever I want?"

"To buy what you need."

"I need a cell phone!" Erica said. "Maggie has a cell phone. It's very handy if she needs to call her mom, or for lots of stuff. She can send messages on her phone, too."

"Who would you send messages to?"

"To Maggie. You said I could buy whatever I wanted if I could afford it."

"Do you want to pay for a phone plan? That costs money, too. Every month."

Erica felt a little disappointed, but she still felt a little better about having to go with Ms. Dench. If she had two hundred and fifty dollars, she could buy really cheap stuff—she didn't need a new jacket this year, and she'd definitely punt on underwear—and she'd have lots left over. Maybe she could just save it until she could convince her mom of the absolute necessity of her having her own phone.

"When is Ms. Dench picking me up?"

"Tomorrow morning. She's going to take you to lunch, too, but I'm going to give you a little extra, and I want you to pay for her lunch as a way of thanking her."

More money! If she could feed Ms. Dench a really cheap lunch, she'd probably be able to pocket the change from that, too. She was going to be rich!

For the rest of the day she thought about the two hundred and fifty dollars. One minute she would buy a phone with the leftovers; the next she was getting a television for her room. It was hard to know which would be better. Or more affordable. She spent a lot of time on the Internet comparison shopping.

The next morning she got up early and currycombed Milkshake. At the beginning of the summer she'd imagined riding him every day, but in the past two months she'd actually ignored him a little. Not that he complained. He was the best horse in the world—part quarter horse, part Appaloosa. And part who knows what else, Laura always said.

After taking care of Milkshake, she saw to the other animals and then went inside to clean up. She wondered where on earth Ms. Dench would want to eat. Her mom gave her thirty dollars for lunch, which probably wasn't a huge amount if they went somewhere like Elm House, which was where everybody went when it was an occasion, like a birthday. There would be no money at all left over if they went to Elm House, so she was hoping she could talk Ms. Dench into a hamburger instead. Or maybe even the $4.99 Pizza Stop lunch buffet—but that was pushing it.

Ms. Dench picked her up at ten, and they drove straight to the Wal-Mart. Her mom and especially Laura sometimes grumbled about Wal-Mart, but Erica loved it. She pulled out one of the chariot-like baskets and made a beeline for the school supplies.

Ms. Dench carried the list of should haves for the sixth grade, and Erica went about plucking the boring necessities off shelves with a heavy heart. Who knew paper was so expensive? Pens, too. She bought the cheapest possible ballpoint pens she could find. Any other year she probably would have picked out folders with cool colors like lime green or purple, or the ones that had foily squiggles and polka dots, but now she reached for the old-fashioned flimsy kind that came only in primary colors.

But even buying the very cheapest stuff imaginable, in no time she had spent forty dollars. And then she came to the Magic Markers. For a moment it was as if her soul was in crisis. She loved markers, loved the way they smelled, loved to spend homework time doodling with them, loved just to look at the color assortments lined up in their plastic package. They almost seemed like a necessity of life. But the ones she wanted were $14.88, which was really over fifteen dollars, with tax. It was outrageous. And depressing.

She tossed them into her basket. There were limits to deprivation.

After finishing off the school supplies, she and Ms. Dench went through the clothes section. There was lots of stuff on sale or clearance already, and Erica grabbed a few things from those racks. But the sneakers set her back. She needed good sneakers, because she wore them every day, and she didn't want to go around looking like a dork in Keds or something. But by the time she was done, her grand total came to one hundred and fifty-nine dollars. How had that happened?

She wondered if she would ever be able to stop resenting footwear.

"You have to buy something besides tank tops," Leanne said as they left the store.

There had been a lot of those on sale. They were really cheap.

"And what about pants? Don't you at least want some jeans?" Leanne added.

"I've got jeans."

"But I'll bet you've grown two inches over the summer. The ones you have will be high-water. You don't want to look like poor . . ."

Here Ms. Dench stopped herself.

"Like Noah Timmons?" Erica asked.

Noah Timmons was a really smart kid in her class, but his parents were really poor, and he was always wearing clothes that didn't fit him. Last spring he'd broken his eyeglasses during recess, and he'd spent the last months of school with silver duct tape holding them together. Noah was pathetic, but he was really quiet and not all that nice, so people, especially the boys, didn't feel too bad about making fun of him.

Ms. Dench suddenly looked stricken, as if she had been caught violating some rule.

"It's okay," Erica said. "Everybody notices Noah wearing shirts with his cuffs past his wrists. And those glasses!" She laughed. "I wonder if he finally got his glasses repaired over the summer."

"He'll have a new pair," Ms. Dench said curtly.

"Have you seen him?"

"No, I talked to his parents. The teachers—all of us—took up a collection in May. I told his mother that it came from the school's emergency fund."

Erica was perplexed. "I didn't know there was an emergency fund." Where had it been when one of the swings on the playground broke and wasn't fixed?

"There isn't. Or wasn't. There is now. We've decided to start up a school need fund, for situations like that. Like when we realized Kim Jenks didn't have a coat."

"Wait. The teachers are just going to give kids stuff?"

"No, it's going to be the school's fund, and a teacher can ask the board set up to oversee it to dispense money for emergency cases. Those eyeglasses were so sad. It was all I could do to keep from crying in front of the whole class sometimes."

Erica was amazed. They had all thought it was kind of funny, especially when the duct tape gave way at odd moments. They had fallen apart once while Noah was doing a really tedious presentation on the solar system.

"So the teachers are paying for all this?"

"We're taking donations first, and then we're going to try to supplement it through the year from things like a dunk tank at the Halloween carnival."

This was big news. "You mean, we'd get to try to dunk the teachers in a tank of water by throwing a baseball and hitting a target?"

"That's right."

Erica grinned. "I'm a really good pitcher."

Ms. Dench frowned. "The thing is, Erica, the teachers' fund works anonymously. In private. I shouldn't have told you about Noah's glasses, but I did because I know you're mature enough to keep a confidence."

"I won't tell."

"You're going to know a little more about what's going on at school because we'll be closer, but some things will have to be just between us."

"Okay."

Ms. Dench turned to her with a big smile. "So now I have a surprise for you. I'm going to treat you."

"To lunch?" Erica asked nervously. "Pizza Stop has this lunch buffet. . . ."

"Nonsense. This is a fun shopping day. We'll go to Elm House. But first I'm going to buy you a nice outfit at Mairzy-Doats."

That statement would have caused a shudder, anyway, just because the two most dreaded words in the world were *nice outfit*. They reminded her of stiff, scratchy Easter dresses and Sears portrait day. But the idea of buying a nice outfit at Mairzy-Doats with Ms. Dench caused an earthquake inside her. As far as she knew, Ms. Dench didn't know Mrs. Robichaux, and she'd like to keep it that way.

"No thanks," she said.

Ms. Dench looked surprised and a little offended.

"I don't want you to waste your money," Erica explained. "What with the wedding and all. I have a nice outfit already. From Easter."

"I'm talking about something you could wear to school that's not jeans. Now that you're experimenting with makeup, you ought to try expanding your wardrobe a little, too. And I want to do something nice for you for being my little helper this summer."

"Helper!"

"Well, whenever you've stayed over, you've taken out the garbage and emptied the dishwasher."

"Yeah, but that's just normal stuff Mom makes me do at home, anyway."

"And I'm sure your mother gives you an allowance. But I don't, so I'm going to give you a nice outfit."

Erica swallowed, feeling desperate. "But I'm hungry. Can't we eat first? I want to go to Elm House."

She'd use up her mom's thirty dollars and even some of her own money to keep Ms. Dench away from Mairzy-Doats.

"It's not even noon yet."

"I know, but . . ."

Ms. Dench turned the car left into downtown Carter's Springs, and Erica slid down in her seat. Maybe it wouldn't matter. Mrs. Robichaux wasn't an idiot. Even if she realized who Ms. Dench was, it wasn't likely she would blurt out, "Of course! You're the woman whose engagement I'm busting up."

Sometimes people hardly said a word to shopkeepers at all. Erica could just make a quick turn around the store and declare that there was nothing there that she wanted. And then they could leave before Ms. Dench could get too far beyond the threshold.

Her pulse was just beginning to settle down when they swung onto the street where Mairzy-Doats was located. But then, just down the block from the store, she spotted her father's truck.

"The clothes here are way too expensive," Erica said in desperation. "You'd just be throwing money away."

"Well, it's my money," Ms. Dench said. "And I feel like throwing it away on you. I know it's been so hard for you, with . . ."

Ms. Dench started choking up.

Great. This was a fine time for Ms. Dench to suddenly get sentimental over how good Erica was being about the wedding.

"But I don't need anything," Erica whined.

Leanne turned on her in teary impatience. "You need some manners, is what you need! When someone wants to show you a kindness, you're supposed to shut up and thank them! All right?"

Erica gaped at her. It was on the tip of her tongue to ask how someone could say thank you and shut up at the same time, but she had a hunch that if she did ask that question, those might be the last words out of her mouth. Ever. She really wanted to live to be twelve, at least.

Leanne unbuckled her seat belt, and it retracted with an emphatic snap. "Come on."

Erica climbed out of the Ford with a heavy heart, trying very hard not to look in the direction of her father's pickup. It could be that he wasn't even in the shop. Why would he be? Anyone (like Leanne) could just walk into the store at any time. And really, the truck was parked closer to the courthouse. He could be there. Maybe he had gotten a speeding ticket and had to pay a fine.

Maybe he was visiting a client who just happened to live in the neighborhood. He sometimes had to go investigate car damage or look at people's houses to estimate insurance costs. There were a hundred squillion reasons he could be parked on this street a discreet yet not-too-inconvenient distance from his secret girlfriend's shop.

Ms. Dench motored up the sidewalk, paused for a moment at the glass door to toss an impatient hurry-up glance at Erica, and then went inside. Her entrance was heralded by the merry jingling of bells on the door.

Even by the time Erica slunk in behind her—to a more muted jingling—Ms. Dench hadn't advanced far. And no wonder. Behind the counter that held the jewelry case that the cash register and the fancy barrette display sat on, Mrs. Robichaux and her dad were perched on a stool together. It was a precarious position; they looked like they were about to fall off, and they had probably been laughing right up till the moment Leanne had busted in on them. Erica could almost see the faded smiles underneath the surprise in their expressions.

The moment seemed to go on forever, leaving all four of them suspended in time while Ms. Dench eyed Jessica Robichaux and Jessica goggled back. When Erica caught her dad's eye, he flashed shock with a hint of betrayal back at her.

It was Ms. Dench who finally spoke, in a strangled tone that made her voice sound an octave higher. She began by nodding with growing vigor, as if her throat were a pump that had to be primed. "I see! I see!"

Mrs. Robichaux and William wobbled guiltily off their stool. Erica's dad barely got out a shocked "Leanne!" before Ms. Dench cut him off. "I expected better of you, William Anderson! This behavior"—she gulped to maintain control—"is unacceptable!"

She pivoted and steamed back toward the door, first passing Erica and then grabbing her hand at the last moment and yanking her along in retreat. Erica spun so fast that it felt like her arm might pop out of the socket.

Leanne didn't slow down until they were halfway to the car, and then she stopped dead on the sidewalk and wheeled around toward Erica. Her face was scarlet, and tears trembled in her eyes. "Did you know about this?"

Erica's mouth opened and closed without any words coming out.

Anger and disgust and hurt warred in Leanne's big eyes. "And here I was trying so hard to be nice to you!" She turned toward her car and then spun back. "Which wasn't easy, believe me!"

The tears broke, and she scuttled the rest of the way to her car. Erica was too stunned to move at first. Once she realized that Ms. Dench was starting the car and pulling away, she ran a few steps forward. But Leanne was either too upset to see her or saw her and didn't care.

Erica hesitated on the sidewalk, unsure what to do next. She couldn't chase Ms. Dench's car. She didn't want to go back into the store and face Mrs. Robichaux and her dad. But she didn't know where there was a phone so she could call the farm.

The only real option was to go back into the store and face the fallout there. But just as she made this decision, the Mairzy-Doats Dress Shop's door opened with an angry jingle and her dad flew out. He stopped short when he saw her standing there. "Thanks!" he burst out. "Thanks a whole heck of a lot!"

Erica threw out her arms. "What did I do?"

He slapped his hand against his pant leg. "I suppose you expect a ride home now. You don't deserve one."

Something grabbed in her throat. Was he actually going to leave her here?

He looked at her in disgust and started walking. *"Come on!"* She hesitated till he turned and barked at her a second time. "Come on! I haven't got all day. I've got work to do."

As she marched after him, her confusion started to turn to anger. Five minutes ago he hadn't been too concerned about all the work he had to do.

She got into the truck, and he flooded the gas for a moment before pulling into the street. His body was rigid with anger. His eyes were fixed stonily on the road in front of him, but apparently he wasn't concentrating, because he nearly ran a red light and squealed to a stop in the middle of an intersection.

"Great!" he yelled as he threw them into reverse. "That's all I need right now is to die!"

He slapped the steering wheel, which honked back at him in protest. "That would just make my goddamned day!"

Erica had been nervous when he was driving, but being stopped with him yelling was even worse. Especially when the light turned green and he was still fuming and sputtering.

"Dad, it's green."

He accelerated with a jerk, and they barreled down the road toward Sweetgum. After a few more moments of silence, he drummed his fingers on the wheel. "What were you thinking bringing Leanne in there?"

Erica wanted to scream but knew instinctively that that would be the exact wrong thing to do. When animals were hysterical, you had to maintain a safe distance and speak softly, if at all. "I tried to talk her out of it, but she insisted. She's crazy."

"You got that right! She's crazy. Bed-bleepin'-bug insane. Just like all women. All of them are just nuts." He threw a warning glance Erica's way. "Don't let that happen to you."

"Mom's not crazy."

"No, your mother's not crazy. She's the sanest person I know. Who I've *ever* known. She was the best thing that ever happened to me, and I . . ." His words broke off, and he shook his head. "It doesn't matter. It's too late."

Erica frowned at him. His jaw was twitching, and he was jerking his head abruptly every so often, like he did when he was really upset.

"Are you okay?"

"*No!*"

She waited a moment before she spoke again, in a softer voice. "Daddy?"

He looked at her, and something in him seemed to melt. His shoulders slumped, and he draped himself over the steering wheel. "I'm so sorry, Erica. I screwed up." He braked the truck and swung onto the dirt shoulder of the road. He dropped his forehead until it was resting on the steering wheel, and when he spoke, every word was punctuated by the raw sound of his breath being laboriously sucked in. "I . . . screw . . . up . . . everything."

She gaped at him for a moment before she realized what was happening. He was crying.

"*Everything,*" he repeated.

Chapter 21

Rue was asleep when Erica got home, but even after she woke up, it was clear that something was not quite right. Laura mentioned that William had dropped Erica off around noon. When Erica finally emerged from her room and appeared downstairs, she was silent on the subject of her shopping trip with Leanne. And if there was any subject usually guaranteed to get Erica talking, it was Leanne.

Instead, she sat eating sample powder-sugar-coated sand cookies one after another and saying nothing.

"What did you have for lunch?" Rue asked her.

Erica seemed to hesitate. "I didn't have lunch."

"You were supposed to take Leanne out."

"We didn't have time. She—she had to leave. Dad gave me a ride home. I put your thirty dollars on the counter."

Voluntarily giving back cash. This seemed odd, too. "Did you have fun shopping?"

Erica shrugged.

"You'll have to show me what you got. When I sent you out with that money this morning, I felt like the hosts of *What Not to Wear*. I wished I had someone to follow you around Wal-Mart with cameras." The statement garnered no reaction. "Is that where you went?"

"Where?"

"Wal-Mart."

"Oh. Yeah." Erica popped another cookie into her mouth, chewed, and swallowed. "But I accidentally left all the stuff in Ms. Dench's car."

"Well, I'm sure you'll be seeing her soon."

Erica scraped her chair back, looking like she was poised to flee.

"Erica," Rue said, stopping her. "You've got to eat something other than cookies."

"I can't now, Mom. I'm stuffed." She rubbed her nonexistent stomach and sped for the side door. "I think I'm gonna take Milkshake for a ride. I'll be back in a little while."

The conversation left Rue with an uneasy feeling. Erica had certainly started acting more secretively this summer. It hurt, but she supposed the discovery of privacy was part of adolescence. Some teenagers barely spoke to their parents at all except to ask for things. She hoped when Erica got older, she wouldn't be like that.

The thought made her freeze in pain, like the moment of shock that came with a bee sting. She sank into a chair and stared out the window, trying to imagine Erica as a teenager. In a way, it wasn't hard. She already had the spirit and sense of injustice down pat. But Rue hoped the sweetness wouldn't disappear completely. It would be a shame to lose the little person who bounded out of bed in the morning like Tigger and who wanted to nurse every stray animal or injured bird in her path.

The most horrible thing would be to never know.

She heard someone coming up the porch steps and started gulping down sand cookies to compose herself.

Heidi came in, stiff and exhausted, and dropped a bushel of peas on the kitchen floor. She stretched, moaned, and made for a chair, which she eased herself into with effort. "Can't . . . straighten . . . back . . ."

Rue cut a glance at the peas. "I guess I know what I'll be doing this afternoon."

Heidi reached for a cookie, lifted it halfway to her mouth, then thought better of it and put it back. "I never thought I'd see the day when I could refuse a cookie."

"Maybe that's a good thing. I ate three just now and feel full as a tick."

"You've been around Laura too long. You're beginning to sound like her."

"It only took thirty-six years."

As if she had overheard them, Laura herself came charging in the side door. "Leanne's coming!"

"You're like a new kind of security system," Rue said, amused. "The Leanne detector."

Laura's warning was followed by the sound of the dogs going nuts outside—their customary greeting to visiting cars.

"I wouldn't be surprised if she had her war on. That Ford was rocketing down our lane at about seventy miles per hour," Laura noted.

Rue and Heidi barely had time to react before the doorbell rang. They heard the door push open, and Leanne came in, followed by the skittering paws of the dogs.

"Hello! Rue?"

"In here, Leanne."

Leanne appeared, red in the face and eyes, and her hair poofing out as if she had been trying to yank it out in hanks. She was attempting to hold two large plastic shopping bags away from the curious snouts of Shelley Winters and Monte. "Would you please call off your dogs?"

Laura slapped her hands together once in a clap that made both dogs and humans jump and turn toward her. She shrugged modestly. "That's all it takes."

Leanne dropped her bags on the kitchen table. "Erica left these in my car. I'm returning them." She sniffed back a wave of emotion. "I guess you heard."

"Heard what?" Heidi asked.

"Erica probably told you."

"Told us what?" Rue asked.

"About the wedding. It's off."

The three of them gaped at her. Even Laura didn't have a re-tort handy.

"*Off?*" Rue repeated. "Are you sure?"

Before the question was even out, Leanne was bobbing her head emphatically. "Oh, it's off, all right. I wouldn't marry that man if he begged me. I wouldn't marry him if he offered me the Hope diamond for a wedding ring." Her teary eyes glistened with outrage. "I wouldn't even marry him if he suddenly turned into Hugh Jackman!"

"What happened?" Heidi asked.

"Sit down," Rue said, coming forward to take Leanne's arm. "You look so upset."

The kindness in her tone made Leanne bristle. When Rue touched her arm, she shook her off like she would a spider. "Let's just say I won't be needing your services. I don't think I need to say more than that, do I? Not to you all, especially."

They all looked at each other, mystified.

Leanne practically tapped her foot with impatience. "If Erica hasn't told you, I'm sure you know William well enough to guess."

"I could guess, but I don't know anything, Leanne," Rue said. "No one does."

"Well, you will soon! Everyone will know soon. Nothing's ever secret in Sweetgum. They'll be yammering about me nonstop at McCaffree's store. People'll stop in to buy gas and talk about the stupid, knocked-up schoolteacher whose fiancé dumped her for that shopkeeper in Carter's Springs, who is a skinny little bitch but who I'm sure people think is a lot better looking than me, so no one will blame William one itty-bitty bit. I might not lose my job, but I'll have to endure stares and sneers and a lot of venom wrapped in homilies. I'm going to be pregnant and alone, and no man will ever want to date me because soon I'll be a stressed-out single mother with a squalling baby, who'll turn into an annoying, shrieking toddler and then a maladjusted brat other teachers will complain to me about, and then it will turn into a sullen, angry teenager who hates me because I can't afford to buy it nice clothes or iPods or whatever stupid gadget kids are gonna want in fifteen years, and we'll be estranged forever and never visit or call or even send e-mails, and I'll wonder what the hell all the sacrifice and pain were for. And when I'm ninety and alone in a county nursing home that smells like urine, I'll remember how all my misery began on this day, with a stupid shopping trip with your scheming daughter!"

Rue, who had been listening with growing sympathy and amazement, jerked back in surprise. "Why blame Erica?"

At the same time, Heidi stepped forward to offer Leanne the plate of cookies. "Sand tart?"

Leanne ignored the cookies. "Ask her."

"I will," said Rue. "But I don't see how an eleven-year-old could destroy an engagement. If she—"

Leanne's demented cackle silenced her. "That just shows you've never taught fifth grade! Believe me, eleven-year-olds are capable of anything, including, it would seem, the vilest acts of treachery!" She sucked in a deep breath and glanced down at the cookies. "Can I have those?"

Heidi nodded.

Leanne snatched them out of her hands. "I'll return the plate."

She lurched toward the door and left them. They all were too stunned to escort her out. They stared at the Wal-Mart bags and then looked at each in befuddlement.

"That must have been some back-to-school shopping trip!" Laura said.

Rue barely heard her. In any case, she was in no mood for joking. Defensive anger was still burbling inside her. *Treachery?* "Where does she get off blaming Erica?"

"I don't know." Heidi shook her head. "She lost me at Hugh Jackman."

Laura figured Erica had seen Leanne's car driving up to the house. It couldn't be just coincidence that she decided to take her longest horseback ride of the summer on that day and didn't return until hunger forced her to late in the afternoon.

Laura met her at the barn, where she was unsaddling Milkshake.

"They say you can't be too cautious." Laura scooped up a kitten and sat down on a square hay bale.

Erica's brows beetled in confusion. "What?"

"Leanne left around three. The coast has been clear for hours."

Erica's face flushed, but she wasn't ready to give anything away before she had to. "What was Ms. Dench doing here?" she asked, with studied casualness.

"Dropping off the fruits of your shopping labors."

Erica looked relieved. "Oh."

"And informing Rue and Heidi that their services won't be needed, because—as best we could piece together—William has deserted her for a certain shopkeeping divorcée in Carter's Springs."

"Oh."

"The lightning's hit the merry-go-round, big-time. What's less clear is your part in all this. Leanne seems to be of the opinion that you were the one who threw the bolt."

Erica dropped the saddle onto its holder on the tack wall and then went back and leaned against Milkshake for support. "Am I in trouble with Mom?"

Laura shrugged her shoulders. "Hard to say. I'm not sure the parents handbook contains a section on what to do when your daughter scuttles your ex-husband's wedding."

"I didn't! I didn't do anything!" A split second later she added, "Much."

"Yeah, the *much* part is what everyone's curious about."

Erica lifted her arms and let them drop again. "It just happened. I didn't even know that Dad took Mrs. Robichaux to the junior prom till Maggie told me."

"And Maggie told you this . . . when?"

Erica lifted her shoulders in all innocence. "I don't remember. A while back."

"Back before your dad offered to take you to Six Flags?"

"Mom was supposed to take us but couldn't."

"And then Leanne was out of town, and Mrs. Robichaux just volunteered to take her place."

"That's right. She volunteered. I couldn't very well tell her not to come, could I? Things just sort of happened. . . ."

"And happened in such a way that Leanne Dench got squeezed out even as she was sewing bridesmaid dresses and picking out china patterns." Laura shook her head in wonder.

Erica looked worried. "Mom is mad, isn't she?"

"Gosh no. Rue's a nut. With her, everybody's innocent until proven guilty."

"It doesn't matter. Ms. Dench blames me, and Dad does too, I think."

"That fits. Heaven forfend he should blame himself."

"He was upset."

"Of course he was. He got caught."

Erica tilted her head. "So Ms. Dench said the wedding was off?"

"Definitely off. She's gone home to map out the rest of her miserably lonely life as a laughingstock, social outcast, and undesirable life partner." Laura experienced a moment of mental whiplash. "Gadzooks—she's becoming me!"

Erica threw out her hands in a kind of defensive supplication. "Is it my fault she's so annoying that Dad couldn't face marrying her?"

"Point taken. But you have to admit, this all worked out the way you wanted."

"Not really. Mrs. Robichaux's weird, too. I'd give anything if things could go back to the way they were before last year, before Mom got sick. Everything was fine then."

"Yeah, I'd give anything for that, too," Laura said.

Erica took her own sweet time feeding Milkshake his carrot rewards. Laura squinted up at the sky, scanning for hawks. The chickens had been spared too many dive-bomb attacks for the past few weeks. She suspected the hawks were just waiting for her to let her guard down.

"I guess I should go inside." Erica's voice dripped with dread.

Laura nodded. "You should. They looked like they needed help shelling peas in there."

"Then what are you doing out here?"

"Do I look like a fool?"

When Erica had trudged away, Laura decided to take Fred back to the chicken house and do an evening egg check. It was so hot these days, she sometimes expected the eggs to be ready cooked by the time she got to them.

She thought about poor Leanne Dench. What a pickle. What a mess everything was.

As she was walking, she looked over and saw Webb's shirtless torso half buried in the old John Deere. He was a crack mechanic, while her stabs at fixing machinery usually ended with a tow truck. He certainly looked better than she did while he was at it, too. His bronzed back glistened with sweat, and she saw the black tattoo on the top of his left arm. She'd first seen it in Guadalajara; he'd told her it was the Chinese symbol for *smile*.

"Why?" she'd asked.

"Because the first time I got leave, I had too many beers and decided at three a.m. that it would be nice to always be wearing a smile."

It made her laugh just thinking about it, and she considered strolling over for a chat.

On second thought, the last thing she wanted to do was talk, since for the foreseeable future all talk would be about Leanne's wedding calamity. That was bound to be a reminder of their own wedding calamity, in which she had played the part of the tornado. It was best to leave it. It was best to stay away from discussions of Guadalajara. Otherwise, he might start thinking that she couldn't get him out of her mind.

"Laura looks disturbed." Heidi's gaze followed Laura's lanky form as it crossed the field toward the lake.

Webb barely looked up. Dylan was getting a wisdom tooth extracted, so Heidi had volunteered to help pick watermelons, but she couldn't take her eyes off Laura. She was alert now to every change in mood on the farm, as if she'd developed an interior Geiger counter for trouble. Right now she heard the cracklings of increased tension.

"She's always disturbed about something," Webb said, hauling an especially large melon to their wheelbarrow.

That wasn't normal, either. Throughout the summer, no matter how irritated he and Laura had seemed with each other, Webb had always seemed to follow Laura with his gaze. Usually with an expression somewhere between exasperated bemusement and full-blown love. He had never been dismissive.

Heidi pursed her lips, thinking. "I wonder what's got her so upset."

"Rue's chemo, maybe."

"She *wanted* her to have it."

"Sure. And now that Rue's laid up, she feels doubly bad. But she would never just come out and say so—not her. She prides herself on being a straight talker, which she is when it comes to needling other people."

Heidi picked up one of the smaller melons and tramped after him. "For someone who couldn't care less, you seem to have her all figured out."

"Twenty-five years of practice."

Twenty-five years! Heidi had never had a relationship last five years. She'd had only two that had lasted five months. "Do you know that if you two were a married couple, you'd be celebrating your silver wedding anniversary?"

When he turned, he looked as if she'd slapped him. "Twenty-five years married to Laura would be about twenty-four years and eleven months and twenty-one days too many."

"But a week would be fine? Just enough to have a honeymoon?"

It was so rare to see Webb glower that she nearly laughed at the sight of his face screwed up in anger.

But she had no doubt that Webb was at least a little right. Rue had been doing poorly, and Laura was bound to feel it. It had been a hard week, anyway. First, they'd lost the wedding job, and the next day Rue had gone to the doctor, who had green-lighted another round of chemo. But unlike with other treatments, when her state of health had seemed to waver, this time she sank like a stone. She stumbled out of bed a few times a day to go to the kitchen, and she still appeared in the living room every night to lie on the couch and watch her movie. But half the time it seemed like she was barely focused on what was going on.

Heidi had made an executive decision to end Laura's banishment from movie time. The day of Rue's chemo, *Cat Ballou* had arrived from NetFlix, and Heidi had waved Laura in at the last minute, knowing that if there was anyone in the world who could make her behave, it was Lee Marvin.

It had worked. Laura had appeared each successive night and had even made it through *Cocoon* without so much as a snide remark.

The night after Heidi had seen Laura walking so forlornly out to the lake, the film was *Song of Norway*. Heidi was a musical fan. Almost anything was watchable to her as long as there was a production number in it. She had survived everything from *The Jazz Singer* to *Xanadu*. But *Song of Norway*, a Florence Henderson musical biopic based on the life of the Norwegian composer Edvard Grieg, nearly did her in.

It nearly did them all in. Erica, the smart one, had said she wasn't interested and hid in her room. Rue faded right away. Thirty minutes in, she actually excused herself. It was so surprising to see her stumbling out before the end of a film that Laura and Heidi gaped at each other in shock. Rue had never abandoned a movie midway on movie night. They had skipped a few nights, or maybe she had dozed off in one or two. But she had never walked out. She really must have felt like hell.

In the next instant, their expressions registered that they were free. They could turn off the DVD player and escape *Song of Norway* forever. But Heidi couldn't bring herself to stop the DVD player, and Laura didn't move.

They both faced forward again with determination and sat like stones to the bitter end, waiting until the very last credit rolled before they stood without a word of relief or criticism.

"Good night," Heidi told Laura.

"Night."

The next morning Heidi drove to the pharmacy in Carter's Springs to pick up a prescription for Rue. Next to the pharmacy was Sally's Sweet Spot, the only place in a twenty-mile radius with an espresso machine. Heidi nipped in; she always found it hard to resist. As if to undermine the vaguely X-rated sound of the name, the interior decor of Sally's Sweet Spot relied heavily on penguin figurines and framed Bible verses. But the coffee was strong and the baked goods were fresh and buttery, so Heidi had developed a fondness for the place. She got a cappuccino and one of Sally's special peach jam biscuits and settled into a corner table for a mental health break. The farm was growing on her, but it was stressful. Rue's downhill slide was painful to watch, and the feeling of Laura constantly circling made it hard to relax.

As she was about to get to work on her peach jammer, she spotted two people making out in the front seat of a white pickup parked outside. She stopped mid-bite and narrowed her eyes, not quite believing what she was seeing.

But it was true. One of those people was Leanne Dench.

Heidi's stare became a slack-jawed gape when the pair untangled themselves and she saw that the object of Leanne's ardor was none other than William. She'd glimpsed him only a few times when he'd dropped off Erica at the farm, but that was definitely him.

What was going on?

The two talked for a few moments; then Leanne slipped out the passenger side and hurried to the bakery door, where she tossed a saucy look over her shoulder. Then she came inside and started ordering enough baked goods to feed an army.

Heidi decided it was time for a refill. When she bumped into Leanne, she did a pretty good imitation of surprise. "What are you doing here?"

Leanne beamed. The change in her demeanor from the last time Heidi had seen her couldn't have been more complete. In place of anger, hysteria, and despair, there was now an ecstatic dementia. "William and I woke up this morning absolutely starving," she confided in a low voice, mindful of a needlepoint sampler about the wages of sin just above the half-and-half pitcher.

"William?"

Leanne put a hand on her arm. "I've been meaning to call y'all. Looks like you have a job, after all!"

Heidi gulped. "Same day?"

"I never did cancel any of the other arrangements. I never had time. William and I got back together almost immediately." She sighed. "I guess all relationships hit a few bumps."

Heidi had grown up as a repeat witness to all manner of conjugal conflict and even disaster. But she had to say, even though William and Leanne had patched things up, a groom cheating on his pregnant fiancée just weeks before the wedding seemed like an especially shaky start. That situation might even have given her mother pause.

"Is something wrong?" Leanne asked.

Heidi hesitated. The Leanne-William wedding seemed like a dicier prospect than it used to. She worried that after all their hard work, the farm would end up with a freezer full of unwanted hors d'oeuvres. And since the last time they had contemplated doing the wedding, Rue's health had taken a definite turn for the worse.

"I probably need to talk to Rue about this," Heidi explained. "She had a chemo treatment recently, and it hasn't gone very well."

To Heidi's astonishment, Leanne was unmoved. "It's not as if she only just realized that she has cancer. She shouldn't have said she would do it in the first place if she didn't think she could follow through."

Heidi's blood pressure spiked. "Of course we can follow through. It's just that I don't want to make a decision without her."

"Well, do you, or do you not, think you can manage it?"

"Of course I do," Heidi said recklessly.

"Then I don't see what the problem is. Honestly, I don't mean to seem unsympathetic, but William and I have been accommodating Rue all summer, driving Erica all over creation and having her visit way more than we agreed to back in May, when Rue pitched a fit and told William that Erica had to stay at the farm."

Heidi didn't know what to say. "I told you, I just want to tell Rue before finalizing things. Maybe you're familiar with the concept of keeping people informed as plans change?"

Leanne rolled her eyes. "There's no reason to be snippety."

They parted with threadbare civility, and Heidi stewed all the way home. In her mind she replayed the scene with Leanne, only with snappy comebacks to Leanne's self-serving statements. She was so preoccupied, she didn't notice the new car parked in the farmhouse yard until she had pulled up right beside it.

It had an Avis sticker on it. Had one of the scheduled guests not received word that the bookings had all been canceled?

She grabbed the pharmacy bag and the extra baked goodie she'd bought for Rue and hurried toward the house. Pulling open the porch's screen door, she stopped in her tracks. Her chest squeezed tight. She had never seen the man sitting in one of the rockers, but she knew who he was.

"Heidi Dawn Bogue?"

Her stomach gave an unhappy lurch. "Mr. Cho?"

He held out his hand. His demeanor relieved her a little. They didn't shake your hand before they arrested you, she was fairly certain. Not that an assistant district attorney could arrest anyone; but he might have brought a policeman with him. Or a U.S. marshal, or whatever. She imagined Tommy Lee Jones hauling her away.

Hamilton Cho's handshake was firm, confident, and once her initial panic left her, replaced by a lower-grade panic, she was able to give the man a closer look. He was wearing a black suit with a white shirt and striped tie. It was a classy look and tailored to emphasize his compact but fit body. She was dismayed to find her thoughts moving in a Marla Boguish direction, but she couldn't help noticing that he was quite good-looking . . . and not wearing a wedding ring.

"Well!" Heidi said, withdrawing her hand. "I can guess why you're here."

His lips twisted into just a hint of a smile. "Then you did receive the letter."

"Well, yes. I did. I even understood a little of it."

"But you chose not to answer it."

"I was trying to decide what to do."

"While you were deliberating, I've been trying to put together a case against Mr. Cavenna. He goes to trial in late September. I need to talk about your involvement with him."

"It's over." She looked around. This seemed an odd place for a DA to take a deposition, however informal, but off the top of her head she couldn't think of a better one. Yet it seemed odd just to sit on rocking chairs. "Would you like a glass of limeade?"

"I've already been offered one, thanks."

"Well, would it be all right if I had one? Also, I have some medication that I need to give to my friend. I won't be a flight risk, I swear."

"All right. I guess waiting a little longer can't hurt. My plane's not till ten p.m."

"The red-eye?" she asked sympathetically.

"I have a very busy caseload right now. I need to get back."

"I'll just be a sec."

She calmly entered the house, throwing him a departing smile, and then lit out at a wobbly run for the kitchen. She dropped the medicine on the kitchen table and assumed the crash position on one of the chairs. "They've found me. I'm done for."

"I left a message on your cell phone," Rue said.

"Damn. I had it on vibrate. I was too busy stewing about Leanne to think straight."

"What about Leanne?"

"We're back in the catering business. The wedding's on again. God knows when she would have gotten around to telling us."

Rue leaned against the counter. Actually, it looked like she was propping herself up. "Good. I'm glad."

"Yeah, it's always good to know about another dysfunctional marriage in the making."

"There's always a chance it could work out."

"Meanwhile, I might be dragged off to the hoosegow before Leanne's big day."

"Surely Mr. Cho's just here to ask you questions. Unless . . ."

Heidi's heart froze. "Unless what?"

"Did he serve you with a subpoena?"

"Not yet." Heidi shivered. "So do I buck up, confess all, and risk the wrath of Vinnie, or hold back and preserve my life?"

Rue looked down at her feet. "I know this is going to sound sort of mom-ish and corny, but in these cases I think it's best to tell the truth."

"There's the whole truth," Heidi said, "and there's the bowd-lerized truth. And then there's the weaselly preserve-one's-life sliver of truth, which I usually prefer."

She poured her drink and left the kitchen, deciding not to make her choice until she absolutely had to.

She returned to the porch and settled herself in a rocking chair.

"Would you call yourself a coward, Ms. Bogue?"

"I am when someone tries to kill me."

"Mr. Cavenna tried to kill you? When?"

"In May, the day I left the bank. The day I left New York. A gypsy cab nearly ran me over just outside your office."

"What were you doing at my office?"

"I was going to tell you of my suspicions that my boss was embezzling, just like Tom Chinske would have if he hadn't been beaten to a pulp."

"But you changed your mind."

"A close encounter with a car bumper is very persuasive."

"Why didn't you report the incident to the police?"

She shot him an amused look.

He attempted a different tack. "Do you know when Mr. Cavenna started deleting or shredding his records?"

"No. And I never looked that closely at what he was doing when I suspected he was covering his tracks, either."

"But you didn't tell your employer?"

"The VP at the bank—our manager—is a friend of Vinnie's. Joe Sanfred. They play golf together. I don't think Tom trusted him, either. And of course, I didn't want to end up like poor Elvin Johnson."

His eyes snapped with interest. "What about him?"

"Vinnie had him killed!"

He squinted at her. "Killed?"

"He was found in an empty parking lot in New Jersey! It was in a newspaper."

Cho released a long-suffering sigh. "This is what happens when bank employees play private eye. Ms. Bogue, Elvin Johnson died of a heart attack in his car in a mall parking lot in Paramus. He wasn't spotted until evening, after the mall had closed, and an employee called the police."

"Oh." She frowned. "Then what does he have to do with Vinnie?"

"We believe Vincent Cavenna never closed Elvin Johnson's account. After the man died, Cavenna began channeling money from accounts of senior citizens through Johnson's account—in increasingly large amounts. Tom Chinske said he suspected the scheme when the wife of one of Cavenna's senior account holders came to him to complain about an unauthorized money transfer. Tom tracked down the account number it went to—Mr. Johnson's—and queried Mr. Cavenna. Later Tom periodically checked up on the Johnson account, which continued to grow. Once Cavenna had put the money into it, we think he would write a bank check off it and deposit the money into other accounts in his own name in other banks."

"But you're still unsure about this?" Heidi asked.

"Mr. Johnson's account was emptied, and no records of recent transactions in it exist."

"Oh."

"Did you ever collect any proof of Mr. Cavenna's wrongdoing?"

"Just what I was going to bring to you back in May."

"Do you have that evidence now?" he asked.

"I'm not sure it will do you any good. I copied my own files, which might not have anything useful on them and gathered up some other papers. I'm not sure if any of it will help with your case."

"Then give it all to me. We can sort it out. I would very much appreciate your help, Ms. Bogue."

"And I would very much like to stay alive a little longer."

He looked around pointedly. "I don't think there are many gypsy cabs around here. Besides, if I had a difficult time tracking you down, I doubt Vinnie Cavenna could swing it."

She wasn't so sure. In his own twisted way, Vinnie had a definite can-do spirit. On the other hand, she didn't quite know how to say no without looking like a sniveling coward. That decided the matter.

It was the root of all her problems. She'd always been a girl who couldn't say no.

Chapter 22

After three days with no word from Maggie, Erica began to feel a little hysterical. The day of the disastrous shopping trip, Erica had called Maggie's cell phone and had received a joyously whispered "Mission accomplished!"

Maggie had had to whisper because Erica's dad had been in the next room, with Mrs. Robichaux. Erica had reacted squeamishly to this news, but Maggie had assured her they were just talking. In fact, she'd been trying to figure out what they were talking about, but even her usual glass-against-the-wall technique hadn't worked.

Erica had then made the mistake of expressing some sympathy for Ms. Dench.

"I thought you hated her!" Maggie exclaimed.

"I do. It all just sort of makes me uncomfortable. Not that I don't like your mom . . ."

An offended sniff could be heard over the line. "Apparently not as much as I thought. Or maybe you don't want to be my sister."

It was true; she still had a hard time thinking of Maggie in that way. Erica wondered if the two of them would get along any better than Aunt Laura and Heidi had in the olden days.

They were certainly off to a bumpy start. Erica had repeatedly left messages on Maggie's cell phone, but Maggie had never called back.

A few days later Erica walked through the kitchen and discovered Heidi making a huge amount of pie dough.

"What's this?" she asked.

"Dough for the wedding. I was going to make it now and freeze it. It will be one less thing I have to do at the very last minute."

Erica picked off a piece of dough and chewed it before the implication of Heidi's statement really sank in. "What wedding?"

Heidi cut her a startled glance. "Uh, Leanne and your dad's?"

"Dad is getting married to *Leanne?*" Her voice was practically a shriek. For days she'd felt almost mournful at the breakup of their engagement, but now that the wedding was back on again, she felt like a gerbil on a wheel. She was back where she was in May. Square one. "How?" she asked. "Why didn't anyone tell me?"

"I thought you knew. And Rue's been so . . ." Heidi's voice trailed off. "She probably thought you knew, too."

"Great!" Erica cried. "No wonder Maggie's not speaking to me!"

She stomped upstairs and called Maggie again. This time Maggie actually picked up and said in a wounded tone, "Oh, it's you."

"What's going on?" Erica asked her. "What happened?"

"What happened is that your father is a jerk. My mom is really depressed."

"I'm sure he likes her better than Ms. Dench."

"So why is he marrying that stupid cow? It shows that he has absolutely no taste. And that he's mean." She added as a parting blow, "And he doesn't really look like Johnny Depp, anyway."

The next time Erica called, Maggie answered but said she was meeting some kids at the pool. Erica suspected she was saying that just to make her feel bad. Since junior lifeguard lessons had ended in mid-July, Erica had no more reason to go to the pool. She didn't want to ask her mom to take her if it was just for fun, and everybody else was busy.

The next day she hooked a ride with Dylan and Herman, who were going to the hardware store in Carter's Springs. They dropped her off at her dad's office, where his secretary, Diana, let her in to see him without making her wait forever, like she usually did.

She flopped down on the chair across the desk from him. "Dad, what happened? I thought you and Ms. Dench were through."

He shook his head, almost acting as if she were crazy to suggest such a thing. "I never said that."

"Well, it certainly seemed that way!"

He looked at her imploringly. "I need Leanne, Erica. Those days I thought we were busted up, I felt lost."

"What about Mrs. Robichaux?"

"It wasn't the same. She's a little flaky, to tell you the truth. Definitely not a dependable person. But Leanne is my rock. I know I've made the right decision. I know you'll think so, too, once you patch it up with your little friend."

"I don't think we'll ever patch it up," Erica said. "She's really mad. She won't speak to me."

"She sounds fickle. A friend so easily lost isn't worth the winning, I say."

She gaped at him. Was he serious? He discarded fiancées and snapped them back up again as if they were old pennies.

"I've got work to do here, hon. . . ."

"Aren't you going to take me to lunch?" she asked. "Dylan and Herman said they'd pick me up in an hour."

"I'm sorry." He dug into his pocket and produced two dollars. "Maybe you can go spend this."

She dragged the money across the desk with her palm. "Okay," she said reluctantly.

Outside the office she debated where to go. In the old days she would have run to Maggie's house, but she wouldn't be welcome there now. She headed for the Dairy Queen instead, where she could at least get out of the heat and eat an ice cream. After her walk in the muggy heat, the blast of cool air was a relief, even though the abrupt change made her headachy. She headed straight for a register to order. Just as the girl behind the counter was handing over a chocolate-dipped cone, a taunting voice hit her like a stab between her shoulder blades.

"Hey, Barkie!"

Kiefer, Luke, and a few of the other boys from junior life-guards were sitting around a table loaded with soda cups and fries and sundaes. Maggie was with them. Their hair was still damp, as if they'd all come from the pool.

Erica approached them with extreme caution. "Hey."

Maggie looked up at her with a smirk. "I thought now that lessons are over, you'd crawl back to your little town, never to be seen again."

"I had to see my dad."

Maggie lifted a finger to her chin. "Oh, but wait—some other Sweetgum kids show up here from time to time." She shot a look at the boy across the table, who had his back to Erica. He turned, and Erica's heart felt like it had just shorted out. "Hey, Jake." She swallowed. "How was camp?"

When Jake didn't answer, several of the boys laughed. "Jake, aren't you going to say hello to your girlfriend?" one of them said.

"Yeah, kiss her, Jake. She said you liked to!"

"Kiss Barkie!"

Jake scowled at her. "She's not my girlfriend. She's just some weird girl from my school."

Maggie crossed her arms and leveled her most contemptuous glance at Erica, who would have been glad if the linoleum floor tiles she was standing on had peeled and the earth had swallowed her. "Are there *any* honest people in your family?"

Embarrassment engulfed her, followed by white-hot anger. Even as she felt herself getting madder and madder, she knew Maggie had a point. Her dad *had* acted like a jerk. She *had* lied about Jake Peavy. There was no defense she could offer, which made everything worse. And now Maggie wasn't going to be her friend anymore, and everyone knew Erica was a liar, and they had told Jake, and Jake would tell everyone in sixth grade, and she would never live it down.

She felt trapped, ashamed, and furious. And for some reason the only response she could think of was to ball her hand into a fist and take a swing at her former best friend.

By the time Erica was staring at herself in her lilac satin dress on the morning of Ms. Dench's wedding, her eye was chartreuse with an undertone of purple. Who would have guessed that under Maggie Robichaux's girly exterior lurked a petite Mike Tyson? Erica had fought hard, but the Dairy Queen's manager had separated them before she could land the crucial blow that would really teach Maggie what a little snot face she was. Then her father had been called to pick her up.

William had been livid.

"Good God almighty!" he yelled at Erica as she slithered into the truck's passenger seat, achy and vanquished. "This is a proud moment of my life, let me tell you. My daughter . . . kicked out of the Dairy Queen! What the heck got into you?"

"She insulted our family."

"So you decided to act like your aunt Laura on steroids? Great! Terrific!" He seethed for a few seconds before doing a belated double take. "What did she say?"

"She said we were all dishonest."

"What?" her father sputtered. "Is that all?"

"*All?*"

"Yeah, well . . ." His jaw worked back and forth for a moment. "Couldn't you have just let it go?"

"No."

He drummed his fingers on the steering wheel. "This is the town I do business in, and thanks to your lack of self-control, you've humiliated me in it. Now people will never stop gossiping about me and Jess."

"That's *my* fault?" Erica crossed her arms and sank down as far as her seat belt would allow. He was criticizing *her* lack of self-control?

Her father fixed his eyes stubbornly on the road and growled, "Things were just starting to calm down a little."

Erica was surprised that, after her brawl with Maggie, her father was allowing her to be in the wedding at all. She had suggested his keeping her out of it as punishment for fighting, but no such luck. Leanne said it would be bad karma to change plans now. As if this whole wedding weren't one big bad-karma exhibit.

She was stuck as part of the wedding, which truly was punishment. Since the fight she'd actually seen Maggie in Sweetgum, walking with Jake Peavy between his house and McCaffree's store. Like they were going together now. And she was sure Ms. Dench had invited the Peavys to the wedding. Jake would see her looking like a Madam Alexander doll with a black eye.

Erica yawned. She'd stayed up late the night before, helping Heidi. But even if she were wide awake, nothing would have prepared her for the sight of Ms. Dench in full wedding regalia. It was still hours before showtime, but Leanne was already finished dressing. She swept into Erica's room in a confusion of bliss and nerves.

"Don't you look pretty!" Leanne said, taking in the putrid purple dress. "I knew that color was you."

Erica stubbed a bare toe against the rug. She had a feeling she was supposed to tell Leanne that she looked nice, too, but she couldn't quite manage graciousness. "I feel so tired."

Leanne's jaw clenched. "Attitude is everything. If you act tired, you'll feel tired."

"But I *am* tired."

Ms. Dench circled her, picking at her sleeves and inspecting her from all angles. "You do realize you should have put your tights on first, don't you? A house is built from the foundation."

"Uh-huh." *Whatever that means.* "I don't want to stand around in them any longer than I have to. I hate tights. They're hot, and the crotch always sags."

Leanne frowned at the word *crotch*. "If you wait too much longer, you'll have to be in a rush right at the end. That's how mistakes are made."

The wedding was still almost two hours away. "I was surprised when Heidi got me up so early to bring me over here."

"Your mother promised me you'd be here by ten." She frowned. "You say Heidi brought you? And you had to help Heidi last night?"

Erica nodded. "What's the matter?"

Leanne's head snapped a little, as if her mind had been some-where else, and her expression changed to a glassy-eyed smile. "Nothing!"

"It's the dress, isn't it? I look like a dork."

"No!" Leanne collapsed onto the bed, then hopped right back up again when she realized she risked wrinkles. "No, it's just . . ."

Her big eyes blinked, the lids slowly swooshing up and down in an unfamiliar movement. The whites of her eyes were veiny red.

It had to be something big. Really big.

"What is it?" Erica moved closer. "Is something wrong?"

She wondered if Leanne wanted to call it all off. She seemed so distracted that when she finally grabbed Erica and clasped her in a hug, the surprise of it knocked the breath out of her.

"Oh, honey!" Leanne's voice quavered. "It's just so wonderful that we're all going to be one family now. Isn't it? We're all going to need each other so much!"

She clasped the back of Erica's head so that her nose was crushed into Leanne's bosom, making it hard to breathe, or even think. *One family?* She finally freed her nostrils and gasped, "Is that all?"

The "one family" bit didn't seem like much to get hopped up about, frankly.

Leanne sniffed, almost as if she were the one who had nearly been suffocated. Then she clamped her two hands on Erica's cheeks and brought them eyeball to eyeball. "Listen here, little bug. I realize we haven't always been the best of friends, but as far as I'm concerned, that's all in the past. I know this coming year is going to be super hard for you, and super sad, but I promise you it's going to bring lots of joy, too."

Erica's heart froze in her chest. What was she talking about? "Why?"

"Haven't you guessed? Your father and I are going to have a baby." Leanne leaned back and rubbed her abdomen as if it were a good luck charm. "By Valentine's Day, you're going to have a little brother or sister."

Erica fixed her eyes on the tummy angled toward her, but it felt like she wasn't really absorbing the words *baby, brother,* and *sister.* At any other moment they would have set her off like cheap fireworks, but there was something else in what Leanne had said that distracted her attention.

"Why is this year going to be super sad?"

Leanne stepped back. She looked surprised. Surprised at Erica's ignorance. "I didn't say it *would* be."

"Yes, you did."

"I'm sure I said it *might*. And, anyway, I thought you . . ."

When she didn't finish, Erica persisted. "What were you talking about?"

Leanne lifted her shoulders in one of those maddening shrugs. "I guess I probably meant a lot of things."

"No, you didn't. You meant one thing." Without conscious thought, Erica allowed the answer to escape her lips. "You meant because of my mother, didn't you?"

Leanne weighed her words carefully before replying. "I suppose that is what I was referring to. Primarily."

"But my mom's having chemo. That's why she's so sick. She went through the same thing last year. She got better. She's going to get better."

Ms. Dench placed her hands on Erica's shoulders. There were tears in her buggy eyes, and her lower lip pooched out like a sad clown's. "Oh, honey, I sure hope so. We all do. We're praying for a miracle."

Erica recoiled. That word—*miracle*—held the force of a blow.

A miracle, a real one, was something that hardly ever happened, except in the Bible or maybe on television. A miracle was water turning into wine, or a homeless man finding a million dollars in a garbage can. A miracle would be having a snow day called on the very morning you have a math test you are doomed to fail because you absolutely don't get fractions. Erica had prayed for a snow day last year—prayed with more dedicated intensity than she'd ever dreamed of applying to studying—and she'd still ended up sweating in a chair over a math test. Because miracles didn't happen to normal people like her.

When adults started jabbering about miracles, what they meant was that things were really, really hopeless. What Leanne had meant was that her mother was going to die.

Erica took another step back.

At the same time, the doorbell rang and Leanne straightened up upbruptly. "Oh! They're here!"

They were her relatives from Houston, whose arrival she had been awaiting all morning. She jostled Erica aside slightly to give herself a final once-over in the mirror. "I'm looking good, if I do say so myself."

Erica stared blankly, barely hearing her.

"And apparently, I have to say so myself, since some other people can't be bothered." Leanne twirled and exited the room in a puff of irritation, which should have given Erica some sense of normalcy. But her insides were in upheaval; her stomach churned, her legs felt rubbery, and she could feel her brain pressing against her skull. She didn't think she'd ever feel normal again.

The hubbub of high-pitched greetings in the living room propelled Erica in the opposite direction. From the hallway she ducked into the kitchen and then sneaked out the back door. She had no idea what she was doing. All she knew was that she had to go, to move, to get out. It wasn't until she had hiked her skirt up and knotted it at her side that she realized she was bicycle bound. She didn't make a conscious decision where to go, either, once she started peddling; only the outraged thoughts running through her mind steered her.

Her head raged in a hopeless argument. Her mother was dying. But she couldn't be dying. But of course she was; it was so obvious.

It had been obvious for a long time, but she'd been too wrapped up in Maggie and her own little drama to see it. She'd been preoccupied with Ms. Dench and the stupid wedding, and attempting to stop Ms. Dench's stupid wedding, and trying to be Maggie's best friend. Thoughts of cute high school boys made her blood boil. Who cared? What did it matter? Why had she wasted time thinking about stupid stuff? So much time.

Why hadn't anybody warned her? Why hadn't Laura said anything to her? Or Webb? Or Heidi? She bet even Heidi knew what was going on. Heidi and her mother hung out together all the time. But what was Heidi to her mother compared to her? It was infuriating. Everyone had kept her in the dark, as if she didn't matter at all. And if she confronted them, they would probably tell her that it had all been for her own good.

Powered by anger, she stood on the pedals in her white patent leather shoes and pumped up a hill. By the time she crested the rise and began to really make speed, her blame was beginning to zero in on her mom. As distracted as Erica had been all summer, there had still been a hundred moments when her mother could have asked her to spend more time at the farm or to help her more, or just given her a few hints about what was going on. Rue had always told her that she had to be honest, but when it came to the most serious thing that had ever happened or probably would ever happen, Rue had hidden the truth. Which was practically the same thing as lying.

Are there any *honest people in your family?*

Were there any honest people in the whole world?

She remembered how her mom had skipped chemotherapy for a few weeks. Why? She couldn't remember now. What was going on? Didn't her mother even want to get better? Was she just giving up?

It was that last thought that made her angrier than anything. How many times had her mother told her that the important thing was not to quit?

She skidded as she turned in to the farm's gate and coasted the rest of the way to the house on a wave of indignation. She was not going to be quiet about this. They'd dismissed her as if she were nothing but a little kid. Now she was going to give them a piece of her mind. She was even prepared to yell at her mom, for hiding the truth from her, for leaving her to learn what was going on from Ms. Dench. And most of all, for not getting better.

If she were Laura, she would have all sorts of colorful expressions for how ill she felt, and a few more for how ill she looked, but Rue doubted any of them would be up to the job. She'd been in bed for twelve hours the night before, but she still was dog tired. Her bones ached, her head felt like it was being squeezed in a citrus juicer, and her stomach pitched and dipped. Memories of Dr. Ajay assuring her that they knew all about controlling the side effects of chemo now—*some patients never even miss a full day of work!*—were never far from her mind. Only the presence of people around her kept her from dissolving into hysteria or crawling into bed and staying there. As it was, she was looking forward to Heidi leaving for the wedding so she could go back to bed again.

Laura had agreed to accompany Heidi to the church and set everything up. Rue felt some guilt for not being up to snuff on the big day, even though Heidi had assured her a hundred times that it was no big deal.

Still, it felt like a big deal not to be a part of something that they had meant to do together. It made her feel she'd failed.

It also made her feel left out, even though she was actually opting out. Rationality flew out the window when your whole body felt like it was being slowly fed through a meat grinder. She struggled to stay in the spirit of the moment as Heidi dashed around the kitchen, assembling, double-checking, and covering.

In trim black slacks, an ironed snowy white shirt, and a red bib apron she'd borrowed from Rue, Heidi looked surprisingly caterer-like. Her normal state of goofy abstraction had been swapped for the moment with crisp efficiency. Earlier Rue had been trying to buoy her confidence in much the same way she would buoy Erica's when she had to perform some dread task, like speaking at assembly, but now she wondered aloud if Heidi might have found her niche.

"It's a shame that we've sidelined the cookbook, but I have to admit, I've enjoyed this," Heidi said. "Certainly more than my job at the bank, or any of the temp work I did before this."

"Maybe that's because this is what you have a talent for."

"The trouble is, I don't think I'd want to spend my life at the mercy of brides."

"You should open your own place, then." Rue thought for a moment. "How about a Sassy Spinster Café?"

Heidi laughed.

"I'm serious."

"What, here?"

Rue shrugged. "Here . . . or somewhere."

Heidi appeared to give it about five seconds' thought, which was probably par for the course in her life. "I could never manage. I have no head for business."

"How do you know?"

"I break out in a sweat whenever I have to balance my checkbook."

"You don't either."

"Okay, but I don't like dealing with money." She frowned. "I probably shouldn't have been working in a bank, should I?"

"There would be more to owning a café than just balancing the books."

"Maybe so, but it doesn't matter. Starting your own business is a leap. I lack courage."

"I imagine courage is like anything else—a muscle you have to work."

"Uh-huh, and mine's atrophied."

Laura came in, reluctantly reporting for duty. "Okay, what's the deal here?"

Heidi looked her over, from her dirty boots to her hair, and shook her head. "No."

Laura turned to Rue for a translation. "What is she saying?"

"I think she's saying no," Rue replied.

"You can't handle food," Heidi said. "You're filthy!"

Laura drew back, offended. "I washed my hands."

Heidi was not impressed. "Your clothes are sweaty, and your boots are disgusting."

"Excuse me," Laura responded tersely. "I still have to keep this place going. Webb's bugged out for the day, and since you stole my guys, I'm it around here." She did a quick spin, as if expecting them to be there. "What have you done with Dylan and Herman?"

"They're already at the church, setting up," Heidi answered, but she was obviously distracted by Laura's hair, which had feathers in it. "You're molting!"

Laura shook her head out like a dog trying to shiver off a few fleas. Two feathers were set alight through the air, and one landed on a platter of hors d'oeuvres. That the platter was covered in cellophane didn't seem to mollify Heidi one bit.

"Look at that!" She shooed the feather off the table. When she was done there, she kept flapping her hands in Laura's general direction. It did seem that Laura had unleashed a cloud of outdoorsy funk. Dust floated in the bright shaft of morning coming through the kitchen window. Even Laura saw it.

"All right," she conceded. "Just give me a minute to change."

Heidi flicked a fretful glance at the kitchen clock. "A minute's about all we have. I need to get the truck loaded—but you need a shower."

Rue stepped forward. "I can help."

"You?" Laura shook her head. "You should go rest. I might be a little untidy, but you look like you've been et by a wolf and shat out over a cliff."

Heidi howled in disgust, but Rue couldn't help laughing. That about described it. "I can still carry a few platters to the truck while you jump in the shower."

Laura looked like she would have argued if Heidi hadn't pushed her toward the door. *"Hurry."*

When she was gone, Heidi glanced at her watch and then

picked up plates with both hands. "Leanne's probably starting to wonder if she should send out for pizzas."

"She's probably wondering if she should send out for a new groom."

Heidi shook her head. "The marriage might be a disaster, but the food's going to be good, dammit."

When she was gone, Rue put one hand on the kitchen table and the other hand on the back of her chair and stood up. She remained upright for about ten seconds before being pushed back down again by a dizzying wave of nausea.

Damn. Why was Zofran letting her down? She would have to call the doctor and ask for something else, but that would take hours. Someone would need to go to Carter's Springs and pick it up for her. Unfortunately, today was a bad day to get anything done that didn't revolve around the wedding.

When Heidi came back and caught sight of Rue still sitting where she'd left her, her brow pinched up.

"I'm sorry," Rue said, bracing herself to take another stab at standing up.

Heidi checked her with a gesture. "Stay right there. We need someone by the phone in case one of the guys—or heaven help us, Leanne—calls from the church."

A kindly lie, Rue knew.

"Oh, and by the way, Erica's here. I saw her riding up on her bike."

Rue lurched to her feet. "But she's in the wedding! She should be at the church."

Heidi's arm shot out to steady her. "Don't panic. I'll take her back with me. They probably won't even notice she's missing."

The phone rang.

Rue tilted her head. "I think they've noticed."

"Don't answer," Heidi said when the phone rang again.

"Why not?"

"Because it's just going to be Leanne and she's going to start complaining and it will make me nervous." Heidi took a breath. "More nervous."

Rue shook her head and took a wobbly step toward the phone. When she reached out to pick up the receiver, she realized that the phone had stopped ringing. *Thank God.* She wasn't certain she was up for words with Leanne right now. In fact, she wasn't sure she was up for much of anything. Her skin was prickly and clammy, and it felt as if someone were performing a Vulcan nerve pinch on her. Her knees felt as if they were going to buckle.

"Oh no!" Heidi sprang forward to catch her, and in the next moment she was holding Rue's sprawled body up by the armpits.

"Rue?" Heidi asked, peering down into her face.

She closed her eyes and swallowed. "I just went light-headed all of a sudden. I'm sorry."

"Don't be." Heidi chuckled, making light of it. "It's like those falling backward trust exercises the PE teacher in junior high school used to make kids do. But I never did. Someone told me that the year before, Laura had actually let some poor girl fall splat to the floor. You wouldn't catch me trusting anybody after that."

Erica skidded into the kitchen. Her hair was windblown and wild, her cheeks were flushed with exercise, and her dress was wrinkled and covered with a film of dust. She had burst in as if her hair was on fire, and yet as she stepped over the threshold, her whole demeanor changed. She stopped short, absorbed the fact that Heidi was holding her mother up, and whatever exclamation was poised on her lips melted away.

"What's wrong?" Her brow scrunched in worry. "Mom?"

Rue forced a smile. "Heidi was just performing an adolescence do-over. Trust falls."

She flicked a glance at Heidi, who brought her up to her feet with a flourish. "Ta-da!"

Erica regarded them distrustfully. "We did that in gym class. Lucy Dewes fell and sprained her wrist."

"Laura hadn't by any chance snuck into that class, had she?" Heidi asked.

"What did I do?" Laura asked, breezing in. Her hair was damp, but at least she had changed clothes and was no longer walking around in a Pig-Pen cloud. Her eyes bugged out in surprise to see Erica. "Hey, fugitive! Leanne's looking for you."

"*You* talked to Leanne?" Rue asked, sliding down into a chair again.

Laura nodded. "She's also wondering where all the food is."

"What did you tell her?" Heidi asked.

"What do you think? I told her to cool her damn jets."

Heidi let out a sigh of irritation. "Let's just get going." She started loading down Laura with plates. "The guys are probably wondering where we are, too."

Laura balanced a plate on each hand and followed Heidi out.

Rue was determined not to be completely useless. Having Erica there gave her a kick in the pants. She didn't want to behave as though she'd taken to her fainting couch. "You got your dress dirty."

Erica suddenly seemed subdued, almost dazed. Rue wondered what had brought her out here in the first place. "Nobody's going to be looking at me, anyway," she said.

"With that eye? You'll be Topic A at the reception."

Erica shrugged. "I don't care. . . ."

Rue had never gotten a clear idea of what exactly had happened at the Dairy Queen. Erica had said that Maggie had called her a liar, but there had to be more to it than that. Kids called each other liars all the time without punches being thrown. But if there was one thing she knew, when Erica had something she didn't want to talk about, getting blood from a turnip was a snap by comparison. It was best to let it drop.

Rue took up a platter and tried balancing it like Laura had the plates, on one hand. Unfortunately, she lacked Laura's strength, and her arm muscles quivered like Jell-O.

"I can get that." Erica took the platter from her.

Rue relinquished it and leveled a curious stare at Erica. "What are you really doing here? Why aren't you in Sweetgum?"

Erica's jaw clenched in a familiar stubborn expression. "I just came back to help."

"Truthfully?"

"Truthfully!" Erica spat out the word as if it were an insult, but when her gaze met Rue's, the spark in her eyes flamed out. "Yeah, that's all."

Rue nodded. She didn't want to argue when Erica was lending a helping hand. But she knew her daughter well enough to suspect that altruism wasn't all there was to it.

Chapter 23

Like when she fell off the monkey bars at school. That was the only way Erica could describe the feeling of rushing into the kitchen and seeing her mother, her face almost green, sagging in Heidi's arms. She looked so helpless, so weak, it had knocked the breath out of her.

Erica crouched between Laura and Heidi on the bench seat of Laura's truck, with a huge chocolate cake perched on her lap and her feet resting on a box of utensils. *Weak* wasn't a word she associated with her mom. Her mom was as tall as Laura and used to seem bigger, because Laura had an alley cat build, whereas her mother looked more like a normal person. She had a little bit of padding. Used to have a little bit of padding. Now she looked like a skeleton with a sack of skin thrown over it.

It had probably been going on all year, this diminishing, ever since the very first operation. Slowly, she'd been losing ground, so slowly it was as impossible to see it in real time as it would be to watch a tree grow. Maybe the doctors had been wrong, and her mother had never really gotten better at all last winter. And now they were determined to poison her to death, when she probably would be better off if they just left her alone. She hated doctors.

She hated herself. She'd felt so stupid, watching her mother trying to hold a platter, which had made her withered arm mus-

cles jiggle. It was only a vegetable platter; her own school backpack probably weighed twice as much.

All her anger, her stupid anger, had disappeared like a puff of
smoke. She knew Heidi and her mom had been lying when they
said they were playing some stupid game. She'd been angry that
people were just pretending that everything was okay for her
sake, because she was a child. But after she'd grabbed the platter
and made out like she'd just come home to help out, she'd understood why no one had pointed out the truth to her before now.
They weren't just pretending for her; they were pretending for
themselves, too. Pretending was what was keeping them going.

She felt dazed, as if she were snapping out of a long dream involving Ms. Dench, junior lifesaving class, Maggie, and Mrs. Robichaux. Everything that had seemed such a big deal, that had
absorbed her every waking hour, actually meant nothing to her.
Nothing at all.

"Shouldn't someone be with Mom?" Erica blurted out. "She's
all alone."

"I'm going back soon," Laura said. "I'm not staying for that
wedding."

Erica wished she didn't have to. She was glad she'd made
them squeeze her bicycle onto the back of the truck. This way
she'd have a way to escape back to the farm when the reception
got too gruesome.

They were greeted in the church parking lot by Dylan and
Herman, sparkly clean and dressed like Heidi in white shirts and
black pants.

Erica handed Herman the cake and then struggled out of the
truck in her dress. "Y'all look like waiters!"

Dylan's cheeks flushed red. "I wouldn't criticize if I were you,
Rocky."

The fellowship room of the church was about midway into its
transformation into a banquet hall. Herman and Dylan had been
busy. Several long tables formed a horseshoe in the center of the
room and to the side, and a couple more tables had been pushed

against the wall. Someone had rounded up what looked like every folding chair in Sweetgum. Only half were actually unfolded; the rest were stacked in leaning clusters against walls and tables. At the same time the five people from the farm were trying to set up, the florist from Carter's Springs and his assistant were piling plants and sprays of flowers everywhere. And then, too, a few stray wedding guests had filtered in to help, or get in the way.

Erica's first instinct was to back away from it all, but Heidi caught her by the arm and propelled her toward a stack of chairs. "You can be the chair unfolder."

Erica wondered if she was supposed to be in the church yet and started to say something. But everything going on here seemed so much more important.

"Oh, and I think Dylan said there were a couple left in that little meeting room down the hall." It was as if the echo of herself barking orders stopped Heidi for a moment. She added, "If you don't mind."

"I don't mind." It beat standing around in the church, just waiting.

She hurried down the hall and ducked her head into doors until she found a room with folding chairs. The trouble was, it was already occupied. A man sat in one of the chairs with his back to her, messing with something inside a briefcase. She cleared her throat a little, and the man slammed the case shut and shot to his feet. Erica gasped, not just because of the suddenness of his movements, but also because of the venomous look in his eye.

"Sorry!" she whispered.

His responding smile didn't quite reach his eyes. "No, I'm sorry. You startled me."

He sounded nice enough, if a little weird. "You're here for the wedding?" she asked.

He didn't say.

It was a dumb question, anyway. Of course he was here for the wedding. He was wearing a suit. He was probably one of Leanne's people—from Houston, by the looks of him. His hair had a dyed streak. Grown men in Sweetgum didn't do hair salons.

"I just need some chairs," she said.

"Be my guest." He gestured toward the chairs as if he were being generous, but in her book being generous would mean actually helping her carry the chairs, which he didn't seem at all inclined to do. The most he did was fold up the one he'd been sitting on and stack it with the others.

"Are you one of Leanne's people?"

"Yeah."

Apparently, the man didn't want to talk about Leanne any more than he wanted to help. She turned and hauled the chairs back to the big fellowship room. She wondered if the guy was actually related to Leanne. Which meant she would be related to him now, too.

Just as she reached the fellowship room, someone snatched her by the arm, hard, and spun her around.

It was her dad. His face was practically purple. "Where've you been?"

"Helping Heidi."

"Jesus Pete!" He started dragging her to the door and then around the side of the church. "Do you know how many people have been hunting for you? Half the family! Even your granny Anderson, who's been here for a solid hour and who you haven't even bothered to say hello to."

"I just got here. I've been helping."

He rolled his eyes impatiently. "You're not supposed to help. You're supposed to stand around with the bridal party."

"Why?"

"Because it's a wedding! That's what you're supposed to do. If you want to help, help Leanne."

She shook his hand off her arm. "What's the matter with you? Are you nervous?"

"No!" he thundered. "I'm perfectly calm, no thanks to your little disappearing act!"

"Sorry."

It wasn't the last time she had to apologize that day, not by a long shot. All her relatives scolded her for not being there to greet them, and exclaimed over her black eye, and criticized her for having stringy, messy hair. Then, when she was tugged into a little anteroom charged with bridal jitters, Leanne noticed Erica's dress had a black, oily streak on the skirt, and she exploded. Two fidgety bridesmaids worked Erica over with Shout wipes and forced her to pull on a pair of panty hose that reached up to her armpits and still bagged at the ankles. She'd left her pair at Leanne's house.

When they were done, Leanne shoved a basket of flower petals into her hands. "Here. Try to stay put for the next five minutes. Maybe now we can get this show on the road."

"You seem as nervous as Dad," Erica observed.

Leanne's face flushed pink. *Wrong thing to say.* "What's *he* got to be nervous about? He's not marrying a lying, philandering cheapskate!"

After that, Erica vowed to stay silent through the rest of the wedding ordeal. When the wedding march began, she scurried up the church aisle, tossing clumps of petals and keeping her eyes glued on the altar. During the wedding itself, she got to sit in the corner of the front pew and peek out at everyone. She scanned the crowd for Jake Peavy, who she knew was there, although he wasn't sitting next to his parents once when she looked. Toward the end she was surprised to see Heidi and Dylan and even Herman hovering in the back of the church, watching.

After the recessional she hurried out as fast as she could and headed straight for the food. She hadn't eaten all day, she remembered.

"Where's Heidi?" she asked Dylan, who was standing by the door.

He rolled his eyes. "Why do people keep asking that? She had to go back for something. It's no big deal. It's not like Herman and I can't handle stuff."

Herman was at the punch bowl, filling glasses as the guests began to flood in.

"Who else was looking for Heidi?" Erica asked Dylan.

"Some weird guy."

Erica remembered the streaky-haired man, and then she saw him, standing in the doorway to the interior hall. She grabbed a Texas-shaped cheese tartlet and went over to him. "Why are you looking for Heidi?"

"I used to know her."

"When she lived here?"

"Yeah."

"That was a long time ago."

The man's eyes narrowed until they looked like little shards of ice. "I know. That's why I wanted to see her. Someone told me she would be here."

"She will. She just had to run out to the farm for a little bit."

"What farm?"

Erica crossed her arms. He didn't know much. "Sassy Spinster Farm."

"Where's that?"

Erica gestured in the general direction with her half-eaten tartlet. "Just down the road, going east. The gate's marked. Everybody knows the farm."

The guy was already turning to leave. His stride was so quick, he walked faster than a lot of people ran.

"She'll be back!" Erica called after him, but it was doubtful he heard.

The wedding horde migrated to the fellowshop room with surprising speed. Nobody was sitting down except a few old folks, but everybody was gathering around the horseshoe-shaped table. The huge wedding cake at the center of the U was like a magnet. People seemed to gravitate toward it more than to the food they could actually eat. Leanne had said she'd spent a king's ransom on the wedding cake, and it looked it. Erica herself had her eye on the groom's cake, which was chocolate. Her mother made really good chocolate cake, with icing that was almost like fudge.

Leanne was the last to enter the room, sweeping in, holding her train in one hand and beaming like a queen before her subjects. Erica's dad trailed behind, a little more subdued, but looking happy.

Amazing, Erica thought. *All that anxiety, and then a few words by a preacher and everything is calm again.*

At the same time the word *calm* crossed her mind, the world suddenly exploded. The blast sounded like a bomb going off. The epicenter was the side table where the groom's cake sat. Or had sat. In the blink of an eye, it was blown to smithereens. There was just a millisecond of shock in the room, and then pandemonium. People screamed. Cake was everywhere. Some icing-covered people ran for the exits, but more people, pelted by baked debris, lunged for the floor. Erica dove behind a chair just in time to see a second explosion.

It was the bridal cake detonating. Something inside it burst, and now the air was raining sponge cake, marzipan, and butter icing. When Erica dared to poke her head up, she saw a hundred wedding guests splayed on the floor, covered in cakey fallout. It was on the floor, too, and clinging to the walls in vanilla and chocolate clumps. Several of the guests cried out in panic as they glanced down at the chocolate icing and fondant dripping down their skin.

Dylan, who'd been crouched right next to her, lifted his head up cautiously. A little chunk of marzipan fell out of his hair. "Whoa! That was awesome!"

Erica nodded. "Awesome." That was the only word for it. "And I can't even get in trouble."

Dylan swung toward her. "Did you do this?"

"No!"

He shrugged. "I don't care. I'm gonna get serious overtime to clean this place up."

"Why would someone make the cakes explode?" she asked. *And who?*

In her mind she was already picturing the likeliest culprit. That weird man. She'd bet a million dollars. He'd acted really odd the two times she'd seen him. She hadn't noticed him during the ceremony, either. He could have sneaked into the fellowship hall while Dylan and Herman were watching the tag end of the wedding.

Where was he?

And then she remembered. He'd left. Right after she'd told him that Heidi would be at the farm.

She'd even pointed out the way.

Airhead. Ditz. Moron.

Heidi called herself every name in the chucklehead lexicon. How could she have forgotten the chocolate sauce? She'd put it right in the front of the fridge. *A quick twenty seconds in the microwave at the last minute*, she'd told herself a hundred times. It was one of the last actual cooking chores on the program.

Of course, it had slipped right out of her mind.

As mishaps went, though, this was pretty minor. Otherwise, things were going like clockwork, if she did say so herself. She wouldn't be surprised if they didn't get a few calls for more work after this day. Or, at the very least, she hoped the reception would be something people would remember.

She nuked the chocolate and was halfway out the door when she remembered she had left her purse in the kitchen. She hurried back through the house, trying not to make too much noise so she wouldn't wake up Rue. Rue had been conked out when she'd arrived, and Laura had given her a warning that her sister was not to be disturbed. As if she needed one.

Laura had then loaded herself and the dogs in her old truck and had headed out to do whatever it was Laura did. Webb had left that morning, mysteriously, to see about a job for the fall; Heidi suspected this was why Laura wasn't exactly in a holiday mood. The last Heidi had seen of her, she'd been muttering something about her pumpkin patch, but she'd driven off in the direction of the pig wallow, which seemed to be her default destination.

She snatched her purse off the counter by threading her right forearm through the handle straps. She was running on fumes.

Of course, the moment she did stop going a mile a minute, she would probably start worrying again. She would have to take stock and decide when she should go back. She had promised Laura that she would stay, but how long could that go on? Vinnie's trial was at the end of September. She was nearly certain she was ready to go back and face Vinnie in a court of law. Rue had ginned up her courage, partly through nagging and shaming, partly by example. A summer on the farm might have taught Heidi next to nothing about farming, but she had learned a thing or two about courage. What Rue faced walking into her chemo room was surely more traumatic than telling a bunch of strangers that your ex-boyfriend was a crook and that you had been a fool.

As she emerged from the house, she saw an unfamiliar car coming up the drive. The screen door slapped shut behind her, and as Heidi stopped on the top step, a cold shiver worked its way through her, scalp to toe. She didn't know the car, but she knew the driver. Knew him even before he stepped out. There was something about the profile . . . And when he turned his head toward her, she was sure. That grim mouth turned down at the corners. Those eyes, cold and businesslike. And then, of course, the hair.

Vinnie's goon.

Damnation.

Her first instinct was to turn and run back inside, lock all the doors and windows, and barricade herself in the house. But old Streaky Hair didn't look like the kind of man who would be intimidated by a button lock. Besides, Rue was asleep inside and weak as a kitten. Bringing a killer into her house would be a great way to repay her for a summer's hospitality.

She didn't really have time to consider alternatives, though. Very methodically, the goon was coming toward her in the blazing heat. Sunlight glinted off of something metal on his person. He had a gun.

Her body was frozen, but her mind was surprisingly calm. This was ridiculous. If Vinnie had sent this man all the way out here to shut her up, he'd wasted his time and money. "You're too late!"

The guy looked surprised that she would stop to speak to him. He continued forward. "Too late for what?"

His voice was astonishingly normal. The man had featured so prominently in her nightmares all summer that she'd expected him to sound more like Darth Vader than an actual human.

"Hamilton Cho got here first. I gave him everything I had." She wondered if with that admission she had just signed her death warrant, but she lifted her chin with something like defiance. "So I'm sorry. You're too late. The evidence is gone."

"But you're still here."

Heavy lids hooded his steely blue eyes from the sunlight, making his face seem expressionless, robotic. It was like she was talking to the Terminator. She'd always preferred sinister figures with a little personality—like Peter Lorre or the Wicked Witch of the West. A personality gave you something to fight against. A weak spot.

The image of the Wicked Witch sinking to the floor in a smoky heap popped into her mind, replacing the image of herself dying at the hands of a man with a bad hairdo. Too bad there wasn't a bucket of water handy.

Or maybe there was something better.

She cradled the Pyrex bowl in her arms.

"Do you like chocolate?" she asked.

The man's stony expression loosened for a moment. He barely uttered a perplexed "Huh?" before she ripped the cellophane off the bowl and launched its contents at his face.

The Three Stooges tactic wasn't going to work any magic, but it gave her the split second she needed to turn and run like hell. In the distance she saw the chicken fence—electric, but not deadly—and veered the other way, toward the barn. If she got there before he caught up to her, she could lock herself in. There had to be something in there to use as a weapon.

As she sprinted across the grass, her world narrowed down to the barn buildings in front of her and the sound of someone running behind her. She half expected to be tackled and brought down like a wildebeest on the savanna. She tossed her purse into the air. The thunk of leather and keys and a said curse let her know she'd actually hit her target.

The only thing she had going for her now was home turf advantage. She darted around the old metal feed storage shed, flinging its door open as she passed. Then, before he had cleared the corner, she sped on into the barn, which was open.

The moment the barn door closed, he would know she wasn't in the feed shed, but maybe she'd bought herself a little time. She slid the metal lock closed—it wasn't much more substantial than the extra slide lock on her old apartment in Brooklyn. Certainly not the two-by-four that barn doors were always barred with in movies. It would take about three seconds for Vinnie's man to bust it down. In those few seconds, Heidi grabbed the first heavy tool she saw mounted on the utility wall and ran to the back of the barn to hide herself in the stall that had been occupied most recently by Erica's goat, Spunky.

Then, to her dismay, she spotted Fred pecking around in the old hay. *What is he doing here?* The bird tilted a nervous glance at her.

Crouched down, she heard the man following, doing exactly as she expected. Running to the door. Pushing it. Pushing it harder. Heidi took deep breaths. Was this how her life was going to end? Gunned down in a barn that stank of goat urine and leather and WD-40, her last moments on earth spent with Laura's chicken? She would be ending her days on the Rafferty farm in Sweetgum, the very thing she'd always dreaded when she was fourteen.

Or was she actually going to hack a man to death with an ax? In the rock, paper, scissors hierarchy of weaponry, could an ax even win over a gun? She had the sinking feeling that a gun trumped everything.

The door crashed open, and she flattened herself against the side of the stall. He knew she was there, but he didn't know where. Surprise was all she had going for her now.

Sweat trickled down her temples, down her back. Hovering against the old cedar planks, all she could hear was her own shallow breath and slow footsteps coming ever closer.

No, there was something else, too.

Fred released a few of his feeble clucks as he bobbed out of the stall to see who had come in. He was probably expecting Laura.

Heidi leaned forward and attempted to shoo him back in, but her flapping hands only made her feather-brained adversary stop and cock his head at her. She sighed and reached her hand out just far enough that her fingertips must have proved an irresistible target. A shot rang out, and fear knocked her back on her heels. He'd missed her fingers, but she felt singed, anyway.

Poor Fred was flapping around in what seemed at first pure birdbrained panic. Then she saw a spray of bright red on his white feathers and more on the floor of the barn. The sight was almost as nauseating as seeing her own blood, and it took her a moment to collect herself. And to prepare for what was coming next. Staying calm was difficult with a hysterical, bloody pet chicken squawking and hopping in a drunken circle in front of you.

Her eyes wouldn't shut, however, and her ragged, shallow breaths counted out her last moments as the footsteps came closer. Her hands tightened around the ax handle, but even as she tried to visualize herself wielding it, the snubbed black barrel of a pistol cleared the stall door. Every muscle in her body froze.

She'd read studies about the human body under extreme stress. All the blood was supposed to go to the muscles to give that extra pep needed to fight or flee. Which meant that even at her most terrified, her reflexes proved useless. She was going to die. She was going to die cowering in this stinky stall, clutching an ax.

It almost made her glad when her life started passing before her eyes, but then that turned out to be disappointing, too. It hadn't been much of a life. Mostly it was notable for what hadn't happened—no serious love affairs, no professional triumphs (no profession at all, really), and certainly no great moments of hero-ism. There was one friendship to speak of. Rue. It was late in coming, but at least at the end she'd found one human being on earth besides her mother who she felt would be sad to see her gone.

Her eyes didn't even bother looking at her assassin's face. She just watched the hand on the pistol, the way it tensed just before it was ready to squeeze the trigger. When that moment came, she forced her eyes shut. A shot even louder than she'd expected cracked through the air. She heard herself shout in surprise at the same time the thug shouted, too. The strange thing was, he kept shouting, while after a split second she was silenced by the fact that she was still all in one piece.

She opened her eyes and looked around the stall door, where her would-be killer was writhing on the ground, crying out in agony a few feet away from poor Fred. The chicken was still hop-ping, although with diminishing strength.

Heidi scrambled to her feet. Laura stood at the door, her trusty pig rifle still trained on the hood lying on the ground. His leg was twisted oddly, and his jeans were bloody at the knee. Groaned and shouted curses spilled out of him.

Heidi tossed the ax down, grabbed the pistol, which the goon had dropped, and ran to Laura. Now that it was over, she felt noodly limbed. The gun in her hand went off, firing into the wall. She shrieked.

"Put that down!" Laura barked at her.

Heidi dropped it, then felt tears gush out of her eyes. She fell against Laura's stiff, wiry arm. "You saved my life! I owe you my life!"

"Don't be stupid," Laura growled. "That jerk just messed with the wrong chicken."

Even as she said it, Fred was flapping drunkenly toward her.

"Come here, little buddy." Laura pushed Heidi away and

knelt down. Over her shoulder, she said, "It's Erica you should thank. She spotted the guy at the church and biked like the wind. I met her coming up the drive. Lucky I had my pig gun handy."

Erica herself materialized at the barn door, holding the dogs by their collars. She sucked in her breath. "What happened to Fred!"

What happened to *you?*" Heidi was tempted to ask. Erica's dress was a mess—was that mud?—and there was white crap in her hair.

But it was no time for worrying about appearances. Laura was inspecting Fred's wounds. One of his legs was dangling in a way that was hard for Heidi to look at. Both man and chicken had taken a hit in the same place.

"Poor Fred!" Erica released the dogs, who immediately swarmed and slobbered over the man on the ground. Their growls mixed with his cries.

"Forget the damn chicken!" he cried out. "My fucking leg!"

"Hey! Language!" Laura brayed. "And just so's you know, I generally don't waste a lot of sympathy on murderers."

"I didn't kill anybody!" he howled. "I didn't even intend to!"

"You practically killed my bird!"

Heidi glowered at him. "If you didn't intend to kill me, then what were you doing chasing me with a gun?"

"I was just supposed to keep you from testifying at the trial. You know . . . take you somewhere."

"Oh! *Just* kidnap me. That's great. Thanks a lot! A real gentleman!"

Laura sneered. "If you were just going to kidnap her, why did you explode the cakes?"

Heidi whipped around. "Cakes *exploded?*"

"Ask Erica," Laura said. "Apparently, it was like Armageddon with baked goods."

"I don't know what you're talking about," the guy said.

Erica nodded. "They both went off. There were bombs in the cakes!"

Heidi looked down at the brown-spattered purple dress. It wasn't mud; it was cake. The cake *she'd* made. And if cake was all over the attendees, then it was probably all over the other food, too. She groaned.

Laura shot her a sharp look. "Call the police. And an ambulance."

For a fraction of a second, Heidi wondered which she wanted the ambulance for, man or bird. "Didn't you guys say it takes forever for ambulances to get here?"

Laura's brows rose, and she looked meaningfully from their gun-toting visitor back to Heidi, and then to someone new standing in the doorway.

Heidi turned. Rue was leaning against the barn door in her bathrobe, clutching a rifle and taking it all in. The commotion had roused her from her sickbed. She was too late for a rescue, but Heidi was moved by the sight of her standing there, baldheaded, in her pink terry bathrobe and scuffs.

"It *can* take a while," Rue said, her mouth tightening in a grim smile. "But really, I don't see the need for a big rush. Do y'all?"

Now that the day she had dreaded for so long was all over, Erica couldn't stop crying. Her dad and Leanne's wedding day had been even more horrible than anticipated—for completely different reasons than she'd expected.

After the ambulance had come and gone, and the police had come and gone, and they all had finally left the barn, Heidi had fallen apart, weeping openly and telling whoever happened to be near her that she now owed her whole life to Laura. (An opinion that seemed to give Erica's aunt no satisfaction at all.) Heidi had sucked down two beers on the porch with Dylan and Herman, who were still wearing their cake-damaged waiter clothing. Heidi had laughed in astonishment as she'd listened to the story of the explosions at the wedding reception, and then she'd started crying again about it being all her fault.

Even though the thug from New York had sworn ten ways to Sunday that he had nothing to do with the exploding cakes, no one gave his story much credence. The police believed he had been trying to create a diversion at the reception so he could snatch Heidi. Then, when Erica informed him of Heidi's whereabouts, he discovered he didn't need the diversion. But by then it had all been set up.

"All that work, for nothing," Heidi moaned as everyone congregated around the kitchen table. "And poor Leanne . . ."

"Oh, for pete's sake," Laura said. "It's not like it was *all* your fault that her wedding reception was a disaster."

Unfortunately, Leanne didn't see it that way. Once word about their visiting gunman from New York had got out, Leanne had called to ream Heidi for luring a mad cake bomber to her wedding reception. No one could quite convince her that Heidi hadn't intended to ruin her wedding all along. Leanne not only wanted all the down payment money for the catering back, but she wanted Sassy Spinster Farm to reimburse her for the bride's cake, too.

"It's so unfair," Heidi said. "The man was just diabolical. Do you know what the cops said the guy used to blow up the cakes? Explosives stuffed in a Wiffle ball and the decapitated head of a baby doll!"

Erica felt the blood drain out of her face. "He used toys?"

"Right," Heidi said. "How sick and twisted is that?"

"Are they *sure* it was the guy from New York?" Erica asked, trying to sound casual.

"Of course!" Heidi said. "Who else?"

Erica sank down in her chair, biting her lip and trying not to think of a certain incident involving a Mr. Potato Head on standardized test day. She had told Dylan that she couldn't be blamed for the explosions. But in a way, she could. They hadn't been part of some crime Heidi was all mixed up in. They were Maggie's revenge.

Telling on Jake Peavy would be tantamount to declaring war. She wasn't sure she could face it. Besides, Maggie had probably put him up to it, and no one knew better than herself how persuasive Maggie Robichaux could be.

Heidi sighed. "I'm going to be bankrupted and shamed."

No one could convince her that even Leanne would be brought around to reason once the dust had settled. No one seemed too convinced of it themselves.

Erica wished she could cry like Heidi—like a fountain spewing for everyone to see. Instead, she had to keep dashing out of the room when she teared up. They were all so focused on the wedding debacle, and what had happened in the barn, but her mind couldn't let go of what she'd learned about her mom today. Everyone, even Laura, assumed she was shaken up over what had happened with the gunman. She didn't contradict them. If she did, they'd only ask her for the real reason she was upset, and there was no way she was going to say the words "My mom's dying." Every time she even thought them, it felt as if her insides were being churned up into hamburger.

She didn't want anyone to notice her at all. All the same, she couldn't stay away from everyone. She craved hearing the day's events rehashed one more time. She sat next to her mom all through dinner and then through the movie.

In honor of their day of suspense, Rue had reached for Alfred Hitchcock. They watched *Rear Window*. Erica had seen it before, but it didn't matter, because she wasn't paying all that much attention. She just sat on the floor in front of the couch, where her mom was curled up, stared at the screen, and chuckled occasionally when she heard other people laughing.

Twice she had to get up. Once she pretended she had to pee, and the other time she microwaved some popcorn, which she had no taste for eating. There might as well have been buttered Styrofoam packing peanuts in the bowl she brought back to the living room.

After the last scene, the TV was shut off and the conversation began again. Heidi was full of talk about how *Rear Window* could apply to the fix she'd been in that afternoon. "I wonder if a few flashbulbs would have done me any good," she said. "I think I would rather have had a gun, or better yet, Laura with a gun."

"You definitely don't want a gun if you're just going to run around shooting walls," Laura said.

"I only shot the wall after the danger was over."

"What a day!" Rue said with a tired sigh. "I wonder if Leanne's calmed down by now."

"The woman probably fumed all the way to Cancun," Laura said. "That'll make for a fun honeymoon."

"You're being awfully quiet," Rue said to Erica.

Erica shrugged. She was glad she was leaning against the couch so her mom couldn't see her expression.

"I would have thought exploding cakes at Ms. Dench's wedding would be right up your alley," Laura observed.

Erica tried not to squirm guiltily. Heidi was looking at her funny. Erica bit at the ragged nail of her thumb. She must have broken it today during all the excitement.

"Are you okay?" Rue asked her.

Erica nodded, not trusting her voice.

"She's probably exhausted," Laura said. "That bike was going a hundred miles a minute. She was the hero of the hour."

Erica scowled at that. Everybody knew that it was Laura who had saved Heidi. "I wasn't thinking about that."

"Then what?" her mom asked.

Erica bit her lip. Why did they insist on making her talk when it was clear she didn't want to? She searched frantically for something they might actually believe, and remembered the other big news of the day. "I talked to Ms. Dench—I mean, Leanne—this morning. She told me her big news. She's going to have a baby."

"I knew there was some reason you came back to the farm!" Rue said. "You looked so upset. You should have said something."

"You knew." Erica looked around at all the faces in the room. No one looked surprised. They all had known about Leanne. "Why does everybody lie to me?"

"No one lied," her mother said.

Erica looked her in the eye. "You knew all along, and you didn't say anything. That's just the same as lying."

Her mom winced. "You're right. Maybe I should have said something earlier, but I didn't think it was my secret to tell."

"Not even to me?"

"I thought your father would tell you."

Erica rolled her eyes. "Oh, right!"

"Anyway, you were having such a good summer . . ."

Was she *crazy*? When Erica thought back on all that had happened, it seemed like the worst few months of her life. All the time she'd wasted hanging out with Maggie and listening to her drone on about cute high school boys and makeup. Who cared? Meanwhile, everything really important had been going on right here, right under her nose.

"It's good Leanne and William are going to be parents," Rue said, leaning forward. She put her hand on Erica's shoulder. "Just think of it as more family for you."

Erica absorbed the words and their unspoken meaning. Now that she'd finally been tipped off, she was alive to every nuance. Her mom was saying that she was going to need more family. But Erica didn't want anyone new. She just wanted to keep what she had already. Was that too much to ask?

She folded her arms. "Babies are boring. They're hardly people at all."

Everybody laughed, which did nothing to brighten Erica's mood. Her mother wrapped her arms around her shoulders in a bony hug, which Erica was only halfway successful in shrugging off. She wished she didn't have to pretend to just be upset about the baby. She wished she didn't have to pretend at all.

"Babies grow up eventually," Rue said. "Faster than you'd think. Pretty soon you'll have a little brother or sister, and you'll barely remember how it was before they were around."

"I'm not four, Mom. Of course I'll remember." Erica glowered down at the rug. "I'll remember everything."

"I guess I was thinking of how it was for me," Rue said.

She and Laura exchanged one of their long looks that was like silent conversation between them.

Rue turned back to Erica. Her eyes were red, and her hand felt like a pincer on Erica's shoulder. "Wouldn't you like to have a sister? Sisters are about the best thing that can happen to a person. They're practically a necessity."

The chirpy pep-talk voice she used seemed to suck the air out of the room. Heidi looked down at her feet. Laura, who was sitting in her usual chair in the corner nearest the door, seemed to sink inside herself. Erica watched Laura's face and the strange change that flashed across it. Her lips flattened and trembled, and streaks of red leapt out on her tawny cheeks. Moisture stood in her eyes, making them appear glassy and bloodshot.

In an instant, what was happening hit Erica like a shock wave. Laura was about to cry.

Her aunt stood abruptly and fled the room without a word.

Heidi leaned forward, grabbed a fistful of popcorn out of the bowl, and stuffed it into her mouth.

Rue leaned back, her eyes wide against her pale skin. She fidgeted with her silver Indian reservation ring, which was so loose that it seemed to be staying on her bony finger just from habit. "Am I wrong?"

Still chewing, Heidi shook her head. "A sister can be a lifesaver," she told Erica. "Even a stepsister. An ex-stepsister. Who hates you."

The three of them sat in silence, trying to pretend that they hadn't just seen Laura leave the room almost in tears. More pretending.

But at least Erica felt a little less alone. She wasn't the only one who couldn't stop crying, she realized now. She was just newer at trying to hide it.

Chapter 24

In the middle of preparations for Erica's birthday, Laura came through the kitchen and stopped when she saw Heidi standing over the food processor. "What are you making now?"

"Eggplant dip." The tomato crisis was under control, and the war against squash seemed to be behind them. Now it was zero hour for eggplants.

On the boom box, Rufus Wainwright was belting out a Beatles tune. The CD was not one of Heidi's favorites, but Rue had picked it. She was propped up on the couch in the next room, dozing.

Where the door had been left open, Fred hopped over the threshold. After he'd lost his foot in the shoot-out, Laura had whittled a prosthesis for him that attached to what was left of his leg. (He was the only peg-legged chicken Heidi had ever seen. Or ever hoped to.) The accident seemed to have made them more attached than ever. Laura had stopped pretending that his days were numbered. Clearly, Fred had a long-term lease at Sassy Spinster Farm.

Heidi found herself almost envying him. Her own future was still unsettled. She had no more idea where she would end up than she'd had when she'd arrived in May. She would go back to testify against Vinnie in September, but after that . . . what?

A few moments after Laura went back outside again, Rue shuffled into the kitchen. She didn't take up her station at the breakfast table—her new spot—but shuffled past Heidi to poke through one of the cabinets. Heidi watched her out of the corner of her eye and would have offered to help, but as sick as she was, Rue's long arms could still reach higher and farther than Heidi's could.

She pulled down an old tin box that bore a fading painted design of morning glories on it. She held it for a moment, tracing the vanishing flowers with her long index finger.

"I was just thinking . . . Chances are we won't be able to finish the cookbook." She looked over at Heidi. "At least not before you have to go back in September. Heaven knows when you'll make your way back here."

"I'll be back," Heidi said. A tension in Rue's voice, in her demeanor, alarmed her. "And like you said, we can always work on the cookbook over the Internet, e-mailing back and forth."

"Or it might be one of those projects that just get back-burnered and then are never finished." Rue shrugged. "In the big scheme of things, I guess it doesn't matter all that much. But in any case, I've been meaning to give you this." She held the old metal box out to Heidi. "It was my grandmother's. My father's mother."

As her hands encircled the box, Heidi froze. "Why are you giving this to me?"

"Look inside."

Heidi lifted the lid. The box was stuffed with yellowing, brittle index cards, all with the same spidery handwriting covering them, sometimes front and back. *Egg custard. Vera's pot roast. Seven-minute icing. Never-fail gravy. Laura's favorite butterscotch cupcakes.*

She snapped the lid back on and put the box on the counter. "I couldn't take this. It's your family's. You should save it for Erica."

"Erica can have my recipe box. It's got most of the same stuff in it, anyway. I copied all the recipes when I first got married."

"Well, then, Laura might want it. It's an heirloom, Rue."

"I already caught Laura tossing it away once during one of her once-in-a-decade decluttering jags," Rue said. "Besides, anyone who cooks like Laura doesn't deserve my grandma's recipes. You'll make better use of them."

Still Heidi hesitated.

"Please?" Rue asked.

Heidi didn't know how to refuse, especially since part of her didn't want to. Even when she had pushed the box away, she had been itching to browse through the old cards and maybe experiment with a few of the recipes. But something in her revolted at the idea of Rue handing her this keepsake. Taking it would feel like a triumph for defeatism. But she could see that her accepting it would gratify Rue.

"Thank you," she said, trying to hold herself together. "Although I don't know what I did to deserve it."

Rue did a quarter turn and pointed to the three-layer coconut cake waiting on its stand for Erica's birthday celebration. "That, for one thing."

They cut into the cake later that evening, and happily, nothing exploded. Although Erica was so enthusiastic about blowing out her twelve candles that for a moment it seemed like she might blast the icing off with sheer lung power.

She'd already received a television from her dad, to be kept in her room at his and Leanne's house. Rue wasn't thrilled at the idea, but she made a good show of hiding it. She and Laura had bought Erica a new saddle for Milkshake, which Erica was over the moon about, and Rue also gave her a little camera, which was put to immediate use. From Webb she received a hardbound copy of *The Adventures of Huckleberry Finn*. Heidi had been a little puzzled over what to give, but she'd finally settled on a manicure set and a leather collar with metal studs for Tortoise.

After Erica had ripped open her presents and demolished two pieces of cake, it was clear that she was itching to go play with her toys. She looked hopefully at her mom. "Can I go put my new saddle on Milkshake?"

"Of course," Rue said.

Erica smiled at Heidi. "I'll take a picture of Tortoise in his new collar."

After she was gone, the adults sat among the boxes and wrapping-paper debris. They'd had the celebration in the living room so Rue could sit on the couch. She'd been having pain in her back—the doctor said it was the tumor on her spine—and she wasn't comfortable sitting up for too long.

Her spirits seemed to be flagging. Heidi struggled to find something to revive the party. "Okay. Your five most essential actors."

Rue perked up. "Essential?"

"Meaning you'd watch them in anything," Heidi explained, "even a Lifetime movie with Melissa Gilbert. And none of them can be Cary Grant."

Rue seemed dismayed by the last stipulation. "Why not?"

"Because everyone would say Cary Grant. It would be a wasted slot," said Heidi.

"It's taken for *granted*," Webb said, earning groans.

Laura shook her head. "He wouldn't be on my list."

"But you're a freak," Heidi told her.

"Okay, I've got it." Rue closed her eyes in concentration. "Jimmy Stewart."

"Excellent," Heidi agreed.

"Fred Astaire."

"Humph."

"Bogie."

"Okay," Heidi agreed.

"Robert Mitchum."

"Going off the rails now, Rue."

"And Anthony Hopkins."

Here, Heidi drew the line. "Anthony Hopkins is *not* essential."

Rue sat up. "Whose list is this?"

"Yeah," Laura said, backing her up. "Come up with your own damn list."

"Well, okay," Heidi said. "Actually my list is almost identical to Rue's. Except that I'd scratch Hopkins and Mitchum and sub Dana Andrews and probably Henry Fonda. And of course, I've always preferred Gene to Fred, as we know, but even so, I really don't think Gene Kelly ranks as an essential, so I'd probably include William Powell instead, just because I'm not sure life would be worth living without the Thin Man movies. And even though I like Bogie a lot, I think I like Paul Newman more."

"You're right," Laura deadpanned. "Those lists are almost identical."

"My list was better," Rue said.

"I'm almost afraid to ask, but what about you?" Heidi arched an eyebrow at Laura. "Who are your five essentials?"

"Easy." Laura held up her clenched fist and ticked them off rapid-fire. "Clint Eastwood, Lee Marvin, the Marx Brothers." When she finished, she was holding up five fingers.

"That's only three," Heidi pointed out.

"I'm counting each Marx Brother as a separate unit, including Zeppo."

"Then that makes *six*," Heidi said.

"Yeah, but I get an extra slot."

"Why?" Rue asked.

"Because I wouldn't have included Cary Grant," Laura replied.

"I don't mean to be hypercritical here," Heidi argued, "but how can Zeppo Marx possibly be considered an essential? Even his own brothers didn't think he was essential."

Laura wasn't budging. "I don't have to apologize for Zeppo to someone who thinks Dana Andrews is one of the five best actors of all time."

"I didn't say *best*. I said he was essential to me."

Webb chuckled.

Heidi turned in exasperation. "Don't tell me you're anti–Dana Andrews, too."

"No, I'm just trying to imagine Lee Marvin in a Lifetime movie," he said.

Rue laughed. "How about Groucho Marx and Melissa Gilbert?"

Heidi shook her head. "Okay, Webb. It's your turn now. Astound us."

Webb crossed his arms, and for a moment his face tensed in concentration. "I'm going to take a job in Amarillo."

If his goal actually had been to astound them, it worked. Looking at their bug-eyed faces, you would have thought he'd just told them that he had decided to join a cult or become a she-male.

Heidi was the first to manage to speak. "What kind of job?"

He hesitated. "With the USDA—the extension office there. They had an opening, and I applied."

This took another few seconds to absorb.

Laura especially seemed to be having a hard time wrapping her mind around the bare facts. "You're going to move to Amarillo?"

"That's it."

"But why?" she asked.

"To make money."

"You can make money here!" Laura continued to gape at him. "But *Amarillo*? Crap Agnes! That's a whole day's drive away. Why go there?"

"I have an army buddy that lives out there. He likes it."

"I think you're out of your mind!" Laura said.

Webb fixed her with a stony stare. "Actually, I didn't tell you so I could get your opinion. I just wanted you to know that I'll be leaving."

"When?" Heidi asked.

"I said I could be there the end of September. They're okay with that."

Heidi wondered where she would be at the end of September. Sitting in a courtroom, she imagined.

"I hope that plan's all right with you all," Webb said.

Laura remained silent, directing all her anger at the rug.

"Of course it's all right," Rue said. "But you'll be missed around here."

Webb stood, seeming to wait for a word of agreement from

Laura, which never came. "Well, I guess I should be going back to my place. Good night."

Heidi watched him go, then looked over at Rue, who had closed her eyes again.

"What do they do at the ag extension exactly?" Heidi asked.

Rue shook her head. "Beats me. I guess anybody's lucky to be getting anything these days."

"Amen to that," Heidi said. "And it's federal. Good benefits."

"Benefits!" Laura spat the word. "Who cares about that?"

"Just about the whole world, except lunatics like you," Heidi said.

"He's going to be a paper pusher. That's not who he is! He might as well put his soul in a jar and stick it under the sink."

"Not everyone wants to be at the mercy of a corn crop all their lives," Heidi said.

Anger flashed across Laura's face, and for a second Heidi wondered if those would be the last words she ever uttered in this world. But in the next moment, Laura leapt to her feet and left the room. A few seconds later they heard the front door slam.

"I can't imagine how barren this place will be in September," Rue said.

"With Webb gone?"

"What about you? Didn't you say that Vinnie's trial is set for late September?"

"I suppose I'll have to go back a little sooner. I don't want to. You'd think after all these months I'd be homesick, but I'm not. I don't kid myself that I belong here, but . . ."

"Where would you go if you could?" Rue asked her.

"I don't know. A town somewhere—not as small as Sweetgum. But definitely smaller than New York City. And I'd like it to be in a place where the weather's not so hot as here."

"Let's see . . . smaller than New York City, not as hot as Texas. I wouldn't call those exacting parameters."

Heidi shrugged. "I'm just rattling things off the top of my head. Even if I found a town that I liked, what would I do there?"

"There's always the Sassy Spinster Café."

"That would take money."

"Did you or did you not work in a bank?"

"Of course I did. That's where my troubles began."

"Okay," Rue said. "Didn't that bank give loans?"

"Sure, to people who had collateral and business plans."

"So draw up a business plan and scrounge up some money. It's been done before, by people more hapless than you."

Heidi leaned back, trying to picture it. A town somewhere, maybe in the mountains or on the beach. She imagined a little city like the one in *Shadow of a Doubt*. Or no, maybe even smaller. Bedford Falls, from *It's a Wonderful Life*. She could take over a defunct diner in a place where everybody knew everybody. When she woke up in the morning, she wouldn't have a sinking feeling in the pit of her stomach that she had failed to become what she might have been. And none of her regulars who came to the café and heard her cracking wise would ever know she'd once been a dithering loser. She'd make really good cobbler and become a local institution.

It could happen. But where would she get the money?

"Dana Andrews?"

Heidi nearly jumped out of her skin. She'd thought Rue had fallen asleep. Now she had to switch gears and go on the defensive for her man. "He's underappreciated," she said. "And besides, he's really cute."

Rue shook her head in disgust. "And you were giving me shit about Anthony Hopkins."

Laura's habit was to pick her sweet corn at the last minute before the farmers' market. The Saturday after Erica's birthday, which might be the last of the corn, Webb came out to help. He and Laura worked back-to-back down a row, carefully twisting cobs off the stalks and tossing them into bushel boxes that were stacked in a red wagon alongside them.

They hadn't talked about his moving since he had announced

his intentions, even though every second they were together, Laura could hardly think of anything else.

"I don't guess you'll miss this," she said.

"What?"

"Getting up early for whatever needs to be done around here. Farm chores."

"Actually I will miss it."

Then why are you leaving? Laura left the thought unspoken, but it was crying out so loudly in her own mind that she almost expected Webb to hear it, anyway.

"Believe it or not, I'll miss a lot of things around here," he told her.

"I believe it." She did a quarter turn. "What I can't believe is that you agreed to go in the first place."

"It's not like I'm going to Uzbekistan. It's just Amarillo."

She harrumphed. "West Texas. A place fit for cows and prairie dogs."

"How do you know?"

"I went there once."

"Really?" he asked. "You might have noticed that they have a city. Full of people."

She didn't respond. Her hands worked while her mind was completely absorbed in the conversation that she and Webb should have been having but weren't. Finally, at the end of the row, she rounded on him as if he had actually been a party to her thoughts. "How can you do it?"

"Do what?"

He was so exasperating. "Go so far!"

"Far from what?"

"From . . ." She shut her mouth, then decided to plow ahead. "From here. From Sweetgum. I thought you liked it here."

"I do."

"What about your mom?"

"She's fine with it. She thinks it's a good idea to get a fresh start. She assumes I'm trying to put some distance between me and Denise."

"Isn't that what you're doing?"

"Only incidentally. Denise isn't really the person I'm trying to get away from."

Laura grabbed an ear of corn and twisted it with more ferocity than was required, practically bringing down the whole stalk. "You don't have to leave on my account. This area's big enough for the both of us, I think."

"I don't."

"Why? Do you think I'd pester you?"

"Just the opposite. If I stayed around here, I would just keep slipping into the same old groove. I'd keep hoping, and you've made it very clear that hoping is a complete waste of time."

"But why not go somewhere where you can do what you love?"

"Like what?"

"Like being outdoors. Working on a farm."

He laughed. "Do you really think I love working out here? Picking and hoeing and fixing your ancient fences and whatever else always needs doing around here? Do you think that I haven't dreamed sometimes about a job in a nice air-conditioned building?"

"Then why have you stuck around?"

His gaze pinned her in place for a moment; then he shook his head. "Can you possibly be that thickheaded? Haven't you ever listened to a word I've said? I'm here because of *you*."

"That's not true. You just needed somewhere to park yourself. This was a stopgap measure."

"I came back here because of you. I agreed to work the summer here because of you. And now I'm leaving because of you. Because I can't stand to be around you, and I can't stand not to be."

"You spent half the summer palling it up with Heidi."

"Because you gave me the cold shoulder! You know you did. Heidi's nice—I wish to hell I could fall in love with her. I don't know what's wrong with me that I like you better. All I can figure is that I'm a masochist, or maybe just an idiot. Maybe both."

"Thank you. That's very complimentary."

"I could shower you with real compliments. You want to hear them?"

"Not particularly."

"You're beautiful."

"Stringy, sunburned, and sweaty," she said. "A real siren."

"It's no joke. Maybe it goes back to the school bus. Maybe I was warped through overexposure to you as a kid, but stringy and sunburned has always been my ideal, because you've been my ideal. I've been running from you or back to you all my life, it seems. You've made me do things that in my saner moments I can see were beyond ridiculous and sometimes almost criminally stupid. Reprehensible things, like getting engaged to a woman I didn't love and then bailing on the wedding. And then going back. Ricocheting around like a lovelorn idiot."

"I thought we agreed not to have this conversation."

"No, I agreed not to tell you that I love you. So I won't. But that's not to say that I can't love things about you. I love the way you stride around the earth like you sprang up from the ground, and the way you probably never spend more than two minutes in front of a mirror each morning but still manage to outshine everyone around you. I love listening to you talk at people. No other human being I know says gadzooks. And I love the way you're hard-boiled, and yet you go to the trouble to fashion a fake leg for a chicken.

"And I have no idea why you have this power over me. I've studied it from every angle, but I can't explain it, except that you—of all the damned people—have always made being on this earth seem worthwhile to me. Even when I was in the desert, I would think of you here, surrounded by green and trees, and I'd think, *I have to get back.* I would have given my right arm to hear you insult someone again."

A crazy kind of happiness took hold of her, making it hard to think. *He's leaving because he loves me. But if he really loves me, maybe he won't leave.*

If she could just say the words. If she could just be sure it wouldn't be thoroughly selfish to say them.

They stuck in her throat. "Gadzooks isn't much to hang your hat on," she managed to rasp out.

"I can't help that." He lifted up his arms and dropped them again. "Anyway, you asked me why I don't stay, so there's your answer."

She looked into his blue, blue eyes, the catnip that drew every woman with a pulse to him. There was a flame in them, an eagerness. He'd laid his cards on the table, and now his face was tensed in anticipation of her response. The longer she hesitated, the more she remembered all her arguments for thinking that she would be poison to him, the more that eagerness began to flicker out. Finally, as he realized that she was going to remain tongue tied, all that was left was a dull stare.

He turned and reached for the wagon handle. "I'll take this load out to your truck."

As she watched him walking away from her, it occurred to her that this might be it. The last chance. One day soon he intended to walk away from her and never come back. That was a thought she just couldn't bear to dwell on.

Somewhere in the distance a door slammed. A voice was calling her name. Heidi's voice.

Webb looked at her again.

Laura bit her lip. Webb's eyes competed for her attention with Heidi's frantic yelling. The hollering grew louder, until it was impossible to ignore her. "I'm over here!" Laura yelled back. She glanced back at Webb. "God, she's irritating," she said under her breath. "She really doesn't annoy you?"

He shook his head and looked away.

Heidi ran as far as she could down their row before being stopped by the wagon. She was breathing hard and almost flapping her hands in agitation. Her face was streaked with tears. "Come quick!" she said. "I can't get Rue to wake up."

Chapter 25

They came to the hospital in shifts, but at night they generally gathered all together until it was boot-the-visitors-out time. Rue would sleep until she was roused by some nurse coming to check her temperature or give her a pill. She was hooked up to a fluid drip, and another with morphine. She was more comfortable here than she had been on her own, but still she ached for home.

When she was alone, she had Heidi's iPod. Her life's sound track, she came to think of it. It was set on random, and she didn't know how to change it, so she would fade out on Ella singing "It Never Entered My Mind" and snap back awake to Placido Domingo. Or Johnny Cash. Also, Heidi had either downloaded or forgotten to erase some things from the iPod's former life, so occasionally she would be startled by Lily Allen, or Weezer. The first time it happened, it was disconcerting. But as her hospital stay stretched to three days, then four, she began to enjoy the wild cards more. A person could get used to anything.

She longed for visitors when no one was there, but when they came, she often felt sorry they'd bothered. She wasn't always up for talking. Her head felt fuzzy, and while she was alone, she simply let her thoughts roam. Odd moments came back to her, like the time she'd stayed out at the lake too long and gotten a sunburn; the soporific feeling of bright sun evaporating lake water off her bare back as she'd floated on a raft seemed as real as life. She remembered the day their school was going to go to the Texas State Fair but Laura got sent home for breaking a badminton racket over Chad Humphries's head. In dreams and daydreams her mother came back to her, and her grandparents, and pets she hadn't thought of in years, and they got all jumbled up in her head with the Sassy Spinster Farm guests and people she saw every week in Sweetgum. It was as if someone had set her brain on random, just like her iPod.

On the afternoon of the fourth day, Dean Martin jolted her awake and she found Heidi sitting next to her bed. At first it seemed like Heidi had popped out of one of her dreams. "I was just thinking about you."

"I was just thinking about *you*," Heidi said. "I brought the RN on duty a double latte, and she finally let slip that the doctor's thinking of sending you home. Isn't that great?"

Rue wasn't sure. "I'm glad you're here."

"Of course I'm here. The farm's pretty dull these days. Erica goes riding all the time, Dylan's doing marching band rehearsal at school, Webb's hardly ever around, and Laura is either here or who knows where. Lately, it's just been Herman and me, planting okra."

"I meant I'm glad you came to Texas this summer. To stay with us."

"And almost got you all killed?"

"I feel like we've made amends. Even Laura."

Heidi weighed that last statement. "Laura says she was just defending Fred, and I'm inclined to believe her. I don't think we're ever going to be cuddly and close."

"That's too bad." Rue felt her eyes drooping closed. Laura could have used a friend.

The next time she opened her eyes, Laura was there, with a wheelchair.

"Where's Heidi?"

Laura looked confused. "At the farm."

"Oh."

"I'm busting you out of here!"

Rue shook her head. "Are you sure?"

"The doctor said. He talked to you, remember?"

Rue did, vaguely, although she still felt doubtful. Yet to her amazement, she lifted her arms and noted that the IVs were gone. Like a puppet whose strings had been cut, she swung her legs over the side of the bed and stood up. She weaved a bit and Laura caught her.

"I brought you your own comfy clothes," Laura said, with an excitement that seemed all out of proportion for discussing a T-shirt and a pair of sweatpants. "No more hospital gowns. Ever."

"How do you know?" Rue asked apprehensively.

Laura shook her head. "I don't follow."

"How do you know I won't relapse and be back tomorrow, or next week?"

"What's the matter with you?"

"Are they sending me home to die?"

Laura's face collapsed. "How can you ask me that?"

Seeing the hurt in her sister's face, Rue was filled with remorse. "I'm sorry. I know that sounded weird. It's just I've been so disoriented. It seems like five minutes ago I was talking to Heidi."

"Heidi's been gone for hours. She's at the farm now, making you 'welcome home' rice pudding." Laura frowned. "Don't you want to go home?"

"Of course." Rue swallowed. "Of course I do."

As she pushed one leg and then another into her sweats, her back pulled sharply. The pain almost made her see spots. She sank down against the bed to finish dressing.

She hated that she'd rained on Laura's parade. There was no excuse for it but fear. Much as she wanted to be at home, the hospital was so much easier. She didn't have to worry about eating, or keeping food down, or trying to do the other basics that sometimes really taxed her at home. At home anything that required preparation was an ordeal. Like a bath.

And there also was an ease here in dealing with people. Drifting in and out as they came and went, she didn't have to focus too hard on them. Now she would be plopped messily into the center of their world again. She would have to be more attentive. She would reattach herself to them all over again.

But maybe that was for the best, too. She had things to do yet. Small things. The hospital wasn't the place for them.

She stood up again, feeling steadier this time. "Let's go."

Laura pointed to the wheelchair. "You gotta go out in one of those. Hospital rules. 'Wheelchairs must be used to escort discharged patients from the building.' "

"You're quoting regulations at me?" Rue asked, amazed. "Have you been body snatched?"

Laura arched a brow. "It's a really stupid rule, isn't it?"

"Probably made to please an insurance company. It's just begging to be flaunted."

Some of the old mischievous spark came back to Laura's eyes. "Or mocked."

"Shall we?" Rue plunked herself down. "Drive. And remember, I've always been a sucker for speed."

Laura maneuvered them out of the room like a pilot taxiing a jet onto a runway. The hallway was empty all the way past the nurses' station.

"Ready?" Laura asked.

"Tallyho!"

Laura started running. *"Yes!"* she cried as they started to gain speed.

Five minutes ago Rue hadn't thought she could stand. Now she was flying. Flying and laughing.

"You still know how to pop a wheelie?"

"You betcha!"

Laura gave them a final shove, and they flew past the nurses' station on two wheels, whooping like they had when they were kids.

The night she got back from the hospital, her mom was all tuckered out. She had let her Netflix list dwindle to nothing, so until the company could send a new batch from the titles she'd hurriedly typed in when she realized her mistake, for movie time they were just left with what was on the shelves. They had recently cycled through all the Fred and Ginger movies, and Erica put her foot down about rewatching them. She wanted to see *The Wizard of Oz*.

The whole room groaned.

Except for Heidi, who was puzzled. "What's the matter with *The Wizard of Oz?*"

"You don't want to know," Webb told her.

Rue poked her head over the arm of the couch, where she was reclining with half the pillows in the house propped around her. "Laura's got a laundry list of complaints about this movie."

Heidi tossed Laura a disgusted look. Erica worried they were about to have a repeat of Audrey Hepburn night. "Honestly, Laura," Heidi said. "*The Wizard of Oz?*"

"It's flawed!"

"I never get to pick the movies," Erica grumbled at her aunt.

"You picked *Free Willy Three*," Laura pointed out. "Nuff said."

"That was months and months ago!"

"And it sucked."

"Not as bad as *Hell in the Pacific*," Erica argued.

"Now *that* was a good movie." Laura sank down in her chair. "But I guess you have a point."

"I vote for *The Wizard*," Heidi said.

Rue seconded the motion.

Webb held up his hands. "I abstain."

"Ha!" Erica snatched the movie off the DVD shelf. "That still makes the vote three to one. We win!"

"But no criticizing while the movie's running," Rue warned Laura. "You can deliver your treatise after the final credits roll."

"I won't say a word," Laura promised.

Heidi frowned at the TV set. "I'm curious now."

"Don't get her started," Erica whispered.

Erica didn't care what Laura thought. She liked *The Wizard of Oz* because it was the first movie she remembered watching with her mom that they both really liked. It was a kids' movie, but it was sort of an adult movie, too.

She climbed onto the couch as the music started and lifted her knees up to her chin. The great thing was, she could watch it a hundred times and it was still good. It was one of the few musicals that didn't seem just like a soppy love story with songs.

But as it turned out, this time around she barely watched the thing. Her mother fell asleep before the tornado sequence, and for most of the time, Erica felt her gaze gravitating to her face. Her mom did this a lot now; it was as if closing her eyes helped her conserve energy. But Laura had told her that last Saturday Heidi had found Rue in her bed and hadn't been able to wake her up. Now just seeing her eyes shut caused Erica to panic. She was afraid what happened last Saturday was going to happen again.

She studied the plane of her mom's high forehead, and her cheekbones, and her wide mouth. She was so thin now that she really didn't look like her mom so much as a work of art representing her mom. She was like a sculpture—something modern that was just the basic outlines.

Rue woke up for the Scarecrow's dance, and during the scene with the angry apple trees, and at the end. Every time she opened her eyes, Erica quickly faced forward, hoping to hide the fact she'd been staring.

When the movie was all over, everybody switched positions and stretched. Heidi was weeping, but this was nothing new. "I don't see what the problem with that movie is," she declared, sniffling. "It's a masterpiece."

Laura shook her head.

"Don't think about it," Rue said. "If you think too hard, you'll spoil it."

"No one's ever accused me of thinking too hard," Heidi replied, earning snorts from Laura. "And I don't want to spoil it, so I won't. It's perfect just as it is."

"Sure." Laura stood. "It's hunky-dory so long as you're not the

Lion, the Tin Man, or the dog." She took her coffee cup into the kitchen, probably for a refill.

Webb followed her with eyes full of wonder. "Laura was probably one of those kids who enjoyed disillusioning other kids about Santa and the Easter Bunny."

"She was," Rue said. "When it came to the tooth fairy, though, she was a dead ender. I think she thought if she believed hard enough, she'd find a twenty under her pillow."

It was a moment before Heidi cleared her throat to speak. Her brow was crinkled. "What *does* happen to Toto?"

"Oh no, not you, too." Rue sighed. "Next thing you know, you'll be kept up nights wondering why Dorothy snubbed the Lion and the Tin Man."

Heidi's eyes widened in alarm. "When?"

"When she says she'll miss the Scarecrow most of all." Erica didn't see what the big deal was. Was it so bad to have favorites?

Laura came back in. "Rationalize it any way you want. It was a crappy thing to say."

Heidi sank a little farther down in her chair. "Oh."

Webb stood up. "As much as I'd love to have this conversation again, I have to get up early tomorrow."

"'Night," Erica said.

After Webb had gone, Erica noticed that Laura looked perturbed for a little bit, until she finally stalked out of the room and went upstairs. Her mother was still on the couch, her eyes closed again. Heidi was staring at the television screen, which wasn't even turned on. Her face looked pinched.

"Maybe she was simply telling the truth," she said slowly, trying to work it out. "Maybe she just liked the Scarecrow better than the other two. He did have a certain appeal. The lion was funny, but after a while he probably got on everyone's nerves. And the Tin Man was sort of a sap." She sighed. "But dreamy. *He* would have been my pick."

Rue laughed. "You're the first person I've ever met to approach *The Wizard of Oz* as if it were *The Dating Game*."

Heidi stood up. "You're right. I think I'll go to sleep before I begin to seem any more pitiful. Good night."

When Heidi left, Erica sat on the floor, using the front of the couch as a backrest. It was nice to have her mom all to herself for once.

"Do you remember when we first watched that movie together?"

"Of course. It was your fifth birthday. I gave you the DVD because it was one of the movies I remembered watching with my mom, back in the bad old days before VCRs."

"And with Laura?"

"Well, sort of. She was almost your age before she finally made it through the whole thing."

"Why?"

"Well, the networks only played *The Wizard of Oz* once a year back then. Every year it was a big deal. And when we were little, we'd all sit down to watch it, but for years Laura never made it past the cyclone, which would send her shrieking out of the room. Then she finally got over that, and the part with the trees scared her. Then it was the winged monkeys in the forest, and I think she was ten before she managed to get past Dorothy locked up in the witch's castle and finally make it to the end. It's about the only instance I can think of where I was actually braver than Laura."

"I can't imagine her afraid of anything."

"I sometimes wonder if that's why the movie drives her so crazy to this day. It reminds her of the few times when she wimped out."

"Did she really have to leave the room?"

"Oh yes." Rue smiled, remembering. "And then my mother and I would be left alone together, and it always made me feel like I was really something. A survivor. That's why I bought it as soon as I thought you were old enough to handle the monkeys. Laura thought I was trying to scar you for life, but you were never a bit scared. You were fearless."

"I wish I'd known my other grandmother."

"She was fun. She loved the late show . . . I guess loving old movies is genetic."

"What else did she like?"

Rue thought for a moment. "Kojak."

"Who?"

"He was a detective. He was bald."

That didn't seem very interesting. "Do you miss her a lot?"

"Oh gosh, yes. She had a hilarious laugh, like something bursting out of her. She was funny, and gregarious—a counterweight to Dad. You probably remember what *he* was like."

Mostly Erica remembered a cranky old guy who made fun of her for being skinny. But she'd heard stories about his temper.

"And even now," Rue continued, "when something funny happens, or something momentous, or even when we're all just together like we were tonight, watching the movie, I can almost feel her in the room with me, as real as life. It's not just that I miss her. It's like *she's* missing being here. Missing us—even you, who she never got to meet."

Erica frowned, wondering if that was what it was like to be haunted. Could people be haunted in a good way?

Her mom reached into the pocket of her robe. "I've been looking for a time to give you this. It's a late birthday present."

She brought out a tiny box wrapped in bright blue paper.

Erica hesitated. "I got a lot of stuff for my birthday already."

"This isn't stuff. It's a special something I want you to have."

Erica untaped the paper way more carefully than she usually did. Most of the time she attacked presents the way she'd seen great white sharks taking out seals on nature shows. One blow and she was done. But the little box made her uneasy. She didn't usually get stuff in little boxes.

The box itself was white, and when she removed the lid, what she saw sitting on a bed of cotton wool made her frown in half recognition. It took her a moment to realize she was staring at her mom's Alabama-Coushatta ring.

She glanced over at her mother's right hand, which suddenly looked conspicuously naked. How come she hadn't noticed?

Her hands trembled a little, so she steadied the box on a couch cushion as she looked up at her mom. "Aunt Laura gave this to you."

Rue's brow pinched with worry. "I shouldn't have wrapped it. It probably got your hopes up for something better."

"No!" Erica cried, frustrated at being misunderstood. She'd made it sound like she didn't want it. "I just . . . It's always been on your finger."

"All my jewelry is going to be yours, you know." She swallowed. "Someday. That's a given. I was worried that this oddball old thing might get overlooked, even though it means more to me than anything else. You remember?"

"Yeah, you said it wasn't because of what it was made of. It was because of who gave it to you." Erica felt frozen. She wanted to hand it back, to tell her mother that there was absolutely no reason she should have it now.

But to give it back to her would be insulting. It would be terrible.

"Well, go ahead," Rue urged. "Put it on."

Erica plucked it off its little cotton cushion. It was too big for her ring finger, so she slipped it on the middle one. The metal—whatever it was—was surprisingly heavy, something she'd never considered in all the years the ring had been riding around on her mom's hand.

Rue pressed her lips together. "Looks like it belongs there."

"It doesn't, though." In spite of her best efforts, Erica felt a tear slide down her cheek. "It's yours. What if Laura sees me wearing it?"

"Oh, I expect she'll understand. That's the way these things get passed along. Maybe someday if you have a sister, or someone you love like a sister, you can pass it along to her."

Erica shook her head because she couldn't speak. Her eyes squeezed shut, and she could only breathe in with a shiver. She wiped her forearm across her face.

Her mom reached down and pulled her up onto the couch as if

she were a toddler. Erica nestled against her bony body with a sob.

"It's strange how you've never been afraid of anything," her mom said, as if they'd never stopped talking about the movie. "That's what's always amazed me about you. It's the way I wish I had been."

If she hadn't been crying, Erica would have laughed. How could her mother say she wasn't afraid of anything when she was falling apart right then and there? She was terrified—of never seeing her again, of being all alone. Couldn't she see that?

Rue rested her chin on the crown of Erica's head like she sometimes used to. "I love you so much."

"I didn't know . . ." Erica's voice broke and faltered. "*I didn't know how sick you were,*" she wanted to say, but she couldn't.

Rue seemed to understand, anyway. "I didn't either. It doesn't matter, though. I've had you here with me this summer. It was more than we expected, wasn't it?"

Erica swallowed back the lump blocking her throat. *More than expected* didn't seem like enough now. There could never be enough time. "If I could, though, I'd do things different."

Rue looked down at her in understanding. "You want to hit rewind and start over. I always think that would be the best. You know how some people wish they could either fly or be invisible? To me the best superpower would be being able to reverse time and do things differently." She frowned. "Of course, if too many people had that power, things could get really confusing. You would never know who was in the process of reversing, or if you were going to fix something that someone else would manage to go back and clean up, anyway."

"That's really weird, Mom."

"No, the really weird thing is, sometimes you don't even have to rewind. Occasionally, someone comes back and you have a chance to do better the second time around."

What was she talking about? Erica wondered sometimes if the drugs weren't making her mom just a little bit insane. All she knew was that she would never get another chance to redo her summer. And now who knew how much time she would have left with her mom?

"Mom, I don't want to move," she said.

"When? To your dad's?"

"No. Tonight. Can we watch another movie?"

Her mom slipped her a wink. "You talked me into it." She switched the television on again and flipped over to TCM, her favorite channel.

They came in on the middle of an old black-and-white movie, a Busby Berkeley musical—the kind that had the big crazy dance numbers that turned people into kaleidoscope figures. Erica stretched out across the couch, resting her head on her mom's lap. She shut her eyes.

"How does someone get the name Busby?" she asked sleepily.

She heard her mom laughing, and then she drifted off, listening to people singing about waterfalls. When she woke up in the middle of the night, the television was off, and she was alone on the couch, with the crocheted afghan cocooning her, as if someone had very carefully tucked her in.

The second time Rue wound up in the hospital, Laura had a hard time prying herself from her bedside. She would usually arrive in the morning. Erica had started sixth grade at the end of August, and Heidi would bring her in the late afternoon. Most of the time they would all stay till visiting hours ended.

Rue thought it was too much. She would tell Laura to go home or to take Erica back earlier. She didn't like Erica to be at the hospital. She was worried Erica wasn't getting her homework done or was stressing out. (Laura didn't have the heart to remind Rue that there wasn't much way to keep her from stressing out when her mother was terminally ill.) From her sickbed, Rue lobbied for Erica to go to the junior high school football games on Friday nights, or to spend more time riding Milkshake on weekends. To do normal things. Not sit in a bare room, watching her mother hooked up to tubes, sleeping.

Laura suspected Rue didn't want Erica to remember her this way. But she knew Rue had to crave seeing Erica as much as Erica wanted to see her. She was torn over whose wishes to honor.

When the subject of a football game came up, Erica finally let Rue persuade her to go. That Friday night Heidi took her, because Laura couldn't imagine enjoying anything knowing Rue was lying in the hospital alone, so sick. Every night after she went home, she was terrified that Rue would be gone by the next morning. But Rue had always been tenacious.

That Friday night she was alone with Rue, who had the usual fluids and morphine drip, and now had an oxygen tube, because it was getting harder for her to breathe. Laura sat next to her bed and read Stephen King books, while Rue, hooked up to the iPod, drifted in and out.

Once she looked up from *Cujo* and saw Rue smiling at her glassily. Laura leaned forward. "Can I get you something?"

Rue ignored the question. "It's funny, your being here."

"Why?"

"Because of you and me."

Rue talked like this more and more now, in little bursts of disjointed ideas. It was maddening, and Laura sometimes wished she would save her strength.

Save it for what, she wasn't sure.

"I feel sick," Rue said, closing her eyes.

"Can I get you anything?" Laura repeated. When Rue didn't respond, her heart thumped erratically; she could taste bile. *"Rue?"*

She had felt this scared once before, she realized—in the wrecked car after the accident. She was on the verge of pressing the call button for the nurse when Rue piped up in a dry voice.

"I know why she says it."

Laura frowned. "Says what? Who?"

"Dorothy. To the Scarecrow. 'I think I'm going to miss you most of all.' " She opened her eyes and smiled a mocking smile. "That line that drives you berserk."

Laura released a long, slow breath. If Rue was talking movies, things couldn't be too dire.

"It's not because she loves him more than the rest." Rue reached out her hand, which had an IV taped to the top of it. On the underside, her wrist still bore a bruise from where the IV had been the last time. She captured Laura's own hand and squeezed it. "It's because he was the one who was with her the longest. Like you are to me."

Laura felt a catch in her throat.

"Scarecrow," Rue croaked.

Laura collapsed from the waist, facedown onto the metal rail guard of Rue's bed. The steel was cold and unforgiving, and she wanted to knock her forehead against it. "Rue . . ."

"The character I've been with longest."

"Stop it!"

"That's what makes it so hard to say good-bye."

Laura bit her lip. "Don't do this to me. I can't stand it. It's impossible. I can't do without you. I've never had to before."

"When I got married," Rue reminded her.

"Even then you were always buzzing in and out."

"I had to check and make sure you and Daddy hadn't killed each other."

"The referee."

Rue stared at her until Laura wanted to look away but couldn't. That penetrating stare. "The farm did okay this summer. You're happy now?"

"No!" Laura cried petulantly. Knowing Rue, she would take any admission of happiness as her cue to float off forever, like Mary Poppins.

With her free hand, Laura reached over to the nonspill hospital mug on the bedside table. One thing this place was good at was keeping mugs filled with ice water. She tipped the straw to Rue's lips. Rue dutifully gave it a few sucks and then quit.

A shadow passed over her face. "Don't lose her."

Laura didn't have to ask who she was talking about. It was the tone. She wondered if she'd ever heard so much pain in three little words. "How could I do that?" She swallowed. "The farm's her home. It's going to all be hers someday, anyway."

"Make her go to college. And finish."

"She will."

Rue closed her eyes. "I hope she forgets me."

"For God's sake," Laura said. "Please."

"I don't want her to brood. I don't want this to screw her up like . . ."

"Like the accident did me?" Laura shook her head. "She's got too much of you in her for that. You don't have to worry. Don't worry about anything. Just concentrate on feeling better."

Rue closed her eyes again. For a moment Laura thought she'd gone to sleep. She leaned back; she felt wrung out. Rue gave her hand another squeeze, then let it go.

Laura tried to read, but she couldn't work up much interest in *Cujo*. Rue was out of it again.

Her head ached. All this stillness. This gloom. Even the flowers crowded on every surface seemed oppressive. This place was driving her crazy.

She got up, paced for a moment, and decided to go to the coffee machine. It was almost eight. She'd stay another hour and then go home. Hear how the Sweetgum Skeeters did.

In the room, Rue was still snoozing, emitting gravelly little snores. Laura crossed to her chair by the bed and collapsed into it. Back to her station. The coffee machine coffee didn't taste very good, but she slurped it down, anyway. She had a forty-minute drive home ahead of her and needed to stay awake.

She glanced over at Rue, who was lying still. So still. Only her chest moved, quietly sucking in air, which then seemed to have a harder and harder time getting back out.

A wave of cold washed over her, and she lunged at the bed, gripping her sister by her shoulders. "Rue?"

Rue's eyes didn't flutter; her lips didn't move.

"Rue, wake up. *Now.*"

But this time she didn't.

Chapter 26

The week of her mother's funeral was so bad that Erica sometimes wondered if people did die from grief. She wore herself out crying even before they left the hospital, and after that her jags were periodic and unpredictable. The slightest thing would set her off, like the first time she came downstairs to breakfast and knew her mom would never be there, making oatmeal and listening to bad music again.

Her dad said she could stay at the farm until she had to go back to school, and she didn't have to go back for another week. She was glad, but having all the time off made her nervous, too. She wondered what kids would say to her when she went back. She kept imagining herself bawling in homeroom, which she knew was a really dumb thing to worry about.

A steady stream of people came through the house. Every time Shelley Winters and Monte went nuts outside, Erica would look out her bedroom window to see who it was this time. She didn't go down. She couldn't stand hearing people say they were sorry. Worse, some of the women actually would take one look at her and burst into tears. She wanted them all to go away. But then, when the house was quiet, she wondered why there weren't more people coming by.

Occasionally, Laura was there to take the visitors' covered dishes and Bundt cakes; she would grumble at them about being up to her eyeballs in Tupperware. When Laura was there, visits were brief.

More often, though, it was Heidi who opened the front door. Acting as the family representative, she invited people inside and listened to their awkward stabs at conversation. The kitchen was just below her room, so Erica could hear snatches of sympathy talk as Heidi served marble cake and sweet tea. "So sad . . . out of her pain . . . motherless . . . better place . . ." It was no wonder Laura tried to make herself scarce. But Heidi knew how to handle them. Occasionally, the visiting mourners would even leave with lunch sacks of what was left over from the garden. *That's what Mom would have done*, Erica thought.

When the actual residents of the farm would meet in the kitchen or the living room, Heidi would announce who'd come by and whatever oddities had cropped up. It was Heidi who had actually met the banjo teacher, who they all had begun to think was a fiction. According to Heidi (Erica had only seen the top of his fuzzy head), his name was Wade and he looked like someone called Gabe Kaplan, an observation that had made Laura laugh for the first time in two days. Heidi was the one who had entertained a former farm guest who had driven all the way from Wichita Falls to deliver a ham. (She'd seen the *in memoriam* notice Heidi had written on the Sassy Spinster Farm Web site.) And it was Heidi who had offered to take care of most of the funeral arrangements. And to Erica's surprise, Laura had let her.

The funeral was held at the Methodist church, but it felt more like an all-church meeting, with the whole adult population of Sweetgum in attendance. The building was as packed as it had been for Ms. Dench's wedding, which seemed a million years in the past now.

Erica was horrified when the preacher and a few other speakers aimed their talk specifically at her. They said they didn't know how to console her about the loss of a mother, but then they went on trying, anyway. She wished she could tell them to save their breath. She wasn't listening. These people didn't really know her mother, anyway. Not like she did.

They were saying the same things they probably said at every funeral, sprinkled with a few personal anecdotes about nice things Rue Rafferty Anderson had done in her lifetime. Random stuff that just made Erica feel more agitated. What did it matter to her if her mom had helped someone who'd had shingles? Didn't they realize that she was going to have to do without the one person who was able to make sense of everything for her? To her, Rue Rafferty Anderson was *everything.* The person who'd taught her to tie her shoes and count, and explained why the sun rose every day, and made her lime sherbet and ginger ale when her throat was sore, and told her why it actually was absolutely necessary to understand fractions, and why Jimmy Stewart was a good actor, while Clark Gable was a guy with a leer who couldn't act his way out of a paper bag. She was the person who'd tried to teach her about patience and neatness and generosity. She'd fed her and encouraged her and made her laugh at herself when things seemed absolutely horrible.

Like now.

She needed her now.

What am I going to do?

She started to tremble with the urge to leap over her pew and run away. She wanted to get as far as possible from the giant oak casket, which she'd been avoiding looking at for thirty minutes now.

Before she could lose it completely, Laura's hand clamped down on hers and squeezed, hard. So hard that Erica could feel the ring her mom had given her digging into her finger. She glanced over at Laura, who was wearing a black dress and black pumps with three-inch heels, which Erica hadn't seen since her grandfather's funeral. It was probably the only thing with a skirt that her aunt owned. She faced the pulpit with a clenched jaw and kept up the pressure on Erica's hand until Erica lifted it to let her know it was okay to let go.

On the other side of Laura sat Webb, suited and shaven, and then Heidi, with a lapful of used Kleenex, and then Leanne and her dad. And crammed into the pews behind her were the people she'd known all her life. Most of the town, and then some people from all over. What would they think if they knew she would swap them all for her mom, or for just another hour with her mom?

Rue would have called her a twisted puppy for dreaming of arranging a hostage swap with God. *"Be civilized,"* she would have said.

And her mom would have actually appreciated all the people who'd taken the trouble to be here. She would have smiled at their anecdotes. Maybe she was smiling, somewhere.

The rest of the time in the church, and all the time at the grave, Erica twisted the heavy ring on her finger and made up a shadow eulogy all her own, involving her own anecdotes. There were hundreds, and they flooded through her mind, blotting out the self-pity and anger that had gripped her for the past few days. She remembered her mom picking her up from school when she'd come down with chicken pox, and the two of them driving to Galveston on vacation, and her mom carving a headstone out of a brick to mark the place where they'd buried her pet guinea pig, Soapy. But in the memory that came back to her most often, her mom wasn't even there. It was the memory of waking up in the night on the couch, tucked in safe by an unseen hand.

The Sunday night after the funeral Erica went to stay at her dad's house. Heidi felt mournful and shaky, but Laura marked the moment with as little fanfare as possible. Erica might be staying with William, Laura insisted, but the farm was her real home. Erica could come and go whenever she pleased. This wasn't the beginning or the end of anything, and she glared if Heidi so much as sniffled.

But it was still awful to watch William taking Erica's suitcase out and driving her away. And for all her brave bluster, after Erica was gone, Laura looked like she'd had the stuffing knocked out of her. She moped around the house. At night she would occasionally slip out like she used to, and later Heidi would hear her coming back in, clomping all the way up to the attic when there was a whole house full of bedrooms below to choose from now.

The week of the funeral Heidi had felt useful. There had been work to do. She had provided a barrier reef between Erica and Laura and the rest of the world. In putting the funeral together, she'd been able to subsume her own grief.

But now, rattling around the empty house with Laura—or more often without her—she felt awkward and more superfluous than ever.

She mentioned this to Laura one morning, as a way of getting around to the announcement that she needed to go back to New York.

Laura seemed taken aback. "Why?"

"Well . . . because."

Laura frowned but didn't seem inclined to argue the matter. "Do what you have to."

"Unless there's stuff you think I should do. Go through clothes, something like that?"

"Forget it."

"Anyway, I thought that I'd just give myself a couple of days."

Laura looked alarmed. "Webb's in San Antonio today. You'd leave without saying good-bye to him?"

Webb had left the night before to attend a wedding of one of his old army buddies. He'd asked Laura to go along with him for the ride, but she wouldn't be persuaded. She'd said she'd be lousy company.

He hadn't pressed her too hard, which seemed sad to Heidi. It was like he was halfway gone already.

"I meant I'd leave a couple of days *from now*," Heidi said, clarifying the matter. "Sunday, maybe?"

"Oh." Laura nodded. "Yeah, that'll be all right."

After lunch Laura went upstairs to her room and didn't come down again. Herman came in twice, looking for her, but when Heidi knocked on Laura's door, she received no answer, and neither she nor Herman was brave enough to risk just barging in. Heidi did her best trying to do the initial work for that week's CSA boxes.

She made a plane reservation for Sunday, flying out of the little airport in Tyler.

With much reluctance, she decided to call her mom to let her know that she was going to be returning to her neck of the woods. Her mother, who had been lobbying for her to come back all summer, now seemed dismayed by the prospect. "What are you going to do?"

"I don't know."

"Are you going to testify at that man's trial?"

"Yes."

"And you're not worried about being killed?"

"Well, I was almost killed here. Here or there—does it really matter?"

"Of course it matters!" Marla yelled. "I mean, you should be trying not to be killed *anywhere*."

"I'll bear that in mind."

Her mother sighed. "Is this about Stephen?"

"No."

"You're not getting back together with him, are you?"

"No."

"Well, that's good."

Heidi shook her head, confused. "You *liked* him."

"Of course. He's perfectly nice. But soooooo dull. Even for you."

"Thanks. In a year I'll probably wish there was a nice, dull Stephen in my life. But for now I just need to figure out where I'm going to park myself." She took a deep breath. *Here goes nothing.* "In fact, I was hoping that you wouldn't mind having a houseguest for a while."

The silence that greeted that last statement was an answer all in itself.

"Mom?"

"Actually, this isn't a good time."

"Why? Is something wrong?"

"No, no. Just the opposite! In fact . . ." Her mother released a breathy giggle. "Well, the truth is, we're engaged."

Heidi frowned in confusion, then felt her facial muscles give way. "Oh no! Mom, no."

"Tom's a good man."

Was it terrible to tell your own mother that someone was *too* good for her? Heidi suspected it was. Still, she couldn't help asking, "Hasn't that man been through enough?"

Her mother laughed gaily. "Apparently not, because he popped the question just last night, and I said yes. Tom says he hasn't been this happy since before Watergate."

"And he does know that you're in Liz Taylor territory when it comes to husbands?"

"Of course. He knew *that* before he spent a week here."

"I'll bet." Marla had never been silent on the subject of her ex-husbands.

"He said he admires my honesty, and I told him, 'Well, doodle-bug, I am what I am.' "

"Congratulations."

"It's not that we don't want you here, you see. It's just . . ."

"That you don't want me there. I see."

"Although it would be great if you could do a little catering for the wedding."

"Wedding?"

"Well, we thought we could have a little ceremony. This is Tom's first time to the altar." She sucked in her breath. "Do you think you could house-sit while we're on our honeymoon? Tom wants to go to the Grand Canyon. Isn't that cute?"

Heidi grunted. "Well, we'll see."

"Don't worry," her mother said. "We'll be back in time for court. That trial's going to be a regular family affair now, isn't it?"

Heidi hung up the phone feeling even less enthusiastic about returning home. She went upstairs to figure out what had happened to Laura. She hoped she wasn't sick.

She knocked on the attic door and heard nothing. She turned

the handle and peered inside, squinting because the room was so dark. "Laura?"

"Go away." Laura's voice sounded muffled, as if her face was buried in a pillow.

"Herman's come in a few times looking for you. He's wondering about the boxes for tomorrow, and if you're going to have a table at the market. He needs to know what to pick, and how much."

"It doesn't matter. He can take a match and torch the whole place for all I care."

Heidi stepped farther into the room. "Are you drunk?"

"No! I'm depressed!"

"Well, yeah . . . of course. That's no reason to take it out on the farm."

Laura bolted up to a sitting position. "Why not? I've wasted my life on this place. I should have run away and joined a circus. Or gone to Alaska or China. *Done* something. Instead, I've been beating my brains out trying to make this place work, and even worse, because I was here, poor Rue frittered away her last years here. She never even liked the farm all that much."

"Then she could have gone somewhere else. She worked before she had Erica, didn't she?"

"As an administrator at a county health clinic. She hated it. Anyway, she thought she was doing me a favor coming back here. She tried to whip the place into shape and make it pay for itself. It killed her."

"That's crazy talk. Rue loved this place. She *liked* living here. She liked the guests, and looking out her window and seeing Erica riding Milkshake, and being around you."

Laura collapsed back against her pillow. She lifted her hands to her face, her elbows sticking straight out, and covered her eyes. "Go away."

"I am. I'm flying out of Tyler on Sunday."

"I mean go away *now*. Leave me alone."

Heidi backed out of the room. She didn't like leaving Laura alone like that—though of course, she didn't particularly want to stand there being abused, either. Still, she quietly grabbed the pig gun on her way out.

The rest of the afternoon she helped Herman. She picked enough produce to fill the boxes and have some to sell at the farmers' market. It wasn't much of a haul. There were just a few melons, peppers, a few tomatoes, pattypan squash, and eggplants for the market. Heidi decided to make some muffins and sell those. It would be her last chance to make a little more for the old place.

She got to work on the muffins. By five o'clock she still hadn't heard Laura stirring. She put a hot muffin and butter on a tray, along with a cup of coffee, then carried it up and set it outside Laura's door. Then she went outside and got Fred.

When she returned, she knocked gently.

"Go away," Laura called.

Heidi let herself into the bedroom, anyway. "I brought you some food," she said. "And I thought you might need a friend."

"Oh, and that would be you?"

Heidi snapped on the overhead light, which worked with a chain. "No, that would be your chicken."

Laura squinted up at her like a rodent who'd been disturbed in its nest. When she heard Fred's clucks, her face softened and she held out her arms. Heidi handed her the rooster and then went and got the muffin and coffee.

"This is crazy," she told Laura, who crumbled a little muffin onto the bedspread for Fred. He pecked it up greedily. "This isn't like you."

"I've never felt this way before." Laura shook her head and took a sip of coffee. "You know what did it? I was standing in the kitchen, and I realized nobody was ever going to call me Laurel Mae again."

Heidi's heart wrenched.

"That stupid name!" Laura exclaimed. "I hate it. Most of the time I hated her for calling me by it. Now . . ."

Her lips clamped tight, and Heidi got the feeling they were holding back a shriek of injustice.

She tried to change the subject. "Herman and I did the pick-ing. And Dylan said he would be at the market to help if you needed him."

"That's nice," Laura said. "Is there any mail I need to tend to?"

"I forgot to pick it up."

Like everyone else's in the area, the farm's mailbox was on the main road so that the mailman didn't have to mess with the lane.

Laura set down her coffee, got up, and shoved her feet inside her boots. "I'll go get it."

She picked up Fred and took him out with her. Even though the box was less than a quarter of a mile away, Laura got in her pickup and drove to the end of the lane, with Fred in the front seat beside her, and then came back. She deposited Fred on the kitchen floor and all the mail on the table. From the pile of let-ters, catalogs, and junk flyers, Laura extracted a familiar-looking red envelope and held it up by her fingertips. Rue's last Netflix delivery.

They both stared at the square envelope with consternation. "I thought she'd frozen the account," Heidi said.

"Maybe this one was already on the way and got held up."

Heidi felt as shaky as Laura looked. It was like getting a mis-sive from the great beyond.

"Whatever's in it, we're watching it," Laura declared. "I don't care if it's *Song of Norway Two*. We're going to watch it. Tonight. We're going to pop popcorn, pour ourselves some liquor, shove this damn thing in the DVD player, and sit our butts down on Rue's couch and watch it."

Heidi bit her lip and nodded. "Movie time." *Last one.*

Laura went outside to finish up work and pay Herman for the week. Heidi made pasta for dinner, because it was easy. The place had enough tomato sauce to last till doomsday.

Both she and Laura picked at dinner. It was just something to get through.

"What was Rue's favorite drink?" Heidi asked her.

Laura thought for a moment. "She always liked fussy old-fashioned drinks. Things with eight ingredients, as long as one of them was a maraschino cherry. The last time I took her anywhere it was to Chester's, and she ordered a Tom Collins. Wade the bartender had to look it up."

"We'll drink Tom Collinses, then."

"Do you know how to make one?"

"You can find anything on the Internet."

After dinner, while Laura popped popcorn, Heidi assembled the ingredients for Tom Collinses. She'd found a little jar of maraschino cherries in the back of the fridge, and the rest was no big deal—lemons, gin, club soda, sugar. There was even an old orange in the hydrator, for garnish. She mixed up an experimental pitcher and poured two glasses.

Laura sipped it and made a face. "It tastes like spiked Kool-Aid."

"I like it."

Laura dumped more gin in her glass, picked up the bowl of popcorn, and marched them into the living room. Heidi settled on the couch while Laura did the unveiling of the DVD. They still didn't know what they were watching.

When Laura pulled the DVD out, she rolled her eyes. "Oh hell."

Heidi immediately thought of Audrey Hepburn. But when Laura flashed the disk at her, she saw that it was actually a pretty good one. "What's the matter with *Dark Victory?*" she asked Laura. "Don't you like Bette Davis, either?"

"Her movies are always so dumb."

"This one is sort of goofy—so over the top, it makes you giggle." Heidi wondered at Rue wanting to watch a movie about a woman dying of a brain tumor. Although . . . "Rue always told me that Bette Davis was her favorite actress."

That settled it. Laura took a breath, put the DVD in the machine, and took a seat on the couch, with her drink. The bowl of popcorn was nestled between them.

The movie was actually better than Heidi remembered. It had a snappy pace, and Laura enjoyed Ronald Reagan playing a drunk and Humphrey Bogart as the Irish stable lad. She wasn't so appreciative of the actor playing the surgeon Bette Davis consults, who diagnoses her brain tumor, falls in love with her, and then realizes her condition is fatal.

"Could they have found anyone more boring?" Laura asked.

Heidi shot her a look. "It's George Brent!"

"So?"

"He's a dreamboat."

"He's really boring."

"Okay, he's a boring dreamboat. At least he's not a drunk, like all the other men she knows."

"True," Laura admitted. "And he's not lurking around barns like Humphrey O'Bogart, either."

Heidi frowned and refilled their glasses from the Tom Collins pitcher. She plopped two cherries in hers.

Maybe it was fitting that the last official movie time they had in this room was a movie Laura would sneer at. It was typical. She felt as if she were taking Rue's place, defending the smarmy, the unbelievable, the over-the-top theatrics of Bette Davis snarling "Prognosis negative!" in a crowded restaurant. When Bette Davis realized she was in love with her boring surgeon after all, Heidi poured out a last round of Tom Collins and dared Laura with a look to utter one snide word.

The odd thing was, though, that Laura didn't. She was slumped on the couch, slurping up sugary gin, and by the time Bette's eyesight started to go, she was looking a little glassy-eyed herself. When a dying Bette bravely sent George Brent off to his medical research conference—to score their big victory over the dark— sniffles came from Laura's side of the couch. Heidi heard it but kept her eyes trained on the screen.

And then Bette, about to die, said good-bye to the dogs.

Laura lost it.

Heidi swung around to look at her—she couldn't help it—but Laura didn't even appear to care. She was draped over the arm of the couch, bawling her eyes out. The angel chorus sound track, instead of being hooted down for its corniness, only seemed to set her off more. Even when the movie ended, Laura kept crying. The sobs coming out of her sounded as if they'd been building up for thirty-six years.

Heidi yanked a tissue out of the box on the end table and handed it to her.

Laura trumpeted into the Kleenex and let out a keening sound that raised the hairs on Heidi's arms. She began to cry, too—not that that was anything new. She'd been crying for a solid week. Laura hadn't wept at all, at least not in front of anyone else. Now she was having a full-throttle meltdown over a movie.

"The part with the dogs *is* really sad. . . . ," Heidi said quietly.

Laura rounded on her. "I don't give a damn about the dogs. I just want my sister back!" She blew into the tissue again. "She should be here!"

"I know."

"No, you don't," Laura snapped resentfully. "You didn't know her as long as I did. You knew her a summer, but I loved her all my life. All my life." She collapsed forward. "All my long, sorry life, and I never once told her what she meant to me."

Heidi grabbed her by the shoulders. "You think she didn't know?"

Laura sucked in a ragged breath. "The last night in the hospital—even then I didn't say anything. She was trying to talk to me, but I told her to stop it."

"It doesn't matter now."

"Yes, it does! I'll never learn. I should have just said it. Said it every time I got the chance. I wouldn't say it to Webb, either, even though I've been eating my heart out all summer. Hell, I should say it to you just for good measure." She looked up at Heidi, her eyes almost frantic. "I love you, okay?"

"Okay . . ."

"No, I mean it. Sort of. I love you. I love the whole world!"

Heidi was glad she'd hidden the pig gun before she'd poured the drinks.

"Listen," she told Laura, "Rue knew you inside out. She knew how you felt—probably better than you ever will."

Laura's head bobbed furiously.

"She loved you how you are." Heidi grabbed a tissue herself and blew her nose. "As crusty and awful as you are. Don't ask me why, but she did."

They were interrupted then by Webb, who burst through the front door. He stopped at the living-room door and gaped at them. They were both red faced and weepy and practically draped over each other, with tissues and popcorn spilling away from them.

"I left the wedding reception early and drove straight back." He was breathing hard, as if he'd actually run back. "I wanted to surprise you, but . . ."

But it looked like they had surprised him instead. His expression was pure disbelief, as if he were looking at a YouTube video of a pit bull nursing a bunny rabbit.

Laura sat up, sending more popcorn cascading to the floor. She rubbed her eyes. "We were just watching a movie."

He glanced over to Heidi for confirmation.

Heidi nodded. "We, uh . . ."

Laura breathed in a ragged breath. "And I was saying that I love you."

"That she loves everyone," Heidi added, clarifying.

"But I really meant just Webb." Laura stared at him with teary, glassy eyes and lifted her hands as a kind of surrender, or summons. "I love you. I've been a mess just thinking about your leaving. If you do go, you might as well rip my heart out and stomp it to little bits under your boot heel while you're at it."

In a moment he crossed the distance to the couch and dropped to his knees in front of her. He held both her arms in a tight grip. "I would never stomp on your heart with my boot heel."

"You should," Laura told him.

"Why?"

"Because I love you. I love you now, and I loved you ten years ago and maybe even before that. I loved you the day I left Guadalajara. I've screwed everything up."

"You're not the only one."

"I thought a person like you deserved better than a person like me."

"I don't know about deserving, but you're the only person I've ever really wanted," he said simply.

Laura slid off the couch like a Baggie filled with liquid and landed with her arms looped around his neck. "Are you going to kiss me or just sit here, squatting and staring?"

Webb flicked a self-conscious glance at Heidi.

"You'd better kiss her before she passes out," Heidi advised.

She reeled out of the room as quickly and quietly as she could.

It had been a long, surprising summer. She had been hit by a car, had fallen from a tree, and had at times been terrified for her life, deliriously happy, or completely demoralized. Her mother was marrying her old coworker, and she was mourning a friend that three months ago she didn't even have. A gunman had chased her down, cakes had exploded, a chicken had been given a pirate leg. But in all the months she'd been here, the one thing she'd never expected to happen, never, ever, ever, was for Laura Rafferty, the stepsister from hell, to tell her that she loved her.

Maybe it really was time to go home.

Chapter 27

Heidi was nattering on so in the backseat of the car that they were in Sweetgum before she even realized they were headed in the wrong direction.

Laura was trying not to let her get on her nerves, since it was the last day she would have to put up with her. And to be honest, Heidi hadn't been nearly as annoying lately as she used to be. She had even been helpful, Laura admitted grudgingly.

And Laura also had to allow that, aside from a wicked Tom Collins hangover, not much had bothered her in the past two days. Despite all that had happened, and the deep sadness she feared would never go away, there had developed inside her an unfamiliar but pleasant hum. The Webb hum. Everything in her life had fallen apart, but now there was this one thing that was working out. He was going to stay and be a farmer by marriage.

"Why are we going this way?" Heidi asked, stopping an excruciating planes, trains, and automobiles breakdown of how she intended to get from the Tyler airport all the way to her mother's house in Stamford. Apparently, she was willing to sleep on Marla's couch rather than go back to Brooklyn. "This isn't the way to Tyler."

"We're taking on another passenger," Laura said.

When they stopped in front of William's house, Erica exploded out the front door. Laura hopped out and gave her a hug, then opened the back door with chauffeur-like formality. Erica slid in and greeted Heidi and Webb, who was driving.

"Congratulations!"

Laura had told Erica that Webb and she had become engaged. In fact, they were planning on getting married just as soon as his divorce came through.

"Boy, am I glad to see y'all!" Erica exclaimed, settling in. "I just spent the longest hour of my life listening to Leanne and my dad trying to pick baby names. She got some test back and discovered it's a girl. She said she wanted to name her something literary, like Portia, but Dad told her she couldn't name a kid after a car."

Heidi laughed.

"Why not name little Leannette after a car?" Laura said. "Some of them have good sounds. How about Mazda Mae Anderson?"

"Lexus Anderson," Webb said.

"Or how about going back in time?" Heidi said. "A good historical name—Edsel Anderson."

"Now she's leaning toward Evangeline," Erica said. "She says we can call it Vangie. I told her that's just weird."

"Speaking of names . . ." Heidi leaned forward so that she was talking right over Laura's left shoulder. "What about the farm?"

"What about it?" Laura asked.

"Well, once you get married, Sassy Spinster Farm won't have any spinsters on it," Heidi pointed out. "Are you going to change its name?"

Webb and Laura exchanged puzzled looks. "I hadn't thought of it," Laura admitted. "What would we name it?"

"Old Boring Married Couple Acres," Webb suggested.

"Too wordy," Laura said. "But I like the sentiment."

"How about Fred's Egg Farm?" Erica said.

"Makes us sound like we're sitting around waiting for our rooster to lay," Webb pointed out.

Heidi had an idea, too. "Why not a tip of the hat to the enemy—Wild Pig Acres."

"No pigs!" Laura insisted.

"Anyway," Heidi said, "when you think of something, I can draw a logo for you. I'll probably have plenty of spare time coming up."

"I think it would be fun to testify at a mob trial," Erica said.

Laura and Heidi corrected her at once. "He's an independent," they said together.

"And *fun* is not the word I would use," Heidi said. "Although probably just as fun as watching my mom get married for the fifth time."

Laura tilted an amused glance at Webb. "Love is just bustin' out all over."

"Seriously, though," Webb said. "What are your plans?"

"Well . . ." Heidi bit her lip. "To tell you the truth, my dream is to open a little café. Which is probably the dream of half the unemployed people in the country."

"If you wanted to call it the Sassy Spinster Café, that's okay by me," Laura told her.

Heidi frowned. "I couldn't."

"Why not?" Laura asked.

"I don't think I've earned it."

"Of course you have," Webb said. "You survived a summer with Laura, didn't you?"

"And you canned an awful lot of tomatoes," Erica pointed out. "I couldn't have done that. Maybe it's like the ruby slippers. You had it in you all along and just didn't know it."

"Until Laura tortured me for a summer," Heidi added.

Laura raised her hand in benediction. "I solemnly declare you a Sassy Spinster. Go forth and bake."

They reached the airport faster than Laura had expected. Her stomach felt slightly queasy, as it always did when she saw airplanes buzzing on a runway. People were not meant to fly.

And good-byes were always so damn awkward.

"Well!" Heidi had tears welling in her eyes when they stood at the point beyond which only passengers were allowed. The tiny airport actually felt more like a depot than a full-blown airport. It contained only a few gates, and jetways were a big new thing. Waiting on the tarmac was Heidi's plane, a twelve-seater, the kind of plane that seemed more mosquito than airliner.

The loudspeaker announced her flight.

"This is it," Heidi said.

Webb gave her a hug. "Take care. And if you ever need another escape hatch . . ."

Heidi laughed. "I promise to look somewhere else."

Erica gave her a hug, too. "Bye, Heidi. Can I come visit you in Brooklyn someday?"

Heidi nodded. "You can visit me anywhere I end up. Anytime."

When it was Laura's turn, they both hesitated. "So . . ."

Heidi smiled. "You're not going to miss me at all, I assume."

"Can't wait to see the backside of you," Laura deadpanned.

Heidi looked like she was about to cry again. "If you ever want to be reminded of how much you dislike me, you're welcome to come visit me in New York."

"I'll bring my pig gun," Laura said. Then she added, "And you know you'll always be unwelcome here. Anytime."

They called for final boarding for Heidi's flight. Briefly, Heidi threw her arms around Laura and gave her a boa-constrictor squeeze, then stepped back, sniffling. So much for sassy.

"Good-bye, Laura!"

"Bye," Laura said, tipping two fingers to her forehead in mock salute.

The three of them watched Heidi until she had disappeared through the jetway. Then they turned and walked slowly out of the airport. By the time they reached their car, they could see Heidi's plane taking off. As it lifted against the background of East Texas pines, Erica glanced over at Webb and Laura.

"You know what?"

"Let me guess . . ." Laura aimed a wry look at her. "You're missing her already?"

"No." Erica squinted at the outline of an airplane skimming into a sky of endless blue. "I feel like someone's missing us."